ANNA SCHMIDT

SAFE HAVEN

THE PEACEMAKERS BOOK 3

SHILOH RUN  PRESS

An Imprint of Barbour Publishing, Inc.

Cover design by Kirk DouPonce, DogEared Design

Published by Shiloh Run Press, an imprint of Barbour Publishing, Inc., P.O. Box 719, Uhrichsville, OH 44683, www.shilohrunpress.com

Our mission is to publish and distribute inspirational products offering exceptional value and biblical encouragement to the masses.

 Member of the
Evangelical Christian
Publishers Association

Printed in the United States of America.

With appreciation to all who make sure that history lives on, this novel is dedicated to the memory of Dr. Willard Schum (October 24, 1931–September 29, 2013), founder of the Safe Haven Museum, Oswego, New York, and to the surviving "guests" of the Fort Ontario Emergency Relief Shelter, who will gather in the summer of 2014 for the seventieth reunion.

# PROLOGUE

Washington, DC
Late July 1944

I t was still dark when the jangle of the phone next to the sofa startled Suzanne Randolph awake. This was the fifth night in a row that she had fallen asleep without bothering to undress or get into her bed. The fact that on this night she had taken the time to go get the pillow and quilt from her bedroom and bring them to the sofa probably indicated this was a long-term move.

Instead of answering the phone balanced precariously on the edge of a makeshift table that was little more than an unsteady stack of coffee-table books with a tray set on top, she burrowed more deeply under the patchwork quilt. Three years earlier—the ink practically still wet on her college diploma—she had been hired by one of the nation's top morning newspapers and moved to the nation's capital, the nerve center for political news.

Her mother had bought the quilt for her as a housewarming present when she moved to Washington, DC, to start her first job. "To keep you warm in the cold, cruel world of politics," she'd said. Her mother had a wicked sense of humor. She also looked at the world through a prism that everything happened for a purpose that would become clear with time.

For the first several months that she worked at the paper, Suzanne took whatever assignment she was given—local council meetings, obituaries, society news about political wives doing their bit for the war effort. Then like an understudy on Broadway, she got her chance to show what she could do. A major story broke in the middle of the night, and she was the first reporter on the scene. Of course the veteran reporters got the credit as well as the bylines. Still, she had filed a human interest piece related to the overall drama, and the paper's managing editor—Edwin Bonner—had been impressed. So impressed that he had begun giving her assignments with a higher profile. In short order her dream of becoming a respected journalist seemed within reach.

Now, of course, she'd managed to ruin all that.

Finally the phone burped out half a ring that was abruptly cut off when apparently the caller gave up. Suzanne pulled the quilt more firmly around her shoulders as she turned over and faced the back of the sofa.

The phone rang again.

She covered her ears and counted the rings as she waited for silence. When it came, she eased back the quilt. Why was she all covered up like it was January instead of July with its steam bath of heat and humidity that was normal for summer in DC? Her apartment windows were wide open, and not a hint of a breeze stirred in spite of the asthmatic whirring of the ancient table fan she'd picked up at a tag sale. Why was she still lying here on a day when she should be up scanning the want ads as she looked for a job—any job?

"You're pathetic," she muttered as she threw back the quilt and lay on her back, staring up at the water-stained ceiling that the super had promised for the last year to repaint. It could be her mother calling, but she and Suzanne's stepfather were on a fishing vacation in Canada so that was unlikely. It could be a friend. That was even less likely, because since the scandal, her so-called friends had avoided her as if she carried some life-threatening disease.

The phone rang again. One of these days Suzanne was sure someone would invent a phone that could be unplugged and silenced, but until then, her only options would be to answer it or rip the cord from the wall. And although the latter was more tempting than she cared to admit, she decided to answer since clearly the caller was not going to give up until she did. Still lying on the sofa, she reached up over her head and fumbled for the receiver. "What?" she barked irritably into the mouthpiece.

"And a good morning to you as well, sunshine." The clipped, precise voice of Edwin Bonner, her former boss, was the last thing she had expected to hear. "You slept on the sofa, didn't you?"

"What are you doing—having me followed? Look, I know I made a huge mistake—"

"*Mistakes* as in the plural form of that word, and they were indeed major."

Suzanne groaned. "Don't remind me." Her first mistake had been trusting Congressman Gordon Langford III. They had been dating for several months when he'd given her the first hint of what he later called the biggest story in Washington. Over the next few weeks, he had played her. Oh, she saw it all after the fact—the notes he left lying around and then snatched away from her as if they were state secrets; the distracted sighs that practically begged her to ask what was going on with him; and the bits and pieces of the story that he surrendered with the plea that "I have to talk to someone or I'll go crazy."

When the first layer of the story broke, Gordon had begged her to write the truth. He had provided her with documentation and details that seemed to contradict the official version of the matter. Because she had thought she was in love with Gordon and trusted him not to do anything that would hurt her—or her career—she had made the cardinal mistake of any rookie reporter. She had failed to check out her sources, instead accepted his version of things, and then turned in a story that she assured Edwin exposed a major politician's corruption.

When Edwin grilled her about whether or not she had "gone down every single back alley," as he liked to put it, to be certain that her information was correct and irrefutable, she had lied and told him she had. Only once the story ran did it come to light that Gordon had manufactured the entire scandal. The story had run on page one of the national news section—above the fold with her name as a byline. That morning she had been so excited that she had bought out the corner newsstand's entire supply of the paper; then she had called both her mother and Gordon.

Her mother had answered. Gordon had not.

By noon of that day, the accused politician's lawyer had contacted Edwin's boss—the paper's publisher—threatening a lawsuit unless the paper printed a full retraction also on page one above the fold and fired Suzanne. Competing newspapers across Washington had had a field day with this ultimatum, and suddenly Suzanne became the news. The accused politician—who Suzanne had little doubt was in fact corrupt although she had no real proof beyond Gordon's assurances that *he* had proof—had become the benevolent hero. He had called a press conference and asked others to forgive Gordon, whom he labeled young and ambitious, and he'd thrown in a plea for forgiveness for the "little lady" because "we all make mistakes, especially when we're in love."

Edwin's voice continued to crackle over the receiver as he apparently laid out the story of her downfall before coming to the real reason for his call. "So now you've decided to hole up in that dump you call an apartment and lick your wounds." It sounded like he was shuffling through papers on his desk. "When's the last time you showered, had a decent meal, and got dressed in something other than your pj's?"

"When did you become my father?"

"When I stopped being your editor," he snapped. "Now, listen up, kiddo. I may have found a way for you to redeem yourself."

"Why do you care?" It was a sincere query. After all, the paper's reputation had taken a blow because of her.

"I've asked myself that very question. The answer is that you have a gift, Suzanne, and when you use it properly, you have the potential to be one of the best reporters I have ever worked with."

She felt her throat close around a lump of emotion that could only be broken up by tears.

"Are you still there?" Edwin asked.

Suzanne made a guttural sound to let him know she was and reached for one of three handkerchiefs wadded into balls on the floor next to the sofa.

"This involves traveling, Suzie. I suspect you should plan on being on assignment for several weeks at a minimum so figure out how to sublet your apartment and how to pack for an extended stay."

She blotted the tears and cleared her throat. "If it involves my going to Siberia, count me out."

"Close. Ever hear of Oswego in upstate New York?"

"No."

"It's a small town north of Syracuse on Lake Ontario. There's this fort there cleverly named Fort Ontario—dates back to the French and Indian War."

Suzanne did not like the sound of this. Ever since the Allies had landed on the shores of Normandy, the tide of war had turned, and the really big stories were in Europe—not some old fort in upstate New York. But Edwin had a thing for history, so she was beginning to understand where this might be going.

"Look, Edwin, I appreciate this, but—"

"Hear me out. You know that announcement that the president made last month about bringing some refugees to America as his guests? The one that mostly got buried in the depths of the papers because of the whole Normandy landing?"

"I was a little busy that month," she reminded him.

"Stop wallowing and try reading the news instead of making it up."

"Okay, that was below the belt."

"Sorry. I'm trying to help you. Do you want my help or not?"

Once again Suzanne felt tears threatening to overwhelm her. "I do," she whispered then sniffed loudly. "Refugees coming to America. . .to Oswego?"

"To Fort Ontario in Oswego."

"When?"

"They are on a ship crossing the Atlantic—scheduled to arrive by the end of the week."

"How many?"

"There were supposed to be a thousand, but officially only 982 made it."

"From?" She felt the stirring of her journalist juices. She was sitting up now, gathering facts.

"The ship sailed from Italy, but my understanding is the group represents at least fifteen or twenty different countries."

Suzanne stood up, picking up the phone and stretching the cord as far as possible as she reached for pen and paper. "Men? Women?"

"And children—whole families in some cases."

"Jewish?" Everyone had finally accepted that the Nazis were specifically targeting the Jews. Some stories Suzanne found impossible to believe, yet apparently those stories weren't the worst of it.

"Mostly Jews but also Catholics, Protestants—I think some Greek Orthodox."

She scribbled as fast as she could. "So they come here and then what?"

"Well now, see that's the story. Then what?"

"I don't understand."

"Roosevelt has labeled them 'guests,' which means they have no legal status here. The State Department is adamant that once the war is over they are to go back to wherever they came from, and FDR has agreed to those terms."

"But that's barbaric. I mean what if their homes and countries have been bombed to smithereens? What if their homes have been taken over by someone else? What if—"

Edwin chuckled. "Now that's much better, Suzie. You're sounding like a real reporter."

"I am a real reporter," she huffed.

"Prove it."

In those two words stood the challenge she didn't realize she'd been waiting to hear—the chance she had been sure had been lost to her forever.

"I will."

"I can't pay you—at least not officially."

"I don't need your money," she shot back, although she was practically broke. Her mind raced even as she struggled to capture all the information that Edwin continued to rattle off at lightning speed.

Refugees traveling on a troopship with wounded soldiers.

As Edwin suggested, I could maybe sublet my apartment and save some money that way.

Crossing the Atlantic in a convoy accompanied by two other ships carrying German prisoners of war.

I have a little savings, and my mom...

Scheduled to stay until war ended, so at least several months.

Months? Where would I live in the meantime? Maybe there is a boardinghouse in Oswego.

"Look, I'm sending you a train ticket and some primary documents by courier."

"I thought you weren't paying me."

"It's a loan. You need to get up there and get settled."

"When are the 'guests' scheduled to arrive in Oswego?"

"Saturday if all goes according to plan."

"Okay, I'll be there. And Edwin? Thanks."

"Don't make me regret this, Suzie. It's an assignment that a lot of reporters could parlay into a Pulitzer."

In his tone she heard a hint of having second thoughts.

"I've learned my lesson," she assured him. "I won't let you down."

This had to be the hottest summer that Theo Bridgewater could remember—at least for Wisconsin. He was harvesting feed corn with his father when he saw his mother come running across the field. She was waving a piece of paper and shouting to be heard above the racket of the harvester. He touched his dad's shoulder and motioned toward his mother.

"Ellie?" Theo's father called out as he shut down the engine and the machine wheezed to a stop in the middle of a row of corn shocks. He jumped to the ground and removed his baseball cap to wipe sweat from his face with a faded bandanna. "What's happened?" Both men started across the already harvested rows to meet her.

"Oh, Paul, they're alive," she shouted, stumbling over the flattened stalks. "They're alive, and they're coming to America. My brother, Franz, and Ilse and little Liesl—they are all alive." She burst into tears as she hugged them both.

Theo met his father's disbelieving eyes. It had been two years since they'd had word of Ellie's brother and his family. The last letter they had received told them that Franz, Ilse, and their eight-year-old daughter, Liesl, were joining Ilse's sister Marta and her family for a skiing holiday in Switzerland. That letter had raised alarms on several fronts, for Theo's parents immediately understood that *skiing holiday* was code for escape. With the war raging, few people could manage a holiday. But of far greater concern had been the absence of any mention of Theo's sister, Beth, traveling with them.

Beth had gone to Munich in the late 1930s to act as a nanny and companion for Liesl. Theo remembered their aunt Ilse as a mousy, nervous woman given to attacks of depression and anxiety. Liesl had been born late in life for Franz and Ilse, and according to Beth she was a lively child who could easily exasperate her mother. But his uncle's last letter had made no mention of Beth, who Theo and his parents had been trying to persuade to come home to America from the day the Nazis first occupied Poland.

Following the news of Franz, Ilse, and Liesl's supposed escape there had been no word for months until they received another letter—this one from Beth. She told them that she was now living on a small island off the coast of Denmark with her new husband—a German doctor named Josef—and their good friend Anja and her family. Her next letter had come to them from Belgium and reported that she and Josef were running a café and expecting their first child. Both letters were carefully worded to avoid providing too much information for the censors, and neither mentioned Franz, Ilse, or Liesl. Also neither letter had included a return address. The letters that Theo's mother sent to the apartment in Munich, hoping they would be forwarded, went unanswered.

Finally, just this past April they had received a long, uncensored letter from Beth reporting that she and Josef were in England with their newborn daughter, Gabrielle. Beth also added that she had had no news from her aunt and uncle. She wrote that she and Josef were doing everything they could to locate the rest of the family but so far had been unsuccessful.

Since then, Beth's letters had come regularly, but there had been no further news of Franz, Ilse, and Liesl, and at every meeting for worship the family attended as members of the Religious Society of Friends, they stood and asked their fellow Quakers to please continue to hold their daughter, her husband and child, and Ellie's brother, his wife, and their child in the Light and pray for their safety.

Now standing together under a broiling sun and cloudless azure sky, Theo watched as his mother released his dad and unfolded the letter with shaking hands. "It's only a couple of sentences," she said, squinting at the thin paper. "But there is no doubt that this is my brother's hand. Paul, see how he has written it?"

"Franz always did have a fine handwriting," Theo's dad replied as he took the paper and shaded the words with one of his large, dirt-encrusted hands so he could scan the contents.

"When do they get here?" Theo asked, and Dad handed him the letter:

My dear Ellie,

Little time to explain. We are scheduled to arrive in New York tomorrow and from there travel with the others to Fort Ontario in a place called Oswego—also in New York. Ilse and Liesl send their love.

The letter's contents raised so many questions—when was "tomorrow"? Who were "the others"? Why were they going to this Fort Ontario, and where was Oswego?

But when Theo voiced the questions, his mother cupped his cheek. "Answers will come," she said. "The important thing is that they are alive, they are safe, and they are here." She took the letter from him and carefully folded it to fit back in the envelope. "I should call Matthew," she said, no doubt already making a mental list of what would need to be done.

"He had that big delivery of lumber this morning," Paul reminded her. "Call Jenny." Theo's brother owned the local hardware store. Their sons' careers had been predetermined. Matthew would take over the family's hardware business after his dad's brother—a lifelong bachelor—retired, and eventually Theo would take over the farm. Matthew had taken to his assignment like a duck to water. Theo was a born farmer, but he was also restless and wanted to find some way that he might make a real difference in the world. In the thirty years that he had been alive, there had been not one but two world conflicts. To Theo's way of thinking, that trend needed to change, and he was pretty sure that what he really wanted was to be a part of that change. He just had to figure out how.

"I'll call Jenny, then," his mother continued. "She'll be home. I want them to come for supper so we can decide what to do next."

It had always been their way to gather together whenever a member of the family faced a new and potentially complicated decision. Theo recalled when they had decided that Beth should go to Germany. Shortly after Liesl's birth, his aunt and uncle had visited them on the farm in Wisconsin and were preparing to return home where Franz was a professor at the University of Munich.

Ellie had worried about Ilse's inability to bond with her new child and had suggested that Beth—freshly graduated from high school—could return to Germany with them to help out. *It will be an adventure,* Theo remembered his mother telling Beth. In those early days of

Hitler's rise to power, no one could have imagined how terrible things would become. And lately as his sister's letters spoke more freely of the journey she had taken since leaving the farm, they were beginning to understand what an adventure it had been—Beth had met this German doctor, married him in the middle of his trial for crimes against the Nazi government, been sentenced with him to a prison camp in eastern Poland, escaped with him and their friend to Denmark, and from there moved to Belgium to await the birth of their daughter while they ran a café. Now they lived in England.

The truth was that Theo was more than a little envious of all that Beth had seen and done. Although he fully appreciated that a great deal of it had been horrible and terrifying, he admired his sister more than he could say for the courage she had shown in the face of such challenges.

Here at home he'd faced his own challenges. In school—even in the years he'd spent studying political science at the University of Wisconsin in Madison—he had had to deal with those who shunned him because of his German heritage and ridiculed him because his Quaker faith did not permit him to enlist. The truth was that he did not believe war was the answer to anything. And if he could, he would dedicate his life to finding ways to show that peace—not war—was the only way to go.

Theo wanted so much more than taking over the family farm.

Ilse Schneider allowed the rhythm of the train to rock her daughter, Liesl, who was finally asleep with her head on Ilse's shoulder. She was almost ten, and years on the run had changed her from an over-exuberant child to one who looked at the world through eyes shadowed with caution and fear. It occurred to Ilse that her daughter was becoming so much the way Ilse herself had been just a year earlier—suspicious, fearful of her own shadow, certain that the world held nothing good.

Liesl was dressed in a thin cotton dress two sizes too small for her, and her hair was braided into a single plait that hung all the way to her waist. She was too thin—they all were—and like most of the children they had crossed the Atlantic with, she had no shoes, her last pair having been destroyed by the process of disinfecting their clothing once they arrived in New York. As they boarded the train in Hoboken, New Jersey, that would take them north to Oswego, someone had found a pair of mismatched socks and given them to Liesl to wear.

Satisfied that Liesl would likely sleep through this endless night, Ilse allowed her gaze to drift to her husband's profile. This proud, quiet man had aged a decade in only a matter of months. His hair was thin and gray, his complexion sallow, and his face etched with lines that spoke of worry and fear and defeat. He wore the jacket of the suit he had been wearing the day they boarded a different train—this one in Munich, leaving their apartment and the city for the last time and starting what was to become the new normal for them for the next year and more. In this new life, they were constantly on the move as they tried without success to get to a place of safety until the war ended. His shirt collar was frayed, as were the cuffs of the shirt that was now too large for his diminished frame. His shoes, Ilse knew, were lined with newspaper to cover the holes in the soles, and they had long ago used the laces for some other purpose. The socks that she had knit for him as a birthday gift years earlier were long gone. He, too, was sleeping, his cheek pressed against the window as the train raced through the night.

In fact, most of the passengers in their packed car—one of several that had left Hoboken the day before—were sleeping. Their journey, which had begun the day they were taken onto a troopship in Italy, had been long, and their many questions had found no answers. Once again they were rushing toward the unknown. Ilse sucked in a breath and slowly let it out. She, too, wore the garb of a person whose life had been ripped apart. She, too, was exhausted and frightened and confused. But she—like her daughter and husband—was not the person she had been back in Munich before the war, in the days when their lives had seemed so settled and the mundane details of their routine had seemed so very important.

What a silly woman she had been! How she had wasted the happy times she could have shared with Franz and Liesl! Too often she had been so very unkind to Beth—the child of her husband's sister and the girl who had taken over whenever the war and life overwhelmed Ilse.

And where was Beth now? She and the young German doctor who had taken up residence in the attic space above their apartment in Munich had been supposed to come with them that day—had been supposed to get on that train. But they had not arrived in time, and Franz had suddenly believed that the young man he had admired and trusted enough to let live with them had in fact betrayed them. That had been the first sign of Franz's paranoia, and he blamed himself for whatever had happened to Beth. Ilse brushed away a tear as she wondered for the thousandth time what had become of the vibrant and beautiful young woman who had willingly stayed with them even after their two countries were at war.

No, Ilse had been a foolish woman in those days—selfish and fearful—but no longer. She smoothed the collar of her cotton dress, shrunken now by that same process of de-infestation that had ruined Liesl's shoes. On her feet she wore a pair of slippers, their leather cracked and peeling and the soles coming loose. She was embarrassed by the way the skirt of her dress barely grazed the tops of her knees when she stood up and by the fact that she was not wearing stockings or a slip.

More foolishness, she thought as she glanced at the other women crowded into the seats of the railway car. She wondered what they had been through. She wondered if some of them would become her friends and she theirs. They were mostly Jewish, and their ways were different from her Quaker faith. But what did that matter in a world gone mad? One of the younger women glanced over at her and smiled. She was traveling with her husband and two young children. The two women had spoken briefly on the voyage from Italy, and Ilse had learned that the woman's name was Karoline and that her marriage to Geza was her second. Franz had learned from the husband that Karoline's first marriage had ended badly and that her ex-husband had insisted on keeping the two children from that marriage with him. Karoline and her family were Jewish, and Ilse understood how worried the young woman must be for the children she had left behind.

Franz snorted. The air was heavy with humidity, and what breeze could be stirred by the movement of the train was hot and seemed to cling to their skin. Franz swiped the back of his hand across his upper lip to dry the sweat that had formed there. He looked over at her and then at their sleeping daughter.

"I can hold her while you sleep," he offered.

Ilse smiled. Franz still expected to see the old Ilse, the woman who could not cope. "She's fine," she assured him and then stroked his cheek with her fingertips. "She's probably dreaming of the Statue of Liberty. I have never seen our daughter struck speechless before, but when she saw that—'the lady,' she called it. . ."

Franz's eyes filled with tears as they had when the passengers crowded onto the deck of the troopship to get their first look at the famous landmark and whispered in their own languages but in unison some version of the word *liberty*. "We're free, Ilse," he murmured. "Free and safe. I just wish that Beth—"

"Sh-h-h," Ilse crooned. "Perhaps she made it out. Perhaps Josef's father. . ."

Josef, the medical student who had boarded with them and fallen in love with their niece, was the son of a powerful member of Germany's secret police—the Gestapo. Despite his position, the man had helped them on more than one occasion—first replacing without question the visa that Beth had claimed to have lost but in reality had given to a friend fleeing the country and then again when he had come to the university to warn Franz that he was about to be fired and perhaps taken into custody. Still Ilse had not trusted him—or his son.

"It's true. I don't think I have ever seen two people more in love than they were—or than I thought they were."

"I have," Ilse whispered as she leaned over and kissed his cheek. "No one could love you more than I do, Professor Schneider, and I know you feel the same."

Franz linked his fingers with hers. "I'm so sorry, my love," he whispered. "So sorry for what I have put you and Liesl through. If I had stayed away from those young people..."

"But you believed they were doing the right thing."

"I had a family to worry about. They did not. And I trusted Josef— he had been one of my brightest students...."

"You stood up and spoke out against evil. This is what we do—what our faith leads us to do. I only wish that I would have been so brave."

Liesl sat up and rubbed her eyes with her fists. "How far is this place?" she asked.

"Soon," Ilse assured her.

"And we can start our new life in America?"

"For now, *Liebchen*," Franz said. "But you must remember that—"

"You must remember that everything will take time," Ilse interrupted. She was not going to allow her husband to worry their daughter by reminding her of the paper they had all had to sign stating that once the war was over they understood that they would be sent back to wherever they had called home in Europe. She was sure that very few people on this train speeding along to Fort Ontario could imagine they had anything left in Europe to call home. Surely the paper had been a formality. Surely once the Americans understood the realities of their situation, they would not be held to that promise. Surely they would be allowed to stay.

PART I

OSWEGO, NEW YORK

AUTUMN 1944

THEY COME TO THE FENCE

OSWEGO N.Y.—The fence is chain link capped by three taut rows of razor-sharp barbed wire, and it surrounds the entire compound. The Fort Ontario Emergency Refugee Shelter is in fact—at least for now—a place where people who have been running for their very lives for the last several months or years are now incarcerated.

A polite term may be "quarantined," and it has been going on for a month. They may not leave the fort nor may relatives and friends who may already live here in America visit them inside the fence.

On one side of the intertwined wire are the "guests" of President Roosevelt—982 men, women and children brought to this small town on the shores of Lake Ontario from war-torn Europe. On the other are a mix of curious townspeople, relatives of someone inside, and do-gooders from agencies that specialize in such work.

Through the small openings in the wire, townspeople might offer a cigarette or a Royal Crown Cola or a stick of gum as a gesture of welcome. In some cases they practice language skills they learned in school, offering halting words and phrases of Italian, French, even German. The relatives are immediately recognizable, their heads bent close to the fence, close to the face of their loved one. The do-gooders come bearing boxes of clothing, toys and candy for the children, books and magazines, as well as newspapers to tell them what is happening back where they came from—where they must return once the war ends.

Those in charge have elected to ignore a hole the young people have created to get down to the lake on hot days or to leave the shelter to meet the friends they have made from town, or to shop for soda and treats at the little grocery store just outside the fence. The grocer says nothing about these illegal forays into his business, and often he adds something to the purchase—a piece of fruit, a box of crackers.

But at the end of the day, those who have escaped the shelter for a few hours return. Amazingly no one has tried to leave for good. No family member on the outside has attempted to orchestrate a permanent getaway. The refugees remain inside and wait. And therein lies the real story. When the war ends, FDR's guests have agreed to leave America and return to what?

CHAPTER I

The first thing Theo noticed when he arrived in Oswego and walked through residential neighborhoods until he reached the fort was the fence. Chain link seemed to run on for miles—certainly it surrounded an area of several acres. Six feet tall. Capped with three rows of barbed wire stretched tight. Behind the fence, rows of whitewashed barracks sat along the cliff that overlooked the lake. Some brick houses positioned on a hill, a small cemetery, and in the background the remnants of the actual fort remained as reminders of a site that had been so important to the security of a young America—through the Revolutionary War, the War of 1812, and even the Civil War. Theo guessed that other buildings might house offices and dining halls, a laundry and a chapel, as well as an infirmary and maybe a recreation center. But overall with the fence surrounding it, the place looked less like a military fort than it did a prison.

Theo had arrived after an overnight bus ride. In their family meeting with Matthew and Jenny back in Wisconsin, they had sat in silence, waiting for guidance as they decided the best way to bring Franz, Ilse, and Liesl home to the farm. After making several telephone calls and scanning the national newspapers in the local library, his father had learned that the refugees would need to remain at the shelter until the war was over. And although with the landing at Normandy in June the tide of war seemed to have turned in favor of the Allies, no one thought for a minute that it would end quickly.

"Well, we can't just leave them there among strangers," his mother had said, her lips set in a tight line that meant she intended to do something for her brother and his family immediately. She had already made plans to reassign the bedrooms of the farmhouse to make room for them. In the end it was decided that Theo would go to Oswego, find a room in a boardinghouse, and do everything he could to persuade the authorities that Franz, Ilse, and Liesl did not need to stay in the so-called shelter—they had a home and family right here in the United States.

The boardinghouse part had worked out fine. Once the owner—Selma Velo—learned that he was Quaker, in spite of the fact that her regular rooms were all filled, she had offered Theo a cot and dresser in the attic in exchange for him mowing the yard and weeding her garden and taking care of other household repairs that her son usually handled. Her son was serving in the Pacific. After supper—shared with the other boarders less one woman from Washington, DC, who had not yet arrived—he had followed his landlady to the basement and unearthed an old fan in need of a new electrical cord.

"My late husband's workshop is out in that shed behind the house. Can you fix this?"

"If I can find the right parts, I can," Theo assured her. He was grateful for the possibility of a fan, because in spite of the fact that he'd propped open the three small attic windows and there was nearly always a breeze off Lake Ontario a couple of blocks away, it was oven hot up there.

"There's a hardware store down on Ninth Street on the way into town," Mrs. Velo explained as she led him to the workshop. "I run an account there. It's closed up for tonight, but tomorrow if you need something..."

"Let me see what I can do tonight," Theo replied. The one thing that he had noticed about Oswego was that everything was close enough that he could walk—even to the fort. That was one of the best things about small towns. On their way to the workshop he saw an old bicycle also in need of repair.

Mrs. Velo saw him looking at the bike. "Use it if you can fix it." Inside the cluttered shed she pulled a chain that turned on the single lightbulb overhead. "I'll leave you to it," she said and headed back across the yard to the house, where a taxi was just pulling into the driveway.

He watched through the square, four-paned window curtained with dust and cobwebs and saw a woman get out of the cab. She was tall and thin with long dark hair. She wore a light-colored skirt and a printed, short-sleeved blouse and sandals with that wedge heel that made Theo wonder how women kept their balance. Over one shoulder, she carried a large purse, and when the cabdriver removed the luggage from the trunk there was one large suitcase and another smaller case that Theo realized was a typewriter.

At supper the regular boarders had quizzed Mrs. Velo about the new arrival. "A reporter?" one man guessed.

"Sort of," Mrs. Velo hedged. "She's a friend of a friend."

"A stranger, then," the woman seated next to Theo huffed.

"We are all strangers," Mrs. Velo said softly, "until we become friends. She is here to write about the refugees."

"I hear the government has spent a lot of money fixing things up for them," the woman—Hilda Cutter—said in a tone that sounded as if she were sharing some huge secret. "New refrigerators and ovens in every apartment and. . ."

Theo had barely paid attention to the rest. Hilda Cutter struck him as a gossip and someone who was always looking for the negative aspects of any situation.

But watching the new arrival as he gathered the tools he would need to repair the fan, Theo recalled Mrs. Velo's vague description of this woman from Washington and he wondered what "sort of" meant. Was this woman a reporter or not? Maybe she was with the government and needed to keep her identity secret. Someone from the government might arrive with a typewriter. She might have connections. Maybe he could talk to her about how best to get his uncle and aunt and cousin out. He turned his attention to the repair of the fan as he planned his approach.

Suzanne followed Mrs. Velo up the steps to the wide porch furnished with several wooden rocking chairs, a porch swing, and window boxes filled with bright red geraniums that lined the railing. The front entrance had a leaded-glass window set into a solid-looking wooden door behind a screen door that Mrs. Velo held open for the cabdriver.

"Just set them down inside there," Mrs. Velo instructed, reminding Suzanne that the cabbie needed to be paid and sent on his way.

She fumbled through the contents of her purse, pushing aside her comb, compact, lipstick, several wadded handkerchiefs, a fistful of pencils held together with a rubber band, a small notebook, and finally her billfold. She paid the driver, adding a less-than-generous tip because she noticed that she had very little cash and it would be Monday before she could get to a bank.

"You have a lovely home, Mrs. Velo," she said, following the woman inside. She was standing in a large foyer with a carpeted stairway on one side leading up to a landing that featured a window seat under another leaded-glass window and then turned to continue the rest of the way to the second floor.

"My late husband was quite handy. When we bought the place, it was a disaster," Mrs. Velo replied as she picked up Suzanne's large suitcase as if it were empty and headed past the stairway toward the back of the house. "Your room is back here," she said.

On the way Suzanne caught a glimpse of a large, dark dining room, its long table covered in a lace cloth, and a far more inviting kitchen with the window over the sink crowded with clay pots that appeared to be filled with herbs. She tried to pay attention as Mrs. Velo ran through the house rules.

"Breakfast is at seven, supper at six. You're on your own for lunch. No food in your room. No hot plates or candles, either. Here's a key to the room."

"Does this also fit the front door?"

Mrs. Velo blinked at her as if she had suddenly spoken in a foreign language. "Nobody in Oswego locks their houses," she said. She crossed the room and raised the blinds before opening the window that overlooked the backyard and a shed. "You'll get a nice breeze off the lake most nights, but in this weather you might want to run the fan." She pointed toward a small table and wooden chair. "I know you asked for a desk, but this is the best I can offer. You're welcome to use the desk in the living room, but be aware that that's for the use of all the boarders."

"This is fine," Suzanne assured her as she set her typewriter case on top of the table and unhooked her bag from her shoulder. "I have the money here for the deposit and first month's rent, although I might not be here an entire month and..."

Mrs. Velo looked directly at her for the first time. "You said you were doing a story on the refugees."

"I am."

"Honey, they are here for the duration of the war, and if you ask me there is no possibility in heaven or on earth that the war will be over before the end of the month." She stood in the doorway, her hand on the knob. "Of course, depending on the story—the depth of it I mean—I guess you could get the gist of things in a week or so, but I rent by the month."

Suzanne flinched at her landlady's lecture. "I understand," she said, handing the woman the envelope with the cash. "Thank you."

The door was half closed before Mrs. Velo opened it again. "You missed supper. I'll bring you a sandwich and some iced tea. At breakfast you can meet the others. You might be especially interested in that young man there," she added, nodding toward the window.

Suzanne saw a tall man leave the shed and walk toward the house. He was carrying a small electric fan. "Your son?"

Mrs. Velo frowned. "My son is in the navy, stationed in the Pacific somewhere. That young man is Theo Bridgewater. His uncle, aunt, and cousin are among the refugees. Like I said, you might want to talk to him."

Suzanne studied the man with interest. "I'll be sure to meet him," she said as she heard the door click closed.

Theo Bridgewater was at least six feet tall, lanky with long arms and legs and a way of moving that made him appear confident and at the same time approachable. He was wearing jeans that looked as if he might have owned them for a decade or more, a short-sleeved cotton shirt with a white T-shirt underneath, and a baseball cap that hid his facial features from her. She could not guess his age, but given his ease of movement, he was not that old.

Then she recalled the conversation she'd had with her landlady about the length of her stay. *"I rent by the month,"* Mrs. Velo had stated emphatically as if Suzanne had suggested that she would expect money back if she left early. *Great, Randolph. You really are getting off on the right foot here.*

Edwin had always told her that she had a habit of getting so wrapped up in her story that she forgot she was dealing with human beings with feelings and opinions of their own. "You come on like a dog with a bone, Suzie. Sometimes it takes a gentler touch."

No one had ever accused Suzanne of being gentle or approachable. Even as a child and teenager she had stated her opinions in such a way that other kids avoided her. Oh, they would elect her to run the student government or manage the school's newspaper, but when it came to friendships—not to mention romantic relationships—most people eventually gave up.

More recently Gordon Langford had given up. "Face facts, Randolph. The man used you and then cast you to the curb," she muttered. As soon as the story he'd urged her to write was published and exposed for the fabricated mess that it was, he had disappeared. Well, not entirely. He had defended himself by saying that "the reporter"—he had referred to her as if they had never met—had twisted his words. He had denied everything, and he had not returned her calls. And why should he? He had achieved his purpose, for in spite of the fact that his accusations could not be proven, he had raised questions about his opponent's integrity.

A light knock at her door proved a welcome interruption as Mrs. Velo presented her with a tray loaded with a tall glass of iced tea, a plate with a multilayered sandwich of ham, cheese, tomato, lettuce, and who could tell what else between slices of thick crusted bread. There was a small dish of sliced lemon, a sugar bowl, a cloth napkin, and a side dish with the most mouthwatering slice of chocolate cake Suzanne thought she had ever seen.

"This is so kind," Suzanne said as she accepted the tray. "I can't thank you enough. I really didn't have a chance to eat and—"

"It's a onetime deal," Mrs. Velo said, retreating into the hallway. But then she winked and added, "Have to be sure you paint me in a good light when you write that story."

Suzanne laughed and realized that it was the first time she had found her sense of humor in days—weeks. "Thank you," she repeated even as she felt tears well.

"Oh, honey, it's just chocolate cake," Mrs. Velo said, coming back into the room and taking the tray from her. She set it on the writing table and then took a seat on the end of the bed and patted the space beside her. "Is this your first big assignment?"

"No." Tears were coming in waves now along with hiccups and sniffles.

Mrs. Velo leaned back to retrieve a tissue from the box on the nightstand. She handed it to Suzanne and then waited while she composed herself.

"I'm so sorry. I must be overtired. I get emotional when I've not had enough sleep, and you've been so very kind, and. . ."

Apparently satisfied that Suzanne was not going to have another breakdown, Mrs. Velo stood up. "Edwin told me that you're good at reporting. He did say you can be a little over-enthusiastic, but it was clear to me that he wouldn't have sent you here if he didn't think you could handle this. You do know that the town is fairly crawling with reporters and photographers?"

"How do you and Edwin—Mr. Bonner—know each other?"

"Eddie grew up here. We went all through school together." Suzanne did not miss the way Mrs. Velo's voice softened, and her eyes got that faraway look people got when they were lost in a memory. "But that's all ancient history," she added, seeming to snap out of her reverie. "Now let me offer one piece of advice, Suzanne. We are like a family, so do not hide away here in your room. Get out and get to know the others and the folks in town. You'll find most people in Oswego can be mighty friendly once they get to know you."

"I will," Suzanne assured her. "Starting with breakfast. I promise. But for now I'd just like to unpack while I enjoy this wonderful meal and then take a hot shower and get to bed. It's been a long day."

"Oh, I nearly forgot," Mrs. Velo exclaimed. "The bathroom. It's at the top of the stairs. There's a hook and latch for privacy." She pulled out the bottom drawer of the dresser and removed a stack of towels. "I'll collect and replenish these every week—Monday is wash day. You're welcome to wash out personal items, but no hanging them in the bathroom to dry." She took a drying rack out of the narrow closet and set it up on a mat in the corner of the room. "If you need to iron something, there's a board built into the wall next to the icebox in the kitchen—the iron is kept on the top shelf of the pantry."

She glanced around as if searching for anything else she might have forgotten. The melting ice settled in the untouched glass of iced tea on the tray. "Well, I'll leave you to it," she said then patted Suzanne's cheek. "It's all going to work out, honey. You'll see."

The door closed for a second time, and Suzanne sat down at the writing table and ate her supper as she gazed out the window and the sunlight faded to dusk.

Will it all work out? And what is "it"? The war? My story? My life?

The train slowed, waking Ilse with the break in its seemingly endless rhythm. Sunlight streamed through the open windows, and in spite of the early hour, it was obvious that this would be another hot, humid day. She sat up and leaned closer to Franz as they stared out the window, eager for their first glimpse of the place they would stay. A murmur rolled back toward them from the front of the car.

"What are they saying?" Ilse asked her husband, whose command of languages far exceeded her own ability to speak only German and basic English.

"There's a fence," he replied. "With the barbed wire on top. Like the camps," he added. His voice became a whisper as he stared out the window at the fence, the low white wooden buildings that stood in rows like soldiers near a small cemetery. The men—some in uniform—hurried around inside the fence. And she knew that Franz was back in the prison camp where he had been taken for questioning and then held for months. The place where he had been beaten and starved. The place where he had suffered much more that he would not tell her. He had escaped from that camp and found her and Liesl in a nearby village, and together they had made their way over the Alps and into Italy just as the Allies were liberating that country.

"It is not the same, Franz," she whispered as she wrapped her arms around his thin shoulders. "This is America. They might have the fence for all sorts of reasons. It is not the same."

But she was less certain as they climbed down from the train and were ushered inside the fence.

As they waited in line to be registered, she fingered the tag they were all wearing—the one with a number and the words *U.S. Army Casual Baggage* imprinted on it as if they were no different from the cardboard suitcases and paper bags that held their belongings. Of course, some travelers clutched fine leather suitcases and satchels as well. The finer luggage pieces bore travel labels from exotic places like Paris and Rome and Monte Carlo. But those were the exception, and she knew that those refugees also wore the casual baggage tags. *When one is an outcast,* she thought, *one has no other identity.*

Ilse looked around. Townspeople lined the outside of the fence, pointing and whispering and watching them as if they were animals in a zoo. Some men held large cameras. News photographers, she guessed. Children, women, and a few men—most of them older—made up the rest of the crowd. Well, why shouldn't they stare? She and the others must seem so very foreign and exotic to these Americans dressed in clean and well-fitting clothes and wearing proper shoes and socks. Some of the women wore straw hats that blocked the sun and shaded their features. Ilse touched her hair and knew that it hung in limp waves. She tugged at her dress, trying without success to lengthen the skirt. They had wanted to look their best for their arrival, but the disinfection process had squelched those hopes, and after riding all night on the train, the clothes they wore were wrinkled and stained with sweat. They must look like exactly what they were—people without a country or home to call their own.

"Mama?" Liesl clung to her arm. "Why are those people staring at us, and why are they behind that fence? Have they been naughty?"

Ilse realized that her daughter's perception of things was that they were free and the townspeople were the ones being held behind the wire fence. The idea made her smile. "They are curious," Ilse replied as they inched closer to the table where men were seated, checking the numbers on their tags against names on lists. She was reminded of all the times that she and Franz had had to show their identity papers while living in Munich. Just going to the market, a person could be stopped and harassed and questioned. Ahead of them, a Jewish family stepped up to the table, and she wondered if they would again be required to wear the ugly yellow felt stars that had labeled them in Europe.

"Welcome to Fort Ontario," the smiling man at the table greeted them when it was their turn. Another man standing next to him translated the words into German and handed Ilse a paper bag stuffed with towels and a bar of soap. He was also smiling. Ilse had noticed that about the Americans. They always appeared so open to new people. Their niece Beth had been like that.

After their names had been checked off, they followed others up a hill to another line and more tables labeled CUSTOMS where they were separated from their few belongings. They had all heard the stories—and some of these people had actually had the experience—of such procedures in the concentration camps. People had been told that the baggage they had checked as they boarded a train would be delivered to them later, but instead, they had been led off to their deaths. For this reason, most of their fellow travelers on this journey had kept what hand luggage they could with them, and they refused the help of boys from town who met their train and offered to carry their baggage for them. The boys reminded her of the youth corps in Germany—the "brown shirts"—but someone explained that they belonged to a group called Boy Scouts that had nothing to do with war or politics.

"I will tag your belongings," the young man explained and went on to assure them that their things would be delivered to their quarters as soon as possible—probably while they were at breakfast. Did they really have a choice?

Franz set down their two suitcases, bound by twine because the edges were coming apart, and stood watching while a man tagged them and then handed him half the tag as a receipt. "This way," their guide and interpreter said as he led them and others toward one of the barracks. Inside Ilse expected to see a barren dormitory packed with rows of bunks perhaps stacked three high like the barracks Franz had described to her after his escape from the prison camp. Instead a hallway led past doors, each with a name on it. She began to recognize some of the names as families they had met on the ship coming across the Atlantic. Franz stopped before the last door. He ran his finger over the small placard that read FRANZ, ILSE, AND LIESL SCHNEIDER.

Their guide—yet another smiling young man wearing pressed trousers and a crisp white shirt—handed Franz a key.

"*Wilkommen*," he said as he continued the tour in German. "Bathrooms are shared—men's on the second floor and ladies' on this level." He opened the door with their name on it and stood back to give them a chance to enter the small apartment.

Ilse could not believe her eyes—two rooms just for them. "Kitchen?" she asked.

The smiling young man explained that all meals would for now be served in the mess hall.

"Mess hall?" Liesl repeated and giggled. "We will eat in a messy hall?" During the years that Beth had lived with them, Liesl had learned basic English, but—like Franz, whose English was fluent—sometimes certain phrases made no sense.

"Dining hall," the man explained. "We'll go there next."

The apartment was furnished with a wooden table and four chairs, a wall shelf that held a few cups and glasses, and a single cot in the room where they stood. Beyond that Ilse could see another room with two more cots and a footlocker at the end of each cot for their clothes. With her imagination, she began decorating the place. She had seen wildflowers on the hillside near the lake as the train pulled in. Perhaps later she and Liesl could go pick some for the table. There were no curtains on the window in the bedroom. *We will have to do something to cover that*, she thought.

"Ilse?" Franz put his arm around her shoulder and turned her back toward the hallway. "He says it is time to eat."

"In the *mess* hall," Liesl announced in English, and once again she giggled. It occurred to Ilse that their daughter had immediately responded to the kindness of the American. She was sure that this was Beth's influence.

The scent of cooking food would have guided them to the dining hall even if their interpreter had not been with them. When they entered the long brick building, they were taken aback first by the noise—people talking in several languages, people laughing and exclaiming over the bounty before them. And indeed it was a feast—

even more impressive than the meals they had been served on the voyage from Italy. The long wooden tables were filled with large glass bottles of milk, bowls the size of Ilse's mixing bowls at home filled with hard-boiled eggs, plates stacked high with sliced bread, dishes of jam and marmalade, and trays that held small boxes labeled CORN FLAKES. Ilse watched in fascination as one of the Americans demonstrated how to open the box and then add milk so that the box became the bowl.

She and Franz glanced at each other and burst out laughing. It felt so wonderful to share a moment like that. For months they had had to settle for scraps or wait in long lines while someone dished up half a cup of watery soup. The bread here was white and soft. While Ilse was not sure she liked it as well as she had the heavier rye bread they had enjoyed from the bakery that occupied the ground floor of their apartment building back in Munich, it was ever so much better than the gooey gray concoction that passed for bread in Europe these days.

Their interpreter explained butter was still rationed. Franz pumped the hand of their guide, thanking him in German and English. Then he led the way to a crowded bench at one of the tables. The people already there squeezed closer together to make room for them. Smiling, they shoved the food into their mouths as if they might never again see such a meal. Ilse saw some people hiding slices of bread and hard-boiled eggs in their pockets as they had at meals on the ship—just in case.

"America," one man kept murmuring to himself as he ate. "America."

Ilse understood his disbelief. But as she looked out the window behind where Franz was filling Liesl's glass with milk for a second time, she could see a large American flag snapping in the breeze off the lake. The only barrier between them and that flag was the fence, its thorny wire making Ilse all too aware that they might be on American soil but they were not yet free.

CHAPTER 2

Theo had risen early and skipped Mrs. Velo's breakfast to get to the fort. He had hardly slept. Aside from the heat that seemed to rise up from the lower floors and stagnate in the attic rafters, the excitement that he was going to find his aunt and uncle—his mother's only brother—and bring them home with him to the farm had kept him up most of the night.

As he stood outside the fence, waiting for the train to arrive, he supposed a stay at the fort was a necessary step on the road to true freedom for his aunt and uncle. But he shuddered to think what their first impressions might be as the train rolled onto the siding and they got their first look at the place that would be home for at least the next several months.

It was nearly 7:00 a.m., and the train was scheduled to arrive before eight. In spite of the early hour, locals had begun to gather on street corners and rooftops to get their first look at the refugees. Inside the wire fence men—some in uniform, others in coveralls—were setting up tables and shouting instructions to one another about the best way to process the new arrivals. Theo heard hammering and saw men carrying paint buckets as they exited the barracks. A man in uniform called out instructions to the painters in German, and Theo was at first puzzled but then realized the men in coveralls were German prisoners of war. How would the refugees react to their presence? Could some of the POWs have been guards in the prison camps the refugees had escaped from?

The soldiers and Americans in civilian dress seemed anxious to get the work done and move these prisoners out before the train arrived. Every once in a while, someone would look in the direction the train would come from and then shout at the POWs to go back to work.

On the bus trip from Wisconsin to Oswego, Theo had stared out at the passing countryside and thought about what the refugees would think of this new land once they boarded the train that would bring them to the shelter. Oswego, like Milwaukee, was on one of the Great Lakes, and he knew from having gone to Milwaukee on vacation with his parents that the expanse of water was so huge that even if the day was perfectly clear it was impossible to see the other shore.

In the distance he heard a train whistle. Immediately the low murmur of conversation among those waiting rose to a higher pitch. They crowded closer and craned their necks to watch for the train that slowly chugged its way onto the siding and stopped. Boy Scouts were lined up at each car's exit along with staffers from inside the fence who had now moved outside to facilitate the arrival. As the refugees slowly climbed down from the train and entered the lone gate that led them inside the shelter, Theo searched for his uncle and wondered if maybe he should have taken time to buy a small gift for Liesl—perhaps a doll. Well, presumably there would be time for that.

In minutes the grounds of the fort were jammed with hundreds of people along with the staff that was trying to get them registered and settled. It was impossible to pick out one individual. And as he made his way along the perimeter of the fence, studying each face, Theo realized that after years of being imprisoned and hunted his relatives were bound to look different—older, thinner. But he had not been prepared for the haunted expressions that he saw—eyes that were ringed with dark circles and that darted from person to person with suspicion; mouths that had clearly not smiled in some time but that were tight, thin lines; skin that was pale and shrunken.

This is what starvation and other constant deprivations can do to a person, he thought. *These are the faces of fear and doubt and uncertainty.* Even though they were safe on American soil, it would take time for these poor souls to believe they were truly safe.

He edged closer to the fence next to a news photographer and a reporter interviewing one of the townspeople. "It's not so different, I guess," the local was saying. "Last year we had the colored soldiers come for training and some boys from the South—couldn't read nor write, but they turned into right good soldiers. Now don't get me wrong— there was some in town who got all upset about those groups. But it all worked out just fine, and so will this." He jerked his head toward the masses of people shuffling toward the tables to be checked in. "May God bless them all," he added and shook his head.

The reporter turned to Theo, and the photographer swung around as well. "How about you?" the reporter asked.

"Not so fast, Andy," a woman interrupted as she pushed her way past the photographer to stand between Theo and the reporter.

"Suzanne Randolph," the reporter exclaimed. "We all thought—"

"Well, think again," she said, not allowing him to finish whatever thought he'd been about to put into words. "I'm working this story, and Mr. Bridgewater here is one of my sources so back off." She gave the reporter a playful push, and he laughed. Then he threaded his way along the fence to find someone else to interview.

"How do you know my name?" Theo asked. He recognized her as the woman he'd seen get out of the cab at the boardinghouse the evening before, but they had not been introduced.

"I missed you at breakfast this morning, but Miss Cutter filled me in. That woman is quite the busybody. You'll want to watch yourself around her."

And you, Theo thought. "What did you mean telling that reporter that I was your 'source'?"

"It means I've got dibs on your story. Believe me, not every reporter would have backed off, but Andy's one of the good guys." She rummaged in the large shoulder bag he'd seen her carrying the night before and after some effort found a small notepad and pencil. "So what is your story, Theo Bridgewater? And is it really just Theo or maybe Theodore or as a boy were you Teddy?"

"It's just Theo," he said, wondering if this woman ever paused for a full breath and looking around seeking a way to escape her questions.

"Miss Cutter—Hilda—said you came here from Wisconsin—does she have that right?"

Theo nodded as he continued to scan the lines of refugees. "Excuse me, please." He pressed close to the wire fence, hooking his fingers through the openings. "Franz Schneider," he called. "Ilse Schneider," he added, thinking that perhaps if he called out their names they would hear him. But there was so much noise, so many people talking in so many different languages, and on top of that was the chatter of the curious townspeople who surrounded him.

"Are those your relatives?" the reporter asked, squeezing closer to the fence herself as she continued to take notes.

"Look," Theo began, not wanting to be rude but also not interested in being the center of her feature story.

"You look," she said, lowering her voice. "From what I know your family will have to stay there until the war is over, and then they will be sent back to wherever they came from—originally. As in before they found themselves on the run or in some camp or whatever."

"I know that, but my uncle and aunt have family right here in the United States so why should they have to go back to where they have nothing?"

She gave him a look of pure pity. "Theo, at least half the people in there have what the government likes to call 'fireside' relatives, meaning a spouse, a child, or a parent already living here, and it makes no difference. They signed a paper stating they understood the ground rules."

"How do you know all this?"

She grinned. "I'm a reporter. It's my job to know. So let me tell your story, and maybe that will help. Nothing in America is more effective than the power of the press," she assured him.

He thought he'd never met a woman with more confidence, but there was also a kind of nervous desperation about her that made him cautious. "I don't know, Miss. . ."

"Suzanne. We're going to be living under the same roof for the time being, sharing meals and such. And if you think Hilda Cutter won't be waiting to grill you about the minute details of why you are here, think again." She shrugged and gave him a beaming smile. "Might as well trust me."

"Hilda Cutter is not a reporter," he reminded her.

"And because of that, she can't help your family members on the other side of this fence. I can at least try."

The lines of refugees were being moved up the hill toward the barracks.

"I'll think about it," he said as he eased his way back through the crowd and looked for some way that he might find a vantage point closer to the barracks. It was no use. They were too far away. A few minutes later, the refugees were led into a large building that someone mentioned was the mess hall.

Suddenly the parade ground was deserted, and the only remaining signs of the people that had crowded onto its soft grass were the piles of baggage and the tables where they had checked into their new home.

What now? He decided to walk back into town and get that present for Liesl and mail the postcard he'd written the night before to let his parents know that he was here. He saw that most of the townspeople had started to leave. The show was over—for now.

Okay, she had come on too strong with the country boy. His eyes had held that deer-in-the-crosshairs look. She hadn't missed the fact that they were beautiful eyes—blue with the long thick lashes that were such a waste on the male of the species. But any way she looked at it, the guy had practically run from her. Of course he was far too polite to be so obvious. A true gentleman. She sighed. A rare breed indeed.

But she was here to work—to resurrect her career. She was able to get the attention of one of the staffers and quiz him. Rumor had it that the following afternoon—Sunday—the camp director was planning a reception. Invitation only but Suzanne knew some press would be included. She was determined to be among the invited reporters.

"Andy," she called out, spotting her fellow reporter across the way. "Can I buy you a cup of coffee?"

"Depends on what that cup of coffee might cost me," he replied.

"A pass to tomorrow's reception would be nice."

He laughed. "Those are readily available. Just show them your press credentials."

She felt the now-familiar heat of embarrassment rising up her neck to her cheeks like the scale of a thermometer. "Well, see that's kind of the problem."

"You're on your own?"

"I have a market for the story once I get it but until then. . ."

Andy frowned. "Look, Suzie, I'd like to help you, but there's nothing so dangerous as a desperate reporter who'll do practically anything to get back in the game."

She had always liked Andy's straightforwardness. "You're right, but then there are reporters—like me—who did do whatever it took to get the story and paid a heavy price. I'm a quick study, Andy. You don't have to worry about me, and you can be certain that the paper interested in buying my story will have it checked word for word and fact for fact."

"Edwin Bonner?" he guessed.

She nodded. "So will you help me?"

"I'll see what I can do, but Suzie, the chances are not good. Beyond that you're on your own."

She kissed him on the cheek. "You're the best," she said.

"If I do this, promise me that you will not mess up," he replied.

"I won't. I promise."

They made arrangements to meet outside the fort's gate the following day and went their separate ways—Andy and the photographer to get some shots of the town and Suzanne to the park near the boardinghouse to work on her plan for the story and eat the apple she had taken from the bowl Mrs. Velo kept by the front door.

An hour later, she stopped working and leaned back, her face upturned and her eyes closed when a shadow darkened the sunlight. She opened her eyes and sat up straight. Standing in front of her was Theo Bridgewater, and he was holding the most beautiful doll she had ever seen.

"It's my uncle, aunt, and cousin," he said without preamble. "Franz and Ilse Schneider and their daughter, Liesl. The doll's for her," he added, holding it out to her. "Do you think she'll like it? I mean there was also a baby doll with a crib and all but..."

"She'll love it," Suzanne assured him. She scooted over to make room for him next to her on the park bench. "What made you change your mind? About the story?"

"I didn't change my mind. I told you I'd think about it. I did, and I can't see the harm. Like you said, it might even help."

Suzanne grinned. "I'm getting a press pass for tomorrow's reception."

"Okay." It was evident that he did not get the significance of this.

"That means I will be on the other side of the fence so I can find your relatives and you can stake out a place along the fence where you can be reunited and you can give Liesl her doll."

Theo's smile was slow to come but when it did, it was like the sun coming out after days of clouds and fog. He was one good-looking guy. Of course, Gordon Langford had also been easy on the eyes.

From the time they first entered the fenced area, Ilse had noticed that the staff always tried to refer to the place as a *shelter* rather than as a *camp*. She suspected they wanted to distract the new arrivals from the fact that their new home had many things in common with the concentration and labor camps that the Nazis had set up back in Europe. The hours of that first day passed in a blur of settling in and enjoying two more incredible meals in the dining hall. Lunch featured meat loaf, mashed potatoes with gravy, and carrots. The main course was rounded out with a salad of fresh, crisp lettuce and tomatoes so juicy and filled with flavor that Ilse could not get enough of them. For dessert they were each given an orange, and afterward she and Liesl walked to the field where she'd noticed the wildflowers growing to pick a bouquet. Franz had gone to reclaim their few remaining possessions.

But when she and Liesl returned to the small apartment with their flowers, Ilse saw a large carton that she did not recognize sitting on the wooden kitchen table. "*Was ist los?*"

"Open it," Franz urged, and she noticed that he was fighting a smile. Liesl climbed onto one of the chairs. "Open it, Mama," she said excitedly.

Ilse pulled the twine loose and spread the flaps of the cardboard box. She took out the first item—a cotton dress perfect for Liesl. It was blue gingham with white daisies embroidered around the neck and hem.

"Oh, Mama, it's beautiful," Liesl exclaimed as she took the dress and held it up to her thin bony body. "What else?" She leaned in to see what other treasures might be inside the plain brown box.

Ilse took out a man's shirt. It, too, was cotton, a muted green plaid with short sleeves. She handed it to Franz and smiled then looked in the box again. Quickly, she identified packages of new underclothes for each of them and some books for Liesl. At the very bottom of the box was a lavender pleated skirt that looked as if it would at last be long enough to meet Ilse's standards in modesty and a white blouse with pearl buttons down the front and lace around the flat round collar and the cap sleeves.

"There's one more item," Franz said as he took the box and started to break it down so that it would be flat. He handed Ilse an envelope. She opened it and unfolded the note inside, and as she did several bills in American currency floated down to the table. "Read it," she said, handing the note to her husband:

Dear Mr. and Mrs. Schneider,

"Your nephew Theo Bridgewater is staying with me in my boardinghouse near the fort. I know that he is trying to find you, and I believe that he has arranged to make that connection at tomorrow's reception. Although he has not yet been able to spot you through the fence, he also told me that many of the people in the shelter arrived barefoot, and he worries that you and your little girl have no proper shoes. The clothes were items I had here that I hope will do, but shoes must be fitted. Please use this money for that purpose or for any other need you may have. May God bless you and keep you safe.

With best regards,
Selma Velo.

"How very kind of this woman," Ilse murmured.

"Mama, I'll wear my new dress tomorrow for the welcome party, all right?"

"Yes. We want to look our very best." She turned to her husband. "Theo is here?" Her voice trembled; she couldn't quite believe the news.

"I'll go to the administration building and ask if I can use the telephone to call this boardinghouse." Franz put the letter back inside its envelope and grabbed his hat from a hook by the door. "Perhaps if Theo is there..."

"Go," Ilse urged, and she smiled at Franz. He was so excited, and after the weeks and months of his depression, she was anxious to encourage anything that might bring her husband all the way back to her. "Liesl and I will wash our hair, won't we, Liesl?"

"Who is Theo?" Liesl asked, and Ilse remembered that her daughter had been little more than an infant when they had all been together on the farm in Wisconsin.

"Theo is Beth's brother and your cousin."

"And he lives here?"

"In America—yes."

"Will Beth be with him? And Josef?"

"No, Liesl." Ilse struggled for words to explain why without putting a damper on the child's good mood. "But perhaps Theo will have news of them."

Ilse had thought so often of Beth and Josef—about her actions toward each of them especially in the early days when Josef had first come to live with them. She had been afraid of everything then and in particular of this former student of Franz whose father was a member of the Reich's secret police. In her paranoia, Ilse was certain that the Gestapo officer had sent his son to spy on them. And when she realized that Beth was falling in love with the young doctor, she was also certain that their niece was doomed. But on that fateful day when they had made a run for the train to take them away from Munich, it was Franz who became convinced that Josef had betrayed him to the authorities. He was sure that Josef was the reason he had lost his position at the university and that they were forced to leave with only the clothes on their back and a small valise.

Franz had sent Beth to retrieve something incriminating that he had left in his office. Later they learned that at that very hour several members of the White Rose resistance movement to which Franz had belonged had been arrested. Franz had admitted to Ilse that Beth and Josef had also been involved in the group, and when they heard nothing from her, they assumed she had been betrayed and arrested. Franz had never forgiven himself for sending her to the university that day. Now Ilse prayed that Theo would have some good news about Beth.

CHAPTER 3

Later that afternoon Suzanne was sitting at her typewriter, a blank sheet of paper rolled into the machine. How was she going to tell this story? She had once been known for the way she could take facts and present them in such a fashion that the people and places associated with the breaking news came alive for readers, meant something to them, stirred their emotions. But then she had gone too far and crossed that very thin line between the realms of journalism and fiction.

"Theo," Mrs. Velo shouted up the stairway. Suzanne startled at the unexpected noise, another part of living in a boardinghouse that she would have to learn to tolerate. "Telephone call for you," Mrs. Velo added in that same raised voice meant to carry all the way to the attic.

Suzanne listened for Theo's steps. They told their own story. They were slow at first, hesitant as if he hadn't heard Mrs. Velo correctly. And as if sensing his indecision, Mrs. Velo called to him again. "Theo, it's for you."

"Long distance?" Suzanne heard Theo ask.

"No. You gonna take the call or not?" Suzanne heard Mrs. Velo set the phone receiver down on the hard surface of the table. "I've got chicken frying that needs my attention."

He ran down the last of the stairs. "Hello?"

Suzanne pictured him standing in the shadowy front hallway of the house where the only phone sat on a small table with a straight chair next to it. There was no privacy, and voices tended to carry up the stairwell and down the hall.

"Uncle Franz?" Theo's voice was almost a whisper, and then it rose to a joyous shout. "Uncle Franz!"

To Suzanne's surprise he conducted the rest of the conversation in German. She caught a word here and there.

Ilse. Liesl. The wife and daughter, she recalled. And then a mention of "Beth."

When Theo's voice became even more muffled, Suzanne realized that she had moved closer to the door of her room to hear him over the spatter of chicken frying and someone cutting grass next door. Her hand was wrapped around the doorknob. She actually leaped back as if she'd been burned.

"Please tell me that you are not so desperate for a story, Suzanne Randolph, that you would stoop to eavesdropping on a private conversation." She sat back down at her typewriter, determined to put words on the blank page. But her thoughts were still on the conversation in the hallway.

She knew the exact moment when Theo hung up. Only seconds later she heard the heavy tread of Hilda Cutter's large brown oxford shoes coming down the stairs. "Good news?" Hilda asked as if she hadn't been listening at *her* door.

"Yes," Theo replied, but he said no more. The next thing Suzanne heard was the screen door creaking open and then shut.

Certain that Theo was on his way for the reunion with his uncle and aunt, Suzanne grabbed her camera, her pocketbook, and key. She was halfway down the hall when she realized she'd left her notebook behind. She ran back for that and then hurried out the door. The secret to any good story was to take a large complicated event like nearly a thousand refugees coming to Oswego and bring it all down to a single family's story. Possibly there were more interesting stories than that of Theo's family, but at the moment she saw Theo as her link to getting close to the refugees. She was not going to miss this opportunity.

Theo was already a block ahead of her when Suzanne emerged from the boardinghouse, having had to pause long enough to be sure that Hilda had wandered into the kitchen where she was giving Mrs. Velo advice on frying chicken in between pumping her for what the landlady might know about Theo and his family. When Theo reached the grounds of the shelter, he moved along the fence, hesitating now and then to stare at the people inside. But he was no gawker like so many of those who had come from town to stand outside the fence. Theo was looking for one man, and Suzanne knew the exact instant he found him.

She edged along the fence, fingering her camera as she glanced around for some unobtrusive spot from where she could photograph the reunion.

"Franz Schneider!" Theo shouted, and the man turned and began to walk slowly toward his nephew, his arms outstretched as if he might be able to wrap them around the fence.

Suzanne stood near a cluster of trees and starting snapping the shutter of her camera.

The older man reached the fence where Theo waited but dropped his arms as he stared at the barrier between them. Then Theo reached up and through the barbed wire that topped the fence, and his uncle reached up and clasped his hand. Both men had their faces pressed close to the wire. Both men were smiling, and she suspected both were crying, as well.

She knew for certain that she was having a lot of trouble focusing the camera because her eyes were blurred with tears.

"Your *Tante* Ilse will never forgive me for not coming to get her so that she and Liesl could share in this moment," Theo's uncle said, alternating between German and English as he and his nephew released their hold over the fence and clutched each other's fingers through the wire.

"We will have other reunions," Theo assured this man who was not anything like the robust professor he remembered visiting the farm all those years earlier. Franz Schneider was only a shell of the man he had been. Not only was he gaunt and emaciated, but his eyes had a hollow, haunted look that Theo suspected might never entirely go away. "Are you settling in?"

Stupid question.

Uncle Franz smiled and shrugged. "It is very nice here," he replied. "We have plenty to eat and a little apartment in that building over there. We can move around the camp—I mean the shelter—freely and they tell us that the fence was here long before we arrived. Once the quarantine is lifted perhaps. . ." He glanced over the buildings around them. "It is a pretty place, this part of New York—different from New York City where we got off the ship."

As suddenly as his thoughts had drifted, he brought them back to the moment at hand. "How is my sister? And tell me more of Beth." He pinned Theo with a hard look—the one Theo remembered his mother calling her brother's "classroom" look. *"It means he wants answers,"* his mother had told him. *"And he wants them now."*

"Mom is fine, and Dad as well. They are both anxious to hear that I've finally connected with you. I'll call them tonight. Beth and her husband and daughter are in England. They are safe, Uncle Franz, and as soon as the war is over they will come home."

"So she made it." The words were a whisper spoken more to himself than to Theo. He smiled with more relief than joy and looked at Theo again. "And she has married?"

"A German doctor—Josef Buch—and they have a little girl named Gabrielle."

"She married Josef?"

This news had upset Franz to the point that he was now shaking. "They are safe, Uncle Franz. I have a letter that Beth sent us to hold for you. I was in such a hurry to see you that I left the boardinghouse without stopping to get either that or the doll I bought for Liesl. She likes dolls, I hope."

"You will bring the doll and Beth's letter this evening after supper. We will meet here again—this time all of us. And you will be at the program and reception tomorrow."

"No, Franz. That's not open to the public, but I'll be right here."

"You are not *public*, Theo. You are family."

"Still, those are the rules. Perhaps after the quarantine is lifted—"

"Quarantine!" Franz spit out the word as if it were something foul he'd eaten by mistake. "If they are so concerned that we might carry some disease, then why are not the government people and those from town working here quarantined as well? They come and go as they please."

"Do you need anything?" Theo was beginning to feel as if he was upsetting his uncle and cast about for something more positive they might talk about. "I can shop this afternoon and bring you whatever you need this evening."

Franz patted his nephew's hand and smiled. "Just come," he said, his voice once again hoarse with emotion. "There will be time for shopping later. We need shoes—your landlady sent us clothes and money for shoes but we cannot go shopping."

"Draw patterns of your feet and bring them to me tonight. I'll take them to the shoe shop in town. Surely they can figure out sizes."

"What a clever boy you are, Theo. Ellie always said that of all her children you were the brightest, and now I begin to understand why."

"Don't let Beth hear you say that," Theo warned, laughing.

"I should get back," Franz said, releasing Theo's fingers. "Your aunt will wonder what has become of me. She worries, you know."

Theo remembered. "I'll see you tonight, then—all of you—and I'll bring the doll for Liesl and the letter from Beth."

They backed away from the fence, and Franz started walking back to the barracks, turning several times to glance back at Theo as if he could not quite believe his nephew was real. Theo raised a hand in farewell and felt a lifting of the responsibility he'd been given by his parents. He had found his uncle, later he would see his aunt and cousin, and after that he would call his parents and give them the good news. Of course he would wait for the long-distance charges to go down, but Wisconsin was an hour earlier than New York so he knew his parents would be awake.

He heard a clicking sound and realized that it had been background noise the entire time he'd been talking with his uncle. He glanced around and saw a camera aimed at him.

"Hey!" He started toward the woman holding the camera. He knew that the refugees had attracted a lot of attention and that there was even a news crew from *Life* magazine staying at the hotel in town, but still. . .

The woman lowered the camera. Suzanne. She adjusted the strap around her neck and waited—for what? Did she expect him to attack? Rip the camera from around her neck and destroy the film inside?

He walked toward her. "Look, Miss Randolph, I know you came here to get a story, but common decency would say you need to ask permission before invading somebody's privacy."

"You have no proof that I was photographing you," she blustered. "I was taking pictures for my article. The fact that you and your uncle just happened. . ." Her voice trembled with the weight of her lies.

"Just don't do it again. We are a quiet, simple people—my family and I. Perhaps it would be best if you find some other story to tell, after all."

He turned to walk away.

"Wait," she called, hurrying to catch up to him. He noticed that she had an athletic stride—not very feminine but at the same time very appealing. "I'm sorry, okay? I admit I heard parts of your phone conversation and I admit that I followed you here. Face it, I'm not all that different from Hilda Cutter."

She looked up at him with eyes that begged for forgiveness and pity, and he couldn't help himself. He laughed. "You can cut the act. I forgive you, but my family is off limits—got it?"

The wide-eyed innocent look shifted seamlessly into a frown of determination. "If that's what you want. But don't forget that it's your family who is incarcerated behind that fence for all intents and purposes. You know what the ground rules are. When the war ends they will be sent back. Sometimes you have to make a little noise to get the powers that be to do the right thing. In this case—because most of the folks in there with your family are Jews—it's going to take a *lot* of noise, but there are Americans who are sympathetic to their cause and willing to speak up for them."

"I don't understand. I mean, I know there are people in town—like Hilda and others—who have their prejudices, but this is a government project and—"

"And you think people who work in government can't be biased against certain ethnic groups?" She did not wait for an answer. "This so-called shelter is nothing more than a token gesture. Do you think that rescuing less than a thousand people when there are tens—perhaps hundreds—of thousands just like them who got left behind makes anything like a real difference?"

Her eyes flashed at him, and she placed her hands on her hips.

"Hey, I'm a Quaker," he said, trying to disarm her. "Peace loving and not up for a fight with you, okay?"

She looked a little surprised at this information. "You're a Quaker? Your relatives in there, as well?" She jerked her head toward the fence.

"Is that a problem? I mean, for your story?" He suddenly thought that with her fiery speech about the Jews, she was intent on telling their story. "How about this: I'm sure my uncle and aunt can introduce you to someone who would be right for your article. Why don't you come here with me tomorrow after the program and reception? You can meet Franz and Ilse, and you can tell them what you're looking for. I'm sure they'll be glad to help out." At least his uncle would. His memory of his aunt was that she was a tight-lipped, cautious woman with a permanent scowl of disapproval etched into her features.

"I'm also a Quaker," she said softly, seeming to ignore his offer to introduce her to Franz and Ilse. "Or I was once."

That explained her passion for making sure the refugees were treated fairly. He was about to quip, "Once a Friend always a Friend," but something in the way she looked away made him abandon that idea.

Somewhere in the distance a clock chimed, and Theo glanced at his watch. "It's getting close to suppertime," he said. "Mrs. Velo will wonder if she should set places for us or not."

"I think I'll get something in town," Suzanne said. "I'm not sure I can handle Hilda tonight."

"Okay. I'll let Selma know. And if you change your mind about coming with me tomorrow after the program. . ."

She smiled at him. "I never said whether I would come or not," she reminded him.

"Suit yourself." He started walking away then turned back and pointed to her camera. "I want to see those pictures and show them to my uncle. We'll decide whether or not you have permission to use them."

The frown was back. "If I decide to use them," she bargained, "then you can see them. Otherwise. . ."

Theo grinned. "Fair enough." He continued on his way, aware that she remained where she was. It was as if he could feel her watching him. Testing that theory, he lifted his hand and waved to her without turning around. "See you later," he called.

And when she instantly replied, "I'll come with you tomorrow," he knew he'd been right.

Ilse was arranging the wildflowers when Franz came into the apartment. He looked agitated, nervous, but at the same time he seemed excited. "What's wrong?" she asked.

"Where's Liesl?"

"I sent her out to meet some of the other children playing on the parade ground. Franz, what has happened?"

He sat down heavily in one of the wooden chairs and rested his folded hands on the table. His hands were shaking, and he was breathing heavily as if he had run a great distance.

"I saw Theo. I called, and he wanted to come right away, and there was no time to get you and Liesl, and. . ."

She placed her hands on his to still them. "What did he say?"

Franz looked at her. "They have heard from Beth. She has married Josef, and they have a child—a daughter."

"Where are they?"

"In England. Theo said there is a letter from Beth to you and me. He will bring it this evening. How could she marry Josef, Ilse? He betrayed us." Franz buried his face in his open palms.

"We don't know that for certain," Ilse said as she moved behind him to massage his shoulders. "We have believed for so long that this was the case because it seemed the only explanation, but what proof did we have?"

"He was the son of a Gestapo agent," Franz reminded her.

"And he was in love with our niece."

"Perhaps. It could have all been an act on his part. You were the one who was suspicious of him," he reminded her.

"But I changed my mind, and after all, it was Josef's father who risked his position to come and warn you—who gave us the opportunity we would never have had to escape had it not been for that warning."

Franz released a heavy sigh. "We will see what her letter says and hold her and her child...."

"And Josef," Ilse added. "We will hold them all in the Light and pray that one day soon we will all be together."

Franz's snort of a laugh told Ilse that he did not believe such a thing was possible. "Theo says that Beth and Josef and the child will come here when the war ends, but we are to go back. Back to what, Ilse? I have no job, and what do you imagine has become of our apartment—our things?"

Ilse sighed. Somewhere along the way, she and Franz had switched roles. Now he was the worrier, the one who could see no hope for their future. It was up to her to find some way to ease his fears before they could infect their impressionable daughter. She leaned down so that her lips were close to his ear.

"Franz, we are here, and for now we are safe. Liesl is free to leave the house and play with other children. We have food and shelter and clothing. Can we not take time to be grateful for these things before we worry about a future over which we have little control?"

She felt the tension ease from his shoulders, and he reached up and patted her hand. "How was I ever so blessed to find you, Ilse?"

She chuckled. "I'll wager there has been more than one occasion over the years we've spent together when you wondered how you had been so cursed," she teased. "Now go find Liesl so she can wash up and we can all go to the dining hall for supper. I overheard one of the kitchen workers say that we are being treated to something called 'steak,' whatever that is."

Steak turned out to be a kind of beef that the women who worked in the kitchen had cut into pieces and made into stew. Upon their arrival, each of the refugees had been assigned to work on one of the crews meant to keep the shelter running smoothly. The shelter director, Joseph Smart, and his staff had handed out the assignments. Ilse and other women with young children had been assigned to the child care center. Franz worked in the fort's hospital. It was small but impressive in the scope of care it could offer. One of the refugees who had been a physician back in Europe served as the medical director.

While they were eating the special meal that did not really seem all that different from the meat loaf lunch they had enjoyed their first day or from the stew Ilse used to make, Mr. Smart and a few of his staff stopped by the dining hall. He moved among the long tables chatting with people, a translator following with him to help bridge any language barriers.

"I don't understand," Ilse heard him say. "Where are the steaks—these people are eating stew. What happened?"

"What is this 'steak'?" a man asked, and others listened closely for the answer, for clearly the director was upset.

"It's a meat—a large slab of meat that when cooked properly is tender and delicious," the translator explained.

"And how is it prepared?" someone else asked.

"Usually it is broiled and then served with a baked potato or perhaps mashed potatoes and a green vegetable like beans or peas. You cook the meat separate from the vegetables because it is in a way a delicacy—something very special."

"This meat came in large slabs," one of the women who worked in the kitchen told him. "We cut it up. We mixed it with the vegetables—that is our way."

Everyone looked at Director Smart, waiting for his reaction. It was evident to Ilse that most people expected him to be angry and to berate the women for their stupidity. That's certainly what would have happened in the camps. But as she watched she saw the corner of Smart's mouth twitch and then he was smiling and then he was laughing as were the people on his staff. "Well, *bon appetit*," he said finally and took a seat at one of the tables while the woman who had told him about cooking the meat served up a plate of stew and handed it to him.

Up and down the long tables, everyone went back to their meal, but they were smiling—not entirely sure of the problem but certain that the man in charge was not going to punish them or deprive them of their meal. It was, Ilse thought, yet another sign that they were safe.

CHAPTER 4

Suzanne was having serious second thoughts about whether or not she had any chance of telling a story about the refugees that could hold up against the work of the other reporters on the scene. She needed to come up with some unique angle, but if she couldn't even get inside the fort...

Andy had been unable to secure a press pass for her to be on the grounds for the ceremony. He had pulled every string he could to no avail. So on Sunday, like dozens of townspeople, she stood outside the fence watching as a drum and bugle corps presented the flag, someone sang "The Star-Spangled Banner," and a local priest gave a prayer of invocation.

The mayor stepped to the podium to give a word of welcome to the refugees standing or sitting on the grass of the parade ground. The director of the shelter—Joseph Smart—along with representatives of various government agencies such as the State Department and the Department of Interior also offered their remarks. Suzanne noted that Director Smart in explaining the decision to translate the day's events into German commented, "We are not at war with the German language, only with the Nazi oppressors." That statement earned him a rousing cheer from the refugees.

Appropriately—given that nearly 90 percent of FDR's "guests" were Jewish—the program ended with a prayer by the rabbi from the synagogue in Oswego. Following the official ceremony, everyone made their way to a row of tables set up with refreshments under the shade of some trees.

"How about something cold to drink?"

Suzanne turned to find Theo standing next to her, offering her a paper cup filled with ice and a slice of fresh lemon and lemonade.

"Selma sent it over," he explained.

"Selma? I notice you're on a first-name basis these days."

He shrugged. "She tries to act tough, but she's quite the softie inside. She said I should make sure you don't stand in the sun too long."

"I learned some time ago to carry my shade with me," Suzanne told him, pointing to her wide-brimmed straw hat before taking a swallow of the sweet liquid. "You look nice."

It was evident that he had recently showered and shaved. His skin was ruddy, and his hair still damp. He wore a plaid, cotton short-sleeved shirt, jeans, and a baseball cap. She was pretty sure that he blushed at the compliment.

"How did your cousin like her doll?"

"I think she really liked it," he said. "She's quite the little talker once she warms up to you. She told me all about the doll she used to have back in Munich and how she and my sister, Beth, used to play tea party and house and how her father had told her that Beth now had her own real baby and. . ." He stopped suddenly and looked down. "Now look who can't shut up," he muttered.

"I brought something for Liesl, as well, if you think it would be all right for me to give her a present."

"Like what?"

She took a tissue-wrapped package from her bag and opened the layers of thin white paper to reveal a rainbow of colorful ribbons. "For her hair," Suzanne explained. "I mean, I guess I just assumed that she would have long hair—pigtails maybe?" She suddenly had doubts. As usual she had simply rushed into buying something she thought a girl would like without finding out anything about this specific child.

"They're perfect," Theo assured her. "She's going to love them. And yes, she has a braid—it's not pigtails, just a single braid."

Suzanne breathed a sigh of relief. "Good." She glanced around, noticing that the reception was beginning to break up as some of the refugees wandered back toward the barracks and some of the dignitaries began to get into their cars. "Is this where we're supposed to meet your family?" she asked.

"Over this way," Theo said, indicating a shaded area. "Here they come now."

Suzanne reached into her pocketbook for her notebook and pen, but Theo put his hand on hers to stop her. "Maybe for this first meeting we could just talk—get to know them?"

"Sure."

She watched the family coming toward the fence. Theo's uncle was probably younger than she had first thought. The mother—Ilse—had fixed her eyes on Suzanne, and it seemed to Suzanne that the woman was sizing her up as to whether she might be friend or foe. The little girl—Liesl—wore a sleeveless blue gingham dress with daisies embroidered on it, a single braid of blond hair that reached her waist, and no shoes. She was also clutching the doll Theo had given her.

"Hello," Liesl said as she ran ahead of her parents to reach the fence first. "I am Liesl, and are you the reporter who is going to tell President Roosevelt about us so he will let us go home to the farm with Theo?"

This was one of those trick questions like a lawyer asking a witness if he still beat his wife. Suzanne smiled and stooped down so that she was more at an eye level with the child. "I am very pleased to meet you, Liesl. My name is Suzanne, and yes, I am a reporter."

She stood again as Theo introduced his aunt and uncle. Handshakes were impossible with the fence so Suzanne just nodded and said how pleased she was to meet them. A dozen questions came to mind, but they were all a reporter's inquiries. Suzanne was really no good at small talk, and she knew that if she started firing away with the things she wanted to know for her article, she could scare them off.

"Miss Randolph brought you a present, Liesl," Theo said when the silence threatened to become uncomfortable.

"Another present?" Liesl looked up at her mother. "It's not even close to my birthday," she added.

Suzanne handed Theo the packet of ribbons, and he passed it over the fence to his uncle, who handed it to Liesl. "What do you say, Liesl?"

"*Danke*—I mean, thank you," the child murmured absentmindedly as she concentrated on opening the paper without damaging it. "Oh look, Mama! Ribbons and so many of them," she added in awe as she fingered each one. "Thank you so much."

"There's a blue one that would go perfectly with your new dress," Ilse said. "Turn around, and I'll tie it onto your braid." She made a bow with the ribbon and lifted Liesl's braid over the child's shoulder to show her the result. "See? It is just right."

The smile Ilse gave Suzanne said that she had made up her mind— Suzanne was a friend. "I wanted to bring something for you and Mr. Schneider," Suzanne said, "but I couldn't think what."

"This is more than enough. There is no need for gifts," Ilse assured her.

Suzanne turned her attention to Theo's uncle, who had remained quiet. "I understand that you are a professor, Mr. Schneider. . .or is it Dr. Schneider?"

"I was a professor, and yes, I have my doctorate, but these days I work in the shelter's hospital. I keep the records there." The smile he gave her was one of embarrassment at his reduced status, and she wondered how many of the people inside the fence felt that same sense of loss. Grief came in many forms.

"And what subjects did you teach back. . .when you were teaching?"

"I taught in the sciences at the University of Munich. Our home was there. It is where I suppose we will be sent once the war ends." His eyes wandered away from her face as if he were already somewhere else.

Suzanne felt that she had some understanding of the man's

sadness. When a person lost the job they were meant to do, it could be demoralizing. And for a man in his prime as Franz Schneider had been, the blow must have been shattering. "I am so very sorry," Suzanne said softly.

"But you are here now," Theo reminded him. He knelt down close to where Liesl had plopped on the grass and was talking quietly to her doll. "Did you name her yet?"

"Lizbeth. That's what Mama told me Beth now calls herself. It starts with the same letter that my name starts with. Lizbeth is in England, and she married Josef, and they have a baby, and—"

Ilse touched the top of her daughter's head. "Enough, Liesl."

"Was all that news in Beth's letter?" Theo asked.

"Yes, all of that and more," Franz replied. He looked directly at Theo and added, "Now we understand. For all these months we had thought that Josef..."

She heard the older man's voice break and wondered what the story behind this puzzling dialogue might be.

"Miss Randolph," Ilse said, covering for her husband, "perhaps one day you will meet our niece. Then you will have a story to tell. I assure you." She laughed. "Beth—for she will always be Beth to me whatever she may call herself—lived with us in Munich. She practically raised Liesl for the first eight years of her life. When we were forced to leave, we were separated and until Theo brought us a letter that she had sent to his parents to hold for us, we had no idea what had happened to her. It is such a relief—a gift really—to know that she is safe and happy."

Suzanne's brain was reeling with angles for that story—Beth's story. But Edwin had sent her here to get the story of the refugees. And besides, Beth and her husband were still overseas, and there was this little matter of a war raging over there.

"Miss Randolph is working on a story for the newspapers about the shelter," Theo said as if confirming her thoughts. "Aunt Ilse, would you be willing to introduce her to some of the other women?"

For the first time since they'd been introduced, Suzanne saw Ilse hesitate. "I really don't know that many people yet. When you have so many people from different countries—different religions and customs, different languages even—it takes time, Suzanne. We've only just arrived here."

All Suzanne heard was that Ilse had not said an outright no. She smiled. "I've got time," she told the older woman. "And meanwhile, you and I can become better acquainted while you tell me your story. You and your husband and daughter will become a voice telling the whole country of the plight of the refugees."

Ilse glanced at her husband. "Franz?"

"We do not wish to do anything that might jeopardize whatever possibility we have to stay in America. Perhaps we should let others be the voice of this circumstance, Miss Randolph. My family has been through enough."

And there was her no.

Back at the boardinghouse, Theo noticed at supper that Suzanne was unusually quiet. Hilda Cutter babbled on about the refugees and the gossip she had heard that morning in church and the trouble there was sure to be once the quarantine was lifted and "those people" were free to go wherever they pleased.

Suddenly Suzanne's head shot up, and she pinned Hilda with her gaze. "*Those people* are not hooligans, Hilda. Theo's uncle, for example, was a respected university professor in Munich. There are doctors and men who were successful in business and women who also had careers. I was told by a fellow reporter that there is even a well-known French actress among the group."

"Well, from what I have heard, most of them are Communists. That is our next great worry, you know. The Communists are little better than the Nazis and—"

"My uncle and aunt are not Communists," Theo said quietly. "They are Quakers like me and my parents and siblings."

He saw Suzanne give him a slight smile before she turned her attention back to her food—food she was moving around the plate with her fork but not really eating.

"A Quaker, eh?" Usually Hugh Kilmer concentrated on his food and paid little attention to the conversation. The other regular boarder, he was a traveling salesman who kept a room at Mrs. Velo's for when he was calling on customers in northern New York State. "You folks the ones who won't fight—won't join up?"

It was a challenge that Theo had grown used to. "We are pacifists, yes, but we serve in other ways."

"Safe ways," Hugh muttered as he stuffed a huge forkful of mashed potatoes into his mouth and continued to stare at Theo. "You have relatives in the camp, then?"

"My uncle and aunt and their daughter—my cousin."

"Germans, are they?"

The words rolled across the room like syrup spilled on the lace tablecloth, sticking to everything as it oozed its way down the table. Theo was aware of all eyes on him—including Suzanne's.

"We are of German heritage, my family, yes," Theo replied and went back to eating, although he had lost his appetite.

"Seems off to me that old FDR would include Germans in those he picked to bring over here," Hugh muttered. A beat of quiet was punctuated only by the clink of flatware on plates and ice shifting in glasses, but with the silence came Theo's certainty that Hugh would finally drop the conversation. He was wrong.

"I mean the French—sure. They're on our side. Even the Polacks and Slavs I can see. After all, Hitler ran straight over them and took over their countries, didn't he?"

"He also took over Germany," Suzanne said, her voice firm and dangerously soft. It was a warning for Hugh Kilmer to shut up, but it came through as clearly as if she had said those words instead.

Hugh turned his attention to her. "You're the reporter, right? From Syracuse?"

"Washington," Suzanne replied, concentrating on cutting her chicken cutlet into bite-sized pieces.

Hugh released a low whistle. "Our nation's capital. Impressive. What paper?"

Suzanne's cheeks reddened as if she was suddenly far too warm and needed air. "I. . .that is. . .there is. . .I am freelancing," she finally managed just as Selma appeared from the kitchen carrying the pitcher of tea that she had gone to refill. "I am not feeling so well," Suzanne murmured as she placed her napkin next to her plate and pushed back her chair. "Please excuse me."

Theo stood as he'd been taught to do whenever a lady entered or left his company. Hugh Kilmer just kept stuffing his mouth with mounds of mashed potatoes.

Suzanne did not return to her room after her abrupt exit. When she left the table, Theo heard the screen door open and close with a soft click. Hilda and Hugh continued to chatter on, apparently knowing each other well. Selma told them all that the other two boarders on the second floor had left that morning for a camping trip and would be gone for a week.

Theo let the conversation flow around him without comment. He was well aware that Hugh Kilmer made some passing references to the "Krauts"—comments Hilda apparently found hysterically funny. Theo cleaned up the last of the peas and potatoes on his plate, washed them down with the last of his tea, and stood up. "Mrs. Velo, if it's okay with you, I'll use the tools in the workshop to repair that rocker on the front porch."

"Oh, Theo, there's no rush, and it's so hot."

"The sun's setting, and there will be a breeze off the lake," Theo replied with a smile meant only for her. He nodded briefly to Hugh and Hilda and left the room. As he went out to the porch to get the chair and carry it to the workshop, he heard Hilda say, "He's certainly a handsome young man."

"Maybe," Hugh replied, taking no pains to lower his voice. "But he should be over there defending his country, not sitting here waiting for somebody else to save him and his Kraut relatives."

Suzanne was not on the porch as Theo had hoped. He had planned to suggest that she sit with him in the workshop while he repaired the chair so they could talk. He glanced up and down the tree-lined street where kids were out playing in the yards while the adults—women mostly—sat on the porches and talked about the heat. There was no sign of her.

It took longer than Theo had expected to find the proper wood to replace the rotted arms on the rocker. Once he had sanded and attached the new arms, they had to be painted, so by the time he pulled the chain to shut off the light and stepped out into the yard, the house was mostly dark. He stood a minute, enjoying the yard filled with the scent of lavender and mint from Selma's herb garden and the soft intermittent glow of fireflies sprinting here and there. Certain that at this hour everyone would be sleeping, he walked around the side of the house and mounted the wooden porch steps.

Suzanne was sitting in the swing that hung from the rafters at one end of the porch. "Hi," he said. "Hot night."

"Nothing stirring," she agreed as she made room for him next to her on the swing. "Sorry about the talk at supper," she added.

"Certainly not your fault, and besides, I'm pretty used to it." He sat down next to her, setting the swing in motion. "Back home my brother and I had to hear a lot of the same stuff."

"Didn't it make you mad?"

Theo shrugged. "I get it that for some people war—fighting—is the only answer."

"And we all know how well that has worked over the centuries," Suzanne said sarcastically.

"People get all worked up—they hear things on the radio, read them in the newspapers. . ."

"Oh, so now this whole thing is my fault, after all?" She laughed.

"I'm just saying that there are all kinds of ways to tell a story depending on the outcome you want to achieve." He chuckled. "It's a little like that game we played when we were little—I think it was called 'gossip'—where a bunch of kids would sit in a line and—"

"The first kid would whisper something to the one next to him, who would whisper what he or she heard to the next, and so on—"

"And by the time it reached the last in line, it was a totally different message than what the first kid had whispered. Seems to me this whole political thing is a little like that. But what do I know? I'm just a farmer from Wisconsin."

They rocked in the swing in silence for several minutes.

"So how do you think I should tell the story?" she asked.

"Depends on what story you plan to tell and on what you believe. If old Hugh were telling the story, it would be about the mistake the president made in bringing these folks here in the first place. If you told my uncle's story it would be a story of fear and anxiety that when the war ended—a good thing—he and Aunt Ilse and innocent Liesl would be sent back to Munich where he has no job and they probably have no apartment and would have to start again."

"Why do you think President Roosevelt did this? I mean, rescued fewer than a thousand people when there are so many thousands in need? And why incarcerate them and send them back? And why—"

He placed his hand on hers. "All good questions and ones I'm sure you plan to work into that story you plan to write. I'm sorry my uncle turned you down."

"He has a point. He and his family have been through so much. It's understandable that he's being cautious, not wanting to rock the boat."

"Tomorrow I'm picking up shoes for them from Mr. Vastano's shop on Bridge Street. If you want to come along when I hand them over the fence, maybe Uncle Franz will have changed his mind."

"No. He needs some time, and I do understand. I'll just have to find another way to report this so that it personalizes it for the readers. Statistics don't get the job done, although they certainly help drive home the point. I need to put faces to those numbers." She stood up. "Either way I have a deadline of sorts. Stories like this can become old news fast, especially when there's a war on. Maybe I'll see if I can find the French actress."

"You'll do fine," he told her, although he had no basis for knowing that. After all, she might be a terrible reporter. And he wondered why she had described herself as a freelance writer when he'd been under the impression that she was on an assignment for a newspaper.

He stood up as well. "Good night, then."

She opened the screen door. "Coming?" she asked.

"No. I think I'll take a walk and maybe it'll cool off a little more before I go up to the attic."

"Good night, then."

"Good night—and Suzanne? Don't let Hugh and Hilda get to you, okay?"

She laughed. "I was just about to tell you the same thing."

CHAPTER 5

I t's not bad," Edwin Bonner said when he called Suzanne at the boardinghouse after receiving her first submission about the arrival of the refugees. "What's your angle? I mean overall. People talking through the fence and all—where are you heading with this?"

Suzanne sat on the chair next to the phone and twirled the cord around her finger. Above her she heard the soft click of Hilda Cutter's door opening and knew the busybody was listening. Leave it to Edwin to raise the one question she couldn't answer. At least not yet. "I'm not sure," she admitted.

"Well, that's refreshing. A few months ago you would have been full of bluster and blarney about your plan."

She winced. Would Edwin ever let her forget the past? Unlikely. At least not until she proved to him that she had changed and would never again go down that road.

"Do you wish to know my thoughts?" he asked.

"Of course."

"I am thinking of a kind of diary approach. Little vignettes about life in the fort. I can get the political angle at this end. But you can perhaps raise questions for people to consider. Not blatantly, of course. Delicately. We have to take this in baby steps. Anti-Semitism is every bit as rampant here on this side of the pond as it is over there—the difference being Americans are more subtle."

"Edwin, that's really getting into a dangerous area." She glanced up the stairway and lowered her voice. "I think if we stick to stories about the refugees as just people like anybody's neighbor or the man who owns the local shoe shop or—"

"That's good. Yes. Stay away from religion and politics."

Suzanne sighed with relief.

"We could run a couple hundred words two or three times a week," Edwin mused absently. "Do you have enough material to do that?"

"More than enough, but at some point Americans are going to have to face facts. We—"

"Baby steps, Suzie," Edwin said softly as if he knew that she was about to protest that she wanted to tell the bigger story—the one they both knew had to do with the State Department's isolationist views and the country's immigration quotas established after the Great War that had set the ground rules. "We'll get there," Edwin promised.

"All right," she agreed reluctantly.

"And keep in mind that just because you write a piece doesn't mean I will publish it."

Any more stumbling blocks you want to put in my way? Suzanne thought, her irritation barely in check. She felt like a schoolgirl who had been called to the principal's office. "You'll want to publish these," she told him.

He laughed. "That's my girl. Get me two more articles by Monday," he said and hung up.

Suzanne returned to her room and sat down at her typewriter. The piece that Edwin had called about had seemed to simply flow from her fingertips that night after she and Theo had sat talking on the porch. Of course now as she read through her copy of the article, she was struck by how much she had left unsaid. She'd not even mentioned people like Hilda. The woman was becoming more blatantly outspoken about "those people" every day, especially now that Hugh Kilmer was back in the house agreeing with her.

Suzanne fit a piece of carbon paper between two sheets of typing paper and rolled them into the typewriter then sat back and stared out the open window. Theo was mowing, and the smell of cut grass floated across the room. She wondered how long it had been since those inside the shelter had smelled fresh-cut grass. How long had it been since they had heard the rhythmic clacking of a lawn mower being pushed in a steady, straight line? How long had it been since the children had been free to play on the newly cut grass?

She closed her eyes and let her other senses take over. Overhead she heard Hilda moving around her room as the music from the woman's radio filtered down through the walls. She wondered what Hilda did all day. She certainly did not seem to have a job, and she rarely left the house except to get her hair done every Wednesday morning, go to the movies—or "picture show" as she called it—every Saturday afternoon, and attend church services every Sunday. Hilda had not received any visitors or phone calls—at least not while Suzanne had been in the boardinghouse.

Suddenly she had an idea. She pushed back her chair and climbed the stairs to Hilda's room. The door was open a crack, so she tapped lightly. "Hilda?"

Hilda opened the door, and the expression on her face told Suzanne that she would have been less surprised to see a ghost standing there. "Yes?" She leaned against the partially open door without inviting Suzanne inside.

"I wasn't sure if you had heard the news or not," Suzanne began and saw Hilda's eyes flicker with interest. "The shelter is holding an open house on Sunday—open to the public, that is. The quarantine will be lifted, and well, you've obviously been curious about. . .the facility." Heaven help her, she had almost said *those people.*

"The government is lifting the quarantine?" Clearly the woman was horrified at the very idea that this might happen.

"That's right, and from what I hear, the children will be allowed to attend the local schools. The principal from the high school—a Mr. Faust—has made all the necessary arrangements. Isn't that good news?"

Hilda snorted derisively. "If you ask me, those people are getting far too much attention. Mixing them in with good Christian children?"

"The occupants of the shelter are not all Jewish," Suzanne snapped and then hid her annoyance at the woman's prejudice with a smile. "I just thought you—and perhaps Mr. Kilmer—might like to tour the place."

"I'll think about it. I have church that morning, and while the calendar might say September, with this heat. . ." She was easing the door shut.

Suzanne stepped back toward the stairway. "Okay, well, just thought you'd like to know." She turned and was down to the landing when Hilda leaned over the banister.

"I've been meaning to tell you something," she said. "I suppose there's little I can do about your typing during the day, but at night the racket is keeping me awake, so no typing after supper." Not waiting for a response, she turned and went back inside her room and closed the door with a definite click.

"But it's fine for you to play your radio and tramp around in those ridiculous high-heeled bedroom slippers you insist on wearing until well past midnight, I suppose," Suzanne muttered to herself as she returned to her own room and sat down at her desk. Oh yes, there was a story here that she had failed to include in that first piece, and it was time the public understood that not everyone—even in Oswego, New York—had welcomed the refugees with open arms.

By the time he finished mowing the lawn, Theo's shirt was completely soaked with perspiration. He turned on the garden hose and held it close to his mouth to drink the tepid water then turned the flow onto his head and neck, shaking himself off like a dog coming in from the rain once he'd finished. When he looked up, Suzanne was standing on the back porch, holding a glass filled with ice and water. "Maybe you don't need this after all?"

Theo grinned and held out his hand for the glass. He drained the water and then dug out an ice cube and ran it over his throat and neck, closing his eyes at the cool relief the melting ice gave him. "Thank you." He looked at her as if really seeing her. "How come you look so cool?"

"I wasn't cutting grass," she pointed out. She sat down on the top step of the porch and shaded her eyes as she peered up at him. "I have a favor to ask."

He propped one foot on the bottom step. "Okay." The one thing he had noticed about Suzanne—other than the fact that she was gorgeous—was that her thoughts rarely strayed far from the business that had brought her here. It was one thing to be dedicated to your work, but Suzanne seemed to be driven as if her very life depended on her success. "What do you need?"

"I was wondering if maybe you would consider letting me attend the open house with you this coming Sunday."

"Well sure, but this isn't like last time. This time everybody can come—in fact I think they want people to come so they can dispel some of these rumors. You don't need me to get you in. . . ."

"I know, but I think maybe that first time I got off on the wrong foot with your uncle and aunt. I do that a lot."

"Why?" It seemed a perfectly reasonable question to Theo, but he saw that Suzanne was a little shocked.

"Why?" she repeated. "I don't know. It's the nature of the business, I guess."

"The business?"

"The newspaper business?" she said, squinting at him.

"So to be a good reporter, a person needs to. . ."

"You're twisting my words. Forget it, okay? I just thought maybe if I went with you I would have a chance to let your relatives see that I can be nice." She got up and headed for the back door.

"I think you're nice," Theo said. "I also suspect that you've got something riding on getting this story about the refugees." He sat down on the step she had vacated. "I've been told I'm pretty good at listening."

He heard the squeak of the screen door and could not tell if she had continued on inside or had let the door close and was still on the back porch. But then she walked to the step and sat next to him. "I kind of got myself in a mess, and you're right: this story is my way back from that. I don't want to. . .I cannot fail. This is my life."

"You mean your life's work—your calling. No job is a life."

"You know what I mean. Everything links to the job, and if it's not there—as my job has not been for the last couple of months—other stuff starts to fall apart."

He gave this some thought. "Maybe there's a plan in this. I mean if you hadn't lost your job, would you be here covering this story?"

"No, I would be in Washington covering something bigger."

"What's bigger than the lives of nearly a thousand people who have been hunted and harassed finding a haven here in America?"

"I didn't mean to belittle the lives here, but the key to what happens to the refugees lies within the halls of power in Washington, and that makes it the larger story."

He tried to frame her words into something that made sense to him. "Seems to me that as the storyteller you get to figure out where the larger story lies. All that finagling down there in Washington is pretty dull reading, but the stories inside that fence. . ." He jerked his head in the general direction of the fort.

"You seem to know a lot about politics."

"For a farmer from Wisconsin?" He grinned.

"That's not what I meant."

He realized that she did not take teasing well. "I majored in political science at the University of Wisconsin."

"Really? I mean from what you told me about the farm, I just assumed. . . ."

"And that's kind of the overall problem with the world, isn't it? We all have this tendency to make assumptions before we have the facts."

"And what are the facts behind being raised on a farm and majoring in political science?"

"When the war first began in Europe, I was pretty sure that eventually we would be in it."

"You assumed?" She gave him a wry smile, and he amended his former thought. She might not take teasing well but she was not above using it herself.

"I assumed," he agreed. "Anyway, I was thinking about how I might be able to serve. I wouldn't be able to join the fight—wouldn't want to. War is never the answer."

"I used to believe that, but in this case. . ."

"There has to be another way, and I guess that's why I went the direction I did. If I could understand how governments work—the science of politics—then just maybe I could figure out a way to make a difference."

"How about helping me gather facts so I can write a story that will make a difference for those folks cooped up in the fort?" She looked up at him. "Let's make a difference together."

He knew that she was really asking for his help in persuading his aunt and uncle to let her tell *their* story. "How about this? How about we go together to the open house and you just enjoy the tour the way I will and everyone from town will? How about you putting aside that little notebook you always seem to have in your hand and leave the camera in your room and for those few hours you're just another visitor?"

"I have a deadline—several of them. My editor wants me to write two or three stories a week. I don't have time."

He placed his hand on hers and then withdrew it at once when he realized that he had not washed up yet after mowing the grass. "How about you try letting the story come to you instead of going in there with some preconceived idea?"

She bristled.

"Or I could help you," he added with a grin.

Ilse looked around the tiny apartment. The floor had been scrubbed, the furniture dusted, the beds were made up with sheets that she had bleached and ironed, and at the foot of each of the three cots was a neatly folded blanket. Their clothes were all stored in the lockers. She had found a glass milk bottle and filled it with flowers for the table, and Franz had helped her hang curtains sent in a box of donated household items from one of the Jewish charities that had been incredibly generous in making sure all the refugees had what one of the ladies had called "the comforts of home."

"It will have to do," Ilse said with a sigh as she wiped the table, which was already spotless.

"It will more than do," Franz replied. "You have turned this place into a real home, Ilse." The now-familiar dreamy expression came over his features, and she knew that he was thinking of the home they had shared back in Munich.

"You look very nice," she said as she straightened the knot of his tie. "You've put on some weight—at least the quarantine accomplished something. Your clothes fit so much better than before."

He chuckled. "Don't you find it amazing how in just a few short weeks—with enough food and some exercise and the lack of fear and worry that we lived with before—everyone is beginning to look less like refugees and more like the people we were?"

"The people we *are*," Ilse corrected him. "You are *Herr* Professor Franz Schneider, and I am your very proud wife. That has not changed."

Franz studied her for a long moment. "You have changed, Ilse. You have become more beautiful."

She felt the blush of a schoolgirl stain her face at his compliment and even more so at the fire of desire that ignited within her. Embarrassed at such feelings, she brushed off the compliment. "We should go out and watch for Theo. Liesl is already by the gate."

When the gates were opened, Ilse was astonished at the number of people who filed through, and it took some time and craning of their necks before they finally saw Theo waving to them from the back of the crowd. He was with the reporter, and it occurred to Ilse that they made a handsome couple—both tall and athletic with those unique American traits of unaffected poise and unconscious self-assurance.

"The reporter is with him," Franz murmured. "I thought we made our position quite clear."

"She might simply be coming to see the place. Theo might have asked her to come with him not as a reporter but as a lovely young woman."

Franz blinked at her as if she had just announced that their nephew might marry this woman. "You are matchmaking?"

"Apparently my skills in that area are unnecessary. It appears to me that Theo is doing quite well without my help." She nodded toward the couple, and they both saw that Theo was laughing at something Suzanne had said and that at the same time he placed his hand lightly on her waist as he steered her through the throng to where they were standing.

Franz frowned. "I do not wish to become a part of her reporting, Ilse. We may be in America, but when we go back to Germany..."

"If we go back."

He stared at her. "You do not want to go home?"

Her attempt at a laugh was so filled with disbelief that it came out a snort. "What home, Franz? We have no home—not here and not there."

"Perhaps not, but you—we—have family. Your sister and the Friends from our meeting."

"Do we know where any of them are? My sister? Her husband and children? The other Quakers from our meeting?"

He wrapped his arm around her shoulder. "Sh-h-h. Here come Theo and the reporter."

She looked up, her bitterness at their situation still a metallic taste in her mouth. Liesl had run to meet Theo, the doll he had given her clutched firmly under one arm. But Ilse found her focus on the woman—Suzanne. She was wearing a cotton sundress that exposed her shoulders, and her hair was piled loosely on top of her head. Her flat sandals exposed her painted toenails, and over one shoulder she carried a large straw purse.

She was a woman who had probably never known real deprivation, real fear. And she wanted to write about them. Franz was right. Not because anything she might write could cause them problems over time, but because how could this quintessential American beauty even come close to being able to imagine the horrors they had experienced?

Suddenly Ilse wanted her to understand. She wanted all these Americans who sat in their offices in Washington and here at the fort making decisions for Franz and her and the others as if they were incapable of thinking or speaking for themselves to grasp the reality of what they were expecting the refugees to do when the war ended. She would not add to Franz's worry by becoming involved directly. Instead she would introduce Suzanne to the one person she had met since coming to the shelter who Ilse knew would not tolerate the reporter's idealism.

She scanned the crowd for Gisele St. Germaine, the French actress she had met in the laundry. With her sarcasm and wry sense of humor, Gisele had had all the women laughing at their situation and snickering at her impersonation of Adolf Hitler. Gisele had made the dictator seem so ridiculous that she robbed him of his power, and afterward the women had talked seriously about how it could be possible that this former housepainter and paperhanger had been able to turn the world upside down.

"Good afternoon, Mrs. Schneider," Suzanne said, extending her hand in greeting. "It's so good to see you again."

Liesl was tugging at Suzanne's arm. "Suzanne?"

"Liesl, this is Miss Randolph," Ilse corrected.

"Oh that's all—" Suzanne caught Ilse's look and changed her words. "That's right, Liesl."

Liesl frowned. "And then am I Miss Schneider?"

Suzanne smiled. "If you like."

Liesl considered this. "No. I am just Liesl."

The public address system squealed, announcing the start of the day's program. Director Smart was approaching the podium, and everyone pressed in closer to the makeshift stage. He outlined the day's schedule—remarks from dignitaries, followed by tours of the shelter's facilities, and then a social hour for everyone to get better acquainted.

But first he made some announcements: the quarantine was officially lifted, and starting immediately, the residents of the shelter would be allowed special passes so that they could go to town to shop or see a movie or have a meal in one of the local restaurants. Furthermore, the children would be attending the local schools. This announcement was met with applause by the residents and a smattering of audible gasps by the locals.

Director Smart explained that the passes would be valid for six hours a day and residents must return to the shelter by midnight. Furthermore, they could not travel beyond the boundaries of Oswego. As he continued speaking, Ilse could not help thinking that in spite of this loosening of restrictions they were still incarcerated, still under the bonds of authorities with no voice to speak for themselves.

As if she'd been hearing Ilse's thoughts, Suzanne edged closer and murmured, "The government giveth, and the government taketh away."

Ilse glanced up at her. She realized that Suzanne looked less like the all-American beauty and more like the cynical journalist—the one in any society charged with challenging and questioning authority. Yes, Suzanne and Gisele together would craft a powerful story—perhaps one that would help the cause of the hundreds of refugees who were now safe, although hardly free.

It was evident to Suzanne that Franz Schneider had his suspicions about her. He was unfailingly courteous but certainly made it clear he had no plans to engage with her on more than a superficial level. For Theo's sake—and perhaps his wife's—he would be polite, but he would offer nothing of himself.

Ilse, on the other hand, surprised Suzanne by seeking her out after the tours and introducing her to a woman who wore an expression that seemed to Suzanne to reflect the same sense of cynicism that Suzanne felt about the world in general. She had a regal elegance about her but also a bohemian casualness that drew attention to her. She was wearing a pair of men's gabardine trousers with a necktie threaded through the belt loops and a crisp cotton, long-sleeved blouse. She had pushed the sleeves up to her elbows and turned the collar up so that it accentuated her long neck. On anyone else in the gathering, the outfit would have come off as pretentious or just sad. On Gisele it was the height of fashion.

"You are French?" Suzanne asked when Ilse left them together while she went to get glasses of lemonade.

Gisele shrugged. "I like to think of myself as a citizen of the world—it comes in especially handy in times like these."

"Your English is certainly impeccable."

"As is my German, my Italian, and of course, my French," Gisele replied with a smile.

Suzanne did not take offense. It had been a stupid thing to say. "Ilse mentioned that you are an actress."

"Among other pastimes. There is not much opportunity for me to ply my acting craft these days. Although Ivo over there seems determined to create the next great acting troupe right here in Fort Ontario." She smiled and waved to a man across the way. "I am inclined to join his little band of thespians. It will certainly help to pass the time. And you, Suzanne Randolph? What is it that you do to pass the days of your life?"

"I am—was a reporter for a newspaper in Washington—the capital city of the United States?"

Gisele smiled. "I am aware of the place where your government makes its policies. Of more interest to me is your use of the past tense. Are you no longer a reporter for this newspaper?"

"It's complicated. I am working as a freelance reporter for now."

Gisele's knowing smile lit her face. "You were dismissed?"

It occurred to Suzanne that Ilse was taking her time getting that lemonade for them. And what had happened to Theo? "Yes, but—"

"And this story—our story—will be your salvation?"

"Well, that just sounds desperate," Suzanne said, trying to laugh.

"Are you good at your craft?"

"Yes. I am quite good," Suzanne replied.

"Then let's work together and tell this story. I am not getting any younger, and it is my understanding that your New York theater prefers younger actresses to grace their stages." She glanced around as if looking for a quieter place for them to go, and her gaze fixed on Theo. "And who is that gorgeous creature coming our way with Ilse?"

Suzanne felt a rush of pure jealousy at the way Gisele was watching Theo as he and Ilse came across the parade ground, carrying glasses of lemonade.

"That's Theo Bridgewater, Ilse's nephew. His mother and Franz are sister and brother. They live on a farm in Wisconsin, and Theo is here to try and get the authorities to let Franz, Ilse, and Liesl come back with him."

By the time she finished this explanation, Theo and Ilse were close enough to hand them the lemonade. "Gisele, this is my nephew Theo Bridgewater," Ilse said.

"So I have been told," Gisele replied, offering her hand to Theo as if she expected the man to kiss her ring—if she had been wearing one.

"Gisele is going to help me tell the story of Fort Ontario," Suzanne explained.

"No. I am going to help you tell the *human* story, Suzanne." She waved her hand to encompass the crowd around them. "The story of who these people were—and still are. That is the story that will get us the freedom we deserve and long for, don't you agree, Theo?"

The man was actually blushing. "I'm just a farmer, Miss St. Germaine. Suzanne is the reporter." *Oh, all of a sudden he's just a farmer?*

Gisele hooked her free arm through Theo's. "Aren't you charming, *mon chéri?* But part of this story is also your story, is it not? And so we shall work together, the three of us."

Somewhere along the way, Suzanne realized that Gisele had taken complete control of the situation. Her smile was radiant and filled with warmth, but her eyes were steely cold, and Suzanne realized that the Frenchwoman had her own agenda when it came to her stay in the Fort Ontario Emergency Relief Shelter. The question was, did Gisele's agenda match hers?

CHAPTER 6

Theo needed to work. It was obvious that it would be some time before the war ended, and until then it was equally clear that nothing would change the current status of the refugees. But his parents were adamant that he stay in Oswego.

"They need family around them right now," his mother told him when he pointed out that it was closing in on harvesttime at the farm and he could be of far more help there. "Matthew can help Dad with that."

There was simply no changing their minds. So Theo began scanning the newspaper's want ads each morning after breakfast. Down the hall he could hear the click of typing as Suzanne composed another article about the people in the shelter. He noticed that there were times when it seemed as if her fingers flew over the typewriter keys—like a pianist playing a ragtime tune. Other times he would hear a few tentative taps with long pauses between and then complete silence. This was one of those mornings.

This was also the September morning that he saw the ad for field-workers to help harvest apples. He'd heard that the crop had been especially abundant this season and orchards around the area were scrambling to get the fruit picked. He pulled a piece of the scrap paper Selma kept on the desk and wrote down the address for the orchard. Then he walked down the hall and knocked on Suzanne's door. It was probably not the world's best idea to invite her along on a job interview, but he'd come to realize that he would take any excuse to spend time with her.

When she opened the door he was a little taken aback. Her hair was a jumble of untamed curls haphazardly pinned up and away from her face. She wore no makeup, and she was dressed in a wrinkled blouse and a pair of dungarees that were baggy on her slender frame. The thick, black-rimmed glasses she wore whenever she was working were perched on top of her head.

"Hi. Want to take a ride with me?"

She frowned up at him and rubbed her eyes with the knuckles of one hand. "Kind of working here," she said, barely concealing her annoyance at the interruption.

He shrugged. "Yeah, well, from the sound of the typing—or the silence of not typing—seems like you might need a break." He held up the paper where he'd written down the orchard address. She glanced back toward the typewriter and groaned. "I'm stuck," she admitted.

"So come for a drive in the country with me and get unstuck. I'm going to check out a job."

"You don't have a car that I know of," she reminded him.

"Selma said if I could get that old truck behind the shed to run I could use it whenever I needed to." He grinned. "Selma likes me."

"Teacher's pet," Suzanne teased. "Okay, when you get that thing running—if I am still here, meaning, if I have not completed this assignment and moved back to Washington—sure, I'll take a drive in the country with you."

"Ah, it won't take that long. I got the thing running a couple of days ago. Just need to pick up some gasoline and we can be on our way." He checked his wristwatch. "How about you be ready in, say, half an hour?"

She laughed. "Did anyone ever tell you that you should run for office? You certainly have the gift of persuasion."

"And I ain't bad-looking, either." Now where had that come from?

He felt his neck and cheeks getting red—a deeper shade than his normal sun-rusted complexion.

"Persuasive and with an ego to match—yep. You are prime material for the world of politics. Go get that excuse for a truck gassed up while I change, and I'll meet you out back."

Even after she closed the door, he stood in the hall for a minute grinning. Then he heard Hilda Cutter coming down the stairs, and he slipped out the back door.

The orchard was not that far out of town, and as the rattletrap of a truck bumped and wheezed its way down a dirt road, Theo saw about half a dozen men in identical coveralls standing on wooden ladders propped against apple trees. A few other men were dressed as Theo was in blue jeans and a cotton shirt. And there were a few soldiers.

"Why are some of the men in those coveralls?" Suzanne asked, reading his mind. "Are they from the local jail or prison or something?"

Suddenly Theo realized exactly who these men were. An article in the paper had described Nazi prisoners of war in the area working on farms and in local canning factories. "They're Germans," he said. "Prisoners of war."

"Here?"

Theo shrugged. "Some of them. We saw quite a few of them back in Wisconsin. They get sent wherever they are needed to fill the void left by so many American workers serving overseas."

He recalled the first day when he had stood outside the fence at the fort, waiting for the refugees to be processed, searching for his aunt and uncle. There had been an incident involving some POWs and the refugees that morning.

He told Suzanne about seeing an American soldier marching a small group of POWs across the crowded parade ground toward the tunnel that led out to Seventh Street and back to town. As they passed by, their murmured conversation caught the attention of some of the refugees, and quickly word spread that these men in coveralls were Nazis. Several of the refugees stopped what they were doing and turned to observe the

POWs, and then one of the refugees shouted a taunt mocking the men in coveralls. When the soldier escorting them heard a POW reply with an offensive slur, he glanced around nervously and ordered the POWs to quicken their step. But the taunts and even some laughter followed them, and the air was charged with hatred on both sides.

Suzanne twisted in her seat, her head out the open window. Once they got past the orchards and reached the cluster of buildings where Theo assumed he would complete his job application, she sat back in her seat. "Those soldiers are just leaning on the fence, talking and smoking. Any one of those POWs could escape," she said in pure disbelief.

"Maybe the other guys—the ones in regular clothes—are also guards." He pulled the truck into a space next to a door with a sign reading OFFICE. "I'll just go see if they have any openings. You'll be okay here?"

As if she hadn't heard him, she opened the truck door and climbed down. She walked to the fence and stared back toward where the men were working.

"This shouldn't take long," he added, and she waved without looking back at him.

Inside the office, which was really more of a corner of the barn, a man wearing overalls and a battered straw hat sat hunched over a pile of papers, a telephone receiver gripped in one hand. "Yeah, well if we don't get this crop picked, it's going to rot. Look Joe, you've got those folks just sitting there in the fort. How about a little help?"

He listened and at the same time motioned Theo to the only other chair in the room. "A dozen or more," he said then leaned back in his chair and smiled at Theo. "That would be fine, Joe. If you can pull that off, then I owe you one." He chuckled at something the person on the other end of the line said and hung up. "Sorry about that. Please tell me you're looking for work."

Theo stood and offered the man a handshake. "Theo Bridgewater, and yes, sir, I could use a job."

"It's temporary," the man warned. "I'm Harry Walls, by the way." He gripped Theo's hand.

"Pleased to meet you, Mr. Walls."

"It's Harry. Can you start tomorrow?"

"Yes, sir. I'll be here. I appreciate this."

"There is this one thing. You got any problem working with the Germans?"

"No, sir."

"How about some of the refugees from over there at the fort? I was just on the phone there with Joe Smart, asking him for help. He thinks he can send some men over. I might need some help keeping the two groups separated."

"My uncle and aunt are refugees," Theo told him. "I don't think you'll have any trouble. Most of the men in the shelter are older—except for the boys, of course, and they're in school so I think it'll all work out."

Harry gave him a look that said he wasn't quite so sure. "Desperate times," he muttered and picked up the phone again.

Theo walked out to the truck, but Suzanne was nowhere in sight. He started down the road toward the orchard and finally spotted her. She was standing at the foot of one of the wooden ladders, her head back as she looked up at a man dressed in coveralls while she spoke to the soldiers by the fence.

Ilse was worried about Franz. His physical health was improving daily, as was Liesl's, but he still drifted into periods of silence and melancholy.

"I am not useful," he told her at night when they lay in the cots they had pushed together so they could whisper without waking Liesl in the next room and without being heard by their neighbors on the other side of the paper-thin partitions that passed for walls between the units.

"You are useful to me and to Liesl," she assured him. "And once we are allowed to leave this place, you can apply for a position with the university that Theo reminded us is near the farm."

"Perhaps." He turned on his side and said no more.

Franz had been elected to the advisory council that had been established shortly after the quarantine was lifted. But that effort at instituting some form of self-government among the refugees had quickly fallen apart. He had also been invited to offer lectures as part of a series of programs for the adults, but he had refused that.

"To what purpose?" he had asked when Ilse urged him to accept the invitation. She had not been able to offer him an answer.

So when Ilse heard one of the other women talking about the possibility that some of the men would be allowed to leave the shelter during the day to work in a nearby orchard, she went to the office of the shelter's director and asked to speak with Mr. Smart. Perhaps if Franz could work for a bit outside the fence, he might see the possibility that one day they would be free—free of the fort and free to pursue the life that had been so savagely interrupted.

She was surprised that Director Smart knew who she was and who Franz was. He even inquired how Liesl was doing in school. The refugees had all been impressed with the way this man made every effort to integrate himself into the community of the shelter. He and his family lived in one of the brick houses on the hill that had once been home for officers serving at the fort. And there had been more than one occasion when he had called this group or that together to apologize for not fully appreciating the differences in their cultures.

All the refugees saw in Joseph Smart an advocate and a warrior—the man who was their best hope for staying in America as truly free people once the war ended.

"Come in, Mrs. Schneider. How can I help you?"

Ilse felt suddenly shy in his presence. He was dressed in a business suit as he dressed every day—as once Franz had dressed for his job at the university.

"I have heard that perhaps some of the men here may be given an opportunity to work outside the shelter."

"And you thought perhaps your husband might be one of those selected?"

From the expression that flashed across the director's features, Ilse knew instantly that he would refuse her. She leaned forward, her voice high and urgent as she pleaded her case. "I am worried about him. He spends a good deal of time alone down by the lake just staring out at the horizon."

"I must be frank with you, Mrs. Schneider. At his age and having suffered the physical abuse he endured while in prison, your husband does not have the stamina required for a day of picking apples."

His voice was so soft and kind that Ilse felt as if she might start to cry. "Please, help me," she whispered, wrapping her fingers in her handkerchief.

The director stood and turned to look out the office window that faced the other community buildings. "I have been thinking that perhaps we could use help in organizing our library, Mrs. Schneider. We have cartons of books donated by the charities that had already brought clothes and household items. Perhaps the townspeople would have books to give as well. It occurs to me that we would be in need of a librarian—someone to record and organize the collection." He turned to face her. "Do you think your husband might be interested?"

"Yes, oh yes. That would be perfect." Ilse stood up and grasped Joseph Smart's hand with both of hers. "Will you ask him? I really don't want him to know I have been here. He is a proud man, and. . ."

The director smiled and patted her hand. "Yes, of course. Your visit will be kept between us, and I will be in touch with your husband. Will that be all right?"

"Oh, Mr. Smart, thank you so much." He really was the kindest man.

Once Suzanne returned from the orchard with Theo, she could barely sleep for all the ideas for articles that were racing around in her brain. What she had discovered about the treatment of the POWs just by asking the soldier guarding them a few questions was mind boggling. But she kept it all to herself, even when Hilda tried to pry at mealtime.

Of course once she learned that Theo and Suzanne had spent the afternoon together, Hilda's interest focused on a possible romance between them. She read movie magazines two and three times over and enjoyed reporting the Hollywood gossip to anyone who would listen. But her main topic of conversation continued to be "those people," making it very clear that she did not consider Theo's family—or indeed anyone who was not Jewish—in that category. Her constant harping on the refugees continued unabated through early autumn.

But one night in October after Edwin had turned down her article about the German POWs for a second time, Suzanne could stand Hilda's diatribe against the Jews no longer.

"Just exactly who do you think is the enemy in this war?" she asked, forcing herself to keep her voice calm and conversational.

"Well, the Nazis, of course," Hilda snapped. "I'm not stupid, Suzanne."

The salesman sprang to Hilda's defense. "Sure, it's the Germans we have to fight, but Hilda has a point. If it weren't for the Jews, we never would have gotten ourselves into this war. If they hadn't completely ruined the economy in Europe with their greed, Hitler never would have come to power. And everybody in this country knows those New York Jews have FDR in their pocket."

Apparently Selma had decided not to remind her boarders of her rule against the discussion of either politics or religion at mealtime. She sat at one end of the table, her head bent over her soup spoon as she blew on the liquid to cool it. But Suzanne saw that her eyes were darting nervously from Hilda to Suzanne and then back again.

The other two boarders said nothing as they, too, concentrated on their meal. And Theo was looking her way, but she saw in his eyes that his message to her was that she should see arguing with Hilda for what it was—a losing battle.

She was inclined to agree until Hilda pushed her advantage. "My guess is that the very newspaper you work for is owned by Jews. They manipulate the news to suit their purposes. Half of them are Communists, and we all know that the Communists are the next big threat to our democracy. Why, just—"

"Hilda?" Suzanne's voice to her own ears was dripping with sweetness. "Remember when you thought the Jews in the shelter were receiving special treatment? Luxuries like expensive appliances and household items?"

Hilda's cheeks reddened. "I admitted that I had been taken in by local gossip," she said grudgingly.

"You were wrong, then?"

"I can see that you are trying to make a point, Suzanne. What exactly is it?" Hilda's smile was more of a grimace.

"My point is that when we don't know all the facts we can be taken in. Take, for example, the German POWs that Theo and some of the refugees—some of the Jewish refugees—are working with in the orchard."

"What about them?"

"Well, a simple comparison of their current status might clarify some things for you. For example, while both the POWs and refugees live in encampments surrounded by fences, the POWs have more liberty when it comes to their daily lives than the refugees enjoy. For that matter, they enjoy some privileges that many American citizens do not. Does that seem right to you?"

The salesman chuckled. "You see, that's what you newspaper people do. You put these so-called facts out there with nothing to back them up." He shoveled another overloaded forkful of spaghetti into his mouth.

"Oh, you want the facts. Okay. Some of the American soldiers guarding the POWs are Negroes, and there are restaurants right here in town that will serve the POWs but will not serve these American soldiers because of their race. Furthermore, the POWs are paid the same daily wage as a United States private—about eighty cents a day. Over a month that adds up to about twenty-four dollars. That's six dollars more than the stipend received by the highest-paid member of the refugee community. They also get clothing twice a year and their officers are not required to work at all. Does that. . ."

"Well now, little lady, we do have this thing called the Geneva Convention," Hugh interrupted. "The idea is that if we treat these Nazis right, then our boys might not suffer when they get captured over there." He pronounced Nazi as *Nat-zee*.

Theo spoke up finally. "Well, you have to admit that it doesn't seem quite fair that the government provides the POWs with things like art supplies and reading materials and two packs of cigarettes a day when the refugees have had to depend on the generosity of the various charities for such things."

"I have heard," Selma said quietly, "that in spite of every kindness shown them, some of the POWs offer the *Sieg Heil* salute when the American flag is raised or lowered."

No one said anything for several minutes, and then Theo stood and placed his napkin beside his plate. "If everyone will excuse me, I have promised to join my uncle and aunt and cousin for a meeting for worship tonight." He looked at Suzanne, and she knew that his invitation to join them delivered earlier that day stood. But although they had both been raised in the Quaker faith, Theo still found solace in practicing that faith while she did not. To her way of thinking to sit in silence and wait for enlightenment when she did not believe there could possibly be a higher spirit offering such enlightenment seemed hypocritical.

She shook her head and got up to help Selma clear the plates and serve the dessert of butterscotch pudding. Behind her she heard Theo exhale a disappointed sigh. They had talked about their differences when it came to faith. Would he rather she pretend?

CHAPTER 7

In mid-October Suzanne decided to make an appointment with Joseph Smart. She wanted to hear his ideas about the shelter and how it was working, and she hoped to get him to reveal some of the thinking of his colleagues back in Washington.

"Here is what I will tell you, Miss Randolph," he said. "The process of reconditioning people who have suffered as these people have is accomplished—if at all—in two stages. The first focus must of course be meeting the immediate need for the basics: shelter, clothing, food. To attend to their physical needs."

"And stage two?"

He gave a wry smile. "Ah, that is the more complex process. It is attending to their psychological needs, their mental health and spiritual well-being. That is a process that we have only just begun."

"In what ways?"

He shrugged. "We offer the trappings of a normal life—sports, films, plays, concerts, classes, and lectures. We offer job training and English lessons—the opportunity to prepare for life after the war. We encourage interaction among the diverse nationalities within the shelter and try to find ways for the townspeople and our guests here at the fort to interact."

"And is it working?"

He leaned forward. "What do you think? You are living in town, are you not? And I have observed you speaking with some of the refugees—Gisele St. Germaine in particular."

Suzanne smiled. "Now there is a woman who speaks her mind."

Smart sighed. "You have no idea." He templed his fingers and studied her. "You are friends with the nephew of one of our families, I believe?"

"Theo Bridgewater. We live in the same boardinghouse. Why?"

"Halloween is coming, and I would like to offer something for the children. Something that would give them the experience of an American Halloween but without—"

"They could go on a scavenger hunt," Suzanne blurted, remembering one of her very favorite Halloweens when her mother had given a party for her entire class. "They could go out in teams and in costume and—"

"Do you think that you and Theo Bridgewater might be willing to facilitate this scavenger hunt?"

She must have given him a blank stare because he quickly added, "You see, Miss Randolph, I believe that in order for you to truly tell the story of the residents of the shelter, you need to spend time with them without that time being for the purpose of an interview or gathering facts for your next article."

He was offering her access to the community in a way few other reporters had experienced. This was huge. "Yes," she agreed. "I mean, yes, I'll talk to Theo, and I'm sure he'll agree to help with the party. And maybe we can get Gisele involved and Theo's aunt and uncle, and I know that Liesl—"

Joseph Smart stood up, signaling an end to their meeting. "Excellent. Put together a plan for me to review."

Suzanne shook hands with him and left the office. On her way out through the tunnel that separated the fort from the town, she thought that really all anyone could offer people forced to live lives of uncertainty while they awaited the end of the war were these momentary reprieves in the form of some kind of event or entertainment. Any way one looked at the situation, they might be in America but they were still a long way from being truly free.

By the end of October, Theo's work for the orchard had come to an end. Harry Walls had told him he would have work in the spring, but until then the POWs could take care of everything.

"Dad, there's really no reason for me to stay," he said when he made his weekly phone call to his parents one Sunday evening. His mother had insisted that he needed to "see this thing through," but he saw little he could do for his uncle and aunt, and certainly it would be at least spring before the war ended.

"I was thinking," his dad was saying, "maybe Mom and I would drive out for Thanksgiving. Would they let us do that? Spend Thanksgiving with Franz and Ilse and Liesl?"

"Sure. I'll ask Selma—Mrs. Velo—if she knows of a room we might rent for you."

"We can stay at the hotel, Son. Why don't you see if that reporter you've told us about has plans? Your mom has been wanting to meet her."

Theo rolled his eyes. Just what he needed—his mom the matchmaker. "I'm pretty sure she'll probably head down to Washington for the holidays."

"But you'll ask her." This was not a question.

"I'll ask her."

"Here's your mom. Plan on us getting there on the day before Thanksgiving, okay?"

"Got it."

There was a muffled exchange between his parents, and then his mother's voice came on the line. "Now Theo, you let your aunt Ilse know that I'm bringing the makings for the dinner with me—everything we'll need."

"Mom, their place is pretty small, and there's not really a kitchen."

"Well, maybe Mrs. Velo would let me borrow her kitchen to prepare everything and then we could—"

"I'll ask her, but Mom, she's running a boardinghouse and needs her kitchen so she can prepare food for her boarders, and—"

"It never hurts to ask. Are you getting some rest?"

Theo was used to the way his mother switched topics with no effort at some kind of transition. "I am, and yes, I am eating enough, and yes, I am going to meeting for worship with Franz and Ilse at the shelter."

"Don't get smart, young man. What about that reporter? Susan?"

"Suzanne. What about her?"

His mother sighed with exasperation. "You know it wouldn't kill you to think about settling down, and from the little you've told us she seems like a nice girl."

"She also lives in Washington," he reminded her.

"Oh, for heaven's sake, Theo, you said she was freelancing. That means she can work anywhere, and believe it or not, we have some pretty good newspapers right here in Wisconsin."

"Okay, how about the fact that we've known each other for less than three months?"

"Your father and I knew we were meant for each other after one date."

It was an old story, and one she was fond of citing whenever she thought Theo was spending too much time alone. "You're not getting any younger, you know."

"Practically ancient," he replied and then decided to give her something that would make her smile. "Suzanne and I are putting together a Halloween scavenger hunt for the children and teens at the shelter."

"Oh, what fun! I wish I could be there to help. I could make a batch of my pumpkin bread and throw in some chocolate chips—all children love chocolate."

"Wish you could be here too, Mom, but you're planning to come for Thanksgiving. That'll be great."

"Don't tell Franz and Ilse, okay? I want to surprise them."

"Sure. I've got to go, Mom. I'll call next week, okay?"

"Same time, same station," she replied and blew him a kiss. "Love you, Theo."

"Love you back, Mom."

The morning of the Halloween party, a large carton arrived addressed to Theo. Inside were a dozen tin boxes filled with his mother's pumpkin chocolate-chip bread made into cookies decorated with orange frosting.

"Oh, that's just perfect," Suzanne squealed when she saw them. "The children are going to love them, and they go perfectly with the gingerbread and apple juice we're serving."

The party was an enormous success. The shelter was filled with laughter and shrieks as the children worked in teams going from door to door in each of the barracks to collect the items on their scavenger list. Later the children gathered in the service club turned recreation hall to bob for apples and enjoy the refreshments while some of the adults entertained them with songs and skits. Suzanne had gotten merchants in town to donate items and gift certificates to be used as prizes for the best costume and for winners of the scavenger hunt, and Theo saw that some of the young people from town had also come for the party.

As they walked home together, Theo removed the fistfuls of straw that Suzanne had tucked into his sleeves and the cuffs of his jeans in her attempt to create a scarecrow costume for him. The truth was the stuff had been scratching him all evening, and he was relieved to be able to throw it away.

Suzanne had dressed up in an old evening gown that Selma had pulled from a trunk in the attic. It had puffed sleeves and a full skirt, and Theo had not missed the way the blue color made her eyes sparkle like Lake Ontario on a clear autumn day.

"We did it, Theo," she said. "The evening was a complete success. I was so sure that somewhere along the way we might do something that would cause someone to get upset."

"That's very important to you, isn't it? I mean, not making a mistake?" He was immediately sorry for asking because her high spirits plummeted at once.

"Well, sure, I wanted everything to be perfect. That's just normal." She sounded defensive and wrapped her arms around her body as if she had suddenly felt a chill.

"I didn't mean it as a criticism. In fact, I sometimes wish I—" He waved off the rest of his statement and put his arm around her shoulders. "Are you cold?"

"A little," she admitted. "Wind off the lake."

"Yeah, well, it is almost November. Speaking of that, my folks are coming for Thanksgiving—they want to surprise Franz and Ilse. Do you have plans? I mean, don't feel like you have to—"

"I'd really like that. It's sweet of them to include me."

They walked the next block in silence, but as they approached the walkway that led to the boardinghouse, she twisted her head so she could look up at him without leaving the circle of his arm around her shoulder. "What were you going to say before when you said 'I wish' but then let it drop?"

"It was nothing."

"Wishes are never nothing. What do you wish for, Theo?"

He stopped in the shadow of the large oak tree in the front yard of the boardinghouse and turned her so they were facing each other, his hands resting lightly on her shoulders. "I wish I could find something in my life that I was as passionate about as you are about your work, Suzanne. I wish I could have that certainty about what my life's purpose might be."

"You do. Once this is all over, you will have the farm."

"What if I want more?"

She reached up and stroked his cheek with her fingers. "Then go after it, Theo. Whatever it is, go after it."

Although Director Smart and his staff had planned a festive celebration for the refugees, Ilse was not feeling especially thankful when she awoke on Thanksgiving Day and wrapped herself in a blanket while she went to boil some water on the hot plate they were allowed so that she could make tea. Franz was still asleep, as was Liesl, and outside the skies were gray and heavy with the promise of snow.

They had been here now for nearly four months, and while most everyone had gone out of their way to make sure the residents of the shelter had plenty of activities to fill their days and evenings, Ilse still felt an absence of anything approaching a normal life—a life with purpose.

Of the three of them, Liesl was faring the best. Was that because she spent her days at school outside the shelter where she had made friends who came to play on the weekends and who invited her to their birthday parties and to their homes—their American homes—to eat or play or study together? Liesl's English was perfect. She spoke with hardly any accent at all, and she had picked up the language so quickly.

Franz had been fluent in English before, but his was still tinged with the formality and inflection of his German heritage. Ilse had faithfully attended the English classes offered in the shelter and was improving, but she was still better with reading the complicated language then speaking it.

And then there was this place—this apartment—that they called home. She had done the best she could to recreate the decor of their apartment back in Munich. Theo had brought them two comfortable chairs, a small side table, and an old radio that he had repaired, and these treasures crowded the small sitting room that also served as Liesl's bedroom.

In the boxes of donations sent by various charities over the weeks after they first arrived, Ilse had found a couple of colorful rag rugs along with the lace curtains and crocheted doilies that she had bleached white to set on the arms of the chairs. On the table that held the radio she had set an ashtray, a small humidor for tobacco, and a pipe stand for Franz's pipe. She had been saving from her monthly stipend to buy him a new pipe for Christmas. But in spite of everything she tried, she could do nothing about the cold that seeped in through the outer walls and window frame or about the constant noise from the apartments next to and above them.

And now winter was coming on with no sign of an end to the war. There had been no change in the government's determination to send them back once the war ended—in spite of a visit by the president's wife and her assurance that she would do all she could to make sure they could stay. Not that Ilse wanted to stay. She missed Munich, missed the beauty of the German countryside, missed the mountains where she and Franz skied in winter. And most of all she missed her sister, Marta, and wondered what had become of her and her family.

When they had fled Munich, the plan had been to go to Marta's home in Eglof, but when they arrived, Marta met the train with the car packed, telling them that her husband, Lucas, and the children had already left, and they needed to leave immediately to join them in the mountains. There they had spent a few weeks believing they were safe, and then one day Franz had awakened her and reported that Marta and her family were gone. There had been a cryptic note about a relative being ill but no information about where they had gone or when they might return.

Franz, Ilse, and Liesl had stayed on in the mountain chalet for another week until Franz had gone into the village one day and heard the news that there were Gestapo agents in the area, searching for traitors. The cheesemaker confided that the agents were questioning locals about anyone who might have come to the village recently and stayed for longer than what might be considered a normal holiday.

They had packed up and left that night, and she had had no word from her sister since. A single tear plopped into the cup she'd been holding while waiting for the water to boil. She wiped her tears away with the back of her hand and went to prepare Franz a cup of tea.

"Mom?" Liesl rolled over in her cot and called to her. She now insisted that calling her "Mom" was the American way. "Did it snow?"

"Not yet." Ilse took a small bottle of milk that they kept stored between the window and screen now that the weather was cold enough to keep it from spoiling. She poured a glass for Liesl and placed it on the table. Then she poured tea into the cup and went to wake her husband.

"Happy Thanksgiving," she said, having practiced the words to get the inflection right. She forced a smile. "Here's your tea. The floor is cold so put on your slippers."

Over the next hour they dressed, took their turn in the bathroom at the end of the hall, and put on their coats, hats, and gloves for the trek to the dining hall for breakfast. Ilse felt a sharp wind off the lake cut right through her coat to her very bones, and she shivered as they made their way back to their apartment following the meal. The day—a holiday—stretched out before them, and she wondered how they might fill the hours.

"Oh my," Franz said, his voice strangled with emotion. He was looking toward the gate where Ilse could see Theo and the reporter and another couple entering the grounds. "Ellie?" he whispered, and then he jogged and called out to the woman who was running toward them. "Oh, Ellie!"

Franz had found his sister.

Ilse had to wonder if she would ever again find Marta.

PART 2

WINTER 1944–1945

HOPE FADING AND FOR ONE— HOPE GONE

OSWEGO N.Y.—As the winter goes on and on—by many accounts the worst winter in memory for this part of New York—the charities that have sent supplies and volunteers and organized programs and pleaded the cause of the refugees have stopped coming. Perhaps like the birds and flowers, they will return in the spring, but in the meantime. . .

The reporters with their photographers documenting each interview have also left. These days there are plenty of rooms available for rent in Oswego. The so-called fireside relatives—spouses, children, parents—of the refugees who are already living in America have had to abandon their vigil and return to their homes and jobs in other parts of the country. The war drags on, as does the debate in Washington about the fate of the refugees.

Meanwhile the citizens of Fort Ontario struggle to stay positive. They must traverse icy alleys of six-foot drifts to reach the dining hall for their meals. They continue to stage concerts and show movies and create crafts with the children. The children bundled like stuffed dolls wait for the bus to take them to and from school and return to the fort to work on their English in the evenings. The shelter's newspaper—the *Ontario Chronicle*—continues to report the news—often tongue-in-cheek. Shelter director Mr. Joseph Smart continues to try and rally spirits as he reminds the residents that the war is going well and that spring will come.

But for Karoline Klein Bleier, with two children from her first marriage left behind in Europe and her new husband and their two children with her in Fort Ontario, the snow and the cold, the guilt she felt for leaving two of her children behind, and the lack of any real progress toward a day when she and her family might leave the shelter was more than she could take. Her husband, Geza, in an effort to lift her spirits, urged her to let him care for their children while she attended the movie being shown after supper that snowy, late-December night.

Finally she agreed to go out. But she did not go to the movies. She did not go to sit with her friend two apartments down from hers as she sometimes did. She went out into the cold, swallowed a handful of pills and did not return.

CHAPTER 8

When Franz described how he and the other searchers had discovered Karoline's body in snow that had drifted so deep she was nearly buried in it, Ilse felt the twinge of panic and deep-seated hopelessness that had once been her constant companions.

The mere mention of those years when she had suffered often from debilitating depression and anxiety haunted her. Her problems were the reason that their niece Beth had left the relative safety of America to come and live with them after Liesl was born. *Would Karoline's life have found a different outcome if she had had the support and courage of someone like Beth at her side?* Ilse now wondered.

By the time Ilse and her family started the two-year odyssey that brought them to Fort Ontario, Beth had been with them for eight years. In so many ways she was like a second daughter or perhaps more like a younger sister. How relieved and thankful she and Franz had been when Theo told them that Beth had made it to the safety of England and that she and Josef had married and now had their own little girl. Had it not been for Beth caring for Liesl, Ilse could not imagine how she would have survived those early years of the war.

But once she and Franz had been forced to flee and go into hiding, gradually Ilse had faced the realities of their situation. Over the months they had spent on the run, she and Franz had in many ways switched roles. Realizing that her only other choice was to surrender, she rediscovered the confidence and strength that had been her trademarks as the young woman Franz had fallen in love with. She found ways to hold her own meeting for worship, although often she was the only attendee. She placed all of her faith in God to show them the way.

Sadly, during this time Franz's faith slipped dramatically, and while he did not suffer from the fear and anxiety that had once plagued Ilse, he did sink into periods of depression that she had feared might lead him to take desperate measures. So often when things seemed darkest he told her that if it weren't for him she and Liesl would be fine. He was the one who had defied the Reich. He was the one who had placed them all in danger.

Now dear fragile Karoline had taken her life. Ilse recalled the days the two of them had worked together in the children's center. It was there that Karoline had told Ilse about her children from her first marriage. She had taken full responsibility for the fact that they had been the victims of that failed union, revealing how her love for Geza Bleier had destroyed her first marriage and how her punishment had been that her two children from that marriage had been taken from her. Her first husband had sole custody.

When Karoline talked about her failure as a mother and her fears for those children left behind and for the two she had with her in America, Ilse tried to console her by talking of how overwhelmed she had been when Liesl was born and how her niece had cared for the child and in many ways been more of a mother to Liesl than Ilse could be in those years. "You will find your way," she had assured Karoline. The woman seemed to take hope from that.

But then Ilse recalled all the times that she had witnessed Karoline sitting alone, staring into space. So many times the young mother had declined invitations to do something with the other women, and her eyes always seemed to brim with unshed tears.

"I should have seen," Ilse moaned. "The children had been so sick with whooping cough, and she had not had sleep for days. We all should have. . . ."

"Sh-h-h." Franz comforted her as they sat across from each other at the kitchen table and held hands. They did not speak for several minutes. Ilse noticed how exhausted her husband looked. He was only in his forties, but he looked like a man of sixty. The war had aged all of them. She was about the same age as Franz's sister, Ellie, yet when she had stood next to Ellie at their Thanksgiving reunion, she had been well aware that she had felt every one of her years and then some while Ellie had looked so young and vibrant.

"Your hands are freezing," she murmured, taking Franz's hands in hers and keeping her voice low so that they did not wake Liesl, asleep in Ilse's bed in the next room. "I'll make you some tea." She started to get up, but Franz gripped her hands more tightly.

"Stay here," he pleaded, and then she felt his tears wetting their joined hands like the first raindrops of a downpour. She leaned across the table and stroked his cheek.

"The children—so very young," he whispered hoarsely. "How could she do that to them? To Geza? He loved her so much." His tone had turned bitter and angry.

But Ilse understood how a young mother might think that killing herself would be the best possible solution for her husband and children. How many times back in Munich had she considered a similar plan? For that matter, hadn't Franz himself tiptoed around the idea?

"Karoline was not in her right mind, and who can blame her? This weather—the constant wind and snow and cold already now in December with months yet to go, not to mention the uncertainty, the hopes raised and then dashed again. And every time there was a new report about what the Nazis are doing to the Jews, Karoline's grief for those children she left behind was inconsolable."

"Why did she leave them?"

Ilse shrugged. "She never told me the entire story, but I know the divorce was bitter and her first husband would not allow her to bring them. Even so, she felt that she had abandoned them."

"But the children could have been safe here with her. And what about the children she had with Geza? What will happen to them?"

Ilse had no answers. And truthfully she was incapable of thinking about the future for Karoline's family. The leaden weight that had dwelt within her during those years of uncertainty in Munich was back, filling her chest with its familiar unbearable and crushing presence. "I wish Theo were still here," she said.

But after their family reunion at Thanksgiving, both Ilse and Franz had insisted that Theo needed to go home where he could at least find work to compensate for the money it had cost to stay in Oswego. "We'll be fine," Ilse had assured them, and they had believed her. Ellie had even commented on how wonderful it was to see her feeling so much better than she had the last time they had been together ten long years ago shortly after Liesl's birth.

So Theo had left, and a few weeks later the reporter Suzanne Randolph had announced that her former editor had offered her a paid position at the paper in Washington. "He says I can come back here when the war ends," she had explained on the snowy afternoon she came to say good-bye. Ilse had not realized how much she looked forward to the time she spent with the lively American and the French actress, Gisele, as Suzanne plied Gisele with questions and gathered material for the stories she assured them would make all Americans aware of their plight.

As 1944 came to a close it seemed that everyone had deserted them—the ladies from the various charities that had provided them with books and art supplies and household goods and helped organize programs, classes, and other activities rarely stopped by, citing the weather, the rush of the holidays, and the difficulty of the drive from Syracuse or other distant places. Even Ruth Gruber, the government liaison who had accompanied them across the Atlantic and who was their most outspoken advocate for the right to stay in America, had gone back to her job at the Department of the Interior in Washington, assuring them all that she could do more for their cause there than by staying in Oswego. The one good thing was that two women teachers who had moved into one of the brick houses on the hill had stayed on and continued to work with all the refugees on their English lessons.

There was a light knock on the door, and with a weary sigh that went beyond physical exhaustion Franz pushed back his chair and went to answer.

"Come in, Gisele," he invited.

The Frenchwoman removed her leather gloves and unfastened the knot in the silk scarf that covered her hair. It was a wonder to all the women in the shelter how Gisele managed to find such beautiful accessories in the bags of donated clothing that had poured into the fort in those first weeks.

"Terrible business," she murmured as she leaned down to kiss Ilse's cheek. She smelled of the cold and cigarettes and the exotic perfume she always wore.

"Sit. I was just going to make some tea."

"Lovely." Gisele shrugged out of the men's gabardine overcoat she was wearing and let it drape over the back of the chair. "I think we need to get in touch with Suzanne. You can be sure that the government will wish to bury this story, and if you ask me, that young woman is one our best hopes for stirring the pot."

"Do you think this is the time for politics?" Franz asked.

"Oh, Franz, at this point everything is an occasion for politics. It is becoming crystal clear that if anything is to be done, we must do it ourselves. Mrs. Roosevelt's visit last September was nothing more than a show for the photographers, and have we seen any results at all from that national radio broadcast a few weeks ago?"

"You have a point," Franz said. "But back in Munich we made the mistake of thinking that people would rise up in protest against Hitler after they distributed the White Rose leaflets, and nothing ever happened." He got the same faraway look in his eyes that always accompanied any memory of his involvement with the Resistance.

"Those young people thought they could change the minds of people in power, and they died for their troubles."

"No one is going to die," Gisele assured him. "This is America."

"Someone already has," he observed. "Karoline Bleier died last night."

"By her own hand, Franz. The government did not murder her as they did those young people back in Munich." Gisele accepted the cup of tea that Ilse handed her. "I mean no disrespect to Karoline, but if her death is to have meaning. . ." She turned to Ilse. "Karoline was already lost when she boarded the *Henry Gibbons* and came here. There was nothing you or anyone else could have done."

"I suppose."

"It is unimaginable that someone like Karoline or indeed any of those of us who are Jewish could have ever envisioned the kind of mass murder Hitler has set in motion," Gisele continued. "Don't get me wrong. We have a long, long history of persecution, but this? This is pure diabolical madness, and the world knows it. Roosevelt knows it, and so do all those high-powered politicians down in Washington and this"—she waved a hand that encompassed the tiny apartment and by inference the entire fort—"this is their answer?"

Ilse smiled. She had come to understand that although Gisele had long ago abandoned any religious aspects of her Jewish heritage, she was very political. She spoke often and at length about rumors of the establishment of a Jewish nation in Palestine and had hinted that this would be her destination once the war ended. She was indeed a woman of the world. But in spite of the fact that Karoline had been Jewish, her suicide had nothing to do with politics or religion. No, this was a tragedy that crossed all national and religious boundaries within the shelter. This was a mother—lost.

"I think that for tonight, we must think only of her poor husband, Geza, and the children," Ilse replied as she removed the kettle from the hot plate and refilled three cups. "Is someone with them?"

"Director Smart and his wife are helping him make the arrangements.

How anyone is going to manage to dig a grave—to find bare earth under all this snow and ice—is beyond me." Gisele blew on her tea. "The truth is I had no real reason for coming here tonight other than that I simply could not stand being alone." As a single woman, Gisele had a bed in the women's dormitory that occupied one of the other barracks. She would hardly have been alone there, but Ilse understood what she meant. The three of them sat around the table, sipping their tea in silence. Through the thin plasterboard walls, they could hear the howl of the wind, and above and to either side of them they heard the murmur of their neighbors' conversations and activities. It occurred to Ilse that in this place it was impossible to be alone. But to be drowning in loneliness was something altogether different.

Suzanne had had to swallow a whole lot of pride with her return to the newspaper. Edwin had made it clear that she would start from the bottom, so she was back to covering activities such as local council meetings and the garden club's annual holiday sale of trees, wreaths, and such. Although she was living and working in the very heart of the nation's capital, Edwin had been adamant that she was to stick to local news that did not include anything to do with politics or the war. He had stopped running her essays about life in the fort, promising to reconsider if something of note happened to change things there. But when Selma Velo called with news of the first suicide in the fort shortly after the New Year, Suzanne was sure that Edwin would immediately make arrangements for her to return to Oswego. After all, he was the one who had sent her there in the first place.

"A woman—a young mother and wife—has taken her own life," she argued when Edwin lifted his thick, dark eyebrows. "Surely—"

"And according to the schedule, you are already late for the meeting of the Parks Committee." He pointed to the large chalkboard that dominated the newsroom and kept track of everyone's assignments and whereabouts.

"Edwin, this could be a big story." She intentionally lowered her voice so she would not seem to be whining or pleading.

The editor leaned back in his chair, and it squealed in protest. "Go cover the parks meeting." He reached for his pen and started marking up an article another reporter had filed.

Suzanne's heart sank, but she knew when she was beat. She trudged toward the door.

"On the other hand, Suzie, if you have no plans for the weekend, I believe there's a night train that you could probably make if the parks meeting doesn't go on all night."

Suzanne grinned. She considered retracing her steps and giving the man a hug, but that might be grounds for him to change his mind. So she stayed where she was, facing the door, her back to him. "I'll check into it. Thanks." He hadn't said anything about how long she could be away, but she would fight that battle later.

Selma Velo had her old room available and was more than willing to rent by the week. She seemed glad to see her. Hilda Cutter was less than thrilled. "I thought you were done with those people and their hard-luck stories."

"It's good to see you again, Hilda." Suzanne carried her suitcase and typewriter into her room and felt a little like she had just come home. She sat on the side of the bed and glanced around. Outside the window she saw the old truck that Theo had restored parked next to the shed. It was covered with snow and looked abandoned.

Like the people at Fort Ontario, she thought. *Like the woman who finally decided that she could stand it no more.*

The boardinghouse was not the same without Theo. For one thing, there was no buffer for Hilda's rampant prejudice against the Jews—her tirades always backed up by Hugh Kilmer whenever he was in residence. The other boarders had moved on, so it was just the three of them and Selma. Selma was distracted by the lack of news from her son serving in the Pacific and rarely paid much attention to the talk at meals.

Suzanne realized that she had gotten used to the times she had spent with Theo during the autumn—sitting on the front porch swing, taking walks together, seeing a movie, or going to watch the high school football game. And where her temper would flare and her voice rise to a frustrated screech when Hilda got going, Theo had a way of changing the subject or making a counterpoint in a way that was both gentle and effective.

Once he went back to Wisconsin and she to Washington, they had exchanged a single letter, but he had warned her that he was terrible when it came to writing. Then she had gotten busy with her work and had made do with a postcard when she really owed him a letter. She had thought of him often, but the weeks had gone by.

And speaking of work, she had a job to do.

"I'm going over to the shelter," she told Selma as she passed by the kitchen. "Don't worry about me for supper. I'll grab something to eat in town."

"Tread easily," Selma warned. "This woman killing herself is not something the powers that be down there in Washington would likely want spread around. And with all the snow and cold, we have all the earmarks of an especially rough winter. That's bad news for everyone, but for the folks at the fort..." She shook her head without finishing the thought and turned back to the stove.

"Good advice," Suzanne replied, sitting on the hall bench to pull on her boots. "I thought maybe I could talk to Theo's aunt and uncle." In Suzanne's mind the Schneiders were more likely to give her the human details of the story while Gisele St. Germaine's take on the suicide would be far more political.

Selma shrugged. "Might be a place to start."

But when Suzanne reached the shelter and trudged up the path to the row of white barracks that were barely distinguishable from the mounds of snow that surrounded them, she had second thoughts. She had no way of knowing if Ilse and Franz had even known the woman. Nearly a thousand people lived in this place, and as with any community it was impossible for them to know everyone. Also, she should have let

Ilse and Franz know she was coming. Of course, the only telephone in the entire compound was in Joseph Smart's office, and in this weather it was unlikely that he would have been thrilled to try and get a message to Theo's relatives. On top of that, darkness came early on these gray overcast days, the path was slippery, and the wind off the lake cut right through her coat so that she wrapped her arms around her body as if trying to prevent the heat from escaping.

She looked up, blinking against the sting of icy snowflakes that had begun falling, and saw someone coming toward her—a woman wearing a silk scarf and dressed in men's trousers and a man's belted overcoat. "Gisele?" she called. She could think of no one but the French actress who would be bundled up in men's clothes and still manage to look completely elegant and feminine.

"Suzanne? What on earth are you doing here?" The two women had come together on the path. "Ah, but Karoline's death is news, is it not?"

"Yes." Suzanne had learned some time ago that it was useless to try and pretend with Gisele. The woman was uncanny in her ability to see through to the truth. "I thought I might try and speak with Ilse and Franz."

"Why? What have they to do with it?"

"I think that Ilse might have been friends with the woman. I remember meeting her once when I was visiting. And the children were there, as well."

"This is not a good time," Gisele said. "Tomorrow is the funeral."

"So soon?"

Gisele shrugged. "It is our way." The simple statement reminded Suzanne that Gisele—like the dead woman and her family—was Jewish.

"But in this weather?"

"People die in all seasons." She rearranged her scarf. "Come. It has started to snow for a change," she said, the sarcasm of her statement obvious. "I'm freezing, and while I cannot promise it will be much warmer in the dining hall, you are welcome to come with me. We can talk there."

"Thank you. I will." Suzanne glanced back at the barracks—at the window she knew belonged to Ilse and Franz. A single lamp glowed behind the lace curtains.

Gisele followed her glance. "I told them I would bring back sandwiches. If you like, you can deliver them. It will give you the opportunity to say hello and catch up on news of Theo."

"I. . .that is.,. ."

Gisele hooked arms with her and started back down the path to the dining hall. "Do not pretend that you are not curious for news of him. You cannot fool the French, *ma chérie*. We practically invented love."

"I have no idea what you are talking about," Suzanne replied, and Gisele's low, throaty laughter echoed across the deserted grounds.

Shortly after Theo returned home to the farm, his father's friend Jim Sawyer, a local attorney active in party politics, invited Theo and his dad to come with him to a political meeting. Theo went more out of boredom than anything else.

Over the months he had lived in Oswego, he had made daily visits to his uncle and aunt while bureaucrats in Washington wrestled with their fate. He had been there when President Roosevelt's wife—the popular and influential Eleanor—made her visit, and he recalled how hopes had been raised by her promise to do everything she could to help those who wished to stay in the United States to do so. But nothing had come of that. He was curious to see whether or not news of the refugees had even made it to Wisconsin.

Much of the discussion that evening revolved around the need to find a viable candidate from their district to run for the House of Representatives in the fall. The current congressman from the opposing political party was retiring after serving several terms.

"This is our chance," Jim Sawyer had told the others. "We need a fresh face, someone not directly connected to the war or to Washington. But the candidate also needs to be someone who knows the system and can figure out how to get things done. Once this war ends, people are going to want to get back to a normal routine and look to the future."

Others disagreed and thought that their best hope to win the election in the fall would be to put forth a war hero as their candidate or at the very least someone who had served in either Europe or the Pacific. But Jim was adamant—and persuasive.

"We're moving into a new era, and people are war weary. They don't want to think about the war. They want to think about the future," he told the others. "The whole landscape of the world will be forever changed once this thing finally ends. This is the time for new blood, new ideas."

Theo thought perhaps Jim should be the candidate, and one of the other men suggested that. "I'm too old, and besides, folks know me. We need somebody young who will make voters think about the possibilities of rebuilding their lives after the war."

"Well, tonight we need to get this mailing out," one of the others announced, and that ended all discussion of an election that was still almost a year away. They turned their attention to the stacks of papers on the table and began stuffing envelopes, sealing them, and applying postage.

As they worked, one of the men asked Theo's dad about his brother-in-law. "I understand that Ellie's brother and his wife and daughter finally made it out of Germany. Will they be coming here to live with you, Paul?"

"Doesn't look likely," Theo's dad replied, and then he explained the terms of the rescue. "Theo knows a lot more than I do about the politics of the thing," he added. "He was out there with them all last fall."

The room had gone quiet except for the rhythmic shuffling of paper as the others continued the work, but everyone was looking at Theo, apparently waiting for him to take up the story. So he did.

He tried to give them a clear and thorough account of the situation. He praised Director Smart and Ruth Gruber from the Department of the Interior, recounting in detail how they had fought to make sure the refugees had more than just the essentials. He also talked about the generosity of the charitable organizations, as well as the Nazi POWs enjoying more government support and liberty than those inside Fort Ontario. He concluded with the story of Karoline Bleier's suicide.

The room went completely still as all work stopped. They all looked at Theo as if waiting for more.

And Theo found that he wanted to tell them more, wanted them to understand the frustration that he felt not only for his aunt and uncle and cousin but for the others as well. He wanted to tell them about the young woman Ilse had told them about in their last telephone call. A mother of two young children who had been through so much and come so close to finally being free to live the life she and her husband had probably thought they would have the day they married.

Finally a man sitting at the far end of the table spoke. "You say the bulk of them are Jews?" The way he said it left little doubt that he thought that explained a lot and was reason enough for the government's plan to send them back.

Theo thought about Hilda and Hugh and their rampant anti-Semitism, and he had to fight the urge to lash out at the man. He thought about how Suzanne had learned that certain government officials—in some cases entire departments—shared those views. Stan was certainly not alone. In fact, he had a lot of company. But Theo's father spoke first. "Come on, Stan. In a country built on the idea that all men are created equal, what does it matter if they are Jewish or Methodist like Jim here is or Quaker like my family? They are people who have been persecuted and starved and chained up like animals in those concentration camps—some say they've seen even worse. Why else are we fighting the Nazis and their kind if not for the right of all people to live free?"

Stan looked away, and a couple of other people around the table cleared their throats uneasily.

"Besides," Theo continued, undeterred by the aura of discomfort that had permeated the room, "there are others there as well—Catholics and Protestants—some who are Greek Orthodox. I expect there are more than a few that would not own up to any faith after what they went through over there. The stories they tell—you wouldn't think such things could be possible in a civilized world."

"I don't get it," another man said as the work resumed. "I mean, the government brings them here and then wants to send them back?"

"It all has something to do with the immigration quotas set following the Great War," Jim Sawyer explained. "This country could have been overrun with those displaced by that war if those restrictions had not been put in place. It'll be worse once this thing is over. Our boys and the Brits are blasting most of Western Europe to smithereens. Even folks who have made it without going through what those poor souls in Oswego have had to suffer are going to want out."

"That makes sense, then. We have to stick to the quotas that are already set," Stan said.

"Still you scoop up these folks and bring them here. . . ," another man began.

Stan interrupted him. "Look, Theo told us they signed a paper. They knew what they were getting into. They agreed to go back."

Theo met the man's fiery gaze. "The question is, back to what?" he said quietly.

The two women at the table who had accompanied their husbands to help with the mailing and who had not spoken a word both stood and, with smiles that were twitching nervously and too bright, suggested it was time for coffee and cake.

Later that night Theo thought about those women and smiled as he imagined Suzanne and Gisele seated at that table. Now, there were two females who would not have been satisfied with the role of stuffing envelopes and serving the men refreshments in silence. They would not have been able to keep quiet. He wondered what Suzanne was doing now that she was back in Washington. He assumed that she had heard about the suicide, and if he knew her at all she would be fairly itching to return to Oswego and get what she liked to call the story behind the story.

They had each managed to write one letter after parting in the fall, but he wasn't much of a correspondent and apparently neither was she. The last communication he'd had from her was a postcard wishing him and his family a happy New Year and ending with a promise to write soon.

Downstairs the telephone rang. It was late for anyone to be calling. He heard his father answer and talk for several seconds to the caller, obviously someone he knew well. Then he heard him say, "Okay, I'll get him," and start up the stairs.

"Theo?" His dad tapped at his partially open bedroom door then stepped inside. "That's Jim Sawyer on the phone. He'd like to speak with you."

"About what?" Theo was already following his father back downstairs.

"He thinks you'd make a good candidate for Congress and wants to know if you're interested." His dad started back toward the stairs. "Hey, Theo? This might be the opportunity you've been waiting for. I think you can do this, Son."

Theo's first thought was that perhaps this was the plan for his life—this was how he could be a part of the change that would have to come with the end of the war. His second was about how disappointed his parents would be when they realized he wasn't really interested in farming. He hesitated. But his father put all his doubts to rest.

In a few words, Dad told Theo that not only was he well aware of his son's ambitions but that he gave those dreams his blessing.

CHAPTER 9

Y ou need a platform," Jim Sawyer told Theo a few days later as the two of them sat across from each other at the diner in Madison. Outside the window Theo could see Wisconsin's impressive state capitol building that occupied an entire city block. Passersby paid little attention to the landmark as they hurried by, clutching their coats close to their necks and hanging on to their hats in the blustery January wind. Theo wondered how the weather was in Oswego, recalling Aunt Ilse's description of the thin walls and the way the cold penetrated even the outer walls of the wooden barracks.

"Are you listening to me, Theo?"

"Yes, sir. A platform. I've got a few thoughts about that."

"Let's hear them."

"Well, in our faith. . ."

Jim held up a hand to stop him. "Can't be mixing religion and politics."

"No, sir. I just—"

"And stop calling me Mister and Sir. If we're going to work together, it's Jim and Theo, got it?"

"Yes, sir—I mean Jim."

Jim rolled his eyes and took a swallow of his coffee as he glanced out the window. A cluster of students from the university strolled by as if it were a balmy day in May. The boys were wearing letter jackets and the girls were clinging to their arms possessively. "Those young folks?" Jim nodded toward the group. "Those are your future, Theo. If we can get you into Congress in the fall with their help, they'll vote for you every election."

"They don't look like they're old enough to vote."

"That's not the point. Before you know it, they will be old enough if they aren't already, and you need to make them feel part of what will be a postwar world, feel like they will have a voice in shaping that world."

For reasons he didn't fully understand, Theo thought about the group of medical students in Munich that his uncle had joined in an effort to inspire others to stand against Hitler. In the months he had spent in Oswego, Franz had talked often about that group. The White Rose was what they had called themselves. They were German young people—mostly university students—who saw a bleak future for their country if things continued the way they were going. Most of them were dead now—tried in kangaroo courts, found guilty, and some of them beheaded.

As he watched the Wisconsin students head on down the street, he wondered if they had that kind of passion. "Okay, forget the part about my faith," he said as if he and Jim had been discussing the matter at length. "Maybe the platform is about building the kind of world we fought for—a world where people can live free regardless of their faith or nationality or color or—"

"You're running for Congress, Theo, not master of the world. You've got to crawl before you walk, and walk before you run."

Theo smiled. "So I'm not 'running' for Congress. I'm 'crawling' in that direction?"

"Don't get smart with me, kid." He squinted as if trying to see Theo more clearly. "Are you sure that you really want to do this? Because it's not too late. We've got time to draft somebody else."

The quick temper that he'd fought most of his life to control flared up. "I can do this," he said, forcing his voice to remain low and even.

Jim visibly relaxed.

"But I am my own man," Theo added.

The squint came back. "Meaning?"

"Meaning I run on a platform that I can wholeheartedly defend."

"Well, of course." But Jim did not seem as convinced as his words indicated.

"And meaning if you're having second thoughts on your end, now would be the best time to speak up."

Theo hoped he sounded confident and determined because he sure didn't feel that way. If Jim Sawyer decided that the party had made a mistake choosing him to groom as their candidate, Theo wasn't sure what he would do. Ever since his dad had called him to the phone that night, he'd been building the dream that a seat in Congress could allow him to start making a real difference—something he'd been wanting to do since the day they had listened to President Roosevelt's radio address to the nation following the attack on Pearl Harbor. In spite of everything he had been raised to believe about the futility of war, there had been a moment when he had wanted nothing so much as to volunteer.

"Theo, you're pretty green when it comes to politics. Take my advice and wise up. This business is a game, and if you want to get anything done—and it's pretty clear that you do—you're going to have to learn the rules of that game."

"Crawl first. Got that part. So are you okay with this?"

Jim smiled. "You took a big risk there. What if I said I wasn't?"

Theo shrugged. "I go back to farming. It's not a bad life."

"Just not the life for you?"

"I won't lie. I'd like to try something else, but I have no problems making an honest living off the land. It was good enough for generations of my family—it's good enough for me."

Jim scooted himself out of the booth and stood. He threw a dollar bill on the table to pay for their coffee. It occurred to Theo that the older man still had not answered his question. He wiped his mouth with the paper napkin and then stood up, noticing that he was a good three inches taller than Jim was.

"You go think through that platform idea and get back to me by next week. Let's get you elected to the United States Congress, Theo Bridgewater," Jim said as he grasped Theo's shoulder and gave it a squeeze. "Once this war is finally over, we're going to need men like you to show us a new way."

The fort's parade ground was a white wasteland set against a backdrop of the enormous Lake Ontario's frozen shoreline as Ilse hurried to the infirmary. Franz had been suffering from a terrible cold and hacking cough for over two weeks now—ever since the funeral for Karoline. He was weak, and the fact that he had little appetite did nothing to help rebuild his strength. She had left him with Gisele while she went to ask for some stronger medicine. She never left him alone these days because he insisted on getting up by himself and trying to make it upstairs to the men's communal bathroom without help. What if he fell?

Two weeks earlier as she had turned the page on the wall calendar that hung next to the door of their apartment she had felt so defeated. January 1945. A new year. By now she had thought that the war would have ended. Certainly every day the headlines in the Oswego newspaper heralded the victories of the Allies. Every day it seemed as if surrender was imminent. By now she had thought that they would be settled somewhere, ready to begin their new life.

Of course that location was uncertain as well, for Franz wanted to stay in America while she wanted to go home to Germany. She wanted to find her sister. She wanted to go back to Munich, the city she had always loved. That was her home—no matter that the Nazis had sullied its image and the Allies had bombed its landmarks. She had been through enough change in her life. All she wanted to do was to go home. If she was destined to start over yet again, she wanted to do it in her own country. But although the Americans occasionally conducted a survey to collect data on what the refugees wanted, they only asked Franz as head of their family. They did not ask her.

The door of the infirmary blew shut behind her with a loud bang. The nurse looked up and smiled. "How is Mr. Schneider?" she asked.

"His fever is down, but he's still so weak, and the coughing is not improved. I wondered if perhaps you might have a stronger medicine? He is not eating because he chokes on the food due to coughing."

The nurse frowned. "I'll have the doctor come see him later today."

The doctor did not arrive until after dark, and by that time Franz's breathing was labored and shallow.

"Pneumonia," the doctor told Ilse. He was a doctor from town that the government had hired to replace the refugee physician as the fort's medical director. "I'll make arrangements for him to be transferred to the fort hospital. They can make him more comfortable."

More comfortable. What about making him well?

But the doctor was already closing up his black bag and starting for the door. Ilse knew that in addition to his work in the fort he also maintained his practice in Oswego. The man always seemed rushed and overwhelmed. She also knew from gossip she'd overheard that he had more than once made negative comments about the Germans.

"Tonight? You will see that he is transferred tonight?"

The doctor sighed and frowned. "I'll make the arrangements. It could be tonight or tomorrow morning. As you are no doubt aware, the fort's facility is small, and I have to be sure there is a bed for him."

Something in his manner caused Ilse to feel fury well up in her, filling her chest the way this American doctor had described the fluid filling Franz's chest. "We may be German, Doctor," she said quietly, "but we are not the enemy. My husband spoke out against the Nazis—it is why we were hunted. It is why we are here."

The doctor paused, and she saw by the slight reddening of his neck above the limp collar of his shirt that she had guessed right. It was hardly the first time that she and Franz had had to defend themselves as "good" Germans.

"Forgive me, Mrs. Schneider. I will make sure that your husband is transferred as soon as possible. Do you have someone to stay with your daughter?"

Ilse was confused. "You are saying that I may be with him?"

He set down his black bag and took her hand between both of his. "The hospital here may be small, but your husband will have the finest care we can offer. Still, I must warn you that he may not recover from this, Mrs. Schneider. You should be with him, and yes, I will make that happen." He studied her for a moment. "You must be strong for your daughter."

Ilse nodded and slid her hand free of his. Only hours earlier she had been thinking of how she and Franz disagreed about where they would live after the war. Now she faced living without him. "Please hurry," she murmured as if speed would make a difference.

After the doctor left, she walked down the hall to the apartment where she had sent Liesl to do homework with friends after supper, not wanting her to hear what the doctor said. On the way back she explained that Papa was going to the hospital.

"Will he die there?" Liesl asked, her voice shaky but matter of fact. What kind of world were they living in where children saw death as an ordinary occurrence?

"The doctor is going to do everything he can to make him well," Ilse replied as they reached their door. "Now go to your father and sit with him while I get Gisele. She's going to stay with you while I go to the hospital with Papa."

Liesl clung to her, suddenly the scared, confused child that she was. "Mama?"

"Sh-h-h." Ilse brushed her daughter's wispy bangs back from her forehead. "Go sit with Papa and tell him about your day. Make him smile the way only you can with your stories about school and your teachers and the other students."

She took her coat and scarf down from the hook by the door, preparing to make the trek across the edge of the parade ground to the single-women's barracks. She hated to ask Gisele to come out in this weather—it was so raw and damp and the wind off the lake was persistent. But the neighbor down the way had children of her own, and Ilse also did not like adding to her burden.

Someone knocked on the door. Was the transport here already? She opened the door ready to explain that they should take Franz and she would follow once she made arrangements for the care of her child, but instead of the orderlies she expected, standing before her was the reporter, Suzanne Randolph, and she was holding a large pot.

When she saw Ilse's face, Suzanne nearly dropped the pot she was holding. Theo's aunt looked absolutely drained as if she could not deal with one more thing. She was wearing her coat and scarf and pulling on her gloves.

"I came. . .I'm leaving for Washington tomorrow, and I came to say good-bye and to see how Professor Schneider is doing."

Ilse motioned toward the pot. "What is this?"

"Mrs. Velo made chicken soup, and there was far too much and she. . .is something wrong?" Behind the distressed woman, she could see Liesl sitting on the side of the bed. She had heard from Gisele that Franz had come down with a terrible cold after the funeral and the lengthy graveside service for the woman who had committed suicide.

She walked past Ilse and set the soup on the table. "What can I do to help you, Ilse?" She had rarely called the older woman by her given name, but this seemed the right time.

Ilse's eyes filled with tears, and she started shaking her head, and then she started to tremble. Suzanne did the only thing she could think to do—she wrapped her arms around Theo's aunt. She was surprised when instead of stiffening Ilse collapsed against her, surrendering completely to her embrace as if it were the one thing she had needed for a very long time. Suzanne pulled out one of the wooden kitchen chairs with the toe of her shoe and eased Ilse onto the seat then knelt beside her.

"Tell me what to do, Ilse." She lowered her voice to a whisper, mindful of Liesl in the next room.

"They are coming to take Franz to the hospital. They are allowing me to go with him and stay until. . . I was on my way to ask Gisele to stay with Liesl. Could you. . . ?"

"I can stay," Suzanne assured her.

"No. You have a train to catch tomorrow, and I don't know when I might return. Please go for Gisele."

"I will stay," Suzanne repeated. "There will be other trains."

"Just until I can send for Gisele."

"I'll just stay. You should be with your husband." She did not add the thought that sprang to mind: *while you still can.*

From the hallway came the voices of men headed toward them. "Mrs. Schneider?" Two men carrying a stretcher stood at the door that had been left open on Suzanne's arrival.

"Yes. My husband is in there." She motioned toward the bedroom and followed the men. Taking Liesl's hand, she guided her back into the front room. "You remember Theo's friend, Miss Randolph?"

Suzanne was stunned by the woman's calm. Now that she was speaking with her daughter, there was no trace of the trembling or tears that she had displayed before. Meanwhile Liesl glanced at Suzanne and then back at the men lifting her father onto the stretcher. Suzanne used her gloves as hot pads and picked up the pot of soup.

"Liesl, what shall I do with this soup? Perhaps I could set it on the hot plate and keep it warm until. . ."

Liesl's gaze was riveted on her father, her small hand searching blindly for her mother's. Suzanne's feeble attempt at distraction had clearly not worked. She moved the soup to the hot plate and set the burner on low heat. Perhaps she could get the child to have some once her parents left.

The men carried the stretcher past them and down the hall. Ilse hesitated then bent down to hug her daughter. "Be very brave," Suzanne heard her whisper and saw the child nod. "I'll be home as soon as I can, but it will be tomorrow. So finish your homework and then to bed with you." She straightened and tweaked Liesl's nose before pulling her coat closed and hurrying away.

Liesl stood in the doorway, watching her go, and then she remained standing there as if she might stay until her parents returned. Suzanne was uncertain what she should do. "Liesl?" She placed her hands lightly on the girl's shoulders and gently turned her away from the deserted hallway.

As soon as the outer door clicked shut, Liesl turned to her and buried her face in Suzanne's skirt, her tears and sobs coming with heartbreaking gasps as she wrapped her arms around Suzanne's legs and clung to her as she might have clung to a lifeline.

"Come on now," Suzanne murmured as she stroked the girl's fine, wispy hair. She would not tell Liesl that everything would be all right. Having seen Franz's gray, haggard face, she wondered if he could possibly recover. "Your mother mentioned homework. Show me what you are studying, okay?"

With a shuddering sigh, Liesl released her grip on Suzanne and sat down at the table. Listlessly she opened a book and pulled it toward her and then took out a sheet of lined paper and a stub of a pencil. "I'm supposed to practice my handwriting," she said, resting her head on one hand as she began to mimic the letters in the book. "My teacher says that most people are right-handed and that I will be at a disadvantage if I continue to use my left."

Suzanne sat across from her, occasionally offering words of praise even though she really wanted to tell Liesl's teacher that there was nothing wrong with being left-handed and by making such an issue of it she was branding the child as different—again. Her mind drifted to Franz on that stretcher and the image of Ilse sitting alone in a sterile waiting room while the doctors tried to save Franz's life.

"Will Papa die?" Liesl asked without looking up from her work. "Lots of people we knew in Munich died, and we saw dead people when we were hiding from the men who wanted to take Papa back to the prison."

All of this information was delivered in a quiet voice that the girl might have used if she had been telling Suzanne about her day at school. Suzanne thought of all the children across Europe forced to witness the horrid realities of war played out on the streets of their hometowns. It occurred to her that regardless of which side the adults in their lives might be on, children living in war zones paid an enormous price—they paid with their innocence and their childhoods.

"My friend Ruthie was in what they call a concentration camp," Liesl continued, still not looking up from her work. "She told me that they had whole days when they had nothing to eat at all and the guards were really mean to her even if she was nice to them. She is Jewish, and the government hated the Jews. I don't know why. Do the American government people hate the Jews?"

Some of them do, and I don't know why, either, Suzanne was tempted to reply. "Unfortunately, Liesl, there are people in every country who don't like people who have a different way about them or look different or come from a different place."

Liesl nodded and leaned back in her chair. "At first some of the other boys and girls in my class were mean to me. They said because I was German that I was their enemy. They called me names, and one boy threw my books in the snow. It happened here at the fort, too—some of the Jewish children would not play with me at first."

Unexpectedly she grinned. "But I set them straight. Cousin Theo told me to tell them that I was a Quaker—a Friend." Her eyes twinkled at the memory. "And then one day Theo came to my school, and he explained all about being Quaker, and after that. . ." She shrugged as if the outcome was evident.

"After that?" Suzanne prompted.

"They played with me. Theo told me that sometimes you just have to explain things so people's questions get answered and then they'll be fine." She went back to her work. "Done," she announced as she closed the book and carefully laid the paper inside a folder.

"Would you like some soup?" There didn't seem to be anything else to offer the girl, and Suzanne realized that the refugees kept little food in their rooms or apartments. They went to the dining hall to eat their meals.

"No, thank you." She glanced at the clock above the table and frowned. "Usually Papa, Mama, and I meet for worship at this time before I go to sleep. Back in Munich there were a whole bunch of people who believed like we do, but they all went away, and here at the fort we're the only Quakers. There are a lot of Jews, and they have their meeting place right here—they call it a synagogue. My friends who are Catholic and others like them can go to services in the churches in town or use their part of the chapel here in the fort. But there's nobody else like us, and we don't have a meetinghouse so we meet here."

"I'm like you," Suzanne found herself admitting. "My family is Quaker, too."

Liesl's eyes widened in surprise. "Theo never told me that. He said that when we could leave here and go back with him to Wisconsin to live on the farm we would be with lots of Quakers but he never said—"

"Well, here I am," Suzanne said.

"Then you know all about sitting in silence and the Light inside us and how that's how we figure out what to do next. So we can hold meeting for worship, after all. Mama says that Jesus used to say all you needed was two or three gathered together, and here we are." She wriggled to an upright position in her chair and closed her eyes as she rested her hands palms up on her knees.

It had been years since Suzanne had sat in silence and supposedly waited for the Light to come her way. But when she saw Liesl squint one eye open, she had no option but to close her eyes and sit perfectly still until Liesl was satisfied.

"We don't have to do a long time," Liesl whispered as if to reassure her.

"Okay," Suzanne whispered back. Other than sounds from the neighboring apartments above and next to them and the wind, the room was silent.

CHAPTER 10

As soon as the call came that Franz had died, Theo and his parents drove through the night to reach the shelter and be with Ilse. Suzanne had made that call, assuring them that Selma Velo had open rooms and would be glad to have them stay at the boardinghouse for as long as necessary. Theo had taken the call. His parents had gone into town, and he was alone in the farmhouse. The moment he had heard Suzanne's voice on the line, he realized how he had missed her.

"Theo? It's Suzanne."

"Hi. How are you? Where are you?" His need for information about her was suddenly voracious.

"I'm back in Oswego. Theo, I'm afraid I have some terrible news."

"Uncle Franz?" They knew he had been ill, but Ilse had assured them that it was just a cold and chest congestion.

"I'm so sorry," Suzanne said, confirming his fear. "It was pneumonia. He was taken to the shelter's hospital last evening but by then. . ." Her voice trailed off. "Your aunt was with him."

"That's good. Liesl?"

"I stayed the night with her in the apartment. Theo, it's a wonder half the people in the camp aren't ill. There is no insulation, and the wind and cold just seep into this place. I spent the night with my coat and gloves on."

Her irritation made him smile. If he knew her at all, he was quite certain that there would soon be an essay about conditions at the fort.

"Sorry," she murmured. "You don't need to hear me ranting just now. Ilse said that she would delay the funeral until your mother can get here. Everyone is being incredibly supportive—the staff, Mr. Smart, the other residents."

"How's Ilse holding up?"

"She's amazing. I mean, it all happened so fast. One minute he's fighting a terrible cold, and the next. . ."

"And Liesl?"

Suzanne hesitated. "She's very quiet—too quiet. And I don't think she has cried. I don't think it's hit her yet that her father is gone."

At that moment Theo had heard the crunch of his father's truck tires on the packed snow. "My folks just got back from town. Tell Ilse we'll be there as soon as we can. We'll leave tonight."

"You're coming, too?"

"Yes. Matthew and his wife can move in here for a few days and take care of things on the farm. Dad will need help with the driving and. . ." *I want to see you*, he almost added.

"Ilse will be so glad. Be safe," she said softly and hung up.

The funeral service for Franz was held in the former service club turned recreation and community hall, and he was buried in the Riverside Cemetery outside the fort—the same place where Karoline Bleier had been laid to rest a couple of weeks earlier. *Free at last* was all Ilse could think as she sat in silence with their neighbors from the shelter and Franz's family from Wisconsin.

She held tight to Liesl's small hand. It worried her how stoically the little girl had taken the news of her father's death.

"Papa is at peace now?" she had asked when Ilse returned from the hospital the day after Franz had been taken there. Suzanne had stayed through the night as she had promised, and her hands rested lightly on Liesl's thin shoulders.

"Yes, Liebchen."

Liesl had run to Ilse and hugged her, but instead of the wails of grief that Ilse might have expected, Liesl said, "We will be all right, Mama."

Her daughter comforting her had been more than Ilse could endure, and she had broken down in sobs. Suzanne had stepped forward then and embraced both Ilse and Liesl. "Come and rest," she said softly. "I'll make you some tea. Liesl, will you help?"

All through the following days as arrangements were made, Liesl had remained stoic. Even now seated beside Ilse at the funeral, she remained dry eyed.

Theo introduced the service, describing the usual ritual for the many people there who had never attended a Quaker funeral. "A funeral in our faith is called 'Meeting for Worship in Thanksgiving for the Grace of God,' and it focuses on two things: honoring the life of the deceased and experiencing the presence of God's spirit in this hour." He glanced at the closed pine casket in the center of several circles of chairs and added, "Everyone who is so inspired may speak regardless of age, gender, or religious beliefs. In our faith all are equal in the sight of God. We ask only that you allow time for silence between each spoken ministry."

Theo took his seat next to his parents, and the silent worship began. After several minutes, Franz's sister, Ellie, stood and spoke of her memories of her brother when the two of them had been children in Germany. Her memorial was followed by more silence.

All Ilse could think about was that Ellie was talking about a stranger. Ilse and Franz had both been nearly thirty when they met at a reception at the university. He had been awarded a prize for his research, and the reception had been in his honor. Ilse's friend who worked at the university had invited her to attend, and the moment she had seen Franz she had felt her heart leap.

In those days he had been so handsome and his eyes—always filled with kindness and curiosity—had met hers when her friend introduced them. He had invited the two of them to join him for a beer at the local *Gasthaus* following the event. Her friend had begged off, citing a headache, but she had insisted that Franz and Ilse go without her. He had walked her home and asked if he could call on her the following evening. Six months later, they had married.

She closed her eyes, remembering their wedding day, remembering the day—years later—when they had learned she was pregnant just when they had given up all hope of ever having a child and how Franz's eyes had filled with tears of joy. She thought of the war years—the first war before she'd known him and then this one. She thought of the times she had wasted wallowing in fear and depression and regretted the worry and pain she knew that she had caused him.

Forgive me, my love.

Breaking the silence, Joseph Smart talked about how Franz had embraced life within the fort despite the challenges. "He was a wonderful teacher and for many of you the key to learning our American ways and language. I believe he was happiest in the hours he spent organizing our little library. I know he preferred that to some of his other chores—shoveling coal in the barracks, for example."

Ilse saw several people smile and nod.

"Franz Schneider was a gentle man and a quiet leader, and he will be missed," Mr. Smart said and sat down.

More silence and then Gisele stood and recounted the time that Franz had told her of his involvement with the White Rose resistance group back in Germany. "I looked at this mild-mannered professor and could not believe what he was telling me, yet I knew of that group, and he was telling me things only a member would know. Franz Schneider was a hero for Germany who was hunted and imprisoned by the Nazis but who never forgot his native roots. There was a time when I—like many others—hated all Germans. Professor Schneider taught me the lessons of forgiveness and discernment."

Ilse thought of how frightened she had been in the days back in Munich when Franz would leave for a "meeting," and she knew that he was not speaking of a faculty meeting or meeting with other Quakers. How angry she had been at him sometimes for risking his life—risking her life and Liesl's. But now she felt such a sense of pride that Franz had never surrendered to the terror and intimidation of Hitler's thugs. In his view they had occupied his country as surely as they had marched into Austria or Poland or France.

After a long silence and as she had requested, her brother-in-law Paul was the last to stand. He removed a paper from his coat pocket and unfolded it then adjusted his reading glasses and cleared his throat.

"In 1693, William Penn—a devout Quaker and founder of the colony of Pennsylvania—wrote these words: 'And this is the comfort of the Good that the grave cannot hold them, and that they live as soon as they die. For death is no more than a turning of us over from time to eternity.'"

He refolded the paper, sat in silence for a moment longer, and then turned to Joseph Smart and offered him a firm handshake, signaling the end of the service. Director Smart walked over to where Ilse and Liesl sat. He murmured words of sympathy and consolation meant only for them. He was a good man—a man who had made it his business to attend every event that involved the refugees, regardless of their faith or traditions. Ilse thanked him for his help. "Franz so enjoyed his work with the library," she said.

"He did us all a great service," the director replied.

"Will we—my daughter and I—need to move to the women's barracks?" Ilse asked. She had always been one to address practical matters as soon as possible.

"No, of course not. You and Liesl are still a family, Ilse."

"Thank you."

Director Smart stepped back to allow others to offer their condolences.

Ilse stood with Ellie and Paul and Theo as those attending the service stopped to speak with them. Because they were the only Quakers in the shelter and there was no gathering of the Religious Society of Friends in the Oswego area, most of those people who grasped her hands and murmured words of comfort were Jewish. It struck Ilse that in life's passages—moments of celebration and sorrow—barriers of religion and politics disappeared. Everyone was on common ground, and that more than anything consoled her, for she knew that Franz would be touched by this outpouring of respect and even affection for him.

When the last person had left the recreation hall, heading for the cemetery in town where Franz would be buried, Ilse realized that it had been some time since she had seen Liesl. Her heart flared with familiar anxiety as she realized that with Franz gone, she and she alone was responsible for raising their child and keeping her safe.

"Coming, Ilse?" Ellie asked. "Paul is getting the car."

"I just have to find Liesl. You go ahead."

Alone in the hall, Ilse turned in a circle, not knowing where to begin to search for her daughter. Then she heard a single note struck on the old upright piano that had been pushed into a corner to make room for the circles of chairs. She followed the sound and saw Liesl sitting on the bench, staring at the keys.

"Papa wanted me to learn to play the piano," Liesl said, her voice little more than a whisper. "I told him there was plenty of time for me to do that later." Ilse realized that for all her taking on of American ways, Liesl had never called Franz "Dad"—he had always been her papa. Liesl started to cry and splayed her hands on the keys, striking a jarring chord that filled the empty hall.

Ilse slid onto the bench next to her and wrapped her arms around her. "You can learn now. You can do it in memory of Papa. Think how pleased he would be."

"I'll practice every single day," Liesl promised. "Do you think Papa will know?"

Ilse hesitated. Some in their faith believed in an afterlife, and others did not. Ilse was unsure of her position on the matter, but she understood that the idea that Franz was somewhere watching Liesl play the piano gave the child comfort. "Yes," she said, hugging her daughter to her. "Papa will know."

As he drove to the cemetery, Theo kept reliving the service that had just ended. After explaining the tradition of the Quaker faith to the mostly non-Quaker gathering, he had thought of sharing his memories of Franz but decided against it. He had barely known his uncle. His sister, Beth, should be the one here speaking of the man she had lived with for eight years in Munich. But Beth was still in England awaiting permission to leave with her German husband and their daughter. Besides, Beth was expecting a second child anytime now.

His mind had wandered as first one and then another person rose to speak. Finally his eyes had settled on Suzanne sitting with Gisele across from the family. Theo was reminded of the conversation they had once had about faith. He'd been surprised to learn that she had been raised as a Quaker and even more surprised to learn that she no longer practiced that or any faith.

"How can you believe in a god who would allow a monster like Hitler?" she had challenged.

"I believe that every person is born with the spirit of God already inside and that it is our choice whether or not we bring that spirit into our daily lives." He knew that she had believed the same thing but something had changed that, and for reasons he could not fully grasp, he thought it had to do with something far more personal than Hitler's regime.

All during the funeral, he glanced up at Suzanne from time to time, trying to decide if perhaps she might once again feel the power of that inner Light. But she sat stone still with her hands folded in her lap and stared out the window behind him. It occurred to him that she had spent a good part of her adult life in Washington, and he wondered if the political world might not be partially to blame for her jaded attitude. Then he wondered if he won election to Congress and moved to Washington, would he suffer a similar loss?

After spending the night in the frigid apartment with Liesl and witnessing Ilse's grief at the loss of her beloved husband, Suzanne had come to a decision. She was going to stay in Oswego and see this thing through to the end. If that meant she had no job—or income—so be it. She still had some savings, and perhaps Joseph Smart or the local newspaper would give her some part-time work.

Obviously the funeral was not the place to broach the subject with the camp's director, but she could at least ask if she could meet with him. So when she found herself standing next to him in line at the meal Gisele and several other women had set up for the mourners when they returned from the cemetery, she asked if it would be convenient for her to stop by his office the following day.

"Another interview, Miss Randolph?" Smart smiled.

"Of sorts," she replied. They agreed to meet at two the following day.

She would have to call Edwin and let him know of her decision, and she dreaded making that call at the boardinghouse where Hilda would no doubt be listening from the upstairs hallway. Perhaps if she made the call while everyone was at breakfast, the table conversation would make it impossible for Hilda to eavesdrop.

She was so engrossed with the details of carrying out her plans that at first she did not notice the man standing alone near the exit. There were dozens of guests all crowding around the buffet to fill their plates and share memories of Franz, but this man drew her attention by the way he stood half in and half out of the room as if he could not make up his mind.

He wore an overcoat that was too small for him, and he carried a fedora. He fixed his attention on Ilse, and Suzanne saw that he watched her with concern. There was something familiar about him, but she could not place him. She had interviewed at least a couple hundred of the residents of the shelter, but this man was not one of them. Still there was something.

She started across the room, weaving her way through the throng to reach the doorway. She wanted to get a closer look, and she had almost reached the exit when the way cleared and she saw that he was gone. She turned to scan the room and almost tilted her plate filled with food onto Theo's shirt.

"No thanks," he said, grinning as he helped right her plate while balancing his plate in one hand. "I have food of my own here."

"That could have been a disaster," she said. "I didn't realize you were there."

"No harm done. How about we find a table?" He glanced around the crowded room where dozens of people were eating and talking. "Franz would have really enjoyed this," he said. "He was always so concerned about the divisions among the refugees—most of them national and making for strained relations on more than one occasion."

Suzanne saw the gathering now through his eyes. In one area was a table occupied by several people, and she realized that they were all from different countries. They were all Jewish, but she recalled how in the first weeks of the camp when a part of the fort's chapel had been converted to a synagogue there had been friction among the two groups. The disagreement had been about how to conduct services, and Joseph Smart had had to intervene and make peace with both groups after he had appeared to take sides with the Slavs when they walked out of a service. Smart had mistakenly thought the service had ended when in fact the Slavs had walked out in protest. It occurred to Suzanne that out of such misunderstandings wars could be made.

She followed Theo as he threaded his way to a small round table in the back of the room, glancing around to see if perhaps the stranger at the door had finally decided to come into the hall. Theo set down his food and procured two empty chairs from the crowded tables around them. Then he waited for her to be seated before taking the other chair and spreading a napkin across one knee.

"How is your mother doing?" Suzanne asked, having dismissed her curiosity about the stranger in favor of focusing on Theo and his

141

parents. "There's been so much attention on Ilse and Liesl, but her loss is great, as well."

"I think she did a lot of her initial grieving on the drive out. She told stories about growing up back in Germany and how Franz had been the perfect older brother—even though they are only a little more than a year apart in age." He glanced over to where his mother was handing a plate filled with food to Ilse. "I think today she is finding comfort in keeping her focus on Ilse and Liesl."

"What do you think Ilse will do now?"

"What can she do? She's here until the end of the war. My dad had a talk with Mr. Smart about maybe under the circumstances she and Liesl could be allowed to come home with us, but that's not going to happen."

"This entire situation is ridiculous," Suzanne fumed. "The people here are supposedly 'guests,' but they sure aren't being treated like that." She attacked her food as if it were the enemy.

"Okay, changing the subject," Theo said mildly. "Did I tell you I might run for Congress?"

If he had announced that he was thinking of making a solo flight around the world in spite of the fact that he had no knowledge of flying an airplane, Suzanne could not have been more stunned. "Congress?"

"Yeah. You know the Senate and House of Representatives that makes laws for the nation?"

"Where did this come from?"

His grin wavered, and he turned his attention to his food. "It's a long shot, I know, but. . ."

She covered his hand with hers. "I'm not doubting you, Theo. The truth is I think you would make an incredible congressman. If there were more people like you making laws, maybe things would be better for everyone."

"Thanks." He told her about attending the political meeting and then being asked to consider running. "The other party has a strong candidate—a war hero. So even if I do run, the chances are not good."

"What made you want to do this?"

He looked over to the table where Liesl sat with her friends. "I realized that what I really wanted was to make a difference for those kids. They're the ones who will be growing up in this world that we make for them in the years after the war ends. I want it to be a better place for them—for Liesl, for my brother's kids, and for mine if I'm lucky enough to have children of my own."

His passion blazed from his eyes.

"Wow," she said. "And here I thought I was the one with big news."

"Like what? You got a byline?" He was one of the few people she had told of her dream to one day rise above the scandal of her past reporting days and earn the right to have her name on a major story, and she could see how excited he was for her.

"Not yet," she admitted. "That's now a long shot. I guess we have that in common."

"A long shot because?"

She sucked in a deep breath as if she were about to take a plunge into deep water.

"I'm going to quit my job at the paper and stay here. I want to see this story through to the end. I want to know what happens to everyone here." She nodded toward the others in the room. "Every single person in the fort." Suddenly nervous, afraid that he would tell her she was out of her mind, she added, "I was thinking that I could write a book." *Might as well go all the way to the deepest end*, she thought.

"That's a terrific idea," Theo said, and when she dared to look up at him she saw that he meant it. "The book idea. I mean, everybody should know the story of these incredible individuals who by circumstances beyond their control have been reduced to a common label—refugees. You can tell the world who they were before, what they had to sacrifice, how they came here, and where they go from here. Ambitious yes, but you can let people see them as the unique individuals that they are. It's a wonderful idea, Suzanne."

She wished then that she had shown more enthusiasm and less skepticism about his plan to run for Congress. "Looks like we're both setting off on new paths," she said. "I'm going to speak with Mr. Smart tomorrow about maybe doing some part-time work here in the fort. If I can be here on a regular basis, it will give me a chance to get to know everyone—well, maybe not everyone, but certainly a lot more of them than I know now."

"You'll have your work cut out for you," Theo warned her. "There are so many stories that deserve telling—so much to learn from these folks." He looked over the gathering and seemed lost in his reflections.

Suzanne took a couple of bites of her meal, waiting for him to come back from wherever his musings had taken him. "Hey," she said in a tone she might have used if waking someone from a dream. "Penny for those thoughts."

He smiled and picked up his fork, but he did not eat. "I was just thinking. I mean if I'm going to run for Congress, there's a lot I need to learn about how things work with the government. It goes way beyond Congress and the president. This whole business here in the fort, for example. The State Department has a hand in this, and Ruth Gruber works for the Department of the Interior, and then there are all the subagencies—the War Relocation Agency for one."

"Okay, I can practically hear the wheels turning in that brain of yours," Suzanne teased. "What are you thinking?"

"I'm thinking maybe I'll stay as well. I can be here as a support for Ilse and Liesl until this thing is over. And in the meantime I can observe our government in action."

"Or inaction as is more likely," Suzanne replied, unable to temper her cynicism.

"Ah, Suzanne. If I stay here, we are going to have to work on getting you to see that glass half-full," he teased, and it occurred to her that just maybe her change of direction for her life might just work out.

CHAPTER 11

"Have you completely lost your mind?" Edwin said when Suzanne called him the following morning. "Not only do you not have the credentials necessary to find a publisher for a book, you seem to be forgetting that you have a reputation in this business that is a long way from being repaired."

She had not really thought about it in those terms. "I could use a pseudonym," she blustered.

Edwin sighed. "Suzie. Suzie. Suzie. Where's your brain? For that matter, where's your loyalty?"

So they had come to the crux of things. When she had returned to Washington and the newsroom in late November, he had assigned her to the local news desk telling her that she needed to work her way up and that it would take time. That same day she learned that the usual local reporter had quit to take a job in Chicago. Edwin had needed her to fill that reporter's place, and once she was there he'd seen no reason to advertise the position.

"My loyalty?"

"Yes. Who gave you a chance when you were basically dead in the news business—at least in this town?"

"You did, and I appreciate that, but—"

"And who let you go back up there to that place to get the suicide story?"

Let me? Edwin had not paid her way, and it had been the weekend when she was free to do whatever she wanted. True, he had given her trip his token blessing by reminding her of the night train.

Edwin kept talking, not waiting for her to answer his question. Apparently it was rhetorical—as was this entire conversation as far as he was concerned.

She decided to take a different path. "Edwin, I'm calling from a shared phone, and I can't really tie up the line. Thank you for everything you've done to help me. I know you think I'm making an enormous mistake, but I just really feel this is something I need to see through to the end."

"I can't hold a job for you, Suzie."

"I understand. Just have Linda pack up my personal stuff and hold it for me. Next time I'm back that way I'll stop by and pick it up," she promised.

"You're doing this in spite of everything. . ."

"Edwin, you know that plaque you hung on the wall in the newsroom? The one that says 'Sometimes to discover new oceans, we have to leave sight of the shore'?"

"You're telling me that you are off to discover new oceans?"

"Something like that."

"Well, take care, Suzie, because you are setting off in a leaky boat."

She laughed. "Bye, Edwin."

"Bon voyage," he muttered, and even as they hung up, she knew that he really did wish her well.

Later after Theo's parents had packed up and started on the long drive back to Wisconsin, she was sitting in the communal living room writing a letter to her mother when Theo came in.

"Am I disturbing you?"

"Not at all." She set her pen and paper aside and curled her legs under her in the large overstuffed chair. "Did your parents get off all right?"

He smiled. "Finally. Mom has this way of taking her time to say good-bye. Dad and I thought she was never going to leave Ilse and Liesl." His smile faded. "She's pretty worried about them. I mean, Ilse seems to have gotten over the way she used to be. . . ."

"Used to be?"

"She had a lot of problems starting just after Liesl was born. That's why my sister, Beth, went to Munich in the first place. From what I know, there were whole days when Ilse stayed in her bedroom, refusing to come out even for meals."

"But now. . ."

"That's just it. She's like a different woman—strong and determined. But with Franz gone. . ."

"That's why you are really staying, isn't it? To be sure she and Liesl are all right?"

"It's a big part of it."

"So what are your plans? I mean, you can't watch over them night and day."

He smiled. "Well, I have to find a job for one thing. Selma is a sweetheart, but I think we've pretty much used up her goodwill as far as staying here for free goes."

Suzanne lowered her voice to a whisper and glanced up at the ceiling. "Don't let Hilda know your parents didn't have to pay. She'll be fit to be tied."

Theo bent to stir the logs on the fire. "How did your call to the newspaper go?"

"My editor thinks I'm making a huge mistake." She stared at the revitalized flame. "Maybe he's right."

Theo sat on the edge of the sofa next to her chair. "You don't strike me as the sort of person who is easily discouraged."

"Maybe not, but I do have a reputation for leaping before looking. And maybe I deserve that reputation."

"Or maybe you're just brave enough to take a chance."

"You give me far too much credit. And look who's talking about courage, Mr. Congressman."

He glanced toward the fire and did not smile at her teasing. "I might be biting off a lot more than I can chew."

"Well, we certainly make an interesting pair—high ambitions and nothing but sheer arrogant gumption to get us there."

"What time is your meeting with Mr. Smart?"

"Two." She looked up at the clock above the mantel. "And speaking of that, I should get ready."

"Good luck," Theo called after her as she left the room.

She felt good about the future. For the first time since the scandal surrounding her story broke, she felt as if she had finally found a story she could follow with certainty—a feel-good piece that could inspire and teach—and this time she wouldn't have to struggle with fudging facts to make the ending turn out right. This time the ending would be what it would be. The story was the people living in the shelter and the lives that had been stripped from them by war.

This time she would get it right.

The phone in the hall rang, and a minute later Selma tapped at her door. "Call from Washington, Suzanne."

"Oh, Edwin," she murmured as she grabbed her coat and pocketbook so she could take the call and still make it for her meeting with Smart, "give up already."

"Hello," she said, drawing out the last syllable in a lighthearted tone. "Suze?"

The voice was male but definitely not Edwin Bonner's.

"Hello, Gordon," she said warily. A dozen questions raced to mind—among them, *How did you find me?* She settled for the obvious. "What do you want?"

Ilse was surprised at the depths of loneliness and isolation she felt after Franz died. Of course she had known she would grieve—and for some time—but this was grief on a level unlike any she had ever experienced. She was surrounded by the other residents of the fort—many of them friends who showed concern for her and for Liesl by stopping by unannounced to visit or leaving little tokens of their concern outside the apartment door.

Ilse was touched by their concern, but the reality was that without Franz she felt as if she were only half the person she had been. For Liesl's sake—and because she knew that it would be what Franz would want her to do—she forced herself to accept the kind invitations extended by these strangers who had once looked on Franz and her with disdain and even outright hatred because of their German heritage. Thankfully it was her constant worry about her child that kept her going.

Liesl had taken to spending long periods of time alone. Rather than going to play with other children in the snow or in the relative warmth of the recreation center, she would sit at the apartment's kitchen table doing homework or reading.

One late afternoon she had disappeared around suppertime. At first Ilse had believed that Liesl had simply gone ahead of her to the dining hall for the evening meal only to get there and find that no one had seen the child. She and Gisele had searched for her, asking her school friends if they had seen her and walking to the library where she had spent hours helping her father catalog and shelve books. But she was not to be found, and the sun had nearly set. Soon it would be dark.

"Let's split up," Gisele suggested. "I'll go to the theater—perhaps she's with Ivo and the others. You go to the recreation center."

With hope fading and images of Karoline Bleier's frozen body racing through her thoughts, Ilse agreed. As she approached the recreation center, she heard the stumbling notes of a simple waltz played on the old upright piano, and her heart leaped with relief. She tiptoed inside and saw her daughter seated at the piano, staring intently at the keys as she worked out the melody.

The old building was cold, and Liesl was wearing her coat and a pair of old gloves with the tips of the fingers cut off. Unwilling to interrupt Liesl's practice, she slipped into the hallway and found the narrow stairs that led to the basement and coal bin. She found a small metal bucket and placed some pieces of coal in it. As she climbed the stairs to the entrance, Gisele came through the front door. Ilse motioned for her to be quiet and then nodded toward the closed double doors that led into the recreation hall. Gisele peeked inside and then closed the door.

"She must be freezing," she whispered.

"I got some coal but I'll need a match to light it."

Gisele reached inside the pocket of her gabardine overcoat and produced a box of matches. The one luxury that Gisele allowed herself was smoking. She was rarely without a cigarette whether she was working, sitting at a meal, or visiting with friends.

Together they managed to light the coals, and Gisele held the door open for Ilse to carry the bucket into the hall. "I'll stop by later," Gisele whispered. "I'll get you both something from the dining hall."

Ilse nodded and crossed the room to where Liesl was still studying the sheet music as she picked out the notes.

"It is so very cold in here," Ilse said calmly as if the two of them had been having a conversation all along.

Liesl's fingers missed the keys she wanted and skittered across the keyboard. "Oh, Mama, I am sorry. I lost track of the time and—"

"I was worried." Ilse held out the bucket. "Here, warm your fingers over these coals."

Liesl did as she was told.

"So you are serious in your wish to learn to play?"

"For Papa."

"Then I will teach you."

Liesl's eyes widened. "I didn't know you could play, Mama."

"I know the notes and how to read music. I am not as gifted as your father was, but I can teach you if that's what you want."

For the first time since Franz had died, Ilse saw the sparkle of excitement light their daughter's eyes. "Oh yes, Mama. Please teach me." She wriggled her fingers to show Ilse that they were all warmed up and ready.

Ilse laughed. "How can I teach you when I am holding a bucket of hot coals?"

Liesl frowned then glanced around the hall. "If we could hang it somewhere," she mused.

"Come. We will begin tomorrow when the hall is open and there is heat. I will not be responsible for setting fire to the building." She wrapped her free arm around Liesl's shoulders as she held the bucket of coals well away from her body and led her daughter to the door. "Gisele is bringing us some supper."

"Does she know about this?" Liesl motioned back toward the piano.

"Yes. Why?"

"I want to be really good at playing before anyone knows."

"There is no shame in learning, Liesl."

"But I don't want to fail and disappoint Papa."

"You could never disappoint your father, and besides, it is in the trying that you will succeed."

Outside she set the bucket on the frozen ground, and Liesl helped her fill it with snow until the coals were extinguished. "Tomorrow," Liesl announced, "I will ask if we can borrow this bucket and use the coals during our lessons. I'll ask Mr. Smart, and I bet he'll know exactly how we can keep the building safe and still have the warmth."

She was so much like Franz had been when Ilse first met him. So sure of himself and always finding a solution for any objection or problem she might raise or set forth to him. It occurred to Ilse that it was Liesl's determination to honor the memory of her father that would in the end be the mother's salvation.

It was amazing how the sound of her name on Gordon Langford's lips brought back every good and bad memory she had of their time together. But Suzanne had learned her lesson. She understood that whatever Gordon wanted had nothing to do with her well-being and everything to do with advancing his political career.

"What do you want, Gordon?" she asked again.

He chuckled. "That's my girl—all business."

She forced herself to remain silent. She forced herself to swallow the accusations and anger she had wanted to hurl at him for months. Just the sound of his voice brought it all back to her. But she remained silent.

"Hey, dollface," he said, letting his voice slide into that sultry register that had once sent chills of longing for his kiss up her spine. "It's me." He waited then let out a long breath. "Look, I know I really messed things up—for both of us."

"You could say that. So once more I will ask, what can I do for you this time, Congressman Langford?"

"So that's the way you're going to play this? No room for forgiveness in that icy heart of yours?"

She glanced up the stairs and lowered her voice. "This is not a private phone, Gordon, so. . ."

"Then meet me."

"You're here? In Oswego?"

Again the laugh. "Yeah, well, until tomorrow. Like I said, things have been a little rough. I got pulled off the Ways and Means Committee and reassigned to Immigration. I'm up here checking out this business of the suicide." He cleared his throat. "So meet me at the hotel. Let me buy you dinner."

This was indeed a step down for him. Suzanne felt a twinge of sympathy.

The clock over the fireplace chimed quarter to two. "I have to go, Gordon. I have an appointment."

"Meet me for dinner—six o'clock. I really want to talk to you. I really want to explain."

How many nights had she stared at the water-stained ceiling in her Washington apartment and imagined his call? Those very words? *I really want to explain.*

"All right—six o'clock. And Gordon? This is dinner only."

"Good to know you haven't changed, dollface—still handing out rules. See you at six."

As she walked to the fort for her morning appointment with Joseph

Smart, she thought about the book she wanted to write. For reasons she did not fully understand especially because her focus was the community at the shelter, she kept thinking about one of the German prisoners of war that she had attempted to interview that day she'd gone with Theo to the orchard.

The man had been older—in fact, he had reminded her a lot of Franz Schneider. Both men seemed worn down in similar ways. Both were quiet to the point of being withdrawn. Both met strangers with a gaze of open suspicion and wariness. When she had tried to speak with him he had smiled politely and climbed the wooden ladder until the branches of the apple tree obscured his upper body.

Even then she had suspected that this man was different from the other prisoners she observed working in the orchard that day. She would have bet that he was a high-ranking officer. He moved with the posture of someone used to giving direction and orders rather than taking them. But prisoners who were officers were not required to work, and this man had been working as hard as anyone.

Those German POWs were incarcerated on a farm not far from Oswego. Before breakfast, Selma had mentioned that she had seen some of them in town as recently as a few days earlier.

"Where did you see them?" Suzanne had been helping Selma set the table. It was not something required as part of her rent, but she thought it made sense to get on Selma's good side in case the day came when she had to ask for an extension on paying her bill. That was more of a likelihood than Suzanne cared to admit. She needed a job.

Her meeting with Joseph Smart did not last long. He turned down her request to work even part-time at the shelter. "Conflict of interest," he'd said.

"How? I no longer work for the newspaper, and—"

"Are you planning to write more stories, Miss Randolph? Or perhaps a book?"

"Maybe." Her tone had been defensive.

"The residents of Fort Ontario are free to speak with you or not as they wish, but many of these people have been traumatized beyond belief by people in authority."

"But I have no authority over them," Suzanne had protested.

"If you are a part of my staff, you may be perceived to have that authority, and I will not impose that on the residents here. They have already been through so much." He had stood then, signaling the end of their meeting. "I have read your essays from earlier, Miss Randolph. You are a gifted storyteller."

Storyteller? I am a journalist.

But instead of protesting, she accepted the director's handshake and left. Now as she folded a napkin to lay on the dinner table, she wondered if perhaps waiting tables might be an option.

"Have you thought about stopping by the newspaper here in Oswego?" Selma asked as if reading her mind. "I know the editor, and I could put in a good word for you."

Suzanne had admitted to Selma that her meeting with the shelter director had been disappointing. "I'll look into it. Thank you."

She returned to her room. With an hour to go before she was supposed to meet Gordon at the hotel, she sat on the side of the bed and stared out the window, thinking about her book. She had no idea how to go about this. In the fall during the weeks she had spent in Oswego talking to a variety of the shelter residents, she would have thought she had gathered enough material to at least make a start. But her curiosity about the prisoner of war kept intruding. Suddenly she knew the answer.

"That man is the start of it," she murmured aloud. "I have to tell both stories." She put on her coat, grabbed her bag loaded with her notebook and stash of pencils, and started out. "I'm off to meet my friend for supper and then I'll be at the library," she told Selma.

"Oh honey, take a night off from work and enjoy being with your friend."

"I can do both," Suzanne replied as she hurried out the front door.

Gordon was waiting for her at a small table set for two. He stood and came forward to greet her. She allowed him to kiss her cheek and tried to ignore how wonderful he looked—his chestnut hair combed back in waves, his suit perfectly tailored to his broad shoulders and the tie she had given him for his birthday. As he followed her to the table, he placed his hand lightly on her waist, and she recalled how Theo had done the same thing the day of the open house at the fort. Why was it that Theo's gesture had felt comforting while Gordon's felt possessive?

"You look wonderful, Suzanne," he said as he held her chair for her. He handed her a menu and then took his seat across from her.

"Thank you," Suzanne replied. She made a study of the menu. Plain fare that Gordon would no doubt disparage. The waiter was filling their water glasses. She handed him her menu, smiled, and said, "I'll have the meat loaf, please."

Both the waiter and Gordon looked startled. The waiter recovered first. "And for you, sir?"

Gordon snapped his menu closed and thrust it at the waiter. "The same." Once the waiter had left, he looked at Suzanne. "Are we in a hurry?"

"I have work to do." She reached for a roll. "So how has your visit to Oswego been?"

He shrugged. "I arrived late last night, met with the director at the fort this morning along with my colleagues, called you, and here we are."

"You leave tomorrow for Washington?"

He relaxed slightly and took a swallow of his water, all the time studying her. "You've changed."

She shrugged. "I suppose that's inevitable when one's life is turned upside down and inside out. I was blessed that Edwin Bonner gave me a second chance."

"Look, Suze, things didn't work out the way I thought they would— for either of us."

She laughed. "You seem to have landed on your feet—still in Congress."

"For what that's worth." He leaned closer. "But I have a plan—one that will revive both our careers."

"Don't do me any favors, Gordon. The last time—"

He dismissed the trashing of her career with a wave of his hand. "This is bigger than that, dollface."

"Will you please stop calling me that?"

The waiter delivered their salads—iceberg lettuce with tomato slices and some shredded carrots topping the french dressing. Gordon attacked his, carving up the lettuce and tomato slices as if they were a tough steak. "I need your help. Suze—Suzanne, okay?"

"I'm listening."

He launched into a tale of a high-ranking German officer that he had traced to the Oswego area. "This man knows things—things that could help end the war. If we can turn him."

"And exactly how do I figure into this?"

"You're here," he said as if the rest should be obvious. "And you have connections with the refugees and maybe some of them knew this man back in Germany and. . ."

The waiter brought their meals and removed the salad plates. In that moment it all became clear to her. Gordon had never meant to cause her harm. He simply hadn't thought things through. He had this way of grabbing onto an idea that was not yet fully formed and moving forward. "The details can always be worked out," he had once told her. "It's the timing that matters, Suze. You have to seize the moment."

She waited until they were alone again. "Gordon, don't do this," she said. "You need to think this through very carefully."

"I have. If we—you—could get to this guy, get him to trust you. . ."

She thought of the man in the orchard. Could he be this man?

"I have no way of meeting this man, Gordon, and besides, I have my own project. I'm writing a book to tell the stories of the refugees or at least as many as I can tell."

"And I have friends in publishing who can get that book in print. Work with me, Suze. Once upon a time we made an incredible team."

"Once upon a time I believed in fairy tales," she said softly and folded her napkin. "Now if you'll excuse me, I have work to do. Thank you for dinner."

He half rose from his chair, but she had already started for the exit. She would not permit herself to get caught up in one of Gordon's schemes—not again.

The library was almost deserted. She passed the librarian's desk and headed for the area where back issues of magazines and newspapers were stored. She took a stack of recent issues of the local newspaper to one of the tables and started methodically going through them page by page. Her purpose was twofold. One, she was on the lookout for any articles about POWs in the Oswego area, and two, she wanted to get a sense of the style of reporting the paper's editors preferred. If she did go for an interview, she would be expected to bring along samples of her work, and she wanted to be sure she chose samples that were a good fit. As for the POWs, it had been her intent well before her conversation with Gordon to learn more about them.

She had been at it for about an hour when a man entered the area and took the chair at the opposite end of the table. He was carrying his hat—a worn brown fedora—as well as the current issue of the newspaper—the one the librarian had fixed onto one of the long wooden poles to set into the current periodicals rack. He laid it on the table and pulled the chair closer as he began to read. There was something familiar about him, but she couldn't place him and decided that she had probably seen him in town.

He was so still that except for the occasional turning of a page Suzanne found it easy to ignore him. But eventually the fact that he continued to read the same paper long past the time when any normal person would have finished made her start to watch him. She kept her gaze lowered, of course, not wanting him to know that she was watching, but gradually the time she spent observing the man far outdistanced the time she was spending studying the papers before her.

She knew she had stepped over the line when he looked up and met her eyes. "I am a slow reader," he said in perfect English colored by a thick German accent. "Did you want this newspaper? I could perhaps read one of those." He motioned toward the stack of papers next to her.

"No. Sorry. It's just. . .I mean. . .you seem to. . ."

"Are you looking for something specific?"

"Well, yes. I'm a reporter—or I was. Anyway I was looking for recent articles about the. . ." She stopped, and her hand covered her mouth as she realized who this man was. "You are. . . You were. . ."

"My name is Detlef Buch, and I am a prisoner of your country." He delivered this introduction without embarrassment or bitterness. "And you are the reporter who came to the orchard last fall when we were picking apples for Herr—Mister Walls."

"That was several months ago. How can you be sure?" She was more than a little wary. Had this man followed her here? And what did he want?

His smile was a mere crooking of his mouth. There was no warmth of joy in it. "It used to be my business to be sure. You are Miss Randolph, are you not?"

He knew her name—a name she did not remember giving as she stood by the fence in the orchard that day. And then she realized that he had also been at Franz's funeral reception. He was following her. She stood up, prepared to flee or at least signal for help. "What do you want?"

"Please do not be alarmed, *Fräulein*. I have thought about what you said that day in the orchard when you spoke to the guards about the POWs and how their story could be very interesting."

"Well, yes, but since that time I have decided to go in a different direction."

He smiled. "And yet you are seeking articles about the prisoners."

"You are very observant, Mr. Buch."

"I wish to know if you might be willing to write my story. You see, Miss Randolph, like many of the people you know here in America, I chose a side in this war. Now I see that it was the wrong side. I will not defend myself by saying that I did not know or that I had no choice. I knew." An expression of utter agony crossed his features. "God help me, I knew."

"And did nothing," Suzanne guessed, relaxing slightly. "Why would

I want to write your story, Mr. Buch?"

He shrugged. "Perhaps because it would be a story that no one else in your country will have the opportunity to write? Perhaps because selfishly I hope that through telling my story I may lessen the severity of my punishment once the war is ended."

Suzanne began to gather her notebook and pencils and purse.

"Miss Randolph, please hear me out."

"Why should I?" She clutched her belongings to her chest, her eyes darting around, seeking the best escape route since he stood between her and the exit.

"Because I will tell you only the facts, and any interpretation or judgment you put on those facts will no doubt be kinder than I deserve."

She could not deny that she was tempted. Standing across the table from her was a man who could give her the story that might lead to the redemption she sought for the career she loved so much. Yet the similarities between this man's offer and the one she had accepted from Gordon that had destroyed her career made her suspicious.

Gordon! Could this man possibly be...

"What was your role in the war?" she asked.

He met her gaze without flinching. "I was a member of Hitler's secret police—the Gestapo."

Okay, Randolph, go now before you get in too deep. She took a step and then hesitated.

The German stepped to one side of his chair as if to leave her a clear passage for escape. "You are right to be cautious, Miss Randolph. After all, I am your enemy."

"Your country and my country are enemies," she replied.

He lifted his eyebrows in surprise. "Another young woman from America once said that," he told her. "She and my son. . ." His voice trailed off and he shook his head as if to banish the thought.

"Is your son also a prisoner of war?"

He looked at her for a long time as if considering his answer. Then very slowly he said, "I do not know what has become of my son. He and that young woman I mentioned stood against the Reich. They married and were sent to a concentration camp but escaped, and the last I heard of either of them they had made it to an island off the coast of Denmark."

Suzanne was surprised at the sympathy she felt for him. In that moment he was not German or a Nazi. He was a father who grieved for his lost child, and that made him no different than any parent in any country.

"Mr. Buch, you are correct in saying that writing about you would be a very different story than anything being done by my fellow journalists."

"Yet you do not trust me."

"These days I cannot afford to trust anyone who promises to tell me his or her story without embellishment. How will I know that what you tell me is true?"

The quirk of his lips that passed for a smile reappeared. "I see your point. But I promise you it is an amazing story. I daresay that young man you dined with earlier—the one from your government—would find it extremely interesting."

"You have been following me. You came to the funeral and—"

He shook his head. "I came to Herr Professor Schneider's funeral. I knew him—and his wife—back in Germany. I had thought to pay my respects but then reconsidered."

She laid down her belongings and pushed the notebook and three of her pencils toward him. "Write down your role in this war or about how you came to be captured and brought here." That was something that she could check for facts. "I will be here tomorrow at this same time. Bring me the pages. I will read them, and then I will decide."

"This is a fair offer," he said as he collected the notebook and pencils and placed them in the patch pocket of his coat. "It has been my pleasure to speak with you, Miss Randolph, whatever the outcome of this conversation may be."

He closed the newspaper and with a slight bow turned away. He replaced the newspaper on the rack, nodded to the librarians, and left.

Suzanne watched him go, and only when he was through the double doors and she could no longer see him did she realize how her pulse was racing with excitement. He was right. This could be the break she was looking for. Perhaps she was not being led to write about the refugees at all. Perhaps Detlef Buch was the reason she had returned to Oswego.

But then there was Gordon.

Theo had news he could not wait to share with Suzanne. That afternoon Joseph Smart had offered him a position on his staff at the shelter. Theo was to have the responsibility of acting as a liaison between Director Smart and the chair of the congressional committee on immigration affairs in Washington. In truth it was little more than a secretarial position, for his job really was to gather the data and forms the committee requested from time to time, but it was a direct connection to Washington. He would have experience in working with a congressional committee. He would perhaps even have the opportunity to meet members of the House or Senate.

But Suzanne had news of her own, and her obvious distress made him reluctant to share his good news until he knew what was upsetting her so much.

"Let's go for a walk," she said after they had finished supper and Hilda and Hugh had returned to their rooms while Selma remained at the table reading the newspaper. "I need to talk to you about something and. . ." She glanced up the stairway and he understood that whatever this was she did not want anyone else to hear.

"I'll get my coat."

Selma had given him a room on the second floor now that she had vacancies, and he was grateful not to have the attic room, which no doubt would have been as cold in winter as it was hot in summer.

"Going out?" Hilda's door was as always partially open, and she called to him as he passed her door on his way back downstairs.

"I am. Do you need anything?"

"No, but it's supposed to snow again so bundle up." Her motherly advice did not surprise him. Hilda liked him. It was Suzanne who ruffled her feathers.

"I will. See you in the morning." He hurried down the stairs to Suzanne, who was waiting for him by the front door.

She was wearing her heaviest coat, a wool scarf, mittens, and a hat that covered her hair, ears, and forehead. As soon as he reached the bottom step, she opened the door and stepped onto the porch.

"What's going on?"

"I met someone at the library today." She told him the story as they walked into town. The streets were mostly deserted, and as Hilda had predicted, a light snow was falling. "His name is Detlef Buch, and according to what he told me, he was someone of importance back in Germany—an officer or high-ranking person in the secret police. It's not hard to envision him in such a role. His whole demeanor suggests a man used to giving orders and having them obeyed."

"He just started talking to you at the library?"

"Not exactly. He. . .I think he has been following me. He was one of the men in the orchard last fall and overheard me interviewing the guards."

"And what does he want of you?"

"He wants me to write his story. I think he believes that if he can just find a way to tell his side, things will go better for him."

"Does he understand that when the war ends it is not the American court but one in Europe that will determine his fate?"

"I have to assume that he does. He is obviously an educated and intelligent man. His English is flawless—something that surely helped him in his position back in Germany."

"So what did you say?"

The details of her meeting with the German POW had been rolling off her tongue like water over a falls, but now she hesitated. "It's not a simple decision for me, Theo. He made the point that his story could be a huge break for any reporter. How many newspeople are going to have the opportunity to sit with someone who was a part of the Nazi regime and ask the key question of why?"

"So you are considering it?"

She released a sigh of utter exasperation as if she could not believe what she was about to tell him. "I am. I told him that he needed to start writing down what he had done in the war. I have friends in Washington who will check the facts for me. If he tells me the truth about his role before he was arrested, then. . ."

"Think this through before you decide, Suzanne. You came here to write the stories of the refugees at Fort Ontario—stories that could help the cause of those who wish to stay in the United States."

"I know, and believe me, I am torn. But what if the real reason I was led back here was to meet this German and write his story?"

Theo smiled. " 'Led back here'? Careful there. You're beginning to sound like a Quaker," he teased.

"I'm serious," she said. "What should I do?"

He took his time considering his answer. "Well, let's think this through together. It seems to me that there are several different questions here. One question has to do with you and your career. Will this help?"

"And the other questions?"

"How will the people at the fort feel if they learn you are writing the story of a POW? Will they understand or might they become more reticent to speak with you about their stories?"

He took hold of her arm and led her into the small café across from the movie theater, where they had gone a couple of times for coffee. She sat in the booth they normally shared, pulling off her outerwear, while he went to the counter and got two mugs of coffee. He set them down and removed his coat and hat, hanging them on the post that separated each booth.

He nodded to two men at the counter who had glanced their way. They returned his nod and went back to visiting with the waitress. No one else was in the café.

"Do you want some pie?" he asked.

"No thanks." She poured sugar from the dispenser into her coffee.

"But if you want some. . ."

He shook his head and took the seat opposite her. "I'm fine with just this." He watched her stir her coffee slowly, drawing the spoon through the dark liquid as she stared out the window at the falling snow. "So those are the questions you need to consider as far as I can see plus one more."

She gave him her full attention. "What?"

"You might want to ask yourself what's in this for Detlef Buch. You said that he appeared well educated and intelligent. Surely he can't believe that a story published in an American newspaper—assuming any paper would agree to print such a story—would do him any good once he returns to stand trial in Europe."

"I hadn't thought of it that way."

"My dad once told me that whenever I had trouble figuring something out I needed to consider it from all sides." He sipped his coffee.

"You're right. It has to be something else. Something more that made him choose me." She studied her coffee as if she were reading tea leaves. "What could it be?"

"Ask him. Make that another condition of considering whether or not to do this."

"I will." She finally took a sip of the coffee. "How do you think Ilse would react if she found out that I was working with a POW?"

Theo shrugged. "I don't know my aunt that well. She's a complex woman who has been through a lot. She also practices a faith rooted in forgiveness and not taking sides. I would imagine after everything she and Uncle Franz went through and after everything she's lost in the bargain, those are two challenges that would be tough for anyone to meet."

He waited until the waitress had come by to offer a refill and then reached across the table to cover Suzanne's hand. "Whatever you decide, take the time you need." He almost encouraged her to join him and his aunt and niece for a meeting for worship but decided that would be going too far. He was about to withdraw his hand when she surprised him by linking her fingers with his. "How was your day?" she asked.

He had a momentary vision of his parents sitting at the kitchen table in the farmhouse long after the last supper dish had been dried and put away and long after he and his siblings had supposedly gone to bed. They would sit there talking for an hour or more, sharing what had happened while they'd each gone their own way during the day.

"Smart gave me a job," he told her.

"Theo, that's wonderful." She tightened her hold on his fingers. "What kind of position is it? Tell me everything."

So he did. They sat in the booth, holding hands and drinking their coffee, until long after the two men at the counter had left and their places had been taken by moviegoers stopping for some pie and coffee after the late show.

"Closing up, folks," the waitress said as she leaned across an empty booth and switched off the neon sign. "Looks like that snow is getting heavier."

Theo glanced out the window and saw that several inches had fallen while they talked. He put on his coat and hat while Suzanne did the same and then handed the waitress payment for the coffee plus a generous tip. "Thanks," he said.

"Anytime," she said. "You two make a nice couple, but then you probably don't need me telling you that. You married or just planning on it?"

Theo's discomfort at the woman's assumption struck him momentarily dumb, but Suzanne seemed to take the comment in stride.

"Married to my work," she told the waitress.

"Pity. I wouldn't kick this one out if he showed up at my door."

"Thanks again," Theo called back over his shoulder as he headed for the door.

Outside Suzanne started to giggle.

"What's so funny?"

"She thought we were married. All the times we've been in there she's been thinking of us as a couple."

Theo had no idea why her words stung so. "Well, maybe in another time and under other circumstances we might have been," he said and thrust his hands into his pockets as he started breaking a trail through snow that now covered their shoes.

They were almost back to the boardinghouse before either of them spoke again.

"Are you mad at me, Theo?"

"Of course not. Just tired. And I told Mr. Smart I would come in early tomorrow." He opened the front door and waited for her to precede him.

A single lamp burned in the front hall. He started toward the stairs.

"Theo? I didn't mean. . . I was embarrassed and didn't want you to think that I took what that waitress said seriously. The truth is. . ."

Theo turned around and pulled her to him, kissing her with all the pent-up feelings he'd kept to himself. Almost from the first time he'd met her he had felt drawn to her in a way that he'd never experienced before. Certainly he had had his share of girlfriends and even a couple of serious romances. But his feelings for Suzanne were far more intense. He wanted to be where she was, know what she was thinking, share his dreams and hopes with her. But he could not deny that their circumstances were unique, and even though she was definitely returning his kiss, he had no idea how she felt about him. So he eased away, kept his hands on her shoulders, and waited for her to open her eyes and look at him.

"Like I said, Suzanne, in another time. . . Good night."

CHAPTER 12

January faded at last into February, and spring was a month closer, but the weather was foul with snow and wind and ice storms. The walls of the barracks were still thin as paper. The grounds were still covered with more than a foot of snow and ice. The gray sky remained threatening and overcast, and darkness seemed to come earlier than usual even though the days should be longer.

Theo spent his days in the offices of the administration building, typing reports or answering calls from his counterparts in various government agencies. The connections he was making in Washington would surely be an advantage in his run for Congress. Of course Jim Sawyer did not agree. He was urging Theo to come home and start "pressing the flesh and kissing some babies." But the election was still months away. He had time, and the work he was doing was important.

He barely saw Suzanne. She spent most of her day moving from building to building and talking to residents of the shelter. As soon as supper ended, she left the boardinghouse for the library. More than once he had offered to walk with her and suggested they could perhaps stop for coffee after she had finished her work there. But she had always refused, citing the uncertainty of her time and not wanting him to have to sit around waiting for her. He was not fooled.

He was fairly certain that she had agreed to meet the German and record his story. Twice he had walked to the library, making sure he left half an hour after she did, and she had not been there, nor had the librarian seen her. On those occasions he had walked back to the boardinghouse, his hands thrust deep in his pockets and his shoulders hunched against the wind, wondering where she was. Where was she going to meet the German?

Theo had mixed feelings about the POWs in general. He knew from working with them in the orchards that some of them were just young men who had signed on to defend their country and been sent to the Russian front. There they had experienced horrors of their own—the brutal winter, the lack of enough food or protection from the cold, the hatred of the Russian army for their country—and them.

Most of them counted themselves fortunate to have been captured by the Americans or British and not the Russians. And it was obvious to Theo that many of them knew nothing of the camps or the persecutions of the Jews and others that had transpired in their leader's determination to rid the world of such people for the sake of a "pure" Aryan society.

But the man that Suzanne was interviewing had been a different type of soldier in Hitler's army. Through Jim Sawyer's contacts and the few that Theo had developed working in the shelter, he had done some checking and learned that not only had Detlef Buch been a high-ranking officer in the dictator's secret police, the Gestapo, as Suzanne had already learned, but he had to have known a great deal about what was going on in those camps. Was he trying to use Suzanne and the power of her pen to save his life?

Discouraged by Suzanne's apparent decision to place her career above her common sense but helpless to come up with any way to dissuade her, Theo decided to go to the shelter and see if Ilse and Liesl might like to go to a movie. For once it was not snowing, and the bitter cold that had held them in its grasp for weeks had finally abated. The theater in Oswego was showing *The Bells of St. Mary's* with Bing Crosby and Ingrid Bergman.

At first Ilse hesitated, and when Liesl pleaded with her to agree, she said perhaps Liesl and Theo should go provided Liesl had completed all of her homework. "I have, but we won't go without you, will we, Theo?"

Since arriving at the shelter and especially since attending school in town and making friends with local children, Theo had noticed how Liesl had blossomed. She was not afraid to state her opinion, and she made it clear that any opportunity she had to go to town was one she fully intended to take.

"Come on, Ilse," Theo coaxed. "It'll do you good to get out of this place for a few hours." Ever since Franz's funeral, Ilse had buried herself in caring for Liesl and her work assignments in the shelter. Theo's mother was concerned that given her history of depression in the past, Ilse might easily become overwhelmed by the realization that she now had the full responsibility for making decisions for Liesl's future and her own.

"Maybe we could have hot chocolate at the café across from the movie house," Liesl suggested, and when she saw Ilse beginning to waver, added, "Come on, Mom, don't be a killjoy. I'll treat."

That made Ilse smile. "And where do you suddenly acquire such riches, young miss?"

"I've been saving the money you give me each week." She ran to the small footlocker that served as her dresser and opened it. "How much is hot chocolate, Theo?"

"Well, a cup of coffee is a nickel but chocolate would probably cost a little more."

Liesl dumped out a bag of coins onto her mattress and carefully counted out the change. "I'll put in extra just in case."

"And I'll treat for the movie," Theo said. "So what do you say, Aunt Ilse? May I escort my two best girls to the picture show?"

Ilse smiled. "We would be delighted."

"Gee, that's swell, Mom. I'll get my coat."

As they walked to town, Liesl kept up a running monologue, pointing out where her classmates lived and which shopkeepers were nice to the refugees and which were not. At the theater she greeted the woman selling tickets as if they were old friends.

"Hi, Mrs. Driver. This is my mom and my cousin from Wisconsin."

The woman sitting in the glass booth smiled. "My daughter, Nancy, is in the same class with Liesl."

"Oh yes," Ilse replied, but Theo noticed that she spoke very softly as if trying to hide her thick accent.

"Two adults and one child," he said, handing over the money for the tickets.

"I am not a child," Liesl huffed.

"You're ten years old," Theo reminded her.

"Going on eleven," she replied, although she had just turned ten a few weeks earlier.

"Oh, I do beg your pardon, Miss Schneider." Theo gave her a little bow and handed her the ticket. Liesl giggled then turned her attention back to Mrs. Driver. "Say hi to Nancy for me."

"I will. You folks enjoy the show now."

Inside they found seats, and Liesl immediately announced she had to go to the bathroom. Ilse stood up, obviously prepared to accompany her. "Mom, I can go by myself," she whispered. "Stay here."

Ilse reluctantly sat down again but not before seeking assurance from Theo that indeed Liesl could handle this adventure on her own.

"I've been dozens of times," she exaggerated.

"She'll be fine," Theo said.

"Come straight back," Ilse admonished her.

Liesl sighed and trudged back up the aisle toward the lobby.

"You should have asked your friend Suzanne to come with us," Ilse said to Theo as around them the theater began to fill with customers.

"She's busy working."

"She is very. . ." Ilse searched for a word.

"Intense?" Theo offered.

"I was thinking dedicated. She comes to the fort every day and spends hours there. It is as if she intends to get every single story. And she also works at night? Well, I suppose she does need the time to transpose her notes. I remember when Franz was preparing his lectures. He would spend hours doing research and then more hours composing the lecture."

For days Theo had felt the need to confide in someone—to seek another opinion regarding his concern about Suzanne and the POW. And now he found himself blurting out the news to Ilse of all people.

"She's interviewing one of the German POWs—a man she spoke to briefly the day she went with me to the orchards. He sought her out a few weeks ago and asked if she would write his story—tell his side of things."

Ilse's eyes widened in shock. "And this she has agreed to do?"

Theo nodded.

"Well, I suppose if the man was only a soldier serving in the army then—"

"He was an agent in Hitler's secret police," Theo said, lowering his voice to a whisper when he saw Liesl coming back to her seat. "His name is Detlef Buch."

To his surprise, Ilse gave an involuntary cry. "You are sure?" she whispered as Liesl inched her way past other patrons to reach her seat and the lights in the theater dimmed.

"I am sure. Why?"

"Because Detlef Buch is your sister's father-in-law. He was the one who told your uncle to flee."

The heavy maroon velvet curtains opened, and a newsreel showing grainy black-and-white footage of the latest war news flickered across the screen, the narrator's voice excited with reports of new victories for the Allies in both Europe and the Pacific and assurances that the war was winding down and "our boys will soon be home."

Theo barely paid attention to the newsreel, the short subject on rationing that followed, or the previews of coming attractions. Surely he had heard wrong. It was impossible that Beth's husband could be the son of a Gestapo agent. Why would his sister allow herself to fall in love with someone like that—much less marry the guy?

But when he glanced at Ilse he saw that she, too, was paying little attention to the images on the screen. Her fist was pressed tight against her mouth, and her eyes were closed, a single tear leaking down her cheek.

Detlef Buch.

Instead of Bing Crosby dressed in the costume of a priest, his blue eyes shining with gentleness and concern, Ilse saw Detlef Buch in his dark wool overcoat, leather gloves, and Bavarian fedora with the jaunty red feather in the band. His dark hair streaked at the temples with gray was always perfectly combed. His eyes were a cold, piercing gray—eyes that could question and mock and judge.

It was true that he had warned them, given them the chance to escape a fate that surely awaited Franz, if not all of them. But at the same time he had apparently been unable to save his own son and Beth from imprisonment. She wondered if he knew that they had escaped and managed to get to England. How horrible would it be not to know the fate of your only child!

As the film flickered across the screen, she could not help but wonder where Herr Buch's wife was. She remembered Josef's mother as a lovely woman filled with self-confidence. In many ways Gisele St. Germaine reminded her of *Frau* Buch.

The music swelled, signaling the end of the movie. Around them women were sniffling and blowing their noses as the lights came up. The mood among the audience as they exited the theater was lighthearted as if for an hour or so they had put aside their worries about the war and the future.

"The café is closed," Liesl moaned.

"I guess we'll have to take a rain check on that cocoa, then. Come on, kiddo." Theo wrapped his arm around Liesl's shoulders. "It's late, and I have to work tomorrow."

"And you have school," Ilse reminded her daughter.

The three of them walked back to the shelter. Ilse suspected that Theo was as anxious to talk about the German with her as she was to ask him what he knew. "Would you like to come in, Theo? I could make us some tea."

In his eyes she saw that she had guessed right.

"May I have some, Mom?"

"Not tonight. It's late, and you need to get to bed so you will be fresh for your spelling test tomorrow."

"Spelling *bee*, Mom. That's what it's called here."

"Forgive me. I am clearly not in touch with the ways of the world." She ruffled her daughter's hair, and Liesl went into the bedroom that she and Ilse now shared. She pulled the curtain across the doorway, and Ilse indicated that Theo should sit at the table while she made the tea. They both kept glancing toward the curtain, where they could hear Liesl getting ready for bed.

She emerged in her pajamas with a toothbrush in one hand and some toothpaste in the other. "I forgot to brush," she said sheepishly. "And I have to go to the bathroom again."

Ilse opened the door and checked the hallway. "All right. Go now and hurry back." She stood in the open doorway while her daughter ran to the end of the hall and into the women's bathroom.

"Are you certain, Ilse?" Theo asked, and she did not need to wonder what he meant.

"I am certain. How many Detlef Buches could there be? Especially ones who were in the Gestapo. This has to be Josef's father."

They were whispering while Ilse kept watch for Liesl's return and anyone else in the hallway. "Let me get Liesl settled, and then we can talk." The tea kettle whistled, startling them both.

"I'll get it," Theo said.

Liesl returned to the room with a frown. "We haven't had our meeting for worship," she announced.

"Theo and I will sit in silence while you go to sleep." She escorted the child into the bedroom and pulled back the covers on the cot that used to be occupied by Franz. "Good night, Liebchen." She hugged Liesl and kissed her forehead before pulling the covers over her.

"Good night, Mom. See you in the morning." Liesl yawned and turned onto her side—the doll Theo had given her when they first arrived cradled in her arms.

Ilse stood for a moment, watching her and thinking about the certainty with which Liesl had simply assumed that all would be well through the night and they would indeed see one another at daylight. She realized that in spite of her own desire to return to Germany after the war, Liesl had taken on many of the traits common to Americans— confidence, self-assurance, and a belief that in the end everything would turn out well for them.

Suzanne had told herself that no matter what the German POW wrote in the notebook she had handed him, she would refuse to write or even hear his story. To get involved with him was to open the door to a possible renewed connection with Gordon.

When she went back to the library that next evening, he was there waiting for her. He sat at the same table in the same chair with the newspaper open before him. As she took the chair opposite him without a word of greeting or acknowledgment, he slid the notebook across the table to her.

"I should tell you," she began, but he held up his hand.

"First, you will read as you promised; then we will talk."

"You are hardly in a position to be setting rules," she whispered.

He smiled, and she realized that he was a man used to setting the rules. "I apologize," he said. "Old habits die hard, as you Americans sometimes say. Please will you not read at least the first of it?"

She fingered the notebook, glanced at him, and then opened it, purposely turning in her chair so that she was not facing him. He went back to reading his newspaper. His handwriting was neat and precise—a reflection of the man himself:

When Adolf Hitler came to power, I was employed in the Ministry of the Interior. My primary responsibility was to oversee Ministry affairs in Bavaria. I was well paid and had what I and my superiors considered a bright future. My wife and I and our only child—a son—bought a home. We entertained often. We traveled extensively. We had a large number of friends. We were by all accounts successful and blessed. But slowly, almost without our being aware, our lives changed. In Germany in the 1930s, everyone's life changed.

She stopped reading, determined to go no further, but there were only a few more lines on the page. She would finish the page and then close the notebook, place it next to him, and leave. He would have his answer. She read on:

In those early days, the changes seemed appropriate. Germany after the first war had been devastated. Hitler proposed revisions to the infrastructure of the government designed to make it more efficient. My superior became the head of the Prussian police and asked me to join him in his new office. Others I worked with were appointed to similar positions in this new agency. My wife and I breathed a sigh of relief that I still had a position—had even been promoted in a manner of speaking.

So he had been ambitious.
Like her.
She turned the page:

Gradually throughout Germany things began to improve and much of the public believed that Herr Hitler was living up to his promise to bring the country back to its rightful position as a world leader, erasing the shame and deprivations of the past. If citizens had questions about the singling out of various groups for special treatment, they did not voice them.

Enough!

"Special treatment?" Suzanne waved the notebook at Detlef Buch.

"Sh-h-h," the librarian hissed, although Suzanne and Detlef were the only patrons.

Suzanne lowered her voice to a whisper as she leaned across the table. "Your government murdered people in cold blood for no reason other than they were against the Reich."

"We did," he replied calmly. Then pinning her with his steel-gray eyes, he added, "I did."

She felt the hairs on the back of her neck tingle. She was sitting across from a murderer—one who did not even try to absolve himself. It did not matter whether or not he had pulled the trigger or directly ordered the death. He was a murderer. She wished she had asked Theo to come with her.

Detlef leaned back and pinched the bridge of his nose. "Fräulein Randolph, if you would please take what I have written and read it through, perhaps you will understand."

"What is there to understand?" She pushed the notebook back across the table. "I will not ease your conscience, Mr. Buch."

He stood up and glanced at the clock. "That is not what I am asking. And now I must leave you. I have my shift to work at the cannery." Without another word he turned and walked out of the library, nodding to the librarian as he left. The notebook was still on the table.

She sat staring at it for a long moment. She closed her eyes and envisioned the fastidious handwriting—the words put down so close together as if he had feared that there might not be enough paper to tell the whole story.

"I will write about how it began," he had said when she had first given him the notebook. "If you are interested and agree, then I will tell you the rest. My English is good in speaking, but writing takes time, and I fear we do not have such time."

But she had read enough. More than enough. Did the man truly believe that he would be forgiven for the deaths he had by his own admission caused simply because in the beginning he had thought Hitler and his maniacal plan was the answer? He was obviously well educated and intelligent. But he was also desperate, she realized.

She spun the notebook around with the tip of her finger. She recognized her anger and also knew that she was judging the man without knowing his whole story—the way others had judged various groups in Germany. And not just Germany. How many people did she know right here in America who formed opinions about entire ethnic or political populations based on nothing more than a difference in belief or conviction?

Was she doing the same thing? Judging this man because she assumed that he was as evil as Hitler and his gang? Hadn't Theo said that making assumptions was at the very root of misunderstanding? She picked up the notebook and opened it to the page where she had stopped reading. An hour later the librarian began flicking off the lights. It was closing time, and Suzanne was only partway through the German's journal. Yet what she was reading was fascinating stuff—information that Gordon would no doubt find useful. Reluctantly she marked the page with a business card she had picked up from the local bank after establishing an account as part of her plan to convince herself that Oswego—not Washington—was now her base of operations.

She had come back to write the stories of the refugees—not the story of some German POW who unlike other POWs was not just a foot soldier in Hitler's army but rather a high-ranking officer in the dictator's reign of terror. As she walked back to the boardinghouse, she thought about her editor. Would Edwin publish the story of a captured Gestapo agent? She was fairly certain that he would. The man was in the business of selling newspapers, and a sensational and controversial story like this one would certainly fill that bill.

Yet it was not Edwin that she wanted to share this story with. It was Theo, and while he would not openly disapprove, he would question. He would find ways to make her stop and carefully consider what this was really all about. Unlike Gordon, Theo would not look at this as an opportunity for advancing his career but rather he would consider all parties concerned—including Detlef Buch.

She had learned the hard way that thinking something through made little difference. And hadn't Edwin preached that a story is about now—not an hour from now or a week or a year? "Seize the moment," was the way he ended every staff meeting.

So she would.

CHAPTER 13

From the moment Ilse told Theo about the connection between the POW and their family, Theo had tried to think how best to break the news to his parents and beyond them to Beth and her husband. They were still in England, but he could send a telegram letting Josef know that his father was alive. On the other hand, if the father had been with the secret police, was it possible that Josef had also worked for them? He could have been an undercover agent spying on those who would stage a resistance or plot to overthrow Hitler's regime. He could have used Beth as his way out of the country.

Ilse assured him that Josef and Beth had been deeply in love and reminded him that Josef had been arrested and sentenced to Sobibor, a death camp in eastern Poland. His father had not been able to save him from that fate. She pointed out that Josef and Beth had escaped from the camp and they had been on the run for their lives for months afterward. Not only that, but they had further risked their lives helping Allied airmen reach safety.

Still, when Theo thought about his brother-in-law being the son of a Gestapo agent, he worried that his sister might still be in danger. Even if Josef were innocent of any wrongdoing, might not the authorities want to question him—and Beth? And would that delay even more the day when she could come home?

His concern extended to Suzanne. Evidently she had decided to pursue things with the German. Feeling it was none of his business, Theo had not spoken to her about it, and he had certainly not mentioned the connection between the POW and his family. In fact, ever since she had established a nightly routine of leaving right after supper for the library and not returning until well past closing time, he and Suzanne had barely seen each other. Hilda and Hugh continued to dominate mealtime conversation, and Theo was surprised when Suzanne did not challenge them as she always had before.

Before she began meeting the German.

Theo felt driven to warn her—to protect her. But he could not name the threat. Detlef Buch would not physically harm her as long as he thought she was doing what he wanted, so he was not the threat. Her editor was not involved in the story as far as Theo knew, so she was not being pressured by her former employer to deliver a story. Yet he had this uneasy feeling that when everything played out, Suzanne was going to end up hurt. . .again.

March quite literally melted into April as the snow finally let up and the temperatures started to rise. Theo spent his time after work climbing through the hole that the refugees had opened in the fence and following the path down to the lake. He walked the shoreline and thought about the future.

Ilse had confided her desire to return to Munich once the war ended. Theo knew that his parents would not think this a wise move, and certainly Liesl had settled into the American way of life so thoroughly that she would be unlikely to want to return to a homeland she had known mostly as a place where she had to watch everything she said or did and where her parents had been so obviously scared and unhappy.

Since Franz's death, Ilse had become more withdrawn and only Gisele St. Germaine seemed to be able to draw her out of her mourning— for her husband, for her homeland, for a life that had once been so predictable and secure. Thinking about Gisele made his thoughts turn to Suzanne. The woman had once accused him of being attracted to the French actress.

"She's been a good friend to my aunt." He'd had no idea why he felt the need to defend himself, and that irritated him.

"Keep telling yourself that's why she's always going to the movies or some function at the shelter with you and Ilse."

He had felt like taking hold of her shoulders as he had done the night he had kissed her. In spite of his annoyance, he had felt like kissing her until she saw her mistake. It wasn't Gisele that he was attracted to. It was Suzanne. But there had been no further intimacy between them since that night, and neither of them had ever mentioned their kiss. Shortly after that shared kiss—and it had definitely gone both ways—she had started slipping off right after supper, turning down all his attempts to find time they could spend together. He had gotten the message. Her career came first.

That was it. She was the threat—or at least her obsession with her career was. Ever since she had told him about the story that had ended her almost meteoric rise in the world of journalism, all she talked about was her work. Her focus was on finding the story that would erase the memory of that embarrassing episode. But from what she had told him about how she had gotten so caught up in the details and possible shock waves of that first story, he wondered if she might not be on the verge of making the same mistake all over again.

Detlef Buch had an agenda, as had the congressman she had gotten that other story from. That man had not cared what happened to Suzanne or her reputation. He had used her ambition to get what he wanted. What if Buch was doing the same thing?

There was one way to stop the man from using Suzanne—or at least to make him think twice: if Theo told him that someone in the fort knew him, knew what he had done. Of course he would never reveal Ilse's name. It would be the knowledge that his so-called facts could be disputed, could be checked that might make him think twice about what he was doing. He might even withdraw his permission for Suzanne to write the story. She would be furious, of course, but it would be for her own good.

"Penny for your thoughts." Suzanne came alongside him, her hands in her pockets and a scarf tied around her unruly hair.

Theo had been thinking about her so much that it was almost as if he had willed her to appear. "Not sure my thoughts are worth a penny." He paused and stared out toward a gray horizon that blended seamlessly into the gray waters. "I haven't seen you down here before."

She shrugged. "I come sometimes. I've seen you, but I didn't want to disturb you."

"So what's different about today?"

"I need a friend I can talk to."

"I'm flattered." He took her hand and tucked it in the crook of his elbow as they started to walk. "Well here I am, so what's going on?"

As if he had somehow opened the floodgates, her words spilled out. She told him all about the meetings with Detlef Buch, about the journal and how it had raised so many questions in her mind.

"Such as?"

"What if I had been in his shoes? What if I had been told to do what my superiors asked or suffer the consequences? What if I had seen others lose their jobs, their homes, their position in the community simply because they dared to question the government's policies? What if—"

"You would still have refused. That is the difference."

"But what if they had threatened my family?"

"Did they threaten the German's family?"

"Yes."

"How?"

"They threatened to send his son to the front lines instead of keeping his service as a medic in relatively safe areas. They threatened to arrest his wife because once when she was a child her parents had entertained 'an enemy of the state' in their home."

"And how do you know this?"

"He told me."

"Exactly. He has told you all of this—what he wants you to know. What has he withheld?"

"Nothing. In his journal he has revealed things that I'm certain could get him sentenced to life in prison or worse. And in the interviews I've had with him, he has answered all my questions without any hesitation."

"Suzanne, this is what he does—what he built a career doing. Why in the world would you trust anything he tells you? The man is fighting for his life."

She stooped to pick up a stone that had been smoothed by lake water over who knew how many years. "I want to understand how a man so obviously intelligent could come to this."

Theo let out a breath and watched the fog of it disappear into the air. "Where are you going to meet him—and do not tell me the library because I checked and you are not going there."

"You checked?" She folded her arms across her chest in a gesture of annoyance. "I'm not Liesl, you know. I'm not ten years old."

"Forgive me for caring. You are here alone, and you do seem to have this habit of going off—"

"Half-cocked?"

"I was going to say you have a habit of going off on your own without anyone knowing where you are or when you might return. I was worried."

She squinted up at him then stuffed her hands into her pockets. "You know, I do have to earn some money for the rent at Selma's."

Relief flooded through Theo. She wasn't spending hours and hours with the POW. She was working. "You got a job? At the paper?"

"No. At the canning factory. It's part-time, but it pays enough to cover rent and essentials and still leaves me the time I need to go to the shelter to gather stories and—"

"And Buch works at the cannery." It was more than a guess.

"Yes. So you see, I am perfectly safe. We work next to each other on the assembly line, so I am able to interview him while I work, and then I get on the bus with other people from Oswego and come home.

Perfectly safe," she repeated.

"But exhausting. Talk about burning the candle at both ends. When do you take time to sleep?"

"I don't need much sleep. Besides, once this is done I'll have plenty of time to catch up."

"And exactly what is 'this,' Suzanne?"

"My book. You see I've finally come up with an angle. I tell two stories—the one of the refugees paralleled with Buch's story. Two sides of the same time period." Her voice quivered with excitement, and she was talking with her hands—something Theo had learned was a sure sign that this was a topic that she felt passionate about. "I can barely wait to sit down each day and type up my notes."

"You would defend this man and his actions?"

"No! I am simply telling the story of how it was possible for him and hundreds—thousands—like him to become caught up in the madness."

"Sounds like a defense to me."

She stopped walking and glared at him. "What do you want from me, Theo? I am a journalist. I write stories designed to inform and teach and help readers come to an educated point of view based on fact."

Theo gave her a wry smile. "And so we have come full circle, Suzanne. How exactly are you proving those so-called facts?" He did not wait for an answer. "I promised Liesl and Ilse to join them for a meeting for worship on Sunday. Gisele is coming as well. If you'd like to come you'd be most welcome."

"Maybe another time."

"Thought so," he murmured as he turned away and climbed the soggy path that led back to the hole in the wire fence.

Suzanne watched him go. What right did he have to judge her? If she wanted to pursue the business with Detlef Buch, wasn't that her right? So she had originally sought his advice, but now. . . And what had he meant by that last comment? "Thought so." As if he had expected that she would refuse any invitation to join in a meeting for worship. Wasn't he the one who had made such a point of not making assumptions without fact?

But he was right—at least about the meeting for worship. Other than the night she had sat with Liesl in the frigid barracks apartment, Suzanne had not attended a meeting for worship or any other form of church service since she had been eighteen years old. As she stood staring out across Lake Ontario, she recalled another lake in another season in another part of the country.

As a teenager her summers had been spent working as a counselor at a camp set on the banks of a large lake high in the Appalachian Mountains of Virginia. But the summer of her eighteenth birthday, she had opted to do something else. Meanwhile at that camp something happened— something that maybe if she had been there would not have happened— something that changed her life. And it seemed to her that everything that had happened in the world following that summer had only served to prove the point. There was no "Light" and there was no plan.

She continued to stand on the rocky beach below the fort where hundreds of people still awaited their fate, until the chill of the day seeped through the fabric of her coat and into her bones. Shivering, she climbed the path back to the hole in the chain-link fence where teenagers from town on one side and from the shelter on the other had created a makeshift if temporary escape.

As she crossed the grounds of the fort—soggy in places where the snow had melted and patches of grass had begun to appear—she saw several people gathered near the administration office and more exiting the barracks and community buildings to join them. Something had happened. Was it possible that the war was over? She quickened her step until she reached the silent throng gathered around the open door of the administration building. A radio had been turned to full volume, and over a mournful composition of funereal music the announcer was saying, "The president died at his home in Georgia."

President Roosevelt had always seemed indestructible despite rumors that the onset of polio long before he had run for the land's highest office had left his legs useless and paralyzed and that when out of the public eye he used canes or crutches and a wheelchair. It was common knowledge that one of the reasons he kept the home in Georgia was to take advantage of the hot mineral springs there.

He had just won an unprecedented fourth term in office. Suzanne tried to picture his running mate—a balding, bespectacled haberdasher from Missouri. Harry Truman was now the president of the United States.

"And so we begin again," Gisele said wearily as she turned away from the broadcast to light a cigarette. "The question is if we were guests of FDR, are we now guests of Mr. Truman?"

"The wording has always been 'guests of the president,'" Suzanne reminded her, but even as she attempted reassurance, she had doubts. Would this new president honor the promises of his predecessor? Only time would tell.

For days after the news of FDR's death was broadcast, everyone in the fort and in town seemed to move through their routine in a kind of disbelief. How could this happen? What would they do now? What would the government do? What did this mean for the war, which had seemed to be winding down at long last?

But Ilse's mind was on another matter. Ever since Theo had told her that Detlef Buch was a prisoner of war and living in the area, she had been unable to get the man off her mind. Her first reaction had been a kind of kneejerk fear and anxiety—the same feelings that had overwhelmed her whenever the man was around back in Munich. But then she would remind herself that this was different. He was a prisoner—not someone in authority. He could no longer bring harm to her or Liesl.

Once she had worked through that, her thoughts went to Beth and Josef. Shouldn't Josef be told that his father was in America? And what of his mother? Where was she? More and more she felt the need to contact Josef and Beth.

So when she saw Suzanne Randolph sitting on the steps of the administration building with Gisele one afternoon just after President Roosevelt's body had been carried by train to his home in Hyde Park, New York, for burial, she crossed the parade ground to speak with the reporter.

Suzanne and Gisele sat with their faces turned to the sun, their eyes closed, soaking in the warmth of spring. Ilse hesitated to disturb them but did not wish to lose her nerve.

"Hello," she called as she reached the walkway that ran around the camp connecting all the public buildings.

Both women blinked and squinted and then smiled. "Come join us," Gisele invited. "I can finally believe that the horrid winter is at long last behind us."

Suzanne scooted to one side, making room for Ilse to sit between them.

"I would like to speak with you," Ilse said, turning her attention to Suzanne. "About Detlef Buch."

Suzanne sat up straight and gave Ilse her full attention. "Theo told you? Look, I know that he thinks I am making a mistake but—"

"I told Theo who this man was—is. I have known for some time now that you have been writing down his story in the same manner that you have been writing stories about the people here in the fort. That is your privilege, and I do not judge your motives. The truth is that I wish to speak with him myself."

Surprise registered in Suzanne's eyes, and Gisele gasped behind her.

"Why?" Suzanne asked. "What possible good could—"

Ilse smiled. "I do not judge you, and you will do me the courtesy of not questioning my reasons. Will you arrange a meeting?"

"You know him?"

"We have family in common. Theo did not tell you?"

"Tell me what?"

"Herr Buch's son is married to my niece—to Theo's sister, Beth. When we were in Munich, he came to our home on at least two occasions." She saw that Suzanne knew none of this. "So Theo is perhaps correct," Ilse said softly.

Surprise had disintegrated to confusion and irritation. "I don't understand. What is it Theo is correct about?"

"That Herr Buch is telling you *his* story but that may not be the whole story. Theo has worried that you are being taken advantage of and he tells me it would not be the first such experience for you."

Gisele leaned forward, her eyes probing Suzanne's eyes. "Why on earth would you agree to consort with this criminal—this man who with a stroke of his pen sent perhaps hundreds or even thousands to their deaths?" She stood up. "I—we have trusted you, and you have gone behind our backs to—"

"To get the other side of the story," Suzanne protested.

"There is no other side to this story," Gisele growled as she stalked away.

Ilse and Suzanne sat on the step without speaking for several minutes. Finally, Ilse could stand it no more. "Will you arrange for me to meet with Herr Buch?"

"Does Theo know you plan to do this?"

"Theo is not my keeper. I am a grown woman, and if I have decided to do this, I hardly need Theo's permission—or yours. But I could use your help in arranging the meeting."

"I'll ask Mr. Buch when I see him at work tonight at the cannery. If he's willing—"

"No! He is not to know of my presence here. I do not wish to give him the choice of whether he wishes to see me. If you will arrange a time for him to meet you—perhaps again at the library?"

"We are to meet there on Saturday at three."

"Then I will get a pass and be there in your place." Ilse got to her feet. "Thank you, Suzanne." And as she walked back toward the barracks, she was already planning exactly what she would say to Detlef Buch.

But on Saturday morning she began to have second thoughts. Gisele had made it clear that she thought Ilse was out of her mind to have anything to do with the Nazi POW. "How can you even think of being in the same room with him, much less sitting civilly across a table from him?" Gisele actually shuddered.

"It feels like something I need to do," Ilse replied as she checked her hair in a hand mirror she had rescued from one of the donation boxes. "I should wear a hat," she murmured and went to the bedroom to get one.

"Do you want me to take Liesl to supper when she finishes practicing the piano?"

"I should be back by then."

"Good. I'm not sure what I would tell her—how I would explain."

Ilse felt a flicker of annoyance as she pulled on white cotton gloves and picked up her purse. "There is nothing you need to explain, Gisele. Not to Liesl or anyone else."

"I apologize, Ilse. I am just worried."

"I know, and thank you for caring. But I feel led to do this and in our faith we do follow those leadings." She opened the door. "Will you walk with me to the gate?"

The two friends linked arms and headed across the parade ground to the tunnel that led out to the street and the town. "What will you say to him?" Gisele asked.

"I have no idea."

"Perhaps 'Fancy meeting you here'? Or maybe, 'Why, Detlef Buch, isn't it a small world?'"

Ilse laughed. She knew that Gisele was trying to ease her nerves, and she was grateful. At the gate they greeted the staff member on duty, and Ilse showed her pass. Gisele waved to her, and Ilse was aware of the click of her high heels on the pavement as she walked through the tunnel and out to the street. She was reminded of all the times she had been walking on a street in Munich and had heard the click of leather heels behind her—all the times she had looked over her shoulder to see a German soldier and been certain that he was following her, about to stop her, demand to see her papers, perhaps even take her in for questioning.

Those days seemed like another lifetime to her now, yet the memories were so very precise, so very fresh.

At the library she paused in the dim lobby to straighten her hat and calm her breathing. Beyond the open doors leading into the reading room she could see a man seated at one of the long wooden tables toward the back of the room. His back was to her as he read a newspaper, but he was also the only man in the room who came close to being the right age.

She moved toward him, her heels now silenced by the carpeted floor. He was about to turn a page when she was within six inches of him. He paused and waited.

"Hello, Herr Buch," she said softly and took some satisfaction in seeing his fingers tremble slightly as he let the page fall back into place. At that moment, she knew exactly why she had wanted to speak with him.

CHAPTER 14

"You let her meet with him alone?" Theo could not believe what Gisele was telling him. He had come to the barracks to find his aunt and instead run into Gisele.

"I did not *let* her do anything. Ilse is a grown woman and perfectly capable of making the choices that seem right to her."

"But do you not understand who this man is? Who he was when Ilse knew him back in Munich?"

"He was—how do you Americans say it—the 'boogeyman'? He is here now as a prisoner and hardly a threat to Ilse or anyone else for that matter. He has been stripped of all authority and that means he no longer has the power to—"

"My aunt is not a strong woman, Gisele. Back in Munich she suffered from—"

"That was the past. These days she is a very strong woman because perhaps she is no longer in Munich and because I am sure she has faced the fact that she must be strong for Liesl's sake." Gisele blew out a ring of cigarette smoke. "Besides, is this Buch person not your sister's father-in-law, and as such is he not family to both you and to Ilse?"

Theo put on his hat. "They were to meet at the library?"

"That was the plan. They were to meet at three, although Buch thought it would be Suzanne coming." She took hold of his wrist and checked the time on his watch. "It's nearly five. I did not realize she had been gone so long." Her tone betrayed her concern. "Perhaps it would be best if you went to the library to see if they. . .if Ilse is all right."

Theo did not bother to answer. He walked away quickly across the parade ground and down the path through the tunnel. He nodded to the gatekeeper and then headed for town. He had gone only two blocks when he saw Ilse coming toward him. He quickened his pace, practically running the last few yards.

"Are you all right?"

She blinked at him as if she did not immediately recognize him then drew in a deep shuddering breath. "Oh, Theo, it's you. No, I am not all right."

"Did Buch—"

"He told me that my sister's husband, Lucas, was working under-cover as a double agent. He was hanged even as the Allies drew close to Munich. He thinks that my sister was arrested but admits that he does not know what happened to her or their children."

Her skin went pale, and she stumbled slightly. Theo took hold of her arm to steady her as he led her to a nearby bench at the bus stop. "Sit down. You've had quite a shock, Ilse." He glanced around and saw a woman sweeping her porch across the street. "Excuse me," he called. "My aunt is not feeling well. Could I trouble you for a glass of water?"

The woman dropped the broom and ran inside. Seconds later she emerged holding a large glass filled with ice water and made her way across the street, dodging traffic as she hurried to them.

"Here, honey," she said, and Theo realized that it was the woman who sold tickets at the movie theater at the same time the woman also made the connection. "Why, you're Liesl's mom, aren't you?"

Ilse accepted the glass of water with a half smile and nodded as she took a sip. "There's really no need to fuss," she said. "I just. . ." She started to stand.

"Sit there," Theo instructed as he took the glass and handed it back to the woman. "Thank you, Mrs. Driver. Sorry to have troubled you."

"No trouble at all. Would you like to come inside? I could send my daughter, Nancy, to the fort to bring Liesl—we could all have supper together. No reason to upset the child by you being delayed."

Somewhere a block or so away a clock chimed five thirty.

"A friend is with Liesl. We'll just sit here a minute until my aunt catches her breath. Thank you."

Mrs. Driver was not anything like Hilda Cutter, who would have lingered until her curiosity about what had caused Ilse's bout of weakness was satisfied. Instead she touched Ilse's shoulder and murmured, "You and your daughter have a standing invitation, Mrs. Schneider. It would be our honor to have you come for supper anytime."

"Thank you, Mrs. Driver. You are so kind."

"It's Mildred, dear. Our children are friends, and I see no reason why we should not be friends as well."

Theo thought Ilse might burst into tears, but she clasped the Driver woman's hand between both of hers. "I would like that," she said. "And I am Ilse."

"Come for Sunday dinner after church this coming Sunday, then." She turned her attention to Theo. "You come, too, and bring that good-looking woman I've seen you squiring around town." She grinned, and to Theo's surprise his aunt actually chuckled. He also must have looked more than a little surprised because Mrs. Driver patted his cheek and added, "Oswego is a small town, honey. Not much happens around here that someone doesn't notice." She started back to her house, turned and waved, and called. "Sunday at one, then."

Ilse nodded and waved back.

She stood up and brushed off her coat before taking hold of Theo's arm. "Come on. Liesl and Gisele will be worried."

He was worried about her. She had visibly aged since he'd last seen her. Clearly the news from Buch had shocked her. "Maybe I can ask Joseph Smart to use his contacts to help you find out what has happened to your sister and the children, Ilse."

"And perhaps Herr Buch is lying," she replied as they reached the gate. "After all, he is a desperate man."

"Then he has admitted his responsibility? He ordered the deaths of others?"

"Not to me, but that is hardly the real issue. His true crime is that he knew about the camps and where the trains were going and all those senseless deaths. Whether or not he pulled a trigger is irrelevant. His crime is that he knew and he did nothing to stop them." She looked toward the dining hall and knelt down with her arms open as Liesl came running to meet her.

The following evening Suzanne sat across from Theo at supper, but he barely glanced at her and he certainly had nothing to say to her. Instead he ate as if this might be his last meal and then excused himself. She heard the front screen door open and shut and his footsteps fade away.

"Excuse me," she murmured, wiping her mouth with her napkin as she left the table.

"Lovers' quarrel," she heard Hilda say knowingly.

Theo was halfway down the block when she caught up to him. "Hey," she said, falling into step beside him. "You seem a little upset. Has something happened to Ilse or Liesl?"

"Not to worry, Suzanne. Nothing that would interfere with your precious story."

She had never heard him sound so sarcastic or bitter. The unfairness of his attitude made her bristle. She was practically running to keep up with his long strides. "Look, I don't know what you think is—"

He stopped and wheeled toward her. "You're right. I don't know what you are doing or why. I don't know why Gordon Langford is sending you letters and calling you several times a week. But I do know one thing—I want you and the congressman to leave my family alone, Suzanne. They have been through enough, and Ilse hardly needs to have to deal with an ex-Gestapo agent at this stage of her life."

"That's what this is about? Well for your information, Theo, it was Ilse who came to me about speaking with Detlef Buch. I tried to dissuade her, but she was adamant. What exactly did you expect me to do?"

"Oh, I don't know. Maybe talk it over with me before you set up a meeting?" He was glaring at her now.

"I'm sorry," she stammered as she became fully aware that his anger at her was based in his fear for his aunt. "The man is a prisoner. He can't hurt them now. From what Ilse told me, he actually helped them once, and besides, he is your sister's father-in-law. Surely he can be trusted not to—"

Theo's laugh was devoid of any real humor. "How can you consider yourself a journalist and be so gullible?" He threw up his hands in exasperation.

That stung. She had told him all about the story that had destroyed her career, the trust she had had for Gordon Langford. Now he was turning her words against her. Once again she had placed her trust in another human being, and once again that person had turned away. Was it any wonder she instinctively kept people at arm's length? But if Ilse had been upset by her meeting with Buch, even if she had been the one to insist on that meeting as well as the secrecy...

"Will you please tell me what happened when Ilse met with Buch? Perhaps I can—"

"Fix it? I don't think so. The man might be a shirttail relative to my aunt and to me, but he is no less than the monster he was back in Germany. He was in the business of hunting people, Suzanne, and my guess is that he takes a certain pleasure in doing so."

He started to walk away, but Suzanne grabbed his shirtsleeve to stop him. "Please tell me what happened. I'll go to Ilse and—"

Theo turned to face her, this time taking hold of her shoulders the way he had the night he had kissed her. But his passion this time was anger, not desire. "Stay away from my family, Suzanne," he growled, and then he released her and stalked away.

She started after him but had gone no more than a couple of steps before realizing that it was fruitless. She considered going to the fort and finding Ilse, but it was already past six. She had to get to the cannery, and if she didn't hurry she would miss the bus. Her wages paid the rent at the boardinghouse and allowed her the time she needed to gather information for her book.

Driven by her realization that at the cannery she would be able to talk to Detlef, she hurried back to the boardinghouse to collect her things. Detlef would tell her what had happened in his meeting with Ilse—of course, he would provide only his version of that meeting. At some point she would need to find a way to get the other side of the story from Ilse.

Buch was already at his station when she arrived. The foreman glanced up and frowned as she hurried to her place on the line. She was sure to get a warning for her tardiness. She fell into the rhythm of the work and waited for Detlef to say something. But he simply nodded as he continued the repetition of the work. It occurred to her that in the few times they had met once she had agreed to hear his story, he had never been the one to instigate the conversation. He always waited for her questions. He would give nothing away. He watched her and waited, like a cat toying with a mouse.

She shuddered as she imagined this man sitting in his office in Germany—a person his men had arrested seated before him, unsure of the crime. In her interviews with others in the fort, she had heard such meetings described—had heard how in many cases the Gestapo agent was unfailingly polite—sometimes even kind, offering water or tea.

Is that how Detlef Buch saw her? Was she just a person he needed to break? She felt a sudden chill and with it the unmistakable need to escape.

Her anxiety built as she launched into the repetitive tasks that were the mainstay of any assembly line. It upset her to suspect that Theo might be right—that once again she had trusted someone and been duped. At least this time the story and her name weren't spread all over the front page of a major newspaper. But would she ever learn her lesson? What if she wasn't the gifted journalist that Edwin had said she was? What if he was wrong and she just wasn't that good? And if that was the case and she could no longer find a place for her writing, who was she?

Instead of making any attempt to ask Detlef about his meeting with Ilse, she worked in silence until the blast of a horn signaled that it was break time. Without a glance at Detlef with whom she usually shared a cup of coffee while she plied him with questions, she hurried off to the restroom. She leaned against the sink and closed her eyes, blocking out her image in the smeared mirror.

"Your boyfriend is waiting, hon," one of the other women said as Suzanne washed her hands at the next sink.

For a moment Suzanne felt hope and relief. Theo had followed her here? Wanted to talk after all? Would rescue her and see her safely home?

"Can't think what you see in that Nazi. He's old enough to be your father, for starters, and you could do a lot better."

"It's not what you think," Suzanne muttered as she ripped the cloth toweling to an unused section and dried her hands.

Back on the factory floor, she walked right past Detlef on her way to the office. She tapped on the door frame, and the foreman looked up from his paperwork. "You were late," he said and turned back to his work.

"I know. I'm sorry. It won't happen again."

The foreman grunted. Suzanne stepped inside the office. He glanced up. "Something else?"

"I was wondering if I could switch positions on the line with one of the others."

He rolled his eyes. "Look, the POWs are—"

"It's not that. Look, if I can find someone willing to switch, would that be okay?"

"I had this feeling you were going to be trouble from the day you showed up. But I need you, so work it out if you can on your own time. Right now get back to work."

"Thank you. I really—"

He gestured toward the door and the factory where the others were moving like cows in a field back to their stations. "On your own time," he repeated.

"Got it." She returned to her station.

Detlef glanced at her with one raised eyebrow. "You are in trouble with the foreman?"

"Not at all." She turned slightly away from him and focused on her work. When the shift ended, she hurried to find the woman from the bathroom. She made her case for making a switch.

"Lovers' quarrel?" The woman grinned knowingly.

It was the second time someone had said that on this day. "Something like that," she said, giving into the fact that it was easier to let it go than to try and explain. "So will you trade?"

"Yeah. Sure."

"Thanks. I'll go let the foreman know."

By the time she spoke to the foreman and got her coat, everyone on her shift had left and the next workers were in place. She hurried out, hoping she had not missed the bus back to town. The last of the workers were climbing aboard as she ran across the road waving at the driver to wait for her. And when she boarded there was only one seat available—the seat next to Detlef Buch.

He pressed himself closer to the window, making room for her. She hesitated and then walked all the way to the rear of the bus to the last row of seats that stretched across the entire width of the vehicle. Two men and a woman seated there moved closer together to make room for her to sit.

"Glad to see you finally came to your senses," one of the men muttered.

Once Ilse got Liesl settled for the night, she joined Gisele outside on the back steps of the barracks. The late April night was unseasonably warm, and Ilse was glad for the breeze. They were facing the lake; the only light came from the tip of Gisele's cigarette and the lights in apartment windows above and to either side of them. If they looked out toward the water, all was darkness—an infinity of blackness and the unknown.

"What will you do?" Gisele asked.

The question was one that needed no further explanation for any of the residents at the fort. As the time came closer for them to leave, it turned out that they might have choices after all. So far none of them involved staying in America, but no longer was their only choice that of returning to the place they had lived before they had been arrested, evicted, or imprisoned.

"I need to go back to Munich. I need to find Marta and the children."

"And Liesl? She doesn't want to go. She thinks of herself as American. Her friends are here."

"But we will have to leave anyway. She cannot stay here, so why not go back to a place we know?"

"She was not happy there. You were not happy there."

"I was a fool in those days." Ilse's voice drifted off as she looked out into the night. "What about you?" she asked, turning her attention back to Gisele, who was crushing out the stub of her cigarette. "Will you go to Paris or to Palestine?"

Gisele sighed. "Does it matter? I know I have been talking about the new state, and if I were ten years younger that might indeed be the best option. As for Paris? Either way I will again be starting over, and I am so very tired of new beginnings. Like your Liesl I have grown used to these Americans and their ways. I would like to stay here—go to New York City and open a little boutique there."

"I can see you doing that. Of course you could also open your shop in Paris."

"Paris will not be Paris for some time once the war ends, and I cannot live on the memory of what the city once was."

"Do you not have family you want to find back there?"

"My family was taken in the first war—brothers, father. My mother died of a broken heart."

"Friends, then—those you told me about working with to get Allied airmen back to England."

"Perhaps." She pushed herself away from the steps and stretched. "The fact is that there is nothing we can count on to still exist from our pasts, Ilse. And so—like it or not—we must make a new future." She bent and kissed Ilse's cheek. "Good night."

Ilse sat alone for some time after Gisele left. She listened to the laughter and conversation coming from the open windows of the barracks until one by one the lamps went out and all was quiet. It was so quiet that she could hear the lapping of the lake against the shore at the base of the hill where the barracks sat. Their "villa on the hill," as Franz had called it.

The sound reminded her of the ocean—the tide coming and going. She thought about Franz, wished he were still with her, and she allowed the tears that she refused to show Liesl or indeed anyone else to fall. "I miss you so very much," she whispered. "You would know what to do. You would decide for us." She buried her face in her hands as the tears evolved into sobs. "I cannot do this alone."

Not alone.

It was as if someone had whispered the words in her ear. She lifted her tearstained face and listened to the wind, to the water, and to the reassuring sound of stillness.

She realized that she had no choice other than to surrender to the will of others and that she would never do. Somehow she would do what needed to be done—protect her child, find her sister, and make a home for them all.

CHAPTER 15

Theo stared at the document before him. Leading citizens of Oswego had banded together to pen a petition to the president and to Congress, recommending that the refugees be permitted to reside in places of their own choosing, accept gainful employment to rebuild their broken lives, and be eligible to apply for full citizenship.

Reading the copy of the petition, Theo felt something he had not felt for some time. Perhaps with the changes in the government following Roosevelt's death—resignations in key departments and the unknown status of Truman's views on the situation—there was reason to hope. He wanted to talk with someone about the changes, consider what they might mean. He wouldn't do that with Ilse or indeed any of the residents of the fort, for they would assume he knew more than he was telling them, and he would not raise false hopes.

The truth was, the one person he wanted to talk about the changes with most was Suzanne. But ever since that night they had argued, she had avoided him. She had taken to leaving for the cannery early and returning late. He suspected she was spending the time before and after with Buch. And the truth was that this idea filled him not with the rage he had felt that night but rather with jealousy and envy.

Gordon Langford had been calling Suzanne several times a week, and he'd seen from the mail that Selma left for tenants on the hall table that she had also begun receiving official-looking letters from Washington. Gisele told him that Suzanne continued to interview various people in the shelter, although as word had spread of her association with Buch, more of the refugees had pulled away and refused to have anything to do with her.

He wished he had not accused her of being so tied to her career that she had lost all perspective when it came to human kindness and understanding. That was not true. And just because the congressman was calling and writing did not necessarily mean that Suzanne was returning his attention. Theo suspected that whatever drove Suzanne was rooted in her past beyond the disaster of the news story that had destroyed her career. Something had happened earlier in her life that lay at the root of her cynicism and devotion to her work.

He had noticed that in spite of her many contacts she did not appear to have much interaction with her family and she did not have any real friends. What was *her* story?

That night he sat on the front porch of the boardinghouse, rocking in the swing until he saw her get off the bus and walk slowly, wearily toward the house.

"Hi," he said as she mounted the steps and started toward the front door.

"Hello." The greeting was guarded and filled with suspicion. She hesitated but did not move away from the door.

"If you're not too tired, I thought we might take a walk. It's a beautiful spring night."

She dropped her shoulder bag onto one of the wicker chairs and perched on the arm. "This is new," she said.

"Yeah, well, sometimes I can act like a spoiled brat—just ask my brother and sister. I realized I had gone a little overboard, but then time went by. You were busy. I had extra duty at the shelter, and—"

"If this is your idea of an apology, you are really bad at it."

"What if I said I miss you—miss what we used to have?"

"And what was that exactly?"

"Friendship?"

She shrugged. "More like two lost souls thrown together."

"Maybe. Seems like we helped each other, though. Back last fall it seemed like we might find our way together."

"Friends," she murmured as if it were a foreign word to her.

"For starters."

She let this linger in the silence. "How is Ilse?"

"Stronger than I gave her credit for."

"I'm glad to hear that."

"So can we go for that walk?"

"Okay."

They covered three blocks before either spoke, but by the second block he had taken her hand and she had not pulled away.

"Ilse gave me your sister's mailing address in England to give to Buch," she said finally.

"She told me she had done that. At first I didn't understand why, but then she reminded me that Beth's husband deserved to know what had happened to his parents regardless of what they had done. I really couldn't argue the point."

"That was. . .right after you and I quarreled. She saw me at the fort one day and handed me the information, but she has refused to speak with me since. She is always cordial when we happen to pass on the grounds or in town, but she does not stop to chat."

"She believes that Buch can either tell her what happened to her sister, Marta, and the children or that he knows how to lead her to someone who can help her. Has he said anything to you?"

"We. . .I haven't spoken with him."

"About my aunt?"

"About anything. I am no longer interviewing Detlef Buch."

Theo tightened his hold on her hand. "Why not?"

"Because you were right. I was walking a dangerous line, and my contact with him has hurt my position with those living at the fort." She walked with her eyes on the ground, not looking at him. "Remember Gordon Langford—the man who ruined my career last summer?"

"Yeah."

"He's now serving on the Immigration Committee for the House. He was here on official business and asked me to meet him for dinner."

"And did you?"

"Yes. It was the same night I ran into Detlef Buch at the library—talk about coincidences. Gordon had just asked me to see what I could find out about a high-ranking Nazi official who was supposedly living in a nearby POW camp. That night when I met Buch, I knew I had found him."

"And?"

"And nothing," she snapped. "You know the rest."

"What about Langford?"

"What about him? He writes and calls. He thinks Detlef is the answer for resurrecting his career."

"As did you once," Theo gently reminded her.

"Yeah, well, somewhere along the way I seem to have grown a conscience. Sorry I can't say the same for Gordon."

"I won't pretend not to be relieved. This is why I wanted you—and my aunt—to be careful how you interacted with Detlef Buch. I don't doubt for a moment that, like your congressman, his first priority is his own future."

"He is hardly *my* congressman." They walked for another block in silence before she asked, "What exactly did he tell Ilse—about her sister?"

"Nothing, but he did recognize her brother-in-law's name and identified him as a double agent who had been captured and hung."

Suzanne shuddered. "And he knew nothing of Marta?"

"He said that he believed she had been arrested. If he knew anything more, he was not giving that information away. Perhaps it is something he sees as information he might trade."

"For what? Ilse has no power."

"I don't know, but this is a desperate man. He is not a simple soldier of the Reich who will likely be set free and returned to Germany once the war ends. Detlef Buch is a war criminal who will be expected to pay for his crimes."

"And what if he, too, was playing both sides?"

"Is that what he told you?"

"Not in so many words, but there are hints in what he has said that perhaps he tried to warn others as he did your uncle and that he made copies of the records he was charged with keeping and smuggled them from the office."

"So he says. Suddenly you of such little faith are willing to take this man at his word?"

"Let's leave my faith out of this." She pulled her hand free of his.

"Okay, sorry. That wasn't fair. It's just that during this time we've been. . .apart, it occurred to me that I know so little about you." This was why he had waited on the porch for her—not to talk about Detlef Buch—or Gordon Langford.

"What do you want to know?"

A thousand questions flooded his brain and finally melded into one. "Who are you when you are not the journalist? Who were you before you were a journalist?"

She did not answer him for a long moment. He waited, giving her the time she clearly needed to form her response. Did she even know herself who she was without the label of "reporter"?

"You are really asking what happened. Where did I lose my way?"

"All right. Start there."

She sucked in a breath and slowly blew it out between pursed lips. "When I was a teenager," she began, "my sister—Natalie—was in a car accident that left her confined to a wheelchair and that damaged her brain to the point that she could barely communicate. The thing was that her mind still worked—she just appeared to be retarded. . . ."

"Natalie was younger?"

"Yes. By the time she entered high school, I was already a senior. She used to tease me about how glad she was that I would finally be going off to college and she could finally have the bedroom we had shared all her life to herself."

Theo saw the wistful smile that flickered across her lips and disappeared. "What happened?"

"The summer after I graduated, Natalie went off to summer camp. We had both attended this camp from the time we were nine, and that summer, Natalie was going to be a junior counselor. She was so very excited. I was supposed to be there as well as a senior counselor, but I got the opportunity to take a writing course at the college in our town and decided to do that instead."

"The car accident happened while she was at camp?"

Suzanne nodded. "She got involved with some boy from the nearby town and started sneaking out after curfew to meet him. He was older, and that night he was drinking and. . ." Her voice trailed off. "My parents were out when the call came. I was the one who answered the phone."

"Oh honey, that must have been awful for you." He reached out to touch her, but she held up her hand, preventing his comfort.

"The next week was a complete nightmare. Natalie had to be transferred to a hospital miles away. She was barely clinging to life for days. My parents never left her side, sleeping next to her bed. I put off starting college for that fall semester so I could work in my father's store in the small town where we lived. Our neighbors and friends were incredible. But that boy—and his parents. . ."

"He must have been injured as well."

She turned on him, her eyes blazing. "Not a scratch and do not defend him. He almost killed—he actually did kill her—and not once did he call or write or come to see her. His father was some bigwig in that town, and the boy was a huge football star who had a scholarship to a major university. The whole thing was covered up. I don't think he got so much as a ticket."

They had circled the area and were again approaching the boardinghouse. The windows were all dark, and the porch was in shadow lit dimly by the streetlamp. "Let's go sit," he suggested.

They sat side by side on the swing. He put his arm around her shoulders and pulled her close. "You don't have to tell me the rest," he said, afraid that remembering what had happened was causing her pain. He was sorry that he had pushed her.

"No. I want you to understand." She settled herself more securely in the curve of his arm. "My parents tried to press charges but were told there was some evidence that in fact Natalie had been driving the car."

"That's ridiculous."

"Yeah, well, one day my dad received an envelope and inside was a check from the boy's father for a great deal of money. Blood money, Dad called it, and he tore up the check. After that I transferred to a smaller college so I could live at home and help out at the store. Mom took in sewing and mending so she could stay home with Natalie, and Dad took a second job as a night watchman. I don't know how we managed, but we did. And gradually Natalie improved."

Theo felt her stiffen as the memory of what came next hit her. "It's okay. Stop if you don't want to remember."

"Natalie improved so much that she was able to go back to school, and in spite of her appearance—the lolling head she could not hold up, the drooling that required constant attention, and the inability to speak—she made her mark. She was able to move herself through the halls in her wheelchair and to write answers to questions on a small slate she carried everywhere. When she was a sophomore, she was elected to the homecoming court."

"But?" Theo's mouth had gone dry.

"I wasn't at the dance and my parents could never really talk about it, but apparently everything was going great. And then Natalie saw the boy she'd been with that night. He had come as the date for one of the senior girls. Natalie had always defended him—she had been so taken with him."

"How could she. . ."

"At night in the room we now shared so I would be there if she needed me, I would see her staring at the photograph that had been taken of the two of them before the accident. One night I couldn't stand it, and I grabbed it and ripped it in half. We had a terrible fight—me screaming at her and her furiously writing notes back to me. The last note shut me up—it said: 'He is a good person, and I still love him.' And then she started to cry, and so did I. So I taped the photo back together and put it back on her mirror."

"So then he shows up at the dance."

"Yeah. Natalie made a beeline for him as soon as she saw him. My mom said her smile was beaming. He was getting punch for his date. Natalie grabbed at his arm and he spilled the punch on his shirt. He said something to Natalie and walked away. After that Natalie told my parents she wanted to go home."

Theo waited. It was her decision whether or not she would—could—tell the rest. He would not push her.

In a voice dead and emotionless she continued. "She didn't speak to any of us for days. She wouldn't eat, and she refused to go to school or leave the house. She put the photo away in her diary, and I thought that at last she had moved on. She even agreed to let Dad carry her downstairs and put her in her wheelchair so she could eat breakfast. The meeting for worship was to be at our house that morning. After breakfast Natalie said she wanted to sit outside during the meeting—she wanted to sit in the grove of birch trees and sketch. We thought this was a good sign," she whispered. She shuddered, and he pulled her closer.

"That's enough for tonight, Suzanne."

"No. Let me finish. The meeting for worship was followed by a meeting with a concern for business, so for two hours we were gathered in that circle. And all the while outside in the birch grove, Natalie was bleeding to death. She had taken a knife from the kitchen while she was at breakfast and once she was alone. . ."

"But I thought—"

"So did we. When I opened her diary after the funeral I found that photograph and along with it her last entry. It read, 'He didn't even

know me. His last words to me were, Get away from me, you freak.'
We were all sitting there—praying and waiting for guidance. Where
was the guidance for one of us to go and check on my sister? That boy
took my sister's life—not once but twice—and he didn't care. How is
that possible, Theo? For a person to feel no remorse at all? Where is the
Light in that?"

She said nothing more for several minutes, and he allowed the silence,
thinking that he had heard enough to have a better understanding of
why she had abandoned her faith.

"That was the first of it," she said, her voice raspy with emotion.
"That next summer I went back to the camp as a counselor. I hoped to
find that boy—to confront him with what he had done to my sister—to
our family. My parents got divorced after Natalie's death, and a few years
later my dad died of a massive heart attack."

"Did you confront the boy?"

"No. His family had moved to California. I finished out the summer
and then went back to school. A few years later, Mom married again.
He's a nice guy and she seems happy. They travel a lot. By that time the
war had started—Hitler and—"

She sat up suddenly, pulling free of Theo's embrace. "Is it really so
difficult to understand how I might find it hard to believe that people
are born with good inside? Some people simply don't stop to think about
how their actions might impact others and some—like that boy who
decided to drink and then drive my sister—are just pure evil. And the
more I got out into the world and began covering stories like those—
stories where if just one person had dared to stand up and speak out and
refuse to take part. . ."

"Kids think they are invincible. They do stupid things." Theo knew
that words he meant as consoling only served to inflame her fury.

"That's an excuse? So the lie is that we are not born with good in us
after all? You want to let the children and teenagers off the hook? Okay,
then answer me this: How do you explain what happened to any one of
the adults cooped up in the fort? They are as innocent as Natalie was, and

yet their lives were destroyed by people—grown-ups who should know better—who are malevolent to their very core." She clenched her fists and pounded them against her knees. "There is no Light in such monsters, not so much as a flicker." She pushed the swing into a jarring motion. "After Natalie died, I finally understood that we are all nothing more than the accident of our birth. Sitting in silence and waiting for some divine inner spirit is meaningless."

Her anger and certainty was like a physical wall that surrounded her, like the fence that enclosed the shelter complete with its barbed wire barrier designed to keep people out. But Theo refused to be restrained. He reached for her, and when she resisted, he pulled her closer, folding his arms around her like a blanket until he felt her body shake with sobs.

No wonder she had elected to focus all of her life on her career. He imagined that she had gone through college just as dedicated to her studies. These things had become her shield.

"You are half right, Suzanne," he said, his lips against her soft hair. "Sitting in silence without eventually finding a way to bring light to the darkness would be meaningless. But you do that in spite of yourself. You have been given the gift of telling stories that make people see what is going on whether or not they want to know. You inspire people, Suzanne. That is your purpose—to move others to action. That and the fact that you never give up. And if you'll let me, I'd like to help."

He set the swing to a calmer rhythm, and they stayed like that until the first rays of dawn lightened the sky.

Ilse was certain that Detlef Buch knew more than he had told her about Lucas and the fate of Marta and the children. After all, they had all left the mountains in the night presumably together. She stopped kneading the dough she was working as she realized her mistake. She and Franz had always assumed the whole family had left together, but what if they hadn't gone to the same place? What if Lucas had sent Marta and the children elsewhere for safety?

At supper she sat with Gisele as she usually did these days. As always the actress was the center of a lively discussion, and finding a quiet moment with her was impossible. But when the meal was over, Ilse sent Liesl to practice the piano and waited for her friend to leave the mess hall.

She told Gisele her theory about her sister. "She could be alive," she said breathlessly as she finished.

"Perhaps but, Ilse, how would you go about finding her?"

"I thought perhaps—with your connections—you might be able to help me."

"My connections are either dead or on the run, Ilse. I cannot help you. Perhaps if I return to Paris when this is all over—certainly then. . ."

"But that could be months from now."

Gisele hesitated then took Ilse's arm. "I know you do not wish to do this, but I think you should speak with Suzanne. From everything you've told me, she and Theo have settled their differences, and you would not be going against Theo's concern about Buch. Suzanne knows people in Washington—perhaps people who are in the government agencies that could help you find your sister and her children."

"Yes, if we work together—combine our forces. . ." She grasped Gisele's hands. "Thank you, dear friend."

That afternoon Ilse obtained a pass and walked into town. First she stopped by the boardinghouse where she left a message for Suzanne. She had no idea how to get in touch with Detlef Buch but hoped Suzanne might help. Then as she headed back to the fort, she decided instead to see if he might be at the library. In fact, he was sitting on a bench in a nearby park that she passed as she climbed the hill on her way to find him. When he saw her, he stood and raised his hand in greeting almost as if he had been waiting for her.

As when they had met that time before, they conducted their conversation in German. "*Guten Tag*, Frau Schneider."

"Herr Buch," she replied when she reached the bench.

He indicated that she should sit and waited for her to do so, ever the gentleman who would not presume to sit down again until she had.

"I will stand," she said.

"Then perhaps we could walk a bit?"

She considered the attention they might draw standing face-to-face against that of walking with him. She glanced around. It was midafternoon on a weekday, and most people were at work. No one else was in the park. "Very well," she said.

He walked with his hands clasped behind his back. She walked with her handbag clutched firmly in both gloved hands in front of her. She was aware of his height and breadth—so much larger than Franz. His was the physique of a powerful and assertive man, while Franz had carried himself with meekness and deference. She shook off the comparison.

"Were you able to contact your son?" she asked.

"I was. I have had a letter from him just yesterday."

"I am glad for you and for him. And your wife?" The words were out before she could censor them.

"My wife is for the time being safe in another country," he said. "We are not in direct contact, but I was able to send word and presumably she knows of our son's circumstances."

I was able to send word. . . . So he did have contacts. This was why she had come to find him.

"And these contacts through whom you were able to send her that message, might they not be able to help me in finding my sister?"

He sighed heavily, glanced up at the blue sky and then back to the flower bed they were passing. He paused and fingered the petals of a daffodil. "Have you ever considered the true power of resilience, Frau Schneider?"

She had little patience for any lectures he might offer. She was on a limited pass, and she had a great deal she wished to accomplish before returning to the fort. "I do not wish to be rude, Herr Buch, but while you may have the freedom to ruminate about the resilience of nature's wonders, I am afraid I do not. Can you or can you not help me find my sister?"

She saw a flicker of something that she realized was respect cross his features. "I will see what I can do, but you need to understand that in spite of outward appearances of my having the kind of freedom to come and go that you do not at present enjoy, I am closely watched and certainly by this time next year I doubt that I will be walking through a park in the company of a beautiful woman. However, it was my pleasure to help you and your family in the past, and if I can. . ."

She stopped walking beside him and turned down a walkway that led back to the street. "Do not presume to use whatever tactics you have used in the past to win favor with me, Herr Buch. If you can help find my sister, I will be grateful, but I will never be in your debt. My family and I owe nothing to anyone who refused to stand up to wrong when they saw it before them. Good day, Herr Buch."

Suzanne had agreed to meet Ilse and Theo in the coffee shop across from the movie theater at three. She checked her watch as she hurried across the bridge. She had been delayed by a telephone call from Gordon.

"How are things in Oswego?" he had asked as if they had been in constant contact in the weeks since they'd met for dinner at the hotel.

"Fine. How are things in DC?"

"Heating up. Looks like the war will be over in a matter of weeks—at least in Europe."

"That's good news."

"It's also why I'm calling, Suze." He cleared his throat, and she realized that as usual he wanted something—something from her. The idea gave her a flicker of disgust.

"What can I do for you, Congressman Langford?"

He chuckled. "Sharp as ever, aren't you? So the thing is, once the war in Europe ends, the Nazis will be sent back to face the music, and we will lose our opportunity to gather what information he has and redeem ourselves." Before Suzanne could respond, he continued. "You would not believe what's going on down here behind the scenes. State and Justice are adamant that the refugees go back period. Interior wants to offer a thing they're calling 'sponsored leave' and let those who can go off to other places in this country and see if they can settle there. The good news is that no one seems to be interested in the Nazi."

"And the president? Where does he stand on the refugee issue?"

"Staying out of it for now, but don't sell Truman short. If you ask me, he's smart enough to let the others fight it out and then he'll step in. But that's not why I'm calling."

"So back to our original question: What do you want from me?"

"I hear through the grapevine that you've taken a factory job. Excellent move."

Suzanne mentally ran through all of her contacts both in Oswego and in Washington, and she could not imagine how Gordon had gleaned this bit of information. "I have to pay the rent," she said.

"And interview the Gestapo guy who apparently also works in the same factory—I get that."

"I've dropped that part of my story," she told him.

"Really? That's too bad."

She decided to ignore this. "I have to get to an appointment, so if we could—"

"Get to the point? Okay, get on board, dollface. The clock is ticking."

So once again he needed her.

"And I am going to need to know what you know," she added as if he had not spoken.

"You'll have what I can give you. You know that this town runs on rumor and gossip so don't expect a lot. Gotta run. They're calling for a vote on the floor." The line went dead.

CHAPTER 16

At Ilse's request Suzanne had renewed her contact with Detlef Buch. "I believe that you can be far more objective than I could ever be. I cannot discount his kindness to our family when he really did not have to help us."

"Maybe Gisele could—"

"I really don't want to involve her," Ilse said. "She has her own life to rebuild."

"Fair enough," Suzanne said. So she had continued her work at the cannery and resumed her habit of riding the bus with Detlef. So what if her coworkers thought they must have patched up their lovers' quarrel? In fact, that was better than them thinking that she was trying to get him to give her information that could help Ilse find Marta.

"New rules," she had told him that first night after her meeting with Ilse. "I will continue to write your story—and find a market for it—in exchange for your help in finding Ilse's sister."

"And if I can deliver nothing that is of use to you or Frau Schneider?"

"You will do everything you can possibly do. I am not naive, Detlef. Ilse told me you were able to get word to your wife that Josef is safe. If you could do that. . ."

"I will try."

For her part Ilse let it be known throughout the shelter that she was searching for her sister. A notice was published in the shelter's newspaper, the *Ontario Chronicle*. Of course, Ilse was hardly the only resident of the fort seeking family and friends. But the article helped. Half a dozen people that she had never met left messages for her or sought her out at mealtime to give her information. One man had known Lucas, Marta's husband, and another had worked with the underground in the area of the ski resort where both families had stayed after leaving Munich.

But in spite of everything, Ilse was no closer to finding Marta and the children than she had been the day she began the search in earnest. Suzanne was losing hope, and she could not imagine what Ilse must be feeling. It amazed her to see how the older woman remained steadfast for Liesl's sake.

"How do you do it day in and day out?" she asked one afternoon when she and Ilse sat across from each other at the coffee shop.

"My faith is strong," Ilse said. "I accept that there is a plan in all of this." She took a sip of her coffee. "Liesl told me that you are also of the Friends' faith."

"It was how I was brought up," Suzanne admitted.

"But you have moved away from those teachings?"

Suzanne eyed Ilse with suspicion, her senses on alert as always for possible betrayal. "Has Theo told you—"

Isle placed her hand on Suzanne's. "My nephew and I do not discuss you." She patted her arm and then cut a bite of her cherry pie. Just before inserting the fork into her mouth, she added, "But since you have raised the subject, how do you see the future for you and Theo?"

Suzanne looked up. Ilse was smiling. "You mean together?"

"Well, of course. He is quite fond of you, and I believe you return those feelings, although it does seem to me that you struggle with that."

"I. . .we. . .perhaps if Theo wins election to Congress and comes to Washington. . ."

"Oh, Suzanne, dear child, you cannot build a future on perhaps."

Suzanne leaned back against the red vinyl cushioning of the booth they shared. "He has a career—perhaps in politics or perhaps in farming. I also have a career."

"And you would not forgo that career for love?"

Put that way, Suzanne was left speechless. Of course she had once dreamed of finding true love, of marrying and having a family, but ever since that summer when Natalie had killed herself, Suzanne had weighed everything in terms of certainty. Only once had she allowed herself to throw that caution to the wind. That had been when she had allowed herself to believe that Gordon Langford loved her—truly loved her.

"You know," Ilse said, "there was a time when I was overly cautious. I was afraid of everything and everyone. Theo's sister, Beth, terrified me. She seemed so reckless and idealistic. Her certainty about what was the right thing to do was overwhelming for me, yet now I see that her faith was so strong."

"Ilse, I have my reasons for moving away from my faith."

"But you must believe in something."

Unnerved by Ilse's probing, Suzanne searched for some way she might change the direction of their conversation without being rude. "I believe that I could use a refill on this coffee," she said and turned to get the attention of the waitress. After the waitress had come and gone, the two women finished eating their pie in silence. As they sipped their coffee, they took turns looking out the window at the steady rain.

"I thought it was April showers that brought the May flowers, and yet the rain has come in May and there are no flowers," Suzanne mused, hoping to relieve the tension between them.

Ilse glanced at the clock over the exit. "I should go. Liesl will be home from school soon, and I promised to help her with her piano practice. Ivo has asked her to play a piece at the variety show he's putting together." She slid her arms into her coat sleeves and then tied a scarf around her hair. She stood up and removed a change purse from her pocket.

"My treat," Suzanne said. "Theo told me that tomorrow is your birthday. I suspect he will want to treat you himself when he returns from Syracuse."

Ilse's smile was sad. "I do not have much to celebrate, do I?" Her eyes brimmed with tears as she clasped Suzanne's forearm. "Do not be too afraid to take a risk, my dear. True love is worth it."

She hurried from the restaurant.

After a day trip to Syracuse to meet with leaders of various religious groups willing to voice their support for allowing the residents of the fort to remain in America, Theo stepped off the train and turned up the collar of his coat against the drizzle. The platform was mostly deserted as he would expect at such a late hour. Inside the station, one lone figure moved back and forth behind the window of the waiting room as Theo made a dash for cover. He reached for the door, hoping there might be a taxi still waiting on the street side of the station.

"You're finally back," he heard a woman say, her voice laced with relief.

He glanced behind him, thinking someone else must have also left the train that was even now pulling out of the station. But then he stopped and turned. "Suzanne? What on earth are you doing here? It must be. . ." He looked at the clock over the ticket seller's cage. "It's past midnight."

"It's also raining cats and dogs, and there are no taxis." She was wearing a rain slicker that he recognized as the one Selma kept hanging by the back door. Her hair was a mass of damp, unruly curls. She was carrying a large black umbrella that she handed over to him as she took his arm. "You must be famished," she said, and he noticed that she seemed a little nervous.

"What's going on?" *Who are you* was more the question he wanted to ask, for Suzanne had never acted this way before. She was—well, the truth was that she was acting as if they were sweethearts. Not that he had any objection to that. He'd been trying to take things slowly over the last few weeks but always in the hope that eventually she would see him as more than a friend—as more than a contact who could help her ferret out the information she needed to tell Ilse's story.

That was the agreement she and Ilse had reached. It had been his aunt's idea. One afternoon as he walked with her back to the fort, she had told him of her plan to tell Suzanne that she had her permission to tell the story of Franz and Ilse Schneider—how they met, fell in love, married, longed for a child, had that child, and found themselves caught up in a war that was not of their making but that was being orchestrated from the very country they had each loved as much as any American had ever loved the United States. Ilse's only requirement was that Liesl was to be left out of the story at least by name and Franz's name as well as her own were to be changed for Liesl's protection.

Theo had tried without success to dissuade her. "You do not need to do this," he had said. "Suzanne will—"

"Suzanne is a woman who is dedicated—far too dedicated—to her career and her ambition for that career. She will work doubly hard if she sees a—how do you Americans say it—a payoff?"

Now as he walked outside with Suzanne and raised the umbrella, holding it high to cover both of them, he wondered what could have happened in his absence to bring on this change in Suzanne. "Did you get something from Buch—some information that may help in finding Marta and the children?"

"No. There's been no change there. I met with Ilse today, and we went over everything, but that only took a few minutes because there is nothing new to share."

"So what did you talk about?"

She shrugged. "Your aunt is a very perceptive woman, Theo. And increasingly she is not afraid to state her opinions—on any topic."

"And today's topic was?"

"Topics, actually. For one, she seemed inordinately interested in my lack of faith. At first I thought perhaps you had told her the story of Natalie and the rest."

"I would never do that."

"That was exactly what she said. Then I realized that her questions grew out of her concern for us—you and me."

"I don't understand."

"She believes that we are. . .fond of one another."

"Can't speak for you but yeah, I like you."

"I think she is looking at our relationship as having moved beyond that stage." She put her hand on his and tilted the umbrella so that his features were exposed to the streetlight they were passing. "Are you in love with me, Theo?"

He would not have been surprised if his reaction had been a feeling of being cornered, trapped. But instead he felt relief. It was finally out in the open. Never mind that he had not been the one to choose the timing or the wording.

"Yes. Yes, I am. Are you in love with me?"

She twisted her mouth to one side as she stared up at him. "I'm thinking about it."

"I'll take that," he said and folded his arms around her, oblivious to the umbrella now dangling upside down.

~⇒

On the eighth of May, Ilse awoke to the sounds of shouting and cheers from the parade ground. Liesl awoke at the same time and stumbled over to Ilse's bed.

"Is it a party for your birthday, Mom? I'll bet Gisele planned it to surprise you."

But even Gisele was not likely to have created such a stir for Ilse's birthday, especially not her first birthday without Franz there to celebrate with her.

"Get dressed," she told Liesl as she threw back the covers and began putting on her clothes. "It must be news—good news."

The hallway of the barracks was filled with sleepy-eyed people coming out of their apartments to investigate the chaos outside. Ilse shielded her eyes from the sun as she tried to make sense of what people were saying.

"It's over!"

"Hitler's dead!"

"We won."

Someone was holding up a newspaper with a headline set in type large and bold enough to be read from yards away. The headline was one word: SURRENDER!

"Oh Mama!" Liesl cried, using the term of address she had always used back in Munich. "This is the best birthday present ever. Everyone will celebrate." She ran off to join her friends, who were dancing in a circle and shrieking with pure joy.

Many of the Jewish residents had begun dancing a folk dance that Ilse had learned was called the *Hora*. It was a lively dance also performed in a circle to music that someone was playing on an accordion and violin. As the circle whirled past her, Gisele spotted her and broke hands with the person next to her, leaving a hole.

"Come on," she urged. "Ilse, it is finally over." Gisele grabbed her hand and pulled her into the circle, and before she knew it, she was dancing with the others, moving with them to the center of the circle with their arms raised high and then back again. She had no idea what the words meant, but she caught onto them quickly and sang and laughed and stumbled round and round with the others until all she saw was the blur of their surroundings racing by as they danced.

Oh, if only Franz might have lived to see this day! The war finally over and the dictators all dead—Hitler by his own hand. She looked at the faces of the people dancing and remembered their stories—so many horrors they had suffered, so many people lost to them forever. By contrast she counted Liesl and herself very fortunate indeed. They had Franz's family, and perhaps now that the war was over in Europe, Marta would come out of hiding or be freed from one of those wretched camps or prisons. The only birthday present that Ilse truly wanted was to be reunited with her sister.

Gradually the dancing slowed and stopped, and although people were still laughing and shouting for the pure joy of it, they had begun to wander away, forming small clusters gathered around a copy of the newspaper or talking in low voices about what this news truly meant for them.

Liesl and her friends were still dancing—a silly little dance called the "Hokey Pokey" that they had learned from their British liberators back in Italy. Ilse moved closer to watch, her arm linked in Gisele's.

Beyond the fence they could hear car horns blaring and people in town celebrating as well. Someone was setting off firecrackers, and somewhere a band was playing. Ilse looked toward the fence and saw a lone figure watching the celebration inside the chain link.

She knew at once that it was Detlef Buch. And she remembered how when they first arrived Liesl had thought those standing outside the fence were the ones imprisoned while she and all the other refugees were free.

Of course they weren't free. The United States government would decide their fate—might already have done so. There had already been a good deal of activity inside the fort, readying things for the day the shelter would be closed for good and they would be held to that promise they had signed nine months earlier.

PART 3

SUMMER-FALL 1945

VE-DAY—HOORAY! BUT WHAT NEXT FOR FT. ONTARIO?

OSWEGO N.Y.—Perhaps no single group of people was more delighted to hear the news of the unconditional surrender in Europe than the residents of Fort Ontario in upstate New York. There nearly a thousand refugees have resided for nine long months, awaiting the end of the war.

They danced, they cheered, they studied newspapers in their native languages to be sure the story was the same. And when they finally came to the full understanding that indeed their war was over, they were faced with a new dilemma: Now What?

There should really be no question. After all, part of the cost of coming here last August was that they promise—in writing—to return to their homes once the war ended. But a lot has changed in those nine months.

For many if not most of them, home no longer exists. The dwellings they once occupied have been either destroyed or given to someone else— perhaps as a reward for turning in the refugee. In many cases their villages and towns have been bombed beyond recognition. Beyond housing, they have no jobs waiting, and with the tens—perhaps hundreds—of thousands of displaced people wandering through Europe, they will have to get in line for housing, for food, for the basics of everyday life.

And there is another line these residents of Fort Ontario will need to join—the line to apply for the chance to legally return to the United States. That's right—these same men, women and children who have lived here for the last nine months, who have proven their willingness to play by the rules, who have made the best of their situation and shown nothing but gratitude for the opportunity given as guests of the president.

They have earned the respect and support of civic leaders in the town of Oswego. Several national charities and nonprofit agencies have also sent letters in support of allowing the refugees to now enter the United States legally as part of the normal immigration quotas.

But the president who extended the original invitation (and set the guidelines for coming and refused to change those rules during his tenure) is dead. His successor has remained silent on the fate of these guests, and for now the original terms stand. They are expected to return to their country of origin.

Put yourself in the shoes of any one of them—people who before they were forced to run or were taken prisoner were talented performers, professionals, heads of businesses. Imagine you are a mother and that your baby was born last month in the fort. Is that child an American by birthright? And if so must the mother and child still go back?

The future for the residents of Fort Ontario is not a case of black and white. It is—for now—a palette of murky grays.

The answers remain with the powers that be in Washington. It is certain that the Fort Ontario Emergency Relief Shelter will close. It is certain that the community created behind that fence will disperse. What is not yet certain is where nearly a thousand displaced people will go to begin yet again.

~≋ CHAPTER 17 ≋~

Joseph Smart resigned at the end of May as director of the shelter and set up the agency Friends of the Fort Ontario Guest Refugees, but he and his family continued to live in one of the officers' brick houses inside the fort. To avoid any accusation of conflict of interest, he made it clear to Theo that until his replacement arrived and was settled Theo was to handle anything that came up.

At the boardinghouse, conversation turned to the war in the Pacific and when that might end, as well. Certainly Selma was focused on when her son might be coming home.

But for Theo and Suzanne and all the residents of the fort, the focus had to be on Washington and what would happen now that the war in Europe had ended. Theo did not miss the irony that on June 6, 1945—exactly one year to the day after the Normandy invasion that had changed the course of the war—Truman transferred responsibility for the shelter and its occupants to the Department of the Interior. Secretary Harold Ickes was known to be sympathetic to the plight of the refugees. He had been the one pushing the sponsored-leave idea. Might this be a turning point for Ilse and the others as Normandy had turned the tide of the war?

Since VE-day Theo had spent most of his time traveling between

Oswego and New York where Joseph Smart had an office for his advocacy group. He tried to get back to the boardinghouse every weekend so that he could have time with Suzanne. They went for rides along the shores of Lake Ontario, sometimes stopping for a picnic or to have supper at a local restaurant in one of the towns situated among the farms and orchards of that part of the state. Sometimes they took Liesl, Ilse, and Gisele along on these excursions, but Theo liked being alone with Suzanne most of all.

They did not discuss the future. For now what they both wanted—needed—was to live in the present. He was surprised to learn that she was an avid baseball fan. She loved listening to him make up silly songs as they sped along on the back roads. But all the while, Theo had an underlying feeling that this could not last.

One June day when he returned to the boardinghouse from a meeting in New York, he saw a note taped to the door of his room. *Call James Sawyer—collect. URGENT!* He stood studying the phone number scrawled on the back of the paper for a long moment.

"Oh, you're back," Hilda Cutter said as she heaved herself up the stairs. "That man has called every single day for the last week." She lifted her eyebrows, clearly expecting an explanation. She had become even more curious than usual about the other boarders ever since Hugh had accepted a new job and moved to Ohio.

"I'll give him a call," he assured her and then went into his room and closed the door.

"Sounds important," Hilda shouted. "Maybe somebody's sick?"

Theo ignored her and breathed a sigh of relief when he heard her door slam. He would call from the fort. The new director would let him make a collect call from there, and that would give him the privacy he needed. Taking off the business suit he wore for travel and for his appointments while in New York, he put on jeans and a long-sleeved white cotton shirt and exchanged his dress wingtips for the tennis shoes that Liesl had talked him into buying when he'd taken her shopping for new shoes.

He did not exactly tiptoe past Hilda's closed door, but he was careful to close the door to his room softly and to walk on the outer edge of each stair so they did not squeak. Downstairs he knocked on Suzanne's door, but there was no answer. So he headed out the back way, picked up the bike resting in the grass, and pedaled off toward the fort.

As he walked the bike through the tunnel and out into the sunlight again, he was taken as he always was by the feeling that he had left one world behind and entered something totally different. He paused for a minute, trying to imagine the fort vacant and unoccupied.

It was difficult, given that the parade ground was filled with children running and playing in the sunlight. A group of Quakers had volunteered to facilitate a summer camp and had organized craft classes and games for the children and teens as well as vocational classes for the adults. Theo watched the activity—it was a village not so very different from Oswego or the devastated communities the refugees had left behind.

Suzanne was sitting in a grove of trees, surrounded by a group of teenagers. He waved and then headed for the administration building.

"Are you running for office or not?" Sawyer demanded when he answered the call. "Cause I gotta say you don't win votes from folks in these parts by staying out there in New York."

"The election is not until November. I thought I would come back in early September and—"

"And that might work if you were running for reelection. But you aren't. You need to decide how serious you are about this, Theo. If we need to get somebody else. . ."

"Don't threaten me, Jim."

Sawyer hesitated and then in a tone that had been reshaped into something approaching conciliatory he said, "Look, it's just that everybody here thinks you are the perfect guy for the job."

Theo couldn't help smiling. "Then what's the problem? Presumably if that's the case, I've got this thing sewed up."

"Let me rephrase," Sawyer said tersely. "Everyone on the committee believes in you. The voters do not know you, and that's the problem—a problem only you can fix."

"I have a job to do here, and trust me, the contacts I am making could prove important down the road."

"Yeah, I get that, but what about the weekends? Come back and attend some events here—press the flesh, kiss a few babies, ride in a Fourth of July parade."

"What about those letters to the editors of area newspapers that I've been sending?"

"Those are great, but folks need a face to put with the name. They may agree with what you say, but they don't vote for a pig in a poke. They want to see what you look like, how you handle yourself on your feet."

"I'll see what I can do," he said. "Set up something for the July Fourth parade."

"And you'll be there? No matter what?"

"No matter what."

But on June 25, word came from Washington that a subcommittee of the House Committee on Immigration and Naturalization would be coming to the fort to conduct a series of hearings. The inference was that these hearings could have a positive impact on the future of the shelter's residents, and everyone was determined to put their best foot forward. Several people were asked to testify, and Theo was surprised to learn that he was one of them. "You represent the family members who already live here in the United States," Joseph Smart reminded him. "You can explain to the committee that many of the residents here in the shelter indeed have places to go and people ready to help them settle into homes and schools and jobs."

Theo thought about the promise he had made to Jim Sawyer. "I need to be back in Wisconsin over the Fourth."

Smart smiled. "If history is any indicator I doubt these men on the House committee plan to spend their holiday in Oswego, Theo. You'll be able to manage both."

In the days before the congressmen arrived, the fort was a beehive of activity. Every building was thoroughly cleaned; the women in charge of the kitchens debated menus for hours; the theater group planned a variety show that would give their visitors a view of life in the camp; and the children used their camp time to set up exhibits of their schoolwork and arts and crafts and to practice songs they could perform for the visitors.

Theo worked between the administration building in the fort and the office of Smart's advocacy agency in New York, gathering data and statistics to present. Suzanne typed up summaries of the histories of several of the residents of the shelter so that Theo could use them as illustrations instead of just offering cold facts and numbers. Everyone worked from early morning until late in the evening, and the atmosphere throughout the shelter was one of purpose and hope—a far cry from the despondent and glum ambiance that had hung over the community like a thick fog for months.

In the rush to have everything ready for the hearings, Ilse set aside her search for Marta and her children. And because they were all so busy, Theo and Suzanne had little private time for being together. Most nights they walked back to the boardinghouse together, but usually they were both too exhausted to do more than share a good-night kiss and go to their separate rooms. Yet Theo felt as if they were growing closer every day. Often as he lay awake at night he would allow himself to fantasize about both of them living and working in Washington. Of course Gordon Langford would also be there. The congressman was coming to the fort for the hearings, and judging by the number of phone messages Selma handed Suzanne, he had not given up pursuing her.

It was his mother who came up with the idea of bringing Suzanne home with him when he came for the Fourth. "We'll show her what life is like in the country," she teased.

"She was raised in a small town, Mom."

"I simply cannot picture that. She seems so. . .I don't know. . . confident and sophisticated."

"Yeah, I can see how you might think that, but trust me. She has doubts and fears like everyone else."

"Well, Ilse has certainly changed her tune when it comes to Suzanne. She absolutely adores her."

Theo had trouble imagining his aunt ever having such a strong emotion about anyone. In spite of whatever progress she might have made in conquering the depression and anxiety of the past, Ilse was still cautious when it came to other people. "I'll see if she can get away, but understand that money is tight for her and—"

"Dad and I will pay her train fare, and she'll eat and sleep here so she'll have no expenses."

Theo's antenna went on alert. "Mom, you're matchmaking."

"Well, of course I am, dear. What are mothers for? Now here's Dad."

Theo's conversation with his father had nothing to do with romance or matchmaking. They talked about the war winding down in the Pacific and about what was happening at the fort. "Well, we're looking forward to having you home, Son. That gal of yours, too."

That gal of yours... Theo couldn't help grinning as he thought about how Suzanne would feel about being called his *gal.*

Ilse's hands shook as she buttoned her dress and checked her reflection in the small hand mirror. Liesl had already left the apartment to join the other children in the dining hall, where the hearings were being held and where testimony from the children was on the agenda for the morning. The Boy Scout troop that had been organized in the shelter would be the first to face the committee of men in suits from Washington. Then the children who were Liesl's age and younger would perform a song followed by testimony from some of the teenagers—two of whom had been accepted into Harvard University for the fall term. Of course it was an honor that they could not accept unless the congressmen could change the minds of others back in Washington. Ilse could not see how these men could harden their hearts against the children, so she had permitted herself a small ray of hope. Theo had convinced her that she should not close the door on an opportunity to stay in the United States by declaring her intent to return to Germany.

"You can always travel to Germany," he had reminded her. "And if you are reunited with Marta and decide that Germany is where you and Liesl should be, you can make that decision then."

No wonder people thought her nephew would make a good representative in the Congress. He had a way of looking at a situation from all sides and making sense of it. Franz had been like that.

"Ready?" Gisele stood at the door of Ilse's apartment, looking as chic as always. "Shall we go and face the masters of our fate?"

Ilse smiled. "According to Theo these men are not all powerful. Something about the need for this subcommittee to make their report and recommendation to the committee of the whole and for that body to make their recommendation to the House of Representatives and. . ." She paused. "And I forget the rest—something about the Senate and the president and. . ."

"It is a first step. We knew that, Ilse. But at least it is movement."

"Nearly a year since we got off that ship and we are just now taking the first step?"

Gisele laughed. "Come along, my friend."

As they walked together to the dining hall, Ilse could not help but think of how much she would miss Gisele once they all went their separate ways. "Whatever happens to us," she said, "we should plan to come back here for a reunion."

"I think that you and I could find somewhere more interesting to get together, Ilse."

"I'm not just talking about the two of us. I am speaking of everyone—the entire village of Fort Ontario."

"That's a wonderful idea, Ilse—and forgive me, but I must say that you are the last person I would ever have imagined suggesting such a thing."

Ilse understood that Gisele was paying her a compliment. "You have inspired me to be more adventurous."

"Oh Ilse, you do not want to imitate me—that will bring you

nothing but trouble." But it was evident that Gisele was pleased.

The two women stepped inside the dining hall just in time to hear the fort's Boy Scout troop giving the pledge to the flag. Ilse studied the faces of the congressmen. They were standing, hands over their hearts, and they were smiling. Surely this was a positive sign.

Across the room she saw Suzanne sitting with a few other reporters. She looked up and smiled, another indication that things were going well. Theo sat just inside the door as he waited for his turn to testify, a stack of folders balanced on his knee. She scanned the room, looking for Liesl, and saw her twisting nervously from side to side, watching the skirt of her dress flare out. And in that moment Ilse realized how her daughter had grown and filled out—a very different little girl than the one she had held on the train coming to Fort Ontario.

Theo's advice had been exactly right. Why would Ilse upset Liesl by taking her back to Germany when it was here in America that her daughter had found confidence and joy and freedom from fear? Once they left the fort—assuming they were permitted to stay in this country—Liesl could go stay with Ellie and Paul on the farm. There was every possibility that Beth and Josef would soon make the journey from England for a reunion with her family. Liesl had been thrilled with that news.

"But what about Josef's family?" she had asked. "Remember that Christmas when his mother came for Sunday dinner and she had a real fur coat and she let me touch it?"

"We'll see, Liesl. One step at a time." Ilse had not told Liesl about Josef's father being a prisoner in a camp nearby, and she had insisted that neither Theo nor Suzanne let anything slip about his presence, either. Her daughter had no idea that Ilse had spoken to the man, much less made it possible for him to contact Josef.

Gisele gripped her arm and nodded to where the children were making their entrance. They lined up before the committee, their hands clasped behind their backs, as one of the women from the Quaker group blew a note into a pitch pipe and the children imitated it. Then together they sang "God Bless America." Looking around, Ilse was fairly certain there was not a single person who was not weeping—or at least trying very hard not to weep. Maybe this was a new beginning for them, after all. Maybe these men in their gray suits, crisp white shirts, and tightly knotted ties would go back to Washington and convince those in power to let them stay.

Almost as soon as she and Theo boarded the train to Wisconsin, Suzanne rested her head on Theo's shoulder and closed her eyes. She had been burning the candle at both ends for weeks now—collecting stories from the shelter during the day, working her shift at the cannery, and coming back to her room to type up her notes or write another of the essays that Edwin had requested.

And there had been the deal she had made with Gordon. When he came as part of the committee for the hearings, he had called her, and she had agreed to see him for dinner at the hotel. This time she was the one with a request.

"I need you to see what you can find out about this woman," she told him, handing him a blurred photograph of Marta and her children. She gave him the facts he needed without telling him the connection to Ilse.

"I don't have time for—" Gordon had been scowling at the photograph, and then he had smiled. "Well, now seems to me what we have here, Suze, is a situation of I scratch your back and you scratch mine."

"I don't understand."

"Sure you do. Each of us needs information the other can get. I find this woman, and you give me the info I need on the Nazi prisoner—and do not tell me you can't because word has it you work with the guy at the local cannery. You've been holding out on me, dollface."

Suzanne stalled by stirring cream and sugar—neither of which she took—into her coffee. If Gordon could find Marta, it would mean everything to Ilse. And Suzanne had come to care for Ilse a great deal.

She wanted to see the woman find some happiness after everything she'd been through.

"Do we have a deal?" Gordon asked.

"If you already know where this man is, why do you need me? Why not question him yourself?"

"Because I suspect you have earned his trust and therefore he is likely to reveal information to you that he would not give me."

She considered her options and found she really had only two—refuse and lose the best chance for Ilse to be reunited with her sister, or agree and betray Detlef. Or perhaps there was a third. . . .

"All right," she said. "And I will provide you the information you want as soon as you get me information on this woman." She tapped the photograph. "Information that is useful."

Gordon was surprised. "You've changed," he said.

"You haven't," she replied.

Now as she allowed the rhythm of the train's rocking, the sounds of metal on metal as the wheels clicked along the rails, and the feel of the hot summer wind rushing through the partially open window brushing her hair and skin to lull her into a half sleep, she thought about that deal she had made.

That night at the cannery she had told Detlef about her deal. As she had suspected, he was anxious to do what he could to help Ilse. "My future is already determined," he said. "But if I could help Ilse. . ."

They agreed to keep the matter between the two of them. Suzanne did not want to raise false hope in Ilse or Theo by telling them about involving Gordon in the search for Marta.

She felt Theo stir as he turned the pages of the report he had delivered to the congressmen, still looking for details he might have left out, although the hearings were over. They were on their way to Wisconsin, to his home. She turned her thoughts to more pleasant matters—a future with Theo.

Surely an invitation to visit his family carried more meaning than a simple invitation to dinner. Theo had even warned her that his mother was a born matchmaker and that she was to simply ignore Ellie's blatant attempts to gather information about where the relationship between them was headed.

So, where are we headed?

Living in the same dwelling, working on the same project, socializing with the same people, the two of them had grown close. They naturally sought each other out whenever they were wrestling with a problem, especially with their work. But the relationship had progressed beyond a workplace friendship. Over the last few weeks, they had spent every free minute together sharing childhood memories, talking about their work and their dreams for the future. They held hands, and those times when they were alone routinely ended in a good-night kiss—often more than one.

If it was hard to say good night when only a flight of stairs separated them, what would it be like once they went their separate ways? Of course, they both hoped that Theo would win the election to Congress. But what if he didn't win? He would go back to farming in Wisconsin. He had told her that.

"We also serve who merely stand in the field," he had joked, but his eyes had reflected the same sadness that she knew he must be seeing in her eyes. He had pulled her into his arms and said, "Look, we are not going to try and predict the future. If the plan is for us to be together, then we will be, and it won't have anything to do with whether or not I get elected."

His certainty had always amazed her, and he seemed equally surprised at her perplexity. "I believe that there is a plan in everything—you know that."

I used to believe that, as well, she had thought at the time, but what possible plan could there have been in what had happened to Natalie and more recently to the millions of people who had been murdered by Hitler simply because they did not conform? Because he needed a scapegoat to excuse his reign of terror?

Her thoughts drifted to Detlef Buch as they always did whenever she thought about the senselessness of what had happened over the last four years. The German had been quieter than usual whenever they met at the library these last few weeks. He had brought her specific names and places that she could feed to Gordon. He had also given her two names to give to Gordon, stating that if these men were still around, they might have more information about Marta and her husband. "They once worked in our embassy in Washington. Of course, that was before ties between our two governments were broken."

"Why would you think they would be available to give information now?"

"Because they were contacts for Frau Schneider's brother-in-law, and more to the point, once the embassy was closed, these men stayed here in America."

She had given Gordon the names, and a few days later he had located one of the men—at least to the point of knowing he was still living in the United States. But the trail had ended there.

The train slowed, rousing her. She sat up and checked her hair and smoothed the skirt of her dress. "Where are we?"

"Chicago. The train will be here long enough for us to get out and stretch our legs a bit—maybe get something to eat." He stood in the aisle and stretched.

"How much longer until we reach Milwaukee and get the bus on to Madison?"

"A couple of hours. Come on. I'm starving."

They ate a snack of peanut butter crackers and cherry Cokes at a newsstand in Union Station that also featured a lunch counter. They talked about the hearings and tried to find clues in the reactions of the congressmen that might offer hints to what would happen next.

"It will be what it will be," Theo said as they reboarded the train. "Let's talk about something else besides the war and the folks at the fort."

"Okay," she readily agreed, but she could not seem to come up with any other topic of conversation. "So, what should we talk about?"

"Well, tomorrow is Sunday, and my folks will be attending meeting for worship. I told them you were a Friend but I did not mention that you—"

"Of course I will go to the meeting with you and your parents, Theo. It would be rude not to go. I am their guest."

"Thank you." His smile reminded her of the first time they had talked and how even then she had been drawn into his eyes as if she were falling into a pool of cool water. He cupped her cheek with his palm. "I mean it. Thank you for everything—for agreeing to come to the farm, for—"

"I wanted to come, Theo. I like your parents, and I'm looking forward to meeting your brother and his family."

Theo groaned.

"What? I thought you and your brother were close."

"We are. It's his wife, Jenny, I'm worried about. She's a bigger matchmaker than Mom is—the woman has been on a mission to get me married off ever since she and Matthew got married. Don't get me wrong—there is not a more caring, sweet woman in the world—but when she makes up her mind that something needs doing..."

"Hey, stop worrying. It's only for a few days, and then we'll be on our way back to Oswego. You can count on me not to go running into the cornfields because your mother and sister-in-law have your best interests at heart."

He grinned and took hold of her hand. "Who told you there are cornfields?"

She nodded toward the window. They had left the city behind, and outside the window a moving picture of barns, farmhouses, and fields rushed past. It was beautiful countryside, but Suzanne thought of what many out-of-towners said about New York City: *It's a nice place to visit, but you wouldn't want to live there.*

As she looked out at the cows grazing in the fields, she knew that the saying absolutely applied to her feelings about living in Wisconsin. She might have grown up in a small town, but these days she was a city girl who was dangerously close to admitting that she was in love with the country boy next to her. She sure hoped he won that election.

CHAPTER 18

Theo's parents met them at the bus station in Madison. Theo did not miss the way his mother greeted Suzanne as if she were already a member of the family. She even insisted that they ride in the backseat together "so we can catch up."

It was Saturday, and they were to take a train back after the parade on Wednesday. Clearly his mom planned to make as much progress as possible during that time toward getting Suzanne and him together on a more permanent basis. He just hoped Suzanne was up for this overdose of family.

"Jim Sawyer called," his dad said, clenching his unlit pipe between his teeth as he drove. "He wants to see you as soon as possible. I told him to come on by the house tonight."

"Dad, we just got here, and—"

"Get it out of the way, Son, and then you and Suzie can enjoy your time here. That is, if your mom and sister-in-law don't take over." He winked at Theo.

Suzie. He'd never heard anyone call her anything but Suzanne. She had once told him that her editor liked to shorten her given name, but she suspected that was more because he was a man of few words and always in a hurry.

Theo could not imagine calling her Suzie. It just didn't fit the woman he had come to know—and love. She was far too serious and intense to be a *Suzie*. He wondered if she would object and made a mental note to ask her about her preference. If she did object, he would have to set his parents straight.

"Matthew and Jenny and the children are coming over for supper," he heard his mother explaining. "You and Jenny are going to get on like sisters—I just know it."

"I'm looking forward to meeting them," Suzanne replied.

"And Jim Sawyer—he's the one who talked Theo into running for Congress—he's stopping by later. I told him to bring Ethel, his wife, and come for dessert. I made a peach cobbler, and Jenny is churning up some vanilla ice cream."

"You make your own ice cream?" Theo heard Suzanne's voice crack slightly.

"Mom, you're scaring her."

"No, not at all," Suzanne protested. "It's just that. . .ice cream from scratch?"

"Well, not every time we eat ice cream, but this is a special occasion and. . ." Now it was his mom who sounded unsure of herself.

"Trust me, Suzie," Theo's dad said, "you have never had ice cream like this. It'll put some meat on you."

"Dad's right," Theo said. "One scoop of that stuff on top of Mom's cobbler and you won't need to eat for a week."

"Sounds like we should maybe start with dessert," Suzanne said. Theo's parents both chuckled, and he saw his mom squeeze Suzanne's hand. They arrived at the farmhouse minutes later, and Suzanne scrambled from the car and spun slowly around, taking it all in. "Oh Theo, it is like a picture postcard—pure Americana."

If he could have risked taking her in his arms in that moment without his mother fainting from sheer joy, he would have. Instead he bent and pulled a piece of grass and stuck it in his mouth. "Aw, shucks, miss, that's just downright kind of you."

She giggled and took a step toward him, and he instinctively knew that she had been about to hook her arms around his neck as she sometimes did—a gesture that almost always led to them kissing.

His dad cleared his throat as he picked up their suitcases. "Show her around the place, Theo. I'll just set these at the foot of the stairs."

"But," his mom started to protest.

"Come along, Ellie. Give these two some time to get settled in."

Hand in hand, Theo and Suzanne walked around the farm. He pointed out the outbuildings and explained the purpose of each then described the different crops coming up in the fields. As they stood by a fence and watched the cows lumber across the pasture toward the barn, he finally stopped talking.

"So peaceful," she murmured after a while.

"Yeah. I've always loved this part of the day here."

"Why this time specifically?"

"I don't really know. The day is coming to a close, and most likely nothing catastrophic has happened. It's almost time to sit down to supper and hear everybody talk about their day. In winter once the cows are in and milked and you're walking back to the house, there's this glow from the lamps—a kind of welcome and warmth that makes the dark and cold bearable. And the promise of what's waiting inside—a fire, maybe a second piece of pie and a glass of milk. . ."

She rested her head against his chest as he wrapped his arm around her. "You do love it here, don't you?"

"I do. It's home. It always will be."

She didn't say anything for a long moment. "So how are you going to feel about living in a city like Washington? I mean you can always come back for holidays and when Congress isn't in session, but—"

He tightened his hold on her. "Ah, but living in Washington will have other benefits like getting to see you every day." He kissed her temple. "Now, how about I show you how to milk a cow?"

"How about you go milk Bessie or Bossy or whatever their names are, and I'll go see what I can do to help your mom get dinner—supper—on the table?"

"Fine, but don't think you can spend all this time here and never milk a cow—and by the way, we have classy names for our animals. That—for example—is Ophelia."

Suzanne laughed and started walking back to the house, and Theo could not help but imagine her making that walk on a regular basis.

Norman Rockwell could have certainly used the scene around the Bridgewaters' dinner table as one of his covers for the *Saturday Evening Post*. It might be titled "This is why we fought!" Certainly the setting outside the warm and comfortable home had taken her breath away with its cream-colored stone accented by forest-green shutters and a porch lined with rocking chairs. This all set against a backdrop of a vibrant red barn, fields of green and gold crops, and a sky that defined the word *azure*. To think such scenes actually existed beyond some Hollywood set!

But it was the gathering of family and friends around a huge oak pedestal table in a dining room that was larger than her Washington apartment, savoring the unique combination of peach cobbler straight from the oven with a scoop of sweet, creamy, cold vanilla ice cream melting over the crust and fruit that touched her heart.

Matthew and Jenny's two toddlers had squealed with delight when Jim Sawyer and his wife arrived, bringing their teenaged daughter, Dora, with them.

"Dora often babysits for the children," Ellie explained. "They adore her, and the feeling is mutual so now we adults can visit in peace." She handed Suzanne a tray stacked with cups and saucers then wrapped her hand in the skirt of her apron to pick up a pot of coffee as she led the way back to the dining room.

They talked about neighbors and friends who had been asking about Theo, and that led to Theo and Suzanne bringing them up to date on what was happening at the shelter.

"Things are a mess pretty much everywhere since Roosevelt died," Matthew commented. "Nobody knows what to expect from this Truman."

"Oh, I don't know. I think the man is just playing it close to the vest until he's had time to catch up," Jim Sawyer said.

"No politics at mealtime," his wife murmured as she placed her hand on his arm. "Suzanne, where are you from originally?"

She had never liked being the center of attention, even in circumstances like this where she had no doubt that everyone seated around the table seemed intent on liking her. "I. . .uh. . .grew up in a small town in Virginia," she said.

"Near Washington?" Paul asked.

"Dad, Virginia is a big state. Suzanne grew up in the mountains."

"Blue Ridge?" Sawyer guessed.

"Appa-latch-chian," Suzanne said softly—aware that in this part of the country it was pronounced as *lay* rather than *latch*.

"I thought those mountains were in New York," Jenny said.

"The range forms the dividing line between the Eastern Seaboard and the Midwest and includes the Blue Ridge among others. In various ways it runs all the way from Newfoundland into Alabama." She hoped she didn't sound argumentative. The truth was that she was exhausted and there were so many people—strangers to her. She wished that she and Theo could have had a quiet dinner with just his parents—at least on this first night of the visit. She realized that she so wanted to make a good impression.

"Suzanne, would you like more coffee?" Theo's mother seemed to know that she was uncomfortable with the direction the conversation had taken. "I promise you," she added, "that we will not grill you any more tonight."

"Nope," Theo's dad said with a wink, "we'll set up the spotlight and continue this whole business out in the barn tomorrow."

Suzanne relaxed.

"Why don't you two go sit on the porch and catch your breath," Ellie suggested. "Jenny and Ethel and I can handle the clearing up, and I know these men want to talk farm business."

"Please let me help as well," Suzanne offered.

"Not a chance," Theo said. "Come with me. I want to show you something." He took hold of her hand and tugged her toward the back door.

"We need to talk, Theo," Jim Sawyer called out, although he was still seated at the table drinking his third cup of coffee.

"Tomorrow," Theo called back.

"Tonight," Sawyer shouted.

Theo let the banging of the screen door serve as his answer as he led Suzanne across the yard to an outbuilding he had skipped on their earlier tour.

"You should talk to him," Suzanne said. "He's only trying to make sure that you're ready."

"I know. But the parade isn't until Wednesday, and it's only Saturday. We've got time." He pulled open the door of the building and pulled a string to illuminate the interior.

"Obviously there's a car under there," Suzanne said, pointing to the tan canvas covering.

"Not just any car. A 1935 Plymouth convertible." He swept away the covering like a magician. "Ta da!"

"I love it," Suzanne said as she ran her finger lightly—reverently—over the ice-blue hood. "Does it run?"

"It will by the time we ride in the parade in it on Wednesday." He rolled up his shirtsleeves and then opened the hood. "Hand me that wrench over there." He pointed to a workbench where hand tools were lined up precisely.

"Where did you get this car?"

"I bought it when I was a senior in high school. Do you like it?"

"I love it."

He grinned. "I was hoping you might."

"But I can't ride in the parade with you, Theo."

"Why not?"

"How would that look?"

"Like I'm one lucky guy?"

"Be serious. You're in the parade because you are a candidate for political office. If I was there, people would wonder who I was."

"And?"

"And you don't want that. And trust me. Mr. Sawyer definitely doesn't want that. He wants the focus to be squarely on you."

She could see by the way the muscles in his forearms tensed that he didn't like being told what he could and could not do. He ducked under the hood and continued working on fine-tuning the engine. "If I can get Jim to agree, will you ride with me then?"

"He'll never agree."

Theo stood up and turned to face her. "But if he does?"

"Theo, if we were engaged or married, then maybe but—"

"That can be arranged," he said as he tucked a strand of her hair behind her ear. She tried to read his expression in the dim glow of the single lightbulb. He had to be kidding around—didn't he?

"Okay, it's been a long, exhausting day and you are clearly starting to show the effects." She kissed his cheek. "I'm going to bed, and you should have that meeting with Mr. Sawyer. I'll see you in the morning."

He moved to the doorway, and she knew he was watching as she started across the yard and up to the house. "Hey, Suzanne?"

She hesitated but did not turn around. "Yeah?"

"I love you."

"Good to know," she said and continued on her way. But she was smiling, and she felt light—as if she could float back to the farmhouse.

After she'd thanked Theo's parents and said her good-nights, she couldn't help but relive that moment in the yard and Theo's words. He hadn't said, "I think I love you." True to form, he had entertained no doubt at all.

But once she had changed into her nightgown and turned out the lights, she couldn't help but consider the doubts that were never far from her mind whenever her life seemed to finally be going in a positive direction. Loving Theo carried with it a host of complications. At the top of the list was what would happen if he didn't win a seat in Congress? That led to questions about whether or not he would understand her need to continue to pursue her career as a journalist or at least as a writer.

The farm was certainly idyllic, but she was not like Theo's mother. She could never be content with the life that Ellie Bridgewater so obviously loved. No, overall it would be best if Suzanne did not allow her emotions to overpower her common sense.

A tap at the door made her sit up, and she reached to turn on the bedside lamp. Pulling her covers to her chin she said, "Come in," and was relieved to see Ellie peeking around the door.

"Oh, Suzanne, forgive me. I thought you might be reading. I know whenever Paul and I travel I have such a hard time getting to sleep, especially that first night."

"Come in. I was just lying here, thinking."

Ellie sat on the side of the bed and pulled an envelope from the pocket of her housedress. "This letter from our daughter Elizabeth arrived a few days ago. As you will see, she had enclosed a letter for Liesl and another for Ilse. Will you see that they receive them?"

"Of course, but why not give them to Theo?"

"I was going to do that, but I overheard Paul and Theo and Jim talking, and it seems likely that Theo will not be returning to Oswego with you."

"Why not?"

"Jim believes that it's important for Theo to spend the time from now until the election here."

Suzanne knew this was necessary, but the idea of returning to Oswego alone. . .of Theo being half a country away. . .

Ellie patted her hand. "I know it's hard, dear, but in the long run it is for the best, don't you think?"

"Yes. Of course."

"Now then, I had one more thing I wanted to tell you—our Friends group takes turns meeting in each other's houses, and I'm afraid that I scheduled the meeting for worship to be here tomorrow. Ilse had once mentioned that you were raised Quaker but these days you were not. . . that is. . ."

"It has been some time since I attended a meeting for worship, Mrs. Bridgewater. Work got in the way. Life got in the way. But lately watching how religion has sustained so many of the residents at the fort, I've had to ask myself whether or not I made a mistake when I turned away. If it's all right with you, I would very much like to take part in tomorrow's meeting."

Ellie smiled. "You will be most welcome, and we will all hold you in the Light." She stood up and glanced around the room, stopping to straighten the shade on the bedside lamp. "Do you have everything you need?"

"Yes, thank you. You and Mr. Bridgewater have been so kind."

Early Sunday morning Suzanne helped Theo and his dad with the chores. They insisted that she at least attempt to milk a cow. "She's a natural," Paul announced. "You better hang on to this one, Son. She's a keeper."

"I plan to," Theo replied.

Again Suzanne wondered if he was teasing. After his warnings about his mother's matchmaking, why would he say such things? Perhaps she had misread his declaration of love? Maybe he had simply meant that he cared for her—as a friend he could count on. When it came to romance, Suzanne had been burned before—most recently and seriously by placing her trust in Gordon Langford. Not that she put Theo in the same category at all, but men had a habit of saying things they didn't necessarily mean the way she might think they were meant. Theo would never intentionally hurt her. Still, she needed to be careful that she didn't get swept up into the whole Norman Rockwell thing.

"This milking thing is hard work," she said lightly. "When's breakfast?"

After a huge country breakfast of pancakes, eggs, sausages, and biscuits, everyone pitched in to wash the dishes and move the dining-room chairs to the living room. They arranged the extra chairs along with the living-room furniture in a circle for the meeting. As soon as everything was in place, Ellie stationed herself by the front door to welcome the others, while Paul took a chair in the circle, signaling the beginning of the meeting and the silence that this entailed. Everyone entered the room in respectful silence and took a seat, although they each smiled and nodded at Theo, who had waited for Suzanne to choose her place and then sat next to her. Within a few minutes the room was full of people—and stillness. At first Suzanne felt anxious and out of place. She was a fraud among these believers, and they didn't seem to notice.

She closed her eyes, willing her hands to relax and fall open on her lap with palms facing up. After a few seconds she became aware of the sounds within the silence—the distant lowing of the cows, the wind playing with a wind chime on the front porch, Theo's steady breathing. Gradually she felt the clamor of work and deadlines and future decisions melt into the silence, replaced by a sense of calm and serenity that she had not felt in a very long time.

After a while Paul stood, and Suzanne waited for his vocal ministry. "I am thinking today," he said, "about what a truly special Independence Day we will be celebrating this year. The war in Europe is over, and we have been brought out of that darkness." In the tradition of Friends everywhere his message was brief—a single observation offered for others to ponder.

He sat down, and as was their custom, the room went silent once again. Now Suzanne found herself thinking about the residents of the fort, especially those she had come to know so well. She centered her thoughts on Ilse. Her husband was dead, her home was gone, and she had nothing more than the possessions she had managed to acquire since coming to America. She was facing such uncertainty for herself and her child.

For the first time in a very long time, Suzanne realized that she was praying for God to watch over Ilse and Liesl and hold them in His Light as they began this new phase of their lives. Then she realized that silent tears were leaking through the lashes of her closed eyes and bathing her cheeks. She let the tears fall, aware that she had sorely missed this simple act of sitting in silence and releasing all of her worries and concerns to the higher power of God's Light.

The Fourth of July celebration at the fort was the residents' first experience with this unique American holiday. Several buildings were festooned with bunting in red, white, and blue, and walking past, Ilse was reminded of the early days of the Reich when every public building had been draped in the brilliant scarlet accented by the black cross of Hitler's Nazi Party. That felt like another time—another life. The war was over, and as had been the case following the first war—the so-called Great War to end all wars—Ilse understood that once again her beloved homeland lay in ruins economically and physically. So it was hard for her to completely enjoy the celebrations these Americans staged to celebrate their independence. She had to wonder if Germany would ever truly be independent again—the rest of the world must hate them so.

"Mom, can we go downtown and watch the parade? Please?" Liesl was wearing a red blouse with navy-blue shorts and a white bow in her hair. Her accent carried only a hint of her German heritage, and now that the war had ended she had stopped asking questions about what would happen to them next. It was as if she had decided to ignore the promise they had made to return to Germany. "Mom? Can we please?"

"Yes, we can go."

Liesl ran to her and gave her a kiss. "Thanks, Mom. I'll go see if Gisele wants to go with us while you change."

"Change?"

"You can't wear that." Liesl scowled at Ilse's faded housedress. "It's a holiday." She ran to the locker that served as their closet and pulled out a white dress that Ilse had worn once. "This one with a red belt."

"I do not have a red belt."

"I'll borrow one from Gisele. . .and a hat." She blew Ilse a kiss and raced out the door.

Ilse watched her go. How she dreaded the day they would return to Munich, dreaded the sadness and distress that such a move was bound to cause Liesl. Yet they had to go somewhere. The fort was to be shut down—the process had already begun. Gisele had once suggested that Ilse tell the authorities who managed the surveys that she and Liesl would go to England where Beth and Josef were—where they had family.

"You can search for Marta and the children from there as easily as you can from Munich," she had argued. "It would be the perfect compromise for Liesl. You have told me how she adores her cousin Beth, and she would still be in an English-speaking country."

But just before Theo left for Wisconsin, he had told her that Beth and Josef had applied for visas to come to the United States. "She doesn't want to say anything to our folks just yet," he had added. "She doesn't want to get their hopes up in case they get turned down." Of course being married to Josef—a German and the son of a Gestapo agent—made the likelihood of rejection more of a probability. If Beth and Josef could not get visas, then going to England might be worth considering.

"Ready, Mom?" Liesl had not even reached the door before she called out.

"Mind your manners, young lady," Ilse scolded her. "You are not the sole occupant of this building."

"Sorry. Why haven't you changed? I brought the belt, and Gisele has a hat for you."

"It is not necessary for me to dress up, Liesl. This is an American holiday."

"And we are guests of the Americans, so it's like a party and we should show respect by looking our best, right?"

Gisele hid a smile. "The child has a point. Go change."

Ilse let out a sigh of frustration and headed for the tiny bedroom, pulling the curtain that covered the doorway closed behind her. She put on the white cotton dress that had a small round collar, a flared skirt that fell to the middle of her calves, and tiny pearl buttons from the neckline to her waist. She threaded the slender red patent leather belt through the belt loops and then stepped into a pair of white sandals. She twisted her mostly gray hair into a chignon low on her neck and positioned the hat—a straw cloche with a red grosgrain ribbon for a band. She looked in the mirror and smiled.

"You look ten years younger, my friend," Gisele said when Ilse pulled open the curtain.

"You look so pretty, Mom," Liesl exclaimed.

Ilse felt her cheeks blush with the pleasure of their compliments and busied herself pretending to look for her handbag. It seemed like a very long time since anyone had told her she looked pretty—something Franz used to tell her daily.

"Thank you both. Shall we go?"

Gisele crooked her elbows, inviting Ilse and Liesl to link arms with her, and like three young girls, they set off for town.

The streets were crowded with people waiting to see the parade. Everyone was in a good mood, laughing and talking in voices high pitched with excitement. As the trio from the fort made their way along the street looking for a vantage point from which to see the parade, Ilse could not help but notice that no one looked at them with wariness or even reserve the way the locals had looked at them when they first arrived. Now the citizens of Oswego greeted them with smiles that were—for the most part—warm and welcoming.

"There's Nancy," Liesl cried out and took off to catch up with her friend and the rest of the Driver family. At that very moment Ilse saw Detlef Buch watching her from across the street.

He tipped his hat and walked parallel to her on the opposite side of the street as the units of the parade moved by. He had something to tell her—she was certain of that. But when Gisele saw him, she took Ilse's arm and led her to where Liesl and Nancy had found a place to stand where they could see the parade more clearly.

When Ilse looked back she saw that Herr Buch had stopped walking, although he was still looking at her. When her eyes met his, he tipped his hat again and disappeared into the crowd.

CHAPTER 19

Two weeks after the Fourth of July, Suzanne was back in Washington, cleaning her apartment preparatory to moving back in. With Theo in Wisconsin and the shelter preparing to close down and soldiers returning from Europe looking for work, there was little for her in Oswego these days. Edwin had offered her some freelance work, and she had taken a part-time job at a shop just down the street from her apartment to make ends meet.

Surprisingly true to his word, Gordon provided her with updates on his search for Marta and also gave her information about the fate of the refugees. The hearings at the fort had resulted in a positive report from the subcommittee. But when the matter was moved to the full committee, the congressmen had rejected the recommendation for sponsored leave and had in fact upheld the original plan for all refugees to return to their country of origin or some other country willing to receive them now that the war was over. It appeared that the United States of America was not one of those countries.

The single bright spot in her days was Theo's nightly telephone calls. She had protested the expense but had to admit that those calls were the highlight of her day.

As she unpacked and got resettled into her apartment, she had turned on the radio to keep her company. A man's voice droned on in the background. Vaguely she recognized the voice of Robert St. John, a well-respected broadcaster for NBC's radio network. She was paying only scant attention to the message when all of a sudden she heard, "But now. . .now they were being invited to America as guests of the United States!"

She ran to the small front room to turn up the sound. Could it be? After all this time was it possible that a national broadcaster was actually talking about the residents at the fort?

"Nineteen of those refugees we invited to this country have sons in our armed forces, fighting for liberty and democracy and freedom. Yet the parents are kept behind wire fences."

The journalist went on talking about how the people in Fort Ontario could only leave the fort for six hours a day, could not even visit family members living in the United States unless those people happened to live in Oswego, had been deprived of the opportunity to accept gainful employment or pursue a career. He called FDR's action a "gesture" and a "token." His tone and inflection left no doubt where he stood on the subject of what should happen for the refugees. He was adamant that they had earned the right to stay.

Suzanne's heart was racing. Finally someone relatively well known was telling the real story of the residents of Fort Ontario, and he was not pulling any punches. He gave the usual excuses—that they had known they would be sent back, that to let them stay could disrupt the economy, that they had come under Roosevelt's administration and now Roosevelt was dead.

"Guests of America? They've overstayed their welcome. Let them go back where they came from," St. John said sarcastically. And then he added a message for his listeners. "If you don't happen to feel that way, drop a card to your congressman." Suzanne leaned even closer to the radio as static threatened to overpower the message. "The fate of these. . .people. . .[*static*]. . .may well depend on whether you care. I hope you do."

An announcer ended the broadcast by reminding the audience that they had been listening to Robert St. John. The refugees could not have chosen a more passionate and effective spokesperson. Over the course of his career, St. John had been beaten up by Al Capone's thugs, had covered London during the Blitz, and had been wounded by the Nazis in the Balkans. His style of delivery could sometimes take on the tone of a fire-and-brimstone preacher, but he always made his point. He was a newsman Suzanne had long admired.

Now she had to wonder if his broadcast would get results. Maybe he had gone too far. After all, Roosevelt had at least made the gesture—token that it was. So although she had no doubt that he would get a reaction, the question was, what kind of reaction. She wished she could talk to Theo but knew she needed to wait for his call. In the meantime she had to speak with someone. So she called Edwin.

"I take it you just heard St. John's broadcast," Edwin said as soon as he knew she was calling. "Pretty powerful stuff there."

"Do you think it will make a difference?"

"Depends on who was listening."

"Truman?"

"Possibly. If you came back here to follow the story, Suzie, then follow it. Will the public speak up, and will it make a difference? Call St. John—maybe he'll give you an exclusive. Good to have you back in town, kiddo." He rang off.

She mentally calculated how long it might take for public opinion to kick in. It was possible that some newspapers might publish a story with excerpts from the broadcast. That would certainly broaden the audience. She still had a contact at the National Broadcasting Company's news department in Washington. She flipped through her roster of colleagues and dialed her friend, who promised to let her know if there was a significant reaction to St. John's broadcast.

Then she made herself a peanut butter and banana sandwich and sat down to wait for Theo's call, while she made notes for the interview she hoped she might get with Robert St. John.

Jim Sawyer had been dead wrong about what people wanted in a candidate for Congress. They might be war weary, but that did not mean they didn't want a soldier—a hero—as their candidate. The other party had figured that out, and Theo found himself running against a former marine who had been sent home after being wounded at Normandy.

The two candidates had a good deal in common. They were about the same age, had college educations, and came from families that were well respected in the district. They were both tall and athletic. Both had an easy smile and a natural grace when it came to meeting people. But one of them had gone to war—and the other had not.

"You can't be thinking that way," Jim argued. "The election is months away, and anything can happen."

"I'm just being pragmatic."

"You're talking like you've already lost—given up. It's starting to come across in your speeches. Stop talking about those people out in the fort in New York. This is Wisconsin. The voters want to know what you plan to do for them, not your aunt in Oswego."

"I talk about my aunt and niece because they illustrate why this country went to war in the first place. I talk about them and others from the fort because every one of them has had to find courage and strength and stand up to evil."

"But those stories have nothing to do with the folks you will represent. They want to know how postwar will affect their lives—farm prices, jobs, their kids."

"I get that but—"

"Look, son, you need to pay attention to what I'm telling you. Either you change your message, or you lose this election. It's that simple. So you decide." He walked away and did not look back.

Theo watched him go. He knew the man was right. He'd seen it on the faces of the small crowds that showed up to hear what he had to say. The minute he started talking about his experience with Smart's advocacy group, they lost interest. Theo had even been heckled once or twice. "What do a bunch of Jews have to do with us?" one man had shouted. "Let them honor the promise they made when FDR brought them here and go home."

Of course, that was exactly the point that Theo had been trying to make—the residents of the fort had nothing to go back to, unlike the people in Wisconsin. Yes, the voters here had survived the Depression and the war, and in some cases they had paid a heavy price for that, but now was a time for rebuilding and for coming together. And it was because Theo knew that these Americans understood hardship and survival that he would have thought they would have responded to his message of coming together in a world where every person could enjoy the freedoms that were the foundation of a democracy.

But he also understood what Jim was telling him. More to the point, he knew that Jim was right. He could not make change by simply wishing people would act in a certain way. As always at the end of the day, he was looking forward to his nightly call to Suzanne. She understood what he was trying to do. They would just have to come up with a simpler way for him to deliver his message—one that would touch the citizens of Wisconsin and get him elected to Congress.

He had barely said hello before Suzanne began telling him about Robert St. John's broadcast. "This is it," she said, her voice almost squeaky with excitement. "Now all across this country people are bound to rise up and insist that Congress act. Oh Theo, finally."

She told him about the story she was working on that would focus on listener reaction to the St. John piece. "I called the station, and if phone calls are any indication, public opinion is running high on the positive side—almost eighty percent. There have even been calls from former servicemen talking about what the refugees would find if they are sent back."

"And the other twenty percent?"

"The usual." She sighed. "Actually think about Hilda and Hugh and you can pretty much know what the negative callers are saying. One caller even said St. John must be a Jew himself. People can be so. . ." She fumbled for the right word.

Theo was glad to hear her so excited. This was the kind of thing she lived for—a good story. "Hey, the good news is that overwhelmingly people want to do the right thing. But the best news is that it sounds like things are coming together for you. You've got the stories of the people at the fort plus Buch's story and now this."

"Plus Edwin has hinted that there might soon be a permanent opening on the political beat in the newsroom." She sounded happier than he had ever heard her sound before.

"That's terrific. As my dad might say, 'You are cooking with gas, lady.'"

"I take it that's a compliment?"

"Yep."

She laughed. "And what's happening on the campaign trail?"

Because he didn't want to rain on her good news, he downplayed his situation. "Moving along," he said. "Wish you could be here with me."

"I miss you, too, but just think, Theo. We'll be able to start the New Year together right here in Washington. You'll be sworn into the new Congress, and I'll be back at the paper doing real reporting, and Ilse and Liesl. . ." She paused. "Where do you think they'll be?"

"No clue. My folks are trying to persuade Ilse to stay if they get that option. She can always travel to Europe if there is word of Marta, but if she stays somewhere in America Liesl will be happier."

"Still so many unknowns," Suzanne said softly.

"Well, here's something you can count on," Theo said. "I love you."

There was a pause that went on long enough to scream her doubt. "Do you mean that?" she said finally.

He felt a prickle of irritation. Of course he meant it. Hadn't he been the one saying it? She was the one. . . . He took a deep breath to calm himself. "Hey, here's another of Dad's favorite sayings: you can take that to the bank."

Another pause. How he wished they were face-to-face!

"Hey, Theo?"

"Yeah."

"I don't think I've ever said this out loud."

Is this it? Finally?

"What's that?" He realized he was holding his breath, clenching his fist the way he did when he really wanted something.

"I am really, really glad you came into my life." She blew a kiss into the receiver. "Sleep tight," she whispered and hung up.

Ever since the Fourth of July parade, Ilse had not been able to get Detlef Buch out of her mind. The way he had watched her from his position across the street as the parade units marched by, she had been certain he wanted to speak with her. But Gisele had also spotted him, and she had steered Ilse away.

"I do not trust that man, and neither should you," she had lectured Ilse as they walked back to the fort together after Mrs. Driver had invited Liesl to come to her house for supper.

"A real American holiday supper, Mom," Liesl had announced. "Please?"

Ilse had given her permission against her better judgment. The more enthralled Liesl became with all things American, the harder it was going to be when the day came that they had to return to Europe. And if by some miracle the United States government changed its mind and permitted them to stay, then she could not argue with the logic presented by Theo and his parents that she and Liesl would move to Wisconsin to be close to family—Franz's family. Liesl's family. But not hers. Franz's sister and her husband were good, caring people, and Ilse knew they wanted only the best for her and Liesl. But she missed her sister. Other than Franz, she had always turned to Marta whenever life's challenges threatened to overwhelm her.

Weeks had passed since the parade, and she still had not been able to find a way to see Herr Buch. If Suzanne were here, Ilse could ask her to arrange a meeting, but Suzanne had returned to Washington right after visiting the farm with Theo. Theo was occupied with his campaign for a seat in Congress. Gisele disapproved of her having any contact with the Gestapo agent, and Ilse did not have an address or telephone number to contact him. So whatever she may have thought about the way he kept watching her at the parade, apparently she had been mistaken. Because although she had no way of contacting him, he knew how to get a message to her. It was certainly no mystery where she might find her.

After she finished her shift in the children's center, she walked slowly across the parade ground toward the barracks. It was hot and humid without the usual breeze off the lake. Her hair clung to her neck, and her dress was damp with perspiration. She was so very tired. She was tired of living in uncertainty, tired of the tiny apartment with its thin walls. She was tired of trying to make what few decisions she had control of without Franz, tired of the meals in the dining hall where even what they had to eat was decided for them. Most of all, she was tired of having to request a pass just to visit her husband's grave. That more than anything made her realize that they were still as far from real freedom as they had been the day they arrived.

They had been here a year, and how her life had changed in that time. She missed Franz so much—missed the companionship of talking things through with him at the end of the day, missed him holding her at night and the certainty that came with his love—the one thing she had always been able to count on no matter what happened.

"Mrs. Schneider?" One of the boys who lived down the hall from her ran across the parade ground, calling her name. She stopped and waited for him to catch up.

"Hello, Rudy," she said.

He held out an envelope to her. "That man at the fence asked me to give you this." He jerked a thumb toward the fence behind them, but no one was there. "I guess he must have left, but he gave me a whole quarter to make the delivery."

After Rudy ran off to continue his soccer game with his friends, Ilse slid her thumbnail under the glued flap of the envelope. Inside was a single sheet of onionskin paper with the following message:

Dear Frau Schneider,

I have been able to learn that your sister and the children were not taken into custody with your brother-in-law as I had first thought. Lucas had made arrangements for their safe passage out of the country. That is all I know or can discern from my limited contacts. I have written to Josef to see what he can find out. I am certain that he will be in touch with you once he has learned further information.

Also I must thank you, for it was through my search for your sister that I learned that my wife is in South America—Argentina. As you may imagine, I long to be reunited with her in much the same way that you wish to see your sister again.

I wish you and your daughter well as you leave your accommodations here in Oswego and begin a new—and hopefully more peaceful—phase of your life together. Your husband was a man of strength and honor, and it has been my great privilege to know you both.

Sincerely,
Detlef Buch

Ilse turned the page over, but the other side was blank. She read through the message again, her heart racing. If Marta and the children had escaped, then perhaps they were safe. A third reading gave her one more piece of news—Detlef Buch was saying good-bye.

She scanned the landscape outside the fence but saw nothing other than the usual activity of cars and trucks passing on the streets that ran past the fort, children riding their bicycles, and neighbors calling out to one another from their porches or front walks. There was no sign of Detlef. How odd that she had come to think of him by his given name rather than as Herr Buch. It was almost as if she had begun to count him among those few people she considered to be her friends.

But of course now that the war was over, he and the other POWs would be sent back to Europe as well. He would be charged and would stand trial. He would be sentenced to prison, perhaps to die. She squeezed her eyes closed, trying to come to terms with what this man had done for her and for Franz. She needed to understand how a monster that knowingly sent hundreds—perhaps thousands—to suffer a certain death could open his heart to warn her husband of his impending arrest and offer her the solace that her beloved sister might be safe.

After supper that evening, she showed the letter to Gisele. "Do you believe him?" her friend asked skeptically.

"Why would he lie?"

Gisele smiled. "Because such men take pleasure in raising hopes and then destroying them. Such men enjoy playing with fragile emotions."

Ilse felt a flicker of irritation. "You do not know him."

"And neither do you, Ilse. He is your niece's father-in-law, but that is pure circumstance—it does not make him family and it does not mean that you must defend him."

Gisele was right, of course. Ilse knew nothing of this man—not really. "I will write to my niece tonight and ask her and Herr Buch's son to see if they can find Marta. Then we will know if the monster deep down still has genuine kindness to offer."

"You amaze me. Your determination to find the good in everyone is touching and even inspiring. But Ilse, have you not suffered enough? Just please be careful, all right?"

"I am not in any danger, Gisele." Ilse could not help but think that sometimes Gisele's inclination toward the dramatic and dark side of life could cloud her willingness to see hope and light.

Gisele shrugged and lit a fresh cigarette. "Your heart is in danger, ma chérie. This man has offered you hope, and he knows it may be false hope."

"But if they escaped, they might have used one of the routes you talked about—the very one that you helped others travel."

"Yes, and it was an escape route well known to the Nazis, to the Gestapo."

"But—"

Gisele placed her arm around Ilse's shoulder, her features softening as she said, "I hope that I am wrong, Ilse. I hope that somehow this man has found some common decency and that he is genuinely trying to help, but experience is a strict taskmaster, and experience tells me that you should prepare yourself for disappointment."

"Still I will write to my niece," Ilse said stubbornly.

Gisele smiled. "And to think you told me that once you were so weak and fearful that at times you could not leave your bed. Look at you now."

The two women stood outside the barracks. The night before them promised to be another in a weeklong siege of sticky and hot August nights, and everyone was reluctant to go inside.

"Have you decided where you will go, Gisele?"

The actress laughed. "I haven't yet decided who I am anymore. Actress? I'm getting a bit old for the roles I once played, and besides, who knows the state of French theater these days? Resistance worker? There is not much call for that now that the war has ended." Again she lifted one shoulder in her trademark shrug as she blew out a long stream of smoke. "For the first time in my life I can see no options, Ilse, and frankly that terrifies me."

Ilse had never once thought of her friend as anything other than self-reliant and confident. Of all the residents in the fort, everyone thought the one who was sure to make a success of the experience would be Gisele. Ilse had never seen this vulnerable side of her friend. She took hold of Gisele's hand.

"We will find our way," she assured her. "You and I." And when she saw tears glisten on Gisele's lashes, she understood that sometimes the people who appear to be strongest need the reassurance and the strength that comes with friendship. "Let's go to town for supper," Ilse suggested and saw by the widening of Gisele's eyes that she had taken her friend by surprise.

"It's not like you to be so. . ."

"Spontaneous?" Ilse laughed. "No, I suppose it isn't. But Liesl is at her friend's house, and we have to eat, so why not?"

Gisele took her time drawing in a last puff of her cigarette before dropping it and crushing out the embers with her shoe. "This would not be your way of perhaps running into Buch, would it?"

"I am not thinking of Herr Buch, Gisele. I am thinking of you and your need to turn your mind from worries about the future."

But when they reached town and took a booth at the café across from the movie theater, they could not help but overhear the chatter between the owner and the patrons at the counter.

"He just walked away, that one. I always said they gave those POWs far too much leeway," one man said.

"I heard that this particular POW was special," another added, waiting for everyone's attention to turn his way. "I heard this one was a high-ranking officer in Hitler's secret police."

Ilse looked at Gisele. "Do you think. . . ?"

Gisele nodded. "No doubt he's been biding his time." She clasped Ilse's hand in both of hers. "Do you understand why you cannot trust anything this man has told you? Written in that note to you?"

"One thing has nothing to do with the other," Ilse protested.

Gisele slumped back. "You are a hopeless romantic, Ilse. At least the man is gone and out of your life finally."

The conversation at the counter had switched to crops, as the men recalled how the POWs had helped with the previous season's harvest. "Won't be needing their help this season," one man commented. "This season our boys will be home to help with the harvest."

"And we will be who knows where?" Gisele muttered.

They ate their supper in silence and walked back to the Drivers' house to pick up Liesl before returning to the fort.

"I'm glad he's gone," Gisele said as they parted ways to go to their respective barracks. "You should probably burn that note. If they are looking for him and realize you—"

"I'll take care of it," Ilse said and gave her friend a hug.

That night once Liesl was in bed, Ilse sat down at the kitchen table to write to Beth and Josef in England. Josef deserved to know what his father had done, for surely he would have no word of him for some time to come—if ever again. Just before she sealed the envelope, she slipped the note that Detlef had written inside with a note of her own asking Josef to see what he might learn about the fate of Marta and the children.

⪻ CHAPTER 20 ⪼

By October Theo had no doubt that he had made a huge mistake when he agreed to run for Congress. His disappointment with the way things worked—or more to the point, did not work—in Washington grew daily as the fate of his aunt and cousin and the hundreds of others caught in the limbo of red tape at Fort Ontario slogged on and on.

In September the government had taken yet another survey, asking the residents of the shelter where they would prefer to go if given a choice—back to their country of origin, to some other country outside the United States, or to some community in America where they had contacts or the residents were willing to help them establish a life there. At the time of the survey two relatively small groups of refugees from Yugoslavia had already asked to be repatriated to their homeland. Theo was well aware that of all the refugee groups the Slavs had always been the most interested in returning home——even if there were no home there. But of those who still called the fort home, overwhelmingly the vast majority had indicated their preference was to remain in America. It made Theo wonder what it would take before the powers in Washington began to consider the reality of the situation. It seemed they preferred to engage in turf wars between various departments—Interior versus State and Justice, and the Congress versus the White House. Clearly no one was willing to take responsibility for making a decision. Was this really the way Theo wanted to spend his days? Two tiny steps forward followed by three giant steps back?

What difference could he possibly make? Surely there was another way. He had been far more effective in his limited role helping Joseph Smart than he could ever be in Congress. There had to be another plan.

He tried not to show his frustration in his nightly talks with Suzanne. Her career had never been on more solid ground or more successful. She had achieved her first byline with her interview of Robert St. John, and a publisher was interested in her book. Edwin Bonner had offered her a full-time position on the national news desk at the paper.

Theo had always understood the importance that Suzanne's work held for her. She trusted in the work—in digging through facts and innuendo and finding a truth that she could put down on paper. She had become especially diligent about checking her facts and finding at least three sources to back them up before writing a single word. The fiasco with Gordon Langford had taught her well. The reality was that she had far more trust in her work than she did in most people.

Of course there had also been those life-changing episodes—first the death of her sister, followed by her parents' divorce and her father's death, and most recently her belief that Langford truly loved her when in fact he was simply using her. Theo had to admit that she had plenty of reason not to trust others. He was still not entirely sure that she trusted him, although he had not given her a single reason why she shouldn't. He could only hope that in time she would come around. He knew she cared for him, but was she even capable of love? Love required two people believing in each other unquestionably. One might disappoint the other, but even then there had to be that rock-solid belief that the disappointment had not been premeditated or intentional.

Suzanne talked a lot in their nightly chats about her vision for their future—a future that involved them both living and working in Washington. Theo was increasingly uncertain that such a future would ever come to be. Every time he sat in on a meeting for worship, he tried hard to open his heart and mind to God's plan for his life. Why would he have been led to run for public office in the first place if he wasn't supposed to do it? Was there some other message in that choice—some lesson he needed to heed? Or just maybe God's plan for Theo was exactly what he had thought it was before Jim Sawyer and Suzanne came into his life—one day he would take over the farm that had been in his family for three generations.

Theo walked to the mailbox to collect the mail and found among the bills and other pieces a letter from his sister, Beth. It was addressed to his parents, and while it was certainly not unusual for Beth to write, the timing seemed off. After all, supposedly she and Josef and their two children were already on a ship crossing the Atlantic on their way back to Wisconsin. Their last communication had been a one-word telegram: Approved!

He studied the postmark and realized the letter had been posted from the station in their little village on the day after they were supposed to have left for Southampton to board the ship. His mother was hanging clothes on the line that stretched from the house to the huge elm tree in the side yard and back again.

"Letter from Beth," he said, handing her the envelope.

She put it in her apron pocket. Beth's letters were always so filled with news and humor that they had taken to waiting until they could all be together to read them. "We'll open it at supper and read it together," she said, squinting up at him. "Theo? What is it?"

"I. . .nothing. . .maybe you should just go ahead and open it now."

His mother gave a nervous laugh, but her smile froze as she studied his face. She fumbled for the letter and handed it to him. "You read it." Her hand shook as she gave him the envelope.

Theo ripped it open and removed the two pages inside. He scanned the contents and then gave his mother the good news first. "They are all well—no one is sick or injured," he assured her.

"But?"

"They are not being allowed to come. Josef's father is an escaped POW, and Aunt Ilse wrote to Josef telling him this so now the authorities think that Josef—and probably Ilse—have knowledge of where he is hiding."

"They are not coming home?" Ellie ran her fingers lovingly over the sheet that Theo knew she had washed in preparation for setting up Beth's childhood bedroom.

"Not now, Mom. Soon," he promised, although he had no way of knowing that. "Once this is all worked out."

She turned back to her laundry, shaking out a pillowcase that matched the sheet and pinning it to the line. "Go tell your father."

That night Theo was late calling Suzanne, and he could not hide his distress over the news his family had received that day. Beth was not coming home.

"But the war is over, and she's an American," Suzanne argued.

"Josef is not an American, and his father is an escaped prisoner of war."

"But Josef is not his father. Besides, couldn't she come with the children? Why are they detaining her?"

"She won't come without Josef," Theo replied and could not help thinking, *Would you go without me?*

"But—"

"It is what it is, Suzanne, and you can't fix it, okay?" He knew he was being unfair, but he was so irritated both at the circumstances his sister and brother-in-law found themselves in and at Suzanne's incurable assumption that something could be done to change that. Would the ripples of this war never cease?

The silence between them was made all the more difficult because they could not see each other's faces, could not reach out a hand to touch the other one in support, could not find the words necessary to break the tension.

"Sorry," she murmured finally.

"No. I'm sorry for snapping at you. It's been a rough day. My folks are devastated. They haven't seen Beth in over five years, and they have two grandchildren they've never held and. . ."

"Why on earth would Ilse—"

"It's not her fault, Suzanne. She wants to find her sister. You can't blame her for going down every possible avenue to accomplish that."

"But I—we—I was working on that and making progress."

Again, the terrible quiet interrupted only by the muffled sound of traffic outside her apartment windows and night birds and crickets outside his.

"Talk to me about your day," he said finally, his tone conciliatory. "Give me some good news."

"I have an offer for the book."

"Really?" He was overjoyed for her. She had worked hard to put the manuscript together, sending him sections to read, and he had found himself enthralled with the story even though he knew most of it already. "Oh, honey, that's terrific."

"It's not firmed up yet and it's an offer from a small press here in the DC area, but it is an offer."

"First a byline and now a book deal—wow! I'm really proud of you."

"The only thing that would make it better would be if you were here with me. I cannot wait for you to move here so we can be together."

Theo did not know what to say. He needed to tell her, but he had hoped not to have to say anything until after the election. If—when—he lost it would be a moot point.

"Theo? What's going on?"

Did she really know him so well? He cleared his throat. "You know if I lose the election—"

"You won't. People love you. I saw the way they wanted to speak with you, be with you at the Fourth of July event. I have told you before, Theo, you are a natural."

"But we have to be realistic, Suzanne. I could lose."

Now she was the one who said nothing for so long that Theo wondered if somehow they had been disconnected. "Are you still there?"

"Even if you don't win, you could still move here. There are plenty of jobs and—"

"Or perhaps you could give Wisconsin a try? We have newspapers and everything." He tried to make a joke of it, but they had danced around this topic for some time now without really discussing it. She had simply assumed that he would come to Washington and refused to consider that there might be any other outcome.

"I know. It's just that right now everything is coming together for me here and—"

"Hey, we don't have to make any decisions tonight. Let's just enjoy your news—a real live book. That's something to celebrate. Does Ilse know?"

"No. I thought of writing to her and Gisele and the others, but I chose to tell Detlef Buch's story as well, and now that he's escaped. . ."

"That's hardly your fault."

"I know, but with Josef being detained and. . . Your folks must be so devastated."

Theo recalled his mother's ravaged face as he gave her Beth's news. "My parents are survivors, Suzanne. Dad was even talking at supper about maybe he and Mom could go to England over Thanksgiving. Things are slow on the farm then, and it just might be a good time for them to get away."

"Would you want to go?"

"I'd love to see my sister and meet my niece and nephew and Josef, but somebody has to milk the cows." He chuckled.

"Yeah, and you'll be getting ready for the swearing-in ceremony in Congress after the holidays. I've found a couple of apartments that might work out for you. Of course with the war over things are starting to fill up fast."

"All I need is a room," Theo assured her. He glanced at the clock. They had talked for nearly an hour. "You need to get some sleep," he said.

"And you don't? As I recall, those cows get up pretty early."

He laughed then sobered. "Suzanne, whatever happens with the election, know that I am so very happy for your success."

"You are going to win that election, and we are going to be together, Theo Bridgewater. Get that straight right now."

"I'd settle for one out of the two—the second one. I love you, Suzanne."

"I know," she said softly, and then she blew him a kiss as she always did to end their calls. He heard the click that told him she was no longer there and quietly replaced the receiver in its cradle. She claimed to believe that he loved her, but did she trust in that love—that it would be there for her no matter what?

Ilse was stunned by the news that Josef and Beth were being denied passage to America. In spite of Ellie and Paul's assurances to the contrary, she felt at fault. If she had not sent the information to Josef, if she had refused to have anything to do with Detlef Buch, surely this would not have happened. Perhaps Gisele had been right, after all. But Ilse found it hard to believe that Detlef would be so cruel—not after all this time.

"You cannot take this on yourself, Ilse," Gisele told her. "The man escaped all by himself. You did nothing to help with that."

"Well, neither did Josef, and yet he and Beth are paying the penalty. I just wish there were something I could do."

I wish Franz were here. Together we could always solve anything. She felt her chest fill with her grief. It seemed as if since his death everything had gotten worse. The war had ended, but they were still here—still not free to make choices for themselves. And almost nightly Liesl quizzed her about where they would go, pleading with her to stay in America— as if Ilse had the power to make that decision.

"Will this nightmare never end?" she whispered, more to herself than to Gisele.

"Come with me," her friend said, taking her by the hand as if they were schoolgirls again. "You need cheering up, and I have just the recipe for that." She led Ilse into the building that had been converted into a performance hall for theatrical productions, the movie nights they held now and then, concerts, and lectures.

Several of the residents who regularly appeared in the shelter's productions were gathered around the piano. They were all talking over one another, and Ilse had to wonder how they could possibly accomplish anything.

"I brought fresh talent," Gisele said.

When Ilse realized that the actress was referring to her, she had to smile. "I cannot sing a note," she protested.

"Not a problem at all," Ivo, the man who usually led these productions, assured her. "At the moment it is your objective opinion that is needed. Come sit." He patted the seat next to him on the piano bench. "We are developing a satirical musical. See what you think of this."

He played an arpeggio on the piano and then nodded to the others, who referred to a song sheet. "We are in a cage without reason," they bellowed. "We are in a cage, a golden cage."

The chorus went on from there, and then one of the men sang alone. "Like a lion in the cage, we are losing health and mood. . . ."

The music stopped suddenly. "That's as far as we've gotten," Ivo said. "Any thoughts?"

All eyes were on her, and everyone was smiling hopefully as if she might actually offer them some viable idea. Their obvious confidence that she might gave her courage. "Well, I will say I never thought of myself as a lion—more as a bird—and an aging one at that." She laughed and realized that she was already feeling a little better.

"If we divided the song into scenes," Gisele suggested. "One when we first arrived and then after the war ended and then—"

"Indeed," Ivo said. "Of course, it is the ending that will have to wait until the last possible moment."

Suddenly the light spirits that had dominated the room dimmed as everyone's smile faded. Surprisingly Ilse did not feel as if she had once again been cast into the depths of depression. Instead she felt as if she were part of a group—a community of people facing exactly what she faced. Some of them also had children who surely wanted to remain in the America they had come to think of as home. She was not alone. "Is there something I could do to help with the production?" she asked. "Behind the scenes, of course."

"Costumes? Do you sew?" Ivo asked.

"Well, of course she sews," one of the women huffed. "Have you not seen her daughter? Liesl is always beautifully dressed, and forgive me but one does not find such fine detail in the donated goods we are forced to rely upon."

"I sew a little," Ilse admitted.

"Excellent. We shall need everyone in the cast dressed in rags for the opening, and then as the show progresses they will become more and more presentable until at the end—"

"At the end we should each dress the role we played in life before all of this," the man who had sung the solo suggested. "Doctors, merchants, lawyers, writers, performers—people who were educated and successful. Let's show them who we were."

"Who we are," Gisele added, and everyone applauded. "I'll help Ilse with the designs and sewing," she added.

Just like that, Ilse found herself part of something that gave her joy and purpose. To some it might be just a silly little amateur production. For Ilse it was a lifeline.

That night as she sat with Liesl while the girl practiced the piano, her mind raced with ideas for transforming the actors in the production from a bunch of ragtag refugees into the proud, gifted men and women they had once been and would be again—if not here in America, then somewhere else in the world. She wondered if those men in Washington debating their fate would ever truly appreciate what they might lose if they held to their plan to send them all back.

"Mom?"

She had been so lost in thought that she hadn't realized Liesl had come to the end of her piece. "What, Liebchen?"

"You were smiling. Were you thinking of Papa?"

"Not just then, but I do think of him often."

"Me, too." Liesl's shoulders slumped. "I miss him so much."

"So do I." She wrapped her arms around this cherished child—her only child. "But do you know what? I believe that every time you play the piano, Papa is listening."

"Do you think he is dancing?"

Ilse laughed. Franz had been a wonderful dancer. "Yes, Liesl. Papa so loves to dance, so you must play for him often. He would be so very proud of the progress you have made in your lessons in such a short time."

"That's what Nancy's mom said when I played for them. She wanted to know who my teacher was, and when I told her it was you, she said that you could give lessons for money. She said you could earn a living doing that. That's how we could make our way when we leave the fort."

Ilse was stunned to realize that Liesl was thinking of such mundane things as how they might earn money. She had thought about such matters, of course, but it had never occurred to her that Liesl might have the same worries.

"We have to have some way to pay the bills," Liesl continued. "I could maybe do some chores for people, but for real money—I mean now that Papa—"

Ilse held her closer. "Sh-h-h. This is not for you to worry about. You just concentrate on doing well in school and practicing the piano. I will see that we have what we need, all right?"

Liesl looked up at her and frowned, and Ilse realized that the child had serious doubts about her mother's ability to provide what the two of them would need. "All right," Liesl said finally, but her words lacked conviction.

That night Ilse sat at the table in their apartment long after the barracks had gone completely quiet except for the occasional footsteps in the hallway as someone made his or her way to the bathroom. On the table in front of her was the local newspaper, a pad of paper, and a pencil. For hours she had scanned the advertisements in the paper, gathering information about what it might cost to feed and clothe herself and Liesl.

Now she studied the listings for apartments for rent. Surely the prices in Oswego would be representative of others in similar-sized towns across the country. She wrote down figures and descriptions on the notepad. Tomorrow she would get a pass and walk or take the bus to some of the addresses. At least then she could see the exteriors of the buildings and the neighborhoods. She would also walk through a food market to get more information for understanding just how much money she would need to earn to care for Liesl and herself.

At the top of the page she had written, "Expenses if we stay in America." After realizing that Liesl was worried about their future and their financial situation, Ilse had decided that the one thing she could do for her daughter was to give her a promise that if the government allowed, they would stay in America. Theo was right. Ilse could always travel to Europe to search for Marta.

So earlier that evening after she and Liesl had held their nightly abbreviated meeting for worship she had sat on the side of Liesl's bed and tucked the covers around her daughter. "Liesl, I have made a decision."

"What decision?"

"If the American government decides that we are allowed to stay in this United States, that is what we will do."

Liesl threw the covers aside as she leaped up to wrap her arms around Ilse's neck. "Oh, Mama, do you mean it?"

Whenever Liesl called her *Mama*, it brought back so many memories of when they had lived in Munich, of when Ilse had relied so much on Beth. It brought tears to Ilse's eyes that something so simple as a promise that depended on the actions of others could make her child so very happy. "You understand that if the government says that we—"

"Have to go back, then we do," Liesl said. "But oh, Mama, surely they will see how good we have all been. If we stay, will we move to the farm in Wisconsin?"

Ilse saw no harm in indulging in dreams for this once. "Would you like that?"

"I don't know. I don't remember the farm. Is it like the fort except with cows and chickens? But then where else would we go? Could we stay here in Oswego? I have a lot of friends here."

"I know. If the Americans say we can stay, then we will have to decide together, but Liesl, there is always the possibility—"

"I know." She sighed heavily, but then she grinned. "Every night from now until we know, I am going to pray really hard in our meetings for worship, and maybe—if God thinks it is for the best—it will all come true."

"I think that is a very good plan as long as you also keep in mind that God may have another way for us, and we must be ready for that as well."

Liesl kissed Ilse's cheeks and hugged her hard before collapsing back onto the pillow, a smile on her face. "I can't wait to tell my friends," she murmured just before she drifted off to sleep.

Ilse had sat beside her for a moment longer and then gathered the newspaper and notepad and started to work. She would plan for staying in America, and if it turned out that Beth and Josef were to remain in England, that would be her second choice because it would be best for Liesl to be around family. But one day—once Liesl was settled—Ilse would return to Munich, for that was her home. That was where she had met Franz, and that was where her memories of their life together lived.

In spite of everything that was going on in her career, Suzanne felt consumed by a melancholy that she could not explain or shake. She missed Theo terribly and was beginning to wonder if in fact she did love him—could trust in his love for her. She lived for the day when the election was finally decided and he could move to DC, for although he appeared to have doubts about being elected, she had none. Who in their right mind would not see that this kind and gentle and incredibly smart man was exactly the kind of elected official the country needed?

"Suzie!"

She roused herself at Edwin's shout and pulled a pencil from her hair as she grabbed her notebook and headed for his office. "Coming."

She couldn't help but notice that these days as she walked through the newsroom her colleagues went on with their work, accepting her presence as normal and right. It was quite a change from just a year earlier when they had deliberately averted their eyes and when she had been all too aware of whispered conversations that seemed to end abruptly whenever she approached.

Now she walked with complete confidence through the newsroom to Edwin's open door. "You called?"

"When was the last time you were in Oswego?"

"Just before the Fourth. Why?"

"So how are you keeping up with what's going on there?"

"I still have contacts there, but really the story is here now."

"Is that so?" He consulted a paper. "Then do you want to tell me about this Gestapo agent who escaped?"

"I wrote about that."

"Yes, in your book. I run a newspaper, Suzie-Q, as in news printed at the time it happens."

"I did the follow-up on St. John's radio broadcast," she said, feeling defensive. It wasn't as if she could decide what stories Edwin would print. She swallowed her resentment. "What do you want me to do?"

"Get your buns up there and find out what's going on. I've got people here who can cover anything that breaks over at State or Justice."

"Interior is in charge now. Secretary Ickes just sent a letter to President Truman and—"

"I know that, and Congressman Dickstein is still pushing for Congress to act. We know all that. What we don't know is what the residents of the fort are doing. Those poor souls are facing yet another New York winter. Go up there and do what you do so well—get me the human side of the story." He picked up his phone and began dialing— his indication that this meeting was over.

Suzanne finished the story due that day then went home to pack. By now she knew the train schedule by heart. She had taken it often enough over the last year. And although she could certainly expense account a hotel room since she was making this trip on assignment from Edwin, she called Selma Velo.

"I'm not sure how long I'll be there, Selma. It might be a week or so but certainly not a month."

"Come on, honey. Stay an hour or a year. I really don't care. My son got home a week ago, and there is not a thing else that matters."

"Oh Selma, I am so happy for you. I'll look forward to finally meeting him, and it is going to be so good to catch up." That was exactly why Suzanne wanted to stay at the boardinghouse. In spite of her disagreements with Hilda, it was in that house that Suzanne knew she would get a bird's-eye view of how the locals were feeling about the residents of the fort now that things continued to drag on months after the war had ended. "See you tonight," Suzanne told Selma and hung up. She was surprised to realize that her spirits had lifted.

Theo! She suddenly realized that she needed to call and let him know of the change in plans. But before she could place the call, her phone rang.

"Hi, dollface."

"The man escaped, Gordon. There's not a lot I can do about that."

"You always go on defense—is it just me or everyone?"

"Just you," she replied sweetly.

"Well, I have information for you. This woman you're looking for is alive."

"And her children?"

"The whole kit and caboodle. Have dinner with me, and I'll give you the details."

"I have to go to Oswego tonight." She glanced at her wristwatch. "Where are you? I can swing by your office or apartment...."

"I'll come to you. You'll need a lift to the train station, right?"

As it turned out, Gordon had no details. He did not know where Marta and the children were—only that they had survived the war.

"But how can you know that and—"

"They turned up on a list of survivors in France. After that the trail ends." He glanced at her as he navigated the streets of Washington. "Give me my due, Suze. I'm doing my best here."

"I know. Thank you. It's good news."

"Good enough to prove that I regret what happened before? Good enough that you might consider starting again?"

"Gordon, we both know—"

"Hey, the war is over. It's a new era. We know we make a formidable team."

And that's the difference, Suzanne realized. *For you it's all about the power of a career, while with Theo it's all about love.*

They had reached the station, and he turned to face her.

"I have to go, Gordon."

"You'll think about it—us?"

A redcap opened the door for her, and the interruption was enough that she did not have to answer. "Bye, Gordon. Thanks for everything."

She boarded the train and stared out the window as the monuments of the capital disappeared and she headed back to the people and story that had saved her career.

CHAPTER 21

Oswego weather in November 1945 was far kinder than it had been the previous year. To everyone's relief, by Election Day there had been only a slight dusting of snow and temperatures had remained mild. The residents at the fort waited anxiously to see whether or not the outcome of the elections might affect them. Ilse was especially anxious for news that Theo had won a seat in Congress. Even though Theo would not represent Oswego, most people at the fort felt as if he were one of their own. They had come to respect him during the months he had worked at the administration office and later with Joseph Smart's advocacy group.

Suzanne had promised to bring the news as soon as she heard. She had come back to Oswego to find out more about Detlef Buch's escape, although there was nothing new there. The man seemed to have simply disappeared, leaving in his wake heartache for Ellie and Paul as well as for Beth and Josef. Ilse understood that she had not caused this, but she still felt guilty. If she had not pressed the man to help in her search for Marta...

But then Suzanne had arrived, confirming the news that Marta and the children had survived. She had been so overcome with relief that she had clasped her arms around Suzanne and hugged her. Both women had cried.

As the days passed leading up to the election, Ilse and Suzanne spent a good deal of time together. They were walking along the lakeshore one day when she asked Suzanne, "What will you and Theo do if he loses the election?"

"But he won't—he can't."

"Yes, Suzanne, he can, and if he does, he will have to face new decisions for his future."

"He plans to farm."

"A respectable profession, although I am not certain that it is the best choice for Theo. His heart does not seem called to such a solitary way of life."

"Exactly." Suzanne's voice rose with excitement. "He has so much to offer. I mean think about what he did while he was here. People really listened to him when he spoke, and he had wonderful ideas, and—"

"Yes, Theo has the gift of helping others more clearly understand the way things are. My late husband also had that gift. Theo reminds me of Franz a great deal. I think that is why I am so very fond of him and Liesl adores him."

"But if he thinks his father needs him on the farm. . ."

"Paul and Ellie want what is best for their children. They know that Theo loves you. They know that your work and life have been in the setting of the city. What they don't know is whether or not you love Theo."

Ilse saw that she had shocked Suzanne with her directness, but in one of her letters, Ellie had spoken at length about the time it had taken for her and Paul to come to terms with Beth's love for a German doctor whose father worked for the Nazi government. Now Ellie had transferred that worry to Theo. *"He is so very much in love with this young woman,"* she wrote. *"But he seems uncertain of her feelings for him."*

So Ilse had seen her opportunity and taken it. It was evident that the question was one Suzanne had wrestled with. What Ilse could not understand was why the struggle if the girl loved Theo. She waited for a response.

"I care for Theo a great deal," Suzanne said softly. "If I were capable of loving anyone. . ." Her voice trailed off.

"Yet you are unable to choose between your feelings for him and your work?"

Suzanne sighed and then smiled tightly. "Hey, perhaps I don't need to choose. After all, everything is a moot point until we know how the election goes, right?"

But was it? If Suzanne loved Theo the way he loved her—the way that Ilse and Franz had loved each other—weren't all obstacles surmountable? "I have to check on Liesl," she said. But as she walked back up the hill to the fort, she thought, *I do not understand you at all.*

It was over. The election was lost. Theo felt bad for the disappointment he'd caused Jim Sawyer and the others who had worked so hard to support him. He had let them down. But Jim was pragmatic in defeat.

"Hey, there's another election in two years. Gives us time to regroup and tweak the message. You ran a good race, Theo. And more to the point, the voters got to know you. You'll be ready next time."

"I appreciate your confidence in me, Jim, but there won't be a next time for me."

"Never say never, son," Jim said as he squeezed Theo's shoulder and crossed the street to where he'd parked his truck. He waved as he drove away, and Theo marveled at his calm acceptance of defeat.

He went to the pay phone in the back of the drugstore and gave the operator the number for the boardinghouse. Suzanne answered immediately, and the operator told him to deposit his coins for the three-minute call. He figured he wouldn't need more than a minute.

"The other candidate won," he said as soon as Suzanne came back on the line.

After a moment of silence, he heard her let out her breath. "Oh, Theo, I am so sorry," she finally said.

"Yeah, well, we knew it was a long shot. How long will you be in Oswego?"

"A few more days. Why?"

"I thought I might come out there."

"Come to Washington instead. I have a friend you can stay with, and I have some vacation coming. I can take time off—show you the sights." Her laugh was forced, and he understood that she had never truly allowed herself to consider what might happen for them if he lost.

"Are you sure?"

"Please come," she said.

"Okay. I'll check schedules and get back to you." The operator interrupted, asking for more money. "You'll tell Ilse?"

"Yes."

He fumbled in his pocket for more coins, but the line went dead before he could deposit them.

That night at supper with his parents, his mother raised the question of his plans for the future.

"I thought I'd go out to Washington and see Suzanne—she's got a friend I can stay with. Might as well see what I missed not getting elected and all." He made a joke of it, anxious to reassure them that he was fine with the election's outcome.

His parents exchanged a look, and he was pretty sure that his mom gave his dad an encouraging nod.

Dad cleared his throat and took a sip of his coffee. "Your mother and I were thinking. Maybe you should look into that overseas opportunity with the Friends that was mentioned at the last meeting for business. They need people, and you know after the first war the Friends did a lot to help displaced people."

The American Friends Service Committee—AFSC for short—had been organized to provide opportunities for conscientious objectors to help rebuild war-torn Europe after the first war. Now with Hitler's reign of terror ended, they were gearing up to once again send relief workers and other aid to Europe to help in the recovery from war.

Theo recalled a letter from his sister during the time she was in Munich. She had written that often when she was stopped for identification and the soldiers had realized she was Quaker they had instantly changed their attitude toward her. In one case a man told her that without the relief the Quakers had offered his family after the first war, he did not know how they would have survived.

"From what I've been reading," Theo's father continued, "this time the relief effort is going to be on a much larger scale. For one thing they're looking for people who can help farmers get their farms back into production. You know agriculture, and you know politics. Sounds to me like you've got some tools that might be of use."

"I thought the idea was for me to help out on this farm."

"Look, Son, I think I've got a few good years left in me, and truth be told, you've pretty much shown your mom and me that farming is not exactly your first love. It's a hard life, Theo, so if you're going to do it, you need to do it because you love it. Can you honestly say that's the case?"

"No, but going off to Europe seems like a pretty big leap from staying here on the farm. Besides, Suzanne—"

Another look passed between his parents, and his father suddenly seemed inordinately interested in cutting his pork chop.

"Suzanne is a lovely young woman," Mom said.

"But?" He felt his defenses rise as he always did whenever Suzanne's name came up. Ever since her July visit, he had noticed that his mother's attitude toward her had cooled.

"But you need to think about what will make you happy."

"She makes me happy."

"Yes, we can see that." His mother glanced at his dad, who was slowly chewing his meat and avoiding eye contact. Mom sighed and continued. "Suzanne strikes your father and me as someone who is still trying to find herself. Our worry is that if you plan your life around hers—"

"Mom, I'm not sixteen, and neither is Suzanne."

"I know that, dear, but—"

"One of the reasons I'm going to see her is so we can talk about the future—whether or not that will be *our* future is pretty much up to her at this point. I love her and want to spend my life with her."

Dad finally looked at Mom and grinned. "He sounds like me."

"It's not the same at all," she protested, her cheeks growing pink.

"Your mom was one tough cookie, Son. I had to work plenty hard to get her to settle down." He reached over and patted her hand. "Thankfully it's all worked out just fine."

"For us," his mom said. "Theo, do not put your life on hold for this woman—for any woman. If it is meant for the two of you to be together, you will be." She looked at her husband, seeking his agreement, and he squeezed her hand.

Theo envied the way his parents looked at each other. How many times had he imagined Suzanne looking at him with such certainty? "I'll look into the thing with the Friends," he promised.

"Good. After all, Suzanne is so fortunate that she has chosen writing as her life's work. A writer can work anywhere, and wouldn't it be wonderful if the two of you could be in Europe, close to Beth until this whole mess with their visas can be cleared up and—"

"I'll look into it, Mom. But first I'm going to Washington."

The residents of the fort followed their normal routine the day after Election Day. They had breakfast in the dining hall, got the children off to school, and went to their assigned jobs. This had been their daily schedule for nearly sixteen long months. This had become normal life, and frankly many of them were beginning to wonder if this might be life for some time to come.

After Ilse had made sure Liesl was on her way to the bus stop, she headed for the recreation hall, where she and Gisele were sorting through the boxes of donated clothing that had accumulated and gone unclaimed for some time. They were looking for pieces they could turn into costumes for the musical production that now carried the title *The Golden Cage*.

"Here she comes," Gisele said, nodding toward a window that overlooked the parade ground. Suzanne was trudging across the grass. "She does not look happy."

They waited for her to open the door.

"He did not win," she said as if she still could not believe it.

"Then clearly there is another plan for his life," Ilse said as she went back to sorting. "And possibly for yours as well," she added quietly.

A week later, Theo stepped off the train in Washington's Union Station and saw Suzanne running to meet him. He grinned and dropped his suitcase to open his arms to her. It had been months since they had been together, but he remembered every detail of her—the scent of her perfume, the feel of her hair against his cheek, the way she fit into his arms.

"Welcome to DC," she said as she rose onto her toes to kiss him. He tightened his hold on her, lifting her off the ground as he returned the kiss and deepened it.

"Now that's what I call a welcome," he said, his voice husky.

"It's that Southern hospitality thing." She ran her gloved fingers over his features as if she needed to be sure he was actually there.

Around them other travelers were sidling by, some giving them annoyed looks while others were smiling. Theo reluctantly broke their embrace and picked up his suitcase. "Where to?"

"I thought we'd go to my apartment and have lunch, okay? You can leave your stuff there for now, and we can go for a walk. Do you believe this day? I mean it's already mid-November and. . ."

She was nervous. He took hold of her hand. "Whatever you say."

Her apartment was compact but cozy, and he got a real kick out of watching her in the tiny galley kitchen. She had made barley soup and corn-bread muffins and a salad. The table that obviously doubled as her desk was set for two.

"Something's missing," he said when they sat down.

She was already half out of her chair. "Salt and pepper," she murmured.

He caught her wrist. "I don't need either. I was thinking that this is the first time you and I have shared a meal—except in a restaurant or at the farm—that either Hilda or Hugh or both weren't there."

She laughed, and he saw her relax for the first time since she'd met him at the train. "Hugh has moved on, much to Hilda's distress, but if you like, I can do a pretty good imitation at least of what I think she might say."

"Pretty sure I can muddle through without that." He took a spoonful of the soup and then another—and another. "This is delicious."

"Well, you don't have to sound so surprised. I *can* cook."

"Good to know." He grinned and held out his bowl for seconds.

After lunch they took his suitcase to her friend's apartment. "Make yourself at home," the young man said. "I'm off to the Pacific on assignment. Now that both wars are over, somebody needs to tell that story."

"Would you ever want to do that?" Theo asked after he had unpacked and changed into more casual clothes. They were walking toward the Smithsonian Museum—a landmark that Suzanne had insisted he needed to see. "Go to faraway places and write whatever story was happening there?"

"It might be fun, at least for a while. But I think it would be exhausting hopping back and forth."

As they approached the museum, he paused and glanced toward the Capitol. "That's where you would have been," Suzanne said. "Where you *should* have been."

He held the door for her. "Apparently not. Apparently there are other plans for me."

They wandered through the exhibits, occasionally pausing to read more about the diorama before them or to peer more closely at something in a display case. Theo felt restless and anxious. He had not really come to Washington to tour museums and monuments. He had come to find out once and for all if Suzanne could see a future for them. "Let's get out of here," he said and knew by the startled look she gave him that he had spoken more gruffly than he thought.

Outside they were greeted by a light, misty shower accompanied by dropping temperatures and a light wind. Theo turned up the collar of his jacket. Suzanne raised the umbrella she had brought along and handed it to him. "Where to?"

"Can we walk to the Lincoln Memorial?"

"Sure."

The mood between them had definitely shifted, and it was all his fault. "Look, Suzanne, I think we both know that we have some decisions to make. The war is over, and so is the election. Soon some sort of decision will be made regarding Ilse and the others. We have no control over that, and in many ways that is no longer a part of our lives."

"Not exactly. I still have the job of reporting that ending." She sounded annoyed, and he realized that they were trudging along rather than strolling the way they had earlier.

"And that's the real issue, isn't it? Your work?" He was really messing this up. Even to himself he sounded as if he were deliberately trying to pick a fight with her.

"My work is who I am," she shot back.

"No. I won't accept that. It is a part of who you are—a key part to be sure. But you are so much more than that, Suzanne. You allow your dedication to your work to overshadow the rest of you. It has become your safety net—your cocoon against having to directly face your own life."

"Oh, so now you are a psychiatrist? Spare me your armchair analysis, Theo."

He stopped at the foot of the steps leading up to the statue of Lincoln. "I love you. Does that mean anything to you?"

"Why do you love me, Theo? It seems to me that at the moment you highly disapprove of me, so how can you call that love?" She stomped up the steps and took shelter under the stone ceiling that covered Lincoln's statue. She folded her arms tightly across her chest and sat down cross-legged on the cold marble floor looking up at the great man's likeness.

Theo followed her and closed the umbrella, shaking it out as he did. They had the place to themselves. He walked to one wall where the words to the Gettysburg Address had been inscribed. Behind him she continued to sit, her knees now drawn up to her chest with her chin resting on them.

"Theo?"

"I'm here."

"I do love you."

He wasn't completely sure he had heard her because she spoke so softly. She could just as easily have said "I don't love you."

He squatted next to her. "Again please?"

"I do love you," she said, and he placed his finger on her lips to stop the *but* that he felt coming. She gently brushed his hand aside. "So what are we going to do?"

His relief that she was not setting conditions was so huge that he lowered himself fully to the floor so that their shoulders touched. "What do you want to do? I mean we could get married."

"That's an option." She said the words as if they were discussing where to go for dinner. "Of course, we'd have to think through some logistics—your work on the farm and my work."

"What if there was another option?"

"I'm listening."

He told her about the AFSC program to help displaced people all over Europe. "Think about it, Suzanne. We could continue doing what we began with the folks at the fort. Europe is pretty compact, so we might even be able to find someplace to live near Beth and Josef and work from there and—"

Now she was the one to stop him with a finger on his lips. "Slow down. What about my job at the newspaper? What about the book? What about your parents and the farm?"

"Details," he said with a shrug. He wasn't sure, but he thought maybe Lincoln was smiling down at them. "Let's make it work."

Suzanne had never felt so completely happy and at peace with her life. Every minute she spent with Theo only confirmed her belief that this was a man she could trust—a man who would love her unconditionally and whose love did not ask any more of her than that she give him her unconditional love in return. And oh, how easy he made that.

The rest of their time together in Washington flew by. They walked and talked and planned their life together. He would return to the farm to manage things while his parents went to England to see Beth and her family over Thanksgiving. She would stay in Washington, awaiting whatever decision would finally be made regarding the residents at the fort. They would spend the holidays together no matter what.

Early in December, her mother called and insisted on coming to Washington. "We have to go shopping, Suze. A wedding requires a trousseau."

"Mom, come for a visit, but Theo and I aren't even engaged, and even if we were, we plan on keeping things simple."

"Nonsense. The war is over. Enough with rationing and deprivation. We have to choose a venue—is there a Friends group in Washington?"

"Yes, but we'll probably be married with the Friends in Wisconsin."

There was a long pause.

"Isn't it terribly cold there, dear?"

Suzanne smiled. Since her remarriage, her mother had made her new home in Arizona. "We probably won't plan an outdoor wedding, Mom."

"But I'll need a winter coat and gloves and a warm scarf and—"

It had always been pointless to argue with her mother. "Okay, Mom. Come to Washington, and we'll go shopping."

She hung up. How long had it been since she and her mother had had such an ordinary mother–daughter conversation? After Natalie's death, her mom's focus had been on grief and the deterioration of her marriage. After Suzanne's dad died, her mom had seemed more the child to her adult, and they had gradually drifted apart. Then after her mom remarried, their relationship had become that of friends who stayed in touch but really did not do the usual family things. Her mom and stepfather traveled extensively, and Suzanne buried herself in work. Now everything was changing for her, and she felt such peace as if finally her life was coming together.

The phone rang again almost as soon as she hung up. Suzanne laughed as she picked it up. It would be so like her mother to call back with something she had forgotten she wanted to say. "Mom, just—"

"Excuse me?" A male voice that she did not recognize interrupted.

"Oh, hello, I apologize. I thought you were my mother and. . .who are you?"

"This is Jackson Anderson with the *New York Times* calling for Miss Suzanne Randolph."

"Speaking," she managed while her mind whirled with ideas for why anyone from the *New York Times* would be calling her.

"Our editorial staff recently became aware of your work with the refugees in Oswego. I was wondering if you might be available to have lunch with me today. I know this is very short notice, but I am only in Washington for the day. Are you familiar with the restaurant the Simpson Bistro?" He named a fancy restaurant in the heart of DuPont Circle and Embassy Row. Even for lunch the place was pricey.

"Well, uh. . ."

"You would of course be my guest, Miss Randolph. Shall we say one o'clock? Would that match your schedule?"

"Sure. I mean yes, that would work just fine."

"Excellent. I'll reserve a table. Thank you, Miss Randolph."

"No, thank you."

The call ended and Suzanne groaned. She must have sounded like such a twit. "No, thank *you*," she said in a high falsetto, mimicking herself. But then reality hit her. She had a meeting with someone from the largest newspaper in America. The man had called her. Someone from the editorial staff of the *New York Times* wanted to take her to lunch. . .in just under two hours.

She glanced in the mirror. She had taken the day off to catch up on laundry and bills and the other mundane trivia of life that so often got put off in favor of her work. She was wearing an oversized sweatshirt and jeans, and her hair was a rat's nest of tangles. She ran to her closet and started pulling clothes out and depositing the rejects on her bed.

She had nothing to wear. She needed a shower. She wasn't sure she had a pair of stockings that didn't have a run in them, and she now had less than ninety minutes to make herself presentable and get to the restaurant.

The shower took less than two minutes, another fifteen to do something with her hair, then ten more for lipstick—smeared the first go-round—and a little rouge and powder followed by a precious half hour to choose something to wear and dress, change her pocketbook to match, grab her coat, and get out the door to hail a passing cab. She arrived at the restaurant breathless and fifteen minutes late, and she couldn't help but be surprised and flattered that Mr. Anderson had waited for her.

Not only had he waited, but as he stood and held her chair for her, he was the one apologizing for the short notice he'd given her for their meeting.

"Let's order, and then we can talk," he suggested.

Later that night she literally sat by the telephone willing it to ring. Theo's parents had decided to extend their stay in England to the middle of December, leaving Theo with the farm to manage. She was happy for them having the extra time with their daughter, especially since Beth and her husband had still not been able to convince the authorities to allow them to travel to America. But she had huge news, and she could not wait to share it with Theo.

Theo had news of his own to share. To pass the time while his parents were gone, he had written to Joseph Smart and learned that his former boss and mentor was well aware of the Quaker relief program just starting up in war-torn Europe. "They'd be lucky to have you on board, Theo. How about I make a few calls?"

Smart's calls had ended up with Theo being offered a position as a team leader for agricultural support and relief in England. "They want you over there after the first of the year. They'll mail you some forms and then bring you out here to meet with the rest of the group."

"You mean I'm hired?"

"Sounds like that's the plan if you want the job. Congratulations."

Okay, but what about Suzanne? How would she handle the news? He thought about how best to present the idea to her as he did the evening chores. He thought about the book she had written. Thousands of stories in England alone just waited to be told. He figured out a budget for how they would live over there—it would be tight, but between his savings and the small stipend he would get from the Friends, she would not have to work. She could spend her time doing what she loved with no one setting restrictions.

Certain that he had worked out the details, he paced through the rooms of the farmhouse until it was time for their nightly call. She answered on the first ring and together they both said, "Wait until you hear—"

He laughed. "You first."

"No, I always go first. You start."

"Okay, how would you feel about living in England for a year or two?" Her lack of response unnerved him, so he hurried to add, "I was thinking that you could take the time to start writing a new book or do a series for the newspaper or—"

"What's happened, Theo?"

He told her about his conversation with Joseph Smart and the strings the former shelter director had pulled to get him a position with the AFSC's relief project. He talked very fast as if by rushing through the explanation he could make her see this as a real opportunity for them both. "What do you think?"

"The *New York Times* offered me a job in their Washington bureau today," she said. "They want me to write a series of essays similar to the ones I did about the residents at Fort Ontario, only these would be about the Americans of Japanese descent who were held in camps on the West Coast during the war." By contrast to his rush of words, she was speaking very slowly as if giving weight to the news she had.

"The *New York Times*. . .that's incredible, honey." This changed everything.

"Yeah. Two incredible opportunities half a world apart. So what are we going to do?"

"We'll figure it out. I mean if we took a year and I went to England and you did this assignment out west. . ."

"A year apart?" She sounded like she might start to cry at any moment. "Oh, why do things have to be so complicated? We've just really come together and now. . ."

She wasn't even hinting that he turn down the relief position, and he would never ask her to turn down an opportunity to write for the *Times*. "We've handled things from long distance for some time now," he reminded her.

She groaned. "When are you supposed to start with the relief project?"

"They want me after the first of the year. How about you?"

"I said I wanted to complete the story of Fort Ontario and they agreed. I really want to see that through. I just feel like we're so close. . . ."

There was a crackle on the line, and suddenly the operator interrupted the call. "Mr. Theo Bridgewater?"

"Yes."

"I have a Mr. Paul Bridgewater on the line calling from England. Will you accept the call?"

Theo's heart pounded. "Suzanne, are you there?"

"Yes. Take the call and then call me back," she instructed and hung up.

"Son?" His father was shouting as if he needed to raise his voice to be heard from an ocean away.

"What's happened?"

"They got their visas. We're coming home, Son. We're all coming home."

Theo had never heard his father cry before, and he was not surprised to hear his own voice break with emotion. "That's great, Dad."

"This is costing a fortune. Your mom will write, but Beth wants to go to Oswego first to see Ilse and Liesl."

"I'll meet you there—just let me know when. Bye, Dad. Give my love—"

The line went dead.

Immediately he redialed Suzanne's number and told her the good news. "I'm going to meet them in Oswego," he said.

"I want to come, too. Is that all right?"

"That is more than all right. I'll let you know as soon as I hear the plans from Mom."

"Oh Theo, I just have this feeling that it is all going to turn out for the best—whatever best is for us. West Coast or England or both, we will find our way."

"Hey, Suzanne?"

"What?"

"Will you marry me—no matter what happens—when the time is right?"

She let out a long sigh. "Oh Theo, I thought you'd never ask."

"So that's a yes?"

"That's a yes, and you can take that to the bank. Good night, my love."

CHAPTER 22

The ship bringing Ellie and Paul as well as Beth, Josef, and their children to America docked in New York on December 20, 1945. Theo and Suzanne were there to meet them, and Suzanne had never felt more a part of Theo's life and his family than she did when she first met his sister.

"Suzanne, thank you so much for coming," Beth said, her accent more European than that of her parents and brother. "I feel as if I know you already, and Josef and I are so very grateful for the support you have shown to Ilse and Liesl."

"They cannot wait to see you—especially Liesl. I don't think she's slept more than a few hours ever since she heard you were coming to the fort."

Josef stepped forward. "I understand that you spent time with my father. Was he well?"

"Yes. He is a very strong man—far younger than his years."

Josef glanced at Theo and then back to her. "Has there been any word? Have they recaptured him?"

"No one has seen him since he escaped," Theo said. "Our friend Gisele—"

"Gisele?" Josef and Beth said the word at the same moment and broke into smiles.

"Gisele St. Germaine?" Beth asked.

"Yes. Do you know her?"

"Yes. She was instrumental in getting our friend Anja and the American airman she had rescued to safety. Anja speaks of her often." She turned to Suzanne. "Anja and Josef and I escaped from a Nazi camp together and then helped Allied airmen get back to England on one of the escape routes that ran across Europe through France and Spain and on to Gibraltar. She and Peter—the American—were married and have been our neighbors the entire time we've been in England."

"Small world," Theo's father murmured, shaking his head as if he could not quite believe what Beth was saying.

"The children are cold," Ellie reminded them. "We should get going."

On the taxi ride to the train station, Suzanne rode with Ellie and Paul and the children, insisting that Theo needed to ride with Beth and Josef so sister and brother could catch up.

The overnight train ride took on the trappings of a party as they shared stories, enjoyed their first dinner together in years, and took turns entertaining the children. They slept sitting up, and Suzanne woke the following morning thinking that in many ways this must have been how Ilse and Franz had felt on that train so many months earlier. For like them, she and Theo were on the verge of a new life—one that hopefully they would find a way to share.

For this stay in Oswego, they had rooms at the hotel. Selma's boardinghouse was once again full, and she and her son were leaving on Christmas Eve to spend Christmas with family in Buffalo. As the train pulled into the station, Beth let out a gasp. "It's Aunt Ilse and Liesl," she said, grasping Josef's arm and pointing out the window.

Sure enough, Ilse and Liesl were scanning the windows of the train, looking for them. The reunion was noisy, with shouts and tears and laughter and hugs. "Oh, this is just the best Christmas ever," Liesl cried as she hugged Beth as if she might never again let her cousin go.

Suzanne felt her eyes well with tears as she stood to one side, witnessing the happy reunion. But then she saw Gordon Langford striding toward her.

"We got him," he announced, ignoring Theo and the rest of the Bridgewater family. "He's in custody here, and the local police chief called me right away. This is it, dollface. This is the break we've been waiting for." He picked her up and swung her around and then planted a kiss on her lips.

In the seconds it took for this to all transpire, Suzanne saw her world crumbling before her eyes. Ellie was looking at her with an expression akin to horror. Paul was making a detailed study of his feet. Ilse had her fist shoved against her lips while Liesl peppered her with questions. But the worst of all was the expression on Theo's face. He stared at her as if she were someone he did not know—had never known—and then he steered his family away.

"Put me down," she ordered Gordon. "Do you have any idea what you have just done? Do you ever have a single thought in your head for anyone except yourself?"

She was furious and embarrassed and scared.

Gordon released her and shoved his fists into the pockets of his overcoat. "Maybe you didn't understand what I just said."

"Detlef Buch has been captured. I got it, Gordon. Those people walking away from us are his family—his son, his daughter-in-law, her parents and brother, and—"

His eyes widened. "And you and the brother. . ." He was clearly beginning to put two and two together. "No wonder you knew so much about the Nazi."

She saw Josef coming their way. "Just please for once in your life shut up, Gordon, and let me try to explain."

But Josef confronted Gordon. "Where is my father being held?"

"He is in custody with the local police, Josef," Suzanne said. "I'm certain that—"

Josef ignored her and took a step closer to Gordon. "You will take me to him immediately."

"No can do. He's being transferred to the nearest military installation tonight."

"I'll take you to police headquarters," Theo said as he joined them and gently took hold of Josef's arm.

"I'll go with you," Suzanne said.

"That won't be necessary," Theo said and walked away, gathering the members of his family and signaling for taxis.

"Do you have any idea what you have done?" Suzanne muttered as she brushed past Gordon to try and catch up with them.

Theo and his family had taken the last two cabs, so Suzanne picked up her suitcase, walked to the hotel, and checked in. But once she had tipped the porter and hung up her coat, she returned to the lobby. She was going to make sure that she knew the moment Theo returned. She only hoped that he would give her a chance to explain.

Ilse stayed with Beth and Ellie and the children while the men were led through a locked door to the cell where Detlef was being held until it was time for him to be transferred. She was astonished at the change in Beth. Gone was the headstrong and sometimes flighty girl she had known in Munich, and in her place stood this composed and serene young woman. She had blossomed into a person of substance and was clearly as devoted to Josef as he was to her. Ilse could not help thinking how that would surely please Detlef.

She realized that she must seem just as changed to Beth. The woman she had been during the time Beth lived with them in Munich was long gone. Once Franz had been arrested and sentenced to prison, she had had to do everything including realizing that Beth would not be with her to watch over Liesl. In those dark days she had had no one but herself.

"Who are you?" Beth's daughter, Gabrielle, asked. The toddler spoke with an English accent.

"I am your mother's aunt and that would make me your great-aunt."

The child broke into a huge grin. "This is excellent," she announced. Ilse smiled. "I agree."

"What shall I call you?"

Ilse was taken by this pint-sized child's curiosity. "Perhaps Auntie?"

"Auntie," she declared. "That is excellent."

"It's her favorite word these days," Beth said as she pulled the child onto her lap and glanced anxiously toward the closed door. "Aunt Ilse?"

"They will be all right, Beth. This is not the same as in Germany."

"I know. Still, one worries," Beth said with a wry smile. "Josef and I had hoped for another venue for sharing this, but we have learned to give and receive news as it comes."

Ilse felt her heart begin to race. "You have news of Marta?"

Beth pulled an envelope from her purse and handed it to Ilse. "We have this letter—addressed to you."

Ilse's hands shook as she accepted the envelope and opened it. Inside was a single sheet of letterhead from a branch of the Religious Order of Friends in France. She scanned the typed message, looking for words that would deliver the news she wanted—needed to know.

"They are safe," she whispered. Her heart pounded. "Marta and the children are living in a small village in France. Marta is helping a group of nuns run an orphanage." She referred back to the letter, reading it more carefully now. "The person who has signed this letter is sending a letter to Marta with your address but has also given me the address for the orphanage so that I can write Marta." She clutched the letter to her chest and gazed at Beth. "My sister," she whispered, her heart so full that there seemed to be no place she could put one more ounce of joy.

"We can send a telegram, Ilse," Beth said. "Just to let her know you have received this news and that a letter will follow. I'm sure the hotel's concierge can help us with that."

"Yes, this is good." Ilse smiled. "Thank you." She took hold of Beth's hand. "I have missed you so much, and when we heard of how brave you were and how you helped others, your uncle Franz was so very proud."

Beth's eyes glistened with tears. "I just wish he were here."

The locked door opened, and all three women stood up. Josef was speaking to a man in military uniform. Paul went immediately to Ellie. "Theo?" Ilse asked.

"He is in custody and will be transferred."

"We knew that," Beth said impatiently. "Is he to be sent back to stand trial?"

"He is a war criminal, Beth, but there is some possibility that our government may intervene."

"That man at the train station?"

Theo shrugged. "No one is saying for sure. What we do know is that he will be transferred later tonight, and after that. . ."

"I wish to speak with him," Ilse said quietly.

"I'm not sure that's wise, Ilse."

But her mind was made up. She stepped up to the officer speaking with Josef. "The man you have in custody saved my family's lives," she announced. "I should like to thank him."

"Ma'am, we really cannot—"

"Yes, you can," Ilse insisted. "It is a simple matter of escorting me to the cell where you are holding him. This may be my only opportunity. It is important for him to know that with all the evil he may have been party to, at least in our case—and in the case of my niece there—he did the right thing."

Two soldiers stood guard on either side of the locked door. The officer glanced at them and then back at Ilse. "Two minutes," he said and nodded to the guards.

The corridor beyond the locked door was narrow and dimly lit. The guards led her past a couple of empty cells to one at the very rear of the hall. They positioned themselves to either side of the locked door. She stepped between them and touched the cold metal of the bars. "Detlef?"

He was sitting on a narrow cot, his face buried in his hands. He looked up and then stood and came to meet her. "This is a pleasant surprise," he said.

"You look terrible. Are you unwell?"

He smiled and ran one shaky hand through his thinning hair. "It is the fate of one who spends several weeks living by his wits with winter coming on. You, on the other hand, look quite well."

"What is to become of you?"

He shrugged. "There is perhaps a possibility that I may redeem myself enough to avoid a death sentence. These Americans seem inordinately interested in learning whatever it is I may know about the Reich."

Ilse thought of the man at the station and suddenly had a thought—one she did not wish to entertain. "Did Suzanne—"

"Turn me in? No, Ilse. We were working together to try and gather the information you needed to find your sister. She knew this congressman who approached her about gathering information from me for his own career advancement, I believe. Suzanne decided to make a trade—information from me for information about your sister. Overall, it worked out quite well, it seems. Josef tells me that Marta and the children are safe in France."

"Suzanne did that? For me?"

"And for your nephew. She is quite in love with him, although she seems incapable of understanding how fragile love can be."

He had rested his fingers lightly on the bars. Ilse wrapped hers around his. "You did agree to her plan? For me? You were always doing things for us—Beth, Franz, me—why?"

Detlef released a long breath. "Perhaps it was because in your niece and my son I saw the possibility of a love story like my own with Josef's mother—one that had a happier ending. Perhaps in Franz I saw the remnants of the man I once thought I was—courageous in the face of unspeakable wrong. Perhaps once Franz died and I realized you faced such uncertainty for your future I wanted to find a way to give you something."

She realized that he was weeping. His voice was strong, but there was no denying the tears that leaked down the lines etched in his face.

"Ma'am. . ." One of the young soldiers glanced at the clock over the door.

"I have to go," Ilse said. "But I wanted you to know that I am so very grateful to have known you."

Detlef laced her fingers with his. "It is I who am in your debt, Frau Schneider. Take care of my son—and my grandchildren—" His voice broke. He released her fingers and turned away.

"Ma'am."

"Yes, all right." The soldiers waited for her to precede them down the hall. "I will write to you, Herr Buch," she called over her shoulder.

"Yes, please," he called back.

To Theo's relief Liesl insisted they go to the fort so she could show Josef and Beth everything and introduce them to Gisele. He really did not want to think about Suzanne or why she had chosen not to mention her renewed connection to Gordon Langford. He fought hard to suppress the myriad negative feelings he was experiencing—feelings of jealousy and betrayal and anger.

But Beth's children were tired after their long journey and needed to be put to bed for the night. For that matter, it had been an emotionally exhausting day for everyone. His mother had been sending concerned glances his way ever since they'd left the station.

"I'm fine, Mom," he assured her.

"I know. It's just that Oswego is a small town, and the hotel is—"

"Maybe Suzanne decided to return to Washington," Paul suggested.

"One can only hope." Ellie sighed.

But when they got back to the hotel, Suzanne was waiting. She fixed her gaze on Theo, ignoring the others. To his relief his dad steered his mom straight to the elevator, and Beth and her family followed.

At the fort, Ilse had taken him aside and told him what Detlef had said. But what Theo could not erase from his mind was the way Gordon Langford had kissed Suzanne—there had been a familiarity and possessiveness in that kiss.

"Will you give me a chance to explain?" Suzanne asked.

Theo stared at her for a long moment—this woman he cared for more deeply than he had ever cared for anyone. "All right." He led the way to a couple of wingback chairs nears the windows that faced the street. Holiday lights blinked in shop windows that had closed for the night.

She began by telling him about the first dinner with Gordon in this very hotel. "He wanted me to—"

"I know all that. Detlef explained it all to Ilse. The question is, why didn't you tell me? Why get involved again with someone who had hurt you so badly before?"

"I didn't get involved with him—not in the way you're implying."

He thought about the kiss on the platform. "Coulda fooled me."

"I seem to remember a similar ambush at Selma's—one where you kissed me without my permission."

"And as I recall you kissed me back. How about today, Suzanne, did you kiss Langford back?"

She slumped back in the chair and stared out the window as he did the same.

The hotel lobby featured a fireplace and a large console radio. At the fort they had heard that President Truman planned to address the nation later that evening, and it was rumored that his topic would be immigration.

"Do you folks mind?" the desk clerk asked as he approached the radio and turned it on.

The president began speaking generally about the numbers of men, women, and children displaced and left homeless by the war. He spoke of the responsibility of all nations to care for and support such individuals. He focused on orphaned children and also on how America needed to set an example. And then he said, "There is one particular matter involving a relatively small number of aliens. President Roosevelt, in an endeavor to assist in handling displaced persons and refugees during the war and upon the recommendation of the War Refugee Board, directed that a group of about one thousand displaced persons be removed from refugee camps in Italy and settled temporarily in a War Relocation Camp near Oswego, New York. Shortly thereafter, President Roosevelt informed the Congress that these persons would be returned to their homelands after the war.

"Upon the basis of a careful survey by the Department of State and the Immigration and Naturalization Service, it has been determined that if these persons were now applying for admission to the United States, most of them would be admissible under the immigration laws. In the circumstances, it would be inhumane and wasteful to require these people to go all the way back to Europe merely for the purpose of applying there for immigration visas and returning to the United States. Many of them have close relatives, including sons and daughters, who are citizens of the United States and who have served and are serving honorably in the armed forces of our country. I am therefore directing the secretary of state and the attorney general to adjust the immigration status of the members of this group who may wish to remain here, in strict accordance with existing laws and regulations."

Theo was not sure he had heard the president correctly, but Suzanne had no doubt.

"They get to stay," she said. "Oh, Theo, they can stay or go or—"

It was over.

"I'm going to the fort," Suzanne announced. She took the elevator up and retrieved her boots, coat, hat, and gloves. When she returned to the lobby Theo was waiting for her.

"Can I come with you?"

They could hear the celebration from a block away. Apparently everyone had decided to gather on the parade ground in spite of the snow. Someone had built a bonfire, and people were laughing and dancing and hugging one another.

Theo and Suzanne stood off to one side, observing the celebration for several minutes. Then Theo took her hand. "Come with me," he said and led her to a spot behind the barracks that overlooked the lake and the lighthouse that was situated several hundred yards offshore. Between the illumination of the full moon and the glow of the bonfire, they were bathed in light.

"Look, I love you," Theo said. "And if you love me as well, then we can work through this." He reached in his coat pocket and took out a long and slender jeweler's box. "I had planned to offer this as an engagement present, but under the circumstances I think perhaps we each need to follow the paths before us—you off to write stories for the *Times* and me off to help refugees in Europe with the AFSC. But while we're finding out whether or not our paths were meant to simply cross or run side by side, I'd like you to have this."

He pulled off his glove with his teeth and opened the hinged velvet box, removed a heart-shaped crystal pendant on a thin silver chain, and offered it to her.

"Your family has doubts," she warned.

"I don't. I love you and will always love you on some level, but you need to follow your path—a path I hope will one day bring you back to me."

She took the pendant from him and touched it to her lips. Behind them someone was playing a violin as the celebration continued.

CHAPTER 23

The day after Christmas Theo had to leave for training at the AFSC's retreat in Pennsylvania while Suzanne returned to Washington to pack her things and once again turn over the keys to her small apartment to a renter—in this case the young man whom Edwin had hired to replace her at the newspaper. Her editor had been surprisingly warm and supportive about her decision to accept the offer from the *New York Times*.

"It's a big step up that career ladder, Suzie. Don't mess it up." For Edwin that was about as close as she could hope to getting a hug of encouragement.

Beth and Josef and the children had returned to Wisconsin with Paul and Ellie for a reunion with Matthew and Jenny, and Ilse and Liesl were back at the fort packing up. In a matter of weeks—once the government had gotten everything in place—they would cross the Rainbow Bridge into Canada where they would receive their visas for legally reentering the United States. Suzanne loved that they would have to cross the Rainbow Bridge in both directions—it felt as if the name alone cast a light and blessing on the process. She hated that she would miss covering this final chapter of their odyssey.

The plan was that once Ilse and Liesl had gotten their visas, they would travel to Wisconsin to spend time with Paul and Ellie and enroll

Liesl in school for the remainder of the school year. Then Ilse would travel back to England with Beth and Josef where she would finally be reunited with her sister, Marta.

"Oh, Theo, everything is coming together," Suzanne said that night. They had continued their nightly phone calls and were both dreading the day when he would leave for Europe and she would leave to follow the *New York Times* assignment. Once that happened, nightly phone calls would be far too expensive.

"I have to be in New York day after tomorrow," she told him. "I'm meeting with the editorial staff and being briefed on what they want from me. They'll put me up for one night in a hotel, and the following morning I'll board the train for California."

"Do you have to spend time with the editors that evening?"

"There's nothing scheduled. Why?"

"I thought I could come up and maybe we could have dinner and—"

"Oh Theo, could you? That would be so wonderful. Are you sure you can get away?"

"I've finished the training, and I was going to head up to Oswego to see how Ilse and the others are doing. I don't actually leave for Europe until January 20. So get me the name and address of the hotel, and I'll meet you in the lobby at six."

On their night in New York City, they enjoyed dinner at a restaurant in Central Park that Theo had heard about. Afterward they started walking through the park and down Broadway, past the theaters, and on until they reached the terminal for the Staten Island Ferry.

"Let's go," Suzanne said, grabbing Theo's hand and pulling him toward the ferry.

"Why would we go to Staten Island?"

"So we can come back—and going and coming we have a fabulous view of the Statue of Liberty."

"Suzanne, it's January."

"I know, but to quote a popular song by Mr. Irving Berlin, 'I've got my love to keep me warm.' Now come on."

They were the last two riders to board and the only two who stayed at the railing as the ferry made its slow voyage across the harbor.

"There she is," Suzanne said, her teeth chattering in spite of the fact that Theo had his arms wrapped tightly around her. She pointed to the famous statue. "Isn't she magnificent?"

"She's beautiful. I can see why people coming here from overseas get all choked up when they see her. What a sight that must have been for Franz and Ilse and all the others when they arrived here all those months ago."

"And think how their lives have changed since then. Who could have imagined?"

He rested his chin on the top of her head. "Do you think when I come back from overseas and you come back from out west our lives will have changed?"

"Probably." She turned so that she was facing him and cupped his cheeks with her gloved hands. "I wish—"

He silenced her by laying his finger on her lips. "No regrets, okay? We are doing the right thing, and when you think about it, this is no different than thousands of scenes like this where one was going off to war and the other staying behind. Those couples were also in love, but they understood that sometimes—"

"I know. I just want to be sure that you don't think I'm putting my career ahead of us."

"Here's what I think. I think that true love allows for each person to find happiness and contentment individually as well as together. You need to go do this, Suzanne—and for that matter, so do I. How can we build a life together until we're sure of what we each want and need?"

"I love you, Theo Bridgewater."

He kissed her. "Good to know," he murmured. "Now could we possibly go inside? I am seriously freezing."

Within days after the president's radio address, Fort Ontario became a beehive of activity. Ilse could hardly believe how things changed almost overnight. The town as well as the fort were filled with extra staff from the Department of Immigration and Naturalization as well as representatives of the various charitable agencies that had helped them settle in during those first hot days of August 1944. Now the charities came to assist with resettlement plans.

The community within the fort took on a true spirit of celebration as almost nightly gatherings were held in the recreation hall. Even Ilse could not help but join in whenever someone started the "Hokey Pokey." And the circle for doing the dance that had helped many of them learn their first English words had never been larger as staffers and agency workers and volunteers from town joined in its joyous silliness.

Ilse had persuaded Gisele to join those who would cross into Canada and back in order to legally enter the United States. "You just never know," she told her friend. "And as Theo has told me, it gives you options. You can return to France, but if things don't work out there, you have your visa to come back."

Liesl was both excited and nervous about going to live with Paul and Ellie and starting the next term in a new school in Wisconsin, but to Ilse's delight, her daughter seemed determined to make the best of the situation. "Theo told me that there's a horse on the farm—one I can learn to ride. And my cousins Matthew and Jenny wrote to ask if I might be interested in doing some babysitting for them. And Aunt Ellie sent me pictures of the farm and the school, and there's a lot of snow, but I like snow, and—"

"It's not forever," Ilse assured her.

"I know. As Papa used to say, 'It's an adventure.'"

Ilse laughed and hugged her child so that Liesl would not see her tears. "That's exactly what he would say."

Suzanne had sent postcards from her new assignment on the West Coast and assurances that she had lots of stories to share with them. Ilse worried about Theo. He had come to Oswego to make sure that she and Liesl had his support. He had even arranged to travel with them into Canada and back and record the whole experience with the box camera that Suzanne had sent to Liesl. But when he thought no one was watching, Ilse did not miss the haunted sadness that came over him. She knew that sadness, for she felt it every time she missed Franz.

The night before they were scheduled to board the buses for Canada, hardly anyone slept. Ilse was aware of the low murmur of voices in the hallway outside her apartment door through the long night, and by dawn most people had already made their way to the dining hall for breakfast. It was hard to believe that when this day ended they would be free to leave—no passes needed, no restriction in time or miles from the fort. They could leave and start living their lives. Theo had already made arrangements for Ilse, Liesl, and Gisele to spend this night in the hotel where he was staying.

The buses were unusually quiet as everyone boarded and found seats. The same anxious uncertainty that had traveled with them from Italy to New York seemed to have returned. Would it all work out? Ilse sat with Gisele across from Theo and Liesl as the bus traveled west toward Rochester and then on to Buffalo following the shoreline of Lake Ontario. As they neared Niagara Falls the chatter and aura of excitement on the bus increased. Then they saw the bridge. At the same time the thunder of the falls filled the air.

"Oh my," Gisele whispered as she stared out at the impressive steel arches.

On the Canadian side, everyone got off the bus and formed a line. Representatives of the Canadian government as well as the American embassy welcomed them to Canada and then handed them the precious document that was their passport to freedom. There was not a dry eye on the bus as they reboarded, clutching their precious proof of legal reentry on the American side of the falls.

"Mom, there's a real rainbow," Liesl squealed as she pressed closer to the window with a view of the falls. Sure enough, a beautiful rainbow arched its way through the mist of the falls. Ilse clutched Gisele's hand. "We are free," she said.

"Finally," Gisele agreed, and for the first time that Ilse could ever remember, her friend—this elegant, cynical, sophisticated woman—giggled like a schoolgirl.

The only thing that could possibly have made the day better for Theo would have been to share it with Suzanne. He could hardly wait for the bus to return to the fort so he could help Ilse and Gisele get their things and go with him to the hotel. Tomorrow they would board a train for Wisconsin, while he headed in the opposite direction, across the Atlantic, to start his work with the AFSC. Tonight would be his last chance to talk with Suzanne for some time, and he planned to memorize the sound of her voice, her laughter. . .even her tears, which he was certain would come when they had to say good-bye.

He had just gotten Ilse and the others settled in their hotel room for the night when the telephone in his room rang. "Mr. Bridgewater?"

"Yes?"

"Could you please come to the lobby? There is a matter of urgency we need to speak with you about."

Now what? He glanced at the small alarm clock he'd set by the bed. He was supposed to call Suzanne in fifteen minutes. "Can this wait? I have a call I need to make and—"

He was aware that the hotel staffer had covered the receiver and was speaking to someone else, but he could not make out what they were saying. "Please sir, if you could come now."

"All right." He had removed his tie and suit coat as well as his shoes, but other than the shoes, he decided not to bother putting on the rest. As he walked quickly to the elevator, he rolled down the sleeves of his white shirt—gone limp after the long day he'd had—and buttoned the cuffs. On the elevator, he ran his fingers through his hair to make it more presentable. There was nothing he could do about the five-o'clock shadow that had sprouted on his face.

The elevator doors opened to a mostly deserted lobby. He headed straight for the front desk. "I'm Theo Bridgewater," he said. "What is this about?"

The desk clerk grinned at him. "You have a guest, sir."

Theo turned to where the clerk pointed and saw Suzanne standing next to a chair that had been facing away from the elevator.

"Hi."

Theo was speechless with surprise. "What. . .where. . .how. . ."

Suzanne ran to him and kissed him. "You know something, Theo Bridgewater? I got out to California and got to thinking about all that stuff you said about finding our individual contentment and such?"

"Suzanne, what are you—"

"Here's the thing. I've had a career—I may still have a career—but it will not be in California or anywhere else that keeps me away from you."

"What have you done?"

"I have chosen us, Theo. I resigned the position with the *Times* and called Edwin—who by the way was delighted to tell me that he was glad I had finally come to my senses. I proposed a series of articles for his paper about the work of the AFSC, and he agreed that it would indeed sell papers so he put in a call to somebody who knew somebody and, well, I'm here."

"But I have to leave—"

"Whither thou goest, my love. It's all arranged."

"You're coming with me?"

"That's the plan." Suddenly she released him and took a step back. "Unless, of course. . .I mean if you'd rather I didn't. . ."

He pulled her back into his arms and kissed her. Then he looked over his shoulder at the desk clerk, who was trying hard to appear as if he hadn't been watching and listening. "Excuse me, but is there a justice of the peace who keeps late hours?"

The clerk grinned. "I'll give him a call. Shall I ask him to come here to perform the ceremony?"

Suzanne and Theo were married in the lobby of the Oswego Hotel at midnight on January 18, 1946, with Gisele, Ilse, and Liesl in attendance. The hotel manager arranged a reception for the wedding party and their invited guests—those on duty in the hotel that night—in the dining room.

The following morning, Suzanne and Theo called their parents with the news and saw Ilse, Gisele, and Liesl to their train. Afterward they settled into a compartment of a train headed east to New York City.

"You're sure about this?" Theo asked, still not quite able to believe his good fortune.

"Theo, I am your wife, and together we are about to do what we both have learned we are very good at: you are going to help a whole new group of displaced people start again, and I am going to tell their stories to the world."

"And when that work is done?"

"It will never be done." Suzanne smiled and looked at him with love-filled eyes. "But somewhere along the way we're going to have children of our own, and when they are old enough, we will tell them about the people of Fort Ontario—about their courage, their patience, and their rainbow ending."

Discussion Questions

1. In the Peacemaker series, historical events and places have been used that many people are unaware of. Talk about what you know of the White Rose in Germany, the concentration camp known as Sobibor, the escape routes across Europe used to get Allied airmen to safety, and the Fort Ontario Emergency Refugee Shelter that is the setting for much of this book.

2. Suzanne is almost obsessed with her career—why?

3. Theo is a man of faith, yet he struggles with his desire for something beyond farming. Discuss whether or not you think his struggle is God driven or ego driven.

4. Ilse is perhaps the character who must make the greatest shift from the woman she was in book one and the woman she has become in this book. How has she come to be this stronger person?

5. The end of the story for Gisele is unresolved—where do you think she goes from here?

6. Detlef Buch is a complex character. How did you feel about him?

7. Herr Buch's story is also unresolved. What do you think happens to him?

8. In the Quaker faith there is the belief that every human being is born with the Spirit of God (or the Light) within and that the task is to maintain contact with that Spirit as we move through our daily lives. They elect to do this through prayer and silence. How do you connect with God's Spirit within you?

9. If there is good in every person, how do we explain evil such as that found in Adolf Hitler and in more modern dictators and tyrants?

10. The backdrop for each book of this series is war, yet the characters are all on a journey to find their personal peace. Talk about how each main character finds that peace in spite of the circumstances.

ACKNOWLEDGMENTS

The secret of happiness is freedom. The secret of freedom is courage.
                              Thucydides, fifth-century historian/general

If there is a way to sum up the stories of this series, this line from
Thucydides is it. This third and final story of the Peacemakers series
has been such a wonderful experience for me. I am one of those weird
people who really enjoys research—especially historical research.
With that in mind I traveled to Oswego, New York, to learn more
of the story of the Fort Ontario Emergency Refugee Center. I was
warmly welcomed by several staff members at the small museum now
housed in what was the administration building while the refugees
were in residence. The museum preserves a wonderful exhibition of
the story of these nine hundred–plus refugees fleeing Hitler and his
regime.

My guide was a lovely young woman—Rebecca Fisher—who
told me that although she had lived in Oswego most of her life, she
had not until very recently known the story of this final use for a fort
and military installation that dated back to the French and Indian
War. As Rebecca led me on a tour of the grounds we saw a remnant
of the barbed wire and chain-link fence that had once surrounded
the installation. The barracks and many of the community buildings
are all gone now, but standing above the shoreline of Lake Ontario, it

isn't difficult to imagine what things would have looked like when the refugees first arrived that August morning in 1944.

I asked Rebecca to be my expert reader for this story and she agreed. On top of that she continued to send me information, data, and wonderfully poignant photographs of life in the fort. I quite simply could not have written this story without her. I must also thank the people of Oswego who seem to have treasured their history and preserved key buildings such as the library and the movie theater that helped me "see" Oswego as it might have been in the 1940s.

I am grateful to everyone at Barbour Books and my editor, Annie Tipton, for this opportunity to tell these stories. I also thank Becky Durost Fish for her editing and revision notes. And always I am so blessed to have had my agent, Natasha Kern, in my corner, believing in me and making dreams come true. I hope you enjoy this story and I look forward to hearing from you. As always you can reach me via my website (www.booksbyanna.com) or by snail mail at P.O. Box 161, Thiensville, WI 53092. All best wishes to you, and may God hold you in His Light.

Anna Schmidt
October 2013

Anna Schmidt is the author of over twenty works of fiction. Among her many honors, Anna is the recipient of *Romantic Times'* Reviewer's Choice Award and a finalist for the RITA award for romantic fiction. She enjoys gardening and collecting seashells at her winter home in Florida.

Other Books by Anna Schmidt

WOMEN OF PINECRAFT SERIES

A Stranger's Gift
A Sister's Forgiveness
A Mother's Promise

THE PEACEMAKERS SERIES

All God's Children
Simple Faith
Safe Haven